INTRIGUE

Seek thrills. Solve crimes. Justice served.

Conard County: Covert Avenger
Rachel Lee

Colorado Kidnapping
Cindi Myers

MILLS & BOON

CONARD COUNTY: COVERT AVENGER
© 2024 by Susan Civil-Brown
Philippine Copyright 2024
Australian Copyright 2024
New Zealand Copyright 2024

First Published 2024
First Australian Paperback Edition 2024
ISBN 978 1 038 92166 6

COLORADO KIDNAPPING
© 2024 by Cynthia Myers
Philippine Copyright 2024
Australian Copyright 2024
New Zealand Copyright 2024

First Published 2024
First Australian Paperback Edition 2024
ISBN 978 1 038 92166 6

MIX
Paper | Supporting
responsible forestry
FSC® C001695

Published by
Harlequin Mills & Boon
An imprint of Harlequin Enterprises (Australia) Pty Limited
(ABN 47 001 180 918), a subsidiary of HarperCollins
Publishers Australia Pty Limited
(ABN 36 009 913 517)
Level 19, 201 Elizabeth Street
SYDNEY NSW 2000 AUSTRALIA

Cover art used by arrangement with Harlequin Books S.A.. All rights reserved.

Printed and bound in Australia by McPherson's Printing Group

Conard County: Covert Avenger

Rachel Lee

MILLS & BOON

Rachel Lee was hooked on writing by the age of twelve and practiced her craft as she moved from place to place all over the United States. This *New York Times* bestselling author now resides in Florida and has the joy of writing full-time.

DEDICATION

To Patience Bloom for many years of kindness,
encouragement and great editing.

CAST OF CHARACTERS

Elaine Paltier—Conard County sheriff's deputy, widowed with three-year-old autistic daughter.

Devlin Paltier—Covert operative for the CIA, off the grid to protect his assets, one of whom has been killed. It's been years since he returned to Conard City or saw his mother.

Lu Paltier—Devlin's mother, lives with Elaine and cares for her autistic granddaughter.

Cassie Paltier—Three-year-old with autism. Has trouble with personal contact and speech.

Beggans Bixby—Ranch owner furious about UFO hunters trespassing on his land, upsetting his cattle. All for two red lights that have been there for years.

Zoe and Kalina—Two female assassins from Eastern Europe who have come to kill Devlin for his part in their brother's death.

Chapter One

Conard County Deputy Elaine Paltier drove along a dusty gravel road on her nightly round of Wyoming's isolated ranch country. Out here, excitement was rare, unless there was an accident or injury, or the weather created a problem. The mountains to the west caught the bright moonlight on their snow-capped peaks, adding beauty to gently rolling foothills and the early spring growth in the fields.

The routine, however, gave Elaine plenty of opportunity to ramble around inside her own head, allowing her to think about her life, her job and mostly her young daughter. Being a single parent had its difficulties, even with help from her mother.

She didn't mind this part of her official duties, though. Each assignment was only for two weeks before she'd be relieved by another deputy. Hardly enough time to find these patrols by herself to be boring.

That night, however, matters got exciting, although indirectly at first. She saw two glowing red spots near the Bixby ranch and wondered if they were tower markers. But who would have erected them since her last two-week tour? And if someone had, she'd have certainly heard about it.

As she got closer, the glowing areas became more orange and bigger.

"Oh, God," she muttered, her heart accelerating. A range fire? But in two different spots? She grabbed her radio to call for backup from the fire squad, but the device hissed and refused to connect. The satellite phone was no better. Dead zones in these distant areas were not uncommon, providing unreliable service that could be maddening and dangerous at times.

Uncommon or not, she had to find a way to summon help. She pressed her accelerator, driving as fast as she dared on the gravel. Range fires could explode with incredible speed, and the green spring growth would offer no protection once a fire started and dried out everything around it.

Seeing the driveway for Beggan Bixby's ranch house, she pulled a sharp right and drove even faster to warn the old rancher—maybe get a better radio signal or use his landline, too.

Were those red blobs growing larger? Elaine couldn't tell, so she turned most of her focus to the looming ranch house. She flipped on her roof lights but no siren, to warn the rancher that she was approaching. All the while, tension increasingly tightened her muscles. A serious range fire could blow up in no time at all.

Then, scaring her half to death, a man appeared in the driveway right in front of her, turning blue and white in the flash of her light bar. He held a shotgun cradled across his breast almost like a baby. Much to her relief, it was clearly cracked open. Not yet a threat.

She jammed her Suburban into Park with a spray of gravel and opened her door, leaning out. "Mr. Bixby?"

Yeah, it was Bixby, in old jeans and a work shirt, with a stained, ancient cowboy hat jammed on his head. He was stomping his feet in anger. "You finally come to get rid of 'em?"

The question put her off-balance. Not at all what she'd expected to hear. *Finally?* "You mean the fire up north of here?" She pointed at the reddish-orange balls of light as she climbed out of her vehicle.

"Hell no. I ain't talking about them."

Elaine looked from him to the glowing light, more orange now. "How can you ignore them? I don't have to tell you about range fires. I need your phone."

"'Tain't no fire."

"How can you be sure unless we go look?" As if it could be anything else. The idea of a range fire made the skin on the back of her neck crawl. A disaster that could reach hundreds of square miles in no time at all. But now she was dealing with a man who'd lost his mind somehow? She had to get to his phone.

But Bixby had a ready answer. "I see them lights a lot. Now, you just do your job and get rid of them SOBs."

She nearly gaped at him. "You want me to get rid of those lights?" How the hell was she supposed to do that without help if it was a fire? And why did he keep dismissing them, then demanding she get rid of them? "I can get a fire truck out here to put them out. But I need your landline. Radio's not working."

Bixby stomped his feet some more and raised his scratchy voice. "You damn useless cop. *Not* the red lights. They ain't no trouble. So when are you going to get rid of them?"

Elaine began to feel some serious irritation, along with a sense of having slipped out of reality. "How am I supposed to get rid of the lights if you won't let me call the fire department?"

"I been calling you guys for more 'n' a month about

this. Y'all ain't done nothing about it. I don't give a rat's patootie about the lights. I keep tellin' ya, they ain't no problem—never have been. You ever listen?"

"Then why do you want me to get rid of them?"

Bixby was clearly reaching the end of his rope. He started to shout. "I ain't talking about them lights. I keep tellin' ya! Get rid of the cussed fools crossin' my fence. I don't want no gawkers cuz of them dang lights. This ain't a ranch like the one on the TV."

Elaine sought to make the connection, then did. In an instant, she *knew* she had fallen down the rabbit hole. She spoke carefully, needing to be sure she understood before Bixby escalated beyond his current anger and frustration. "I saw that show once."

"Well, I ain't that place, and I'm getting sick of freakin' trespassers climbing my fence and bothering my herd. Damn it, I got cattle to raise."

Elaine looked to the north, saw the lights were still there but didn't seem to have grown. They didn't resemble a range fire, which by now would have been a whole lot larger. Just lights, like Bixby had said. Her tension eased as she gave her full attention back to the old man. "Bet you got gawkers tonight." The idea of people chasing balls of light amused her. Clearly Bixby didn't share that feeling.

"Hell yeah." Bixby spat on the ground. Chewing tobacco. "Swear I'm gonna shoot one or two of them soon as I get a chance. Hell, I can't afford no security guys to protect my fence and my herd. I'm it."

Elaine's stomach tightened with apprehension. "Mr. Bixby, you don't want to kill somebody and put yourself in jail."

"I got a right to shoot anybody who comes on my land."

That was debatable, and would require a judge and

maybe a jury. She realized she wasn't going to be able to talk or scare him out of murderous intent—not right now. Her hands tightened with a sense of urgency, seeking a way to calm the situation.

She glanced north again at the lights, more curious now than anything. "What are they?"

"Damned if I know. Been showin' up from time to time all my life, but they ain't hurt no one and nothing. Seems like they ain't no problem, and I'm happy to leave them alone. But things might not be so simple if them jackasses keep crossing my fence and taking pictures and all that other stuff they do. Bunch of lunatics."

Elaine sighed, now having a clear picture of the *real* problem here, and it wasn't just a couple of lights or orbs or whatever they might be called. No, it was people who wanted to climb his fence—maybe even cut it—and wreak havoc on a rancher's land and herd.

Bixby spat again and resettled his shotgun in his arms. "Used to call 'em UFOs," he said. "Now they got a new name—UAPs. Don't make no difference. No little gray or green men ever been seen. Nothin' ever seen but them balls. Bet you can't even take a good picture of one."

Elaine studied Bixby, thinking he was a little more informed than a man who simply wanted to keep trespassers out. *UAPs?*

A recent term not yet in common vernacular as far as she knew. Maybe he'd been talking to some of these trespassers. Arguing with them. Given this man, it wouldn't surprise her. Maybe the only surprise was that he hadn't killed one of them yet.

Bixby glared at her in the lights from her vehicle. "What the hell you gonna do about them, Deputy? Them trespassers. I complained before, but you never even sent anyone out here. So what are you going to do?"

Since it was unlikely that half the Conard County Sheriff's Department could come out here to guard Bixby's land from trespassers, Elaine had no answer.

Which apparently didn't surprise Bixby. "Ha," he said. "What good are all you folks? Ya think I don't pay taxes like everyone else around here?"

"It's more about manpower," Elaine said finding a reasonable response, although minute by minute, Bixby was looking closer to a frazzled edge.

"Wouldn't take many of you to convince them jerks to stay away."

Well, he had a point there. A few deputies talking to these invaders might scare them off. Briefly.

"They'll just come back eventually," Elaine said honestly.

Bixby went off into a cussing fit that would have amused Elaine a whole lot more if he hadn't been holding a shotgun.

When he ran out of words and rage and fell briefly silent, Elaine spoke heresy. "You know, Mr. Bixby, those balls of light are hardly harmless to you and this ranch if they're causing these trespassers to overrun you."

Bixby glared at her again as if she were a fool. "They didn't bring them jerks. Like I said, the lights been there on and off my whole life. Even my cattle ain't bothered by them."

Bixby spat again, and this time he cocked the shotgun and waved it. "You get yourself out of here. Useless. Just useless."

Elaine started to turn, her back prickling with awareness of that shotgun. Leaving was the only choice to avoid a possibly dangerous confrontation. She'd only taken two steps toward her Suburban when Bixby spoke again.

"I know you," he said. "Elaine Paltier, George Henley's girl. Dang, wouldn't your daddy be ashamed of you right now."

Elaine stiffened but kept walking to her vehicle, then climbed in and switched off all her flashers. Bixby could go to hell.

Yet as she swung her vehicle around to continue her patrol, she saw the red lights again. Then she saw them wink out.

She braked and waited for five minutes or so, but they never reappeared.

A mystery that would always remain a mystery, she supposed. But she had a real life to deal with, and she resumed her patrol at an easy pace. Eventually her radio and satellite phone returned to normal function.

After a few more minutes, she returned to normal as well, smiling into the night. Red lights, trespassers and Mr. Bixby.

What a story!

Chapter Two

In the morning, after Elaine had finished filing her report at the office, the laughter and snickers began to run around among the other deputies. She couldn't hide her own smile as she listened to the would-be comics filling in the blanks of her encounter with Beggan Bixby.

She had, of course, written the terse report of a police officer: name, date, time, description of complaint and her response. Bare bones. Basic.

But the other deputies in her office had no trouble imagining a scene that went far beyond the report. Elaine had to laugh along with them because they were coming close to what had actually happened. And it was ridiculous—*so* ridiculous—except for one thing.

"Guys," she said, "we still have to do something about the trespassers at the Bixby ranch."

Lev Carson hooted. "Which trespassers? The orange blobs?"

Still smiling, Elaine left as another round of laughter filled the office. She had no doubt two or three of her colleagues would head out to the Bixby ranch that day to deal with the invaders, laughter or not.

But Elaine's thoughts had already moved on. She was seriously looking forward to seeing her three-year-old daughter, who would be fresh out of bed, getting ready for her breakfast and still smelling of that sweet baby smell she hadn't yet outgrown.

Cassie made everything worthwhile. Everything.

MIDMORNING, ELAINE WAS still yawning her way through her third cup of coffee and Cassie was still in her pajamas having splashed milk from her cereal onto a coloring book. The damp spots and curling paper didn't bother Cassie a bit. With her tongue stuck out in concentration, her mop of blond curls all awry, she worked on a unicorn that filled the entire page. Cassie's choice of colors was bold and on the wild side.

Her late husband's mother, Lu, had gone to the grocery. Lula was Elaine's lifesaver. After Caleb Paltier's death in a construction accident, Lu had moved right in, taking charge of Cassie and the house while managing not to make Elaine feel like she had lost control. Making it possible for Elaine to continue working and paying the bills.

Except that, for a long while, Elaine hadn't cared about being in charge of anything. That was changing at last, and Lu was sliding into second place with a smile. Not that Elaine wanted Lu to feel that way, but she needed some control of her own life beyond her job. Needed to feel there was some kind of future for her and Cassie.

Then the doorbell rang. The old thing sounded more like a sick frog than a chime. Something she needed to take care of.

There weren't always enough hours in the day. Simple repairs like the doorbell had been put on hold for entirely too long. And some of them had waited because getting herself out of bed had, for a while, been a chore. The feeling still visited her sometimes, but infrequently now.

Smothering another yawn, she tugged the tie of her gray sherpa robe more tightly around herself. She wondered who it might be since most of her neighbors didn't drop by when they knew she'd been on the graveyard shift. Still, maybe someone had a serious problem. The thought brought her fully awake.

She opened the door. And stared, even though she recognized the man. But she hadn't expected to see him.

"Devlin?" she said almost uncertainly. Her late husband's brother? The last time she had seen him had been at Caleb's funeral.

"Hi, Elaine," he answered with a smile. "I guess Mom didn't tell you I was coming."

No, his mom hadn't. But so what? As her mind whirled with surprise, she realized she was being rude by not inviting him in, letting him stand there in the chilly morning air. "Come in," she said, trying to be gracious, forcing a smile. "Heavens, it's been forever!"

He entered and she stepped back, taking him in. He wore a denim shearling jacket, jeans and hiking boots. More casual than she was used to seeing him. He looked thinner, too. A lot thinner. And older, as if life had treated him roughly. Only his short dark chestnut hair appeared the same, and it was now dashed with some gray.

Devlin hardly looked like Caleb. They might have come from different families, although they didn't, but there was still enough similarity to make her heart stumble. But no, this would do no good. She yanked back from sorrow and forced her smile to widen. "Your mom went to the store, but Cassie is in the kitchen. Come on and have some coffee."

He shrugged out of his jacket and hung it on a hook near the door.

As she turned to lead the way to the kitchen, she paused. "I'm afraid Cassie won't remember you," she added, to fill a silence that might become awkward.

"I'd be surprised if she did. She was, what—eighteen months the last time I saw her?"

At the funeral. Nearly two years ago. And during that time, Devlin had sent only a few emails. Any relationship that might have grown between them had been stymied by his duties abroad with the State Department.

Of course, he'd kept in better touch with his mother— occasional phone calls, an actual letter or two. No reason he should keep in touch with Elaine. She was another part of Caleb's life he had barely been exposed to.

Devlin spent a few quiet minutes talking to Cassie, who looked slightly frightened by the big stranger, but then he had the sense to look away and leave her alone while he directed his attention to Elaine.

"Mom says your job is keeping you really busy."

She nodded as she brought him a mug of steaming coffee. "'Busy' is mostly a good thing. But I guess you know that, given *your* job."

Elaine could have sworn that he almost winced, but then his face smoothed over. "Well," he answered, "I hope you don't mind that I'll be around for a few weeks, maybe a month."

Startled, she froze as she set the mug before him. "Is something wrong?"

His mouth twisted. "There is something very wrong when my sister-in-law asks that. But you're right. I've been a stranger. And yeah, something is wrong. You can call it 'strongly recommended leave.' It seems someone decided it was high time I took a vacation."

She sat in the chair beside Cassie and eyed him. "You do something wrong?"

He shook his head. "Trust me, I did not. Nope, the chief just decided I'd saved up too much vacation time for it to be healthy. Told me to go breathe some fresh air."

At that, she gave a half smile. "It happens. So why not Tahiti or the Caribbean? Great vacation spots. Better than here." Then she bit her lip, hoping she hadn't sounded as if she wanted him to leave. She didn't want that. His mother didn't deserve that.

He looked down at his mug, then raised a face that reflected faint sorrow. "I got to thinking about Caleb. About you. About Cassie. About my mom. I've been a prodigal son for too long."

Elaine was sure Lu would agree with that. She wondered if her mother-in-law had applied some pressure to Devlin. Then, if so, why now? Why not in past years?

She nearly sighed. The law officer was taking over again, asking a bazillion questions she'd never, in this case, be able to ask out loud.

But as she sat there in the lengthening silence, a certainty grew in her. Something was definitely wrong with this trip, no matter what he said. This was not a simple visit to family.

As she drained her coffee, she remembered basic courtesy. Much as she hated to cook, she asked, "You want something to eat?"

Devlin shook his head. "I stopped at Maude's before coming over here."

Elaine rose to get more coffee. Weary or not, sitting still had suddenly become difficult. Nothing was right. She just wished she knew what was wrong.

"The diner must have been a trip down memory lane for you."

He chuckled at that. "Maude hasn't softened much, has she? And her daughter is damn near a clone. She bangs those dishes around almost as sharply as Maude does."

"A lot of us wonder how the dishes survive." Having topped off their mugs, she sat again at the table. Cassie remained totally involved in her coloring. But that was Cassie. *Special needs. On the spectrum.* God, she hated those words. Cassie was Cassie, a lovely child who had some quirks. Elaine had trouble seeing it any other way. She had certainly come to hate labels.

Especially when those labels seemed like a huge barrel into which people could toss anyone who didn't fit someone's idea of *normal*. What the hell was *normal*, anyway?

"Elaine?" Devlin spoke quietly. "Is something wrong?"

Abruptly she realized that her face had tightened into a scowl. She forced herself to brighten her expression. "Just tired," she answered. "Graveyard last night."

He raised his brows. "Then what are you doing up? Why not catch some sleep?"

She shook her head. "Best thing to do to make the switch back to days is stay up all day after I finish my last graveyard. I'll sleep tonight, and then tomorrow will be close to normal."

"Makes sense." He nodded and sipped his coffee. Then he glanced at Cassie, seeing that she was still busy coloring. "Quite some concentration there."

Elaine nearly winced. "Yeah," was all she said.

He looked down briefly as if he'd heard something in her tone, but then he raised his face with a smile. "When will Mom be back? Maybe I should just go get settled in the motel and come back later."

"The motel?" God. Elaine had no trouble imagining Lu's response to that. Well, she pretty much had the same reaction to the idea herself, just milder. "Damn, Devlin, this is your home now. You think Lu wants you sleeping at the La-Z-Rest?"

"Hardly my home," he replied. "I've been here so rarely over the last fifteen years I can barely claim the *town* as home."

And the house he'd grown up in had been sold by Lu when she moved into the Paltier house to take care of Elaine and Cassie. Elaine would have bet that Devlin didn't have much of a home for himself anywhere, not with him being overseas with the State Department. Kinda sad, even though she wasn't in much of a mood to feel sad for Devlin. Dang, the guy had taken off all those years ago and basically made a stranger of himself, even to his own mother.

But the thing that concerned her right now was her mother-in-law. "No, you stay here. You can argue about it with Lu if you want, but I won't hear of it. Get your stuff out of your car. There's a small bedroom in the back that you can have."

A room she had once shared with Caleb as an office and now was hers alone. Computer, papers, bills…all stuff that could be moved, and there was a daybed for him to sleep on.

"I don't want to impose—"

"Maybe not," she interrupted him. "But this is the way it's gonna be."

At that, he smiled again. "Total deputy," he remarked. "Giving orders."

She might have flushed, but rather than feel embarrassed, she started to become irritated. *Lack of sleep,* she told herself.

"Whatever," she said. Then she rose. "I'm going to get dressed. Cassie? Wanna come with me?"

Cassie slowly lifted her head from her coloring book and looked at Devlin, then dropped her crayon and slid off her chair. She walked beside her mother. No touching.

Well, that was as clear as a sign in flashing neon, Elaine thought as she headed for her bedroom with her daughter. The girl clearly didn't want to be alone with the stranger. She wondered if Cassie would become comfortable with Devlin. Or if she even should.

Devlin, after all, had a track record of seldom being around.

She heard him call out, "I'm going to step outside."

Good. Easier than having him in here and trying to fill in conversational blanks.

OUTSIDE, BRIGHT MIDMORNING sunlight flooded the world and the remaining chill of spring defied the greening leaves. Devlin looked around and wondered if he'd lost his mind.

Coming to see his mother, well, that was normal. Even after all this time. She'd been torn up by Caleb's death, and Devlin had done what he could to comfort her in the aftermath. But he was confined by his job's demands. By other people's lives depending on him. By information he absolutely couldn't turn over to a backup. A week. Just a week for his grief over Caleb. A week when he'd hardly left his mother's side, except to try to spend a little time with Elaine, who was grieving as much as anyone and totally absorbed in her small daughter. Little help he'd been.

This visit would be much longer and he knew it, but the situation was different. This time, lives didn't depend on his return. Far from it. Right now they depended on his absence.

God. He could barely stand thinking about it. Trust had been shattered, and shattered badly.

But now he was here, making a nuisance of himself. He had the distinct, unsurprising feeling that Elaine would be happier if he'd stayed away. What was he if not a reminder of her late husband? Besides, he'd never really gotten to know Elaine. In school she'd been four years behind him; then he'd left for college and his current job. They were damn near strangers.

And Cassie. She might be his niece, but he'd done a lousy job of being her uncle. He'd been a rotten godfather, too. That implied some obligation, as did the blood relationship. What business did he have now of developing a relationship with such a young child, who might not see him again for a year or more? Or even longer?

Damn, he should have gone elsewhere. Anywhere. Somewhere he could be sure of not messing up the lives of his family.

Devlin, without thinking about it, reached for the pack of cigarettes he used to carry in his breast pocket. His flannel-shirt pocket felt empty. Of course. He'd quit ages ago. A habit was harder to get rid of than a physical addiction.

He shook his head a bit, stepping down onto a cracked sidewalk, giving serious thought as to whether he should stay in this house. The motel was an option, one he should at least check out.

Except for his mother. He shook his head again and considered Lu. He knew she'd been annoyed for some time over the fact that he came home so seldom. Hell, to be honest about it, he rarely came home at all. A trip for his brother's wedding? Another for Cassie's baptism? Not a record to be proud of.

Then Caleb had died, which he was sure had just about killed his mom, and he still hadn't come home except for a week for the funeral. A while after he'd returned overseas, she'd emailed him to tell him she was selling the house.

It did her no good, she said, to be rattling around in that big old place by herself. Besides, Elaine and her grand-daughter needed her help.

So here she was. Here *he* was. In the house Caleb had bought for his new family. A house his brother would never share with them.

God!

Just as he'd made up his mind to take his car and head to the motel, his mother pulled up in the driveway. She still drove her aging silver Volvo. It wasn't until Lu climbed out that she saw Devlin.

Her mouth dropped open; then her purse fell to the ground, and she opened her arms and hurried toward him. Devlin met her halfway, lifting her off her feet in a bear hug. Only then did he realize just how much he had missed her.

When he set Lu on her feet, she stepped back, holding his forearms, and said, "Let me get a look at you, boy."

It gave him a chance to look at her as well. The last couple of years had taken some weight off her. Maybe too much? Her hair had turned almost completely gray, and the lines had deepened in her face. Her skin looked soft and smooth, though, as if it had never really aged. Bright hazel eyes looked up at him from above a mouth that had once sung him lullabies and kissed his small hurts.

She was beautiful to him, and always would be.

"How long you here for?" she demanded as her smiling eyes scoped him. "Damn, it's good to see you. But how long? A few days? A week?"

Her small expectation caused a pang in him. "Longer this time," he promised. "Maybe a month or more."

For the second time, Lu's mouth dropped open; then her face creased with concern. "You get fired?"

Under other circumstances, he might have laughed. Shame pricked him as he realized he'd neglected Lu to the point that she thought he must have been fired if he was going to visit for more than a few days.

He shook his head. "I built up too much unused vacation time. The bean counters booted me out the door and told me not to come back until I'd used most of it."

"Smart bean counters," she said, then laughed. "You'll be staying here, of course. We've got a little room."

"Elaine was pretty definite about it."

Lu nodded. "She would be. She's got a good heart. And Cassie. Did you meet Cassie?"

"She's beautiful, but busy with her crayons."

He saw something like sorrow flit over his mother's face, but it swiftly left and her smile returned.

"Well, since you're here, help me with the groceries."

Just like old times, he thought as he rounded the back end of the Volvo and opened the trunk. Help with the groceries. Ever since he was old enough to lift a bag.

Except now the bags were reusable, with handles.

Elaine helped put everything away, the two women chatting companionably. Cassie sat in a chair at the table and simply watched.

He'd heard from his mom some time back that Cassie had some developmental problems, but the subject had been skimmed over as if minor. After watching Cassie color so intently despite his arrival, despite his conver-

sation with Elaine, he wasn't sure it was exactly minor.
Especially now, when the child seemed totally focused
on the process of putting groceries away. No chatter, no
moving around, no attempts to help or curiosity about the
items being stored. Just focused observation.

But then, what did he know about young children? Zip.

Once everything was put away, Lu started a fresh pot
of coffee. "Now to get Devlin settled," she said briskly.

"The office," Elaine responded. "I'll start moving some
things out of the way."

Devlin straightened. "I can help with that."

Elaine shook her head. "There's not much. You'd just
get in the way. How about you get your suitcase?"

Passing by, Lu patted his cheek. She had to reach up
because he'd outgrown her by nearly a foot. "It really isn't
much. Now, go get your things."

A corner of his mouth lifted. She was still his mother
and acting as if he were still ten. He kinda liked it, actually. It had been so many years—maybe too many. A
grown man, he stood on his own two feet and leaned on
no one. He also had no one to care for him in the small,
important ways.

"Okay," he said, and turned to go out to his car. He'd
started to think he should cut this visit short, to maybe
a week or so, and go to another town, a place where he
wouldn't be creating a tidal wave of complications for
these two women.

Then he realized he was trying to slip into an old habit,
one that had made him a stranger to his own mother.
Move on and move along, and make no deep emotional
connections no matter where he landed. He couldn't afford to care deeply.

Except he already had an emotional connection here,

and he couldn't leave yet. Not when his mother kept looking at him and getting a huge smile on her face.

Move along? No, not yet.

FROM HALF A world away, two people had come looking for him, trying painstakingly to follow his travels. To find out where he'd gone and where he remained.

The search might have been more difficult except they had contacts of their own. When fairly certain they had been given most of the information they needed, travel became their primary goal. Their primary purpose.

They couldn't wait too long, or their target might move again. The way he'd been moving for weeks now.

The desire for vengeance drove them. It was a hungry master.

They ignored everything else.

Chapter Three

Elaine headed to work three days later, thinking Devlin's visit wasn't as much of an imposition as she'd almost feared. As houseguests went, he ought to get a gold star. No messes or forgotten dishes anywhere so far. Everything he'd brought with him tucked away neatly in her office. Even last evening, he'd made himself nearly invisible.

It was almost as if he wasn't there, except for when he sat with Lu and carried on a mostly one-sided conversation. If Devlin had much to say about his life, Elaine doubted she'd ever hear it.

Cassie had begun to relax around him, too, to judge by breakfast this morning, although she wasn't yet interested in making him part of her life. She watched but didn't talk. Lu let her be while still trying to make sure she felt like part of it all.

Lu, Elaine often thought, was amazing, an angel.

At her work office, however, her thoughts did a quick one-eighty turn. Bixby, the rancher, was a big part of the conversation still.

Detective Guy Redwing, along with deputies Connie Parish and Kerri Canaday, filled her in.

"Bixby wasn't kidding about those trespassers, Elaine," Connie said. "They were camping out there on the Selvage side of the fence. I'd guess the Selvages haven't noticed yet."

Elaine plopped down in one of the office chairs. She'd wondered, in some small, unkind part of her brain, whether Bixby had been exaggerating. Evidently not. "Seriously? How many?"

Guy shrugged. "Maybe six or seven that we saw. Anyway, we moved them out yesterday afternoon. Gave them a trespass warning, including the part about how the landowners might shoot them on sight. They left."

"They'll be back," Kerri remarked, stroking the white fur of her service dog, Snowy. "Nothing they said made it sound otherwise."

Guy shook his head. "Damn fools. And all because there's some lights in the sky. Could be almost anything."

"You'd think," Elaine said. "I saw them when I was out there. I got a real scare thinking they might be part of a range fire, but Bixby told me he's been seeing them most of his life and they don't hurt anything."

Kerri cocked a brow at her. "So you saw them, too?"

"They were what made me pull into Bixby's place. I thought, like I said, I was seeing a range fire. Damn radios and phones wouldn't work, though."

Connie snorted. "Typical. They almost never do out there."

No news there, Elaine thought. "Well, I guess we'll have to keep an eye on this before someone gets shot. Bixby was sure ready when I was out there. Waving his shotgun, spittle flying."

"You can't blame him," Connie said. "It's hard enough making money off a ranch these days without fools interfering. Ethan, my husband, is working Micah's sheep ranch with him. Well, you guys know that. All I was gonna say was, wool isn't doing much better than beef, either."

Elaine nodded. She glanced over at the coffee urn and saw Velma, the dispatcher who must be at least half as old as the county, sitting at her console and puffing on a cigarette below the *No Smoking* sign that was tacked to the wall. That was Velma—she'd been the department's dispatcher for as long as anyone could remember, and no one was going to fire her. Nobody even thought about it.

But Velma's presence meant Velma had made the coffee in the big urn. The bottles of various antacids that lined the coffee bar attested to the quality of the brew. Which meant that if Elaine wanted coffee she could enjoy, she needed to take her thermos across the way to Maude's diner.

She could have laughed, but then she'd have to explain why. Nope. Not in Velma's hearing. She turned her attention back to Connie, Guy and Kerri. "I guess I should stop and talk with the Selvages on my patrol today. Unless you did yesterday?"

Guy shook his head. "The loonies were still gone after we scared 'em off the day before. Can't prove they'll be back. So what could I say to Lew? Hell, for all I know, Lew Selvage won't care. He's got a much bigger spread than Bixby. Healthier, too."

Elaine blew out a long breath that briefly puffed her cheeks. "Okay, I'll stop and talk to Lew. He's got hired hands he needs to warn. I hope we can get through this without any corpses."

Connie shook her head. "You know I'm not bloodthirsty, but you gotta wonder about people who think they have a right to run all over private land."

"Without getting hurt," Elaine added. "Like it or not, it's the same as breaking into someone's house."

"Well, not quite," Kerri said dryly, making Elaine laugh.

She picked up her thermos, then headed down a few doors across from Main Street and entered Maude's diner. It was properly known as the City Café, but Elaine didn't think she'd heard anyone call it that in her entire life.

It was not a large diner, more of a cozy place, but large enough to be a breakfast gathering spot for a lot of retired older men, and later for a lunch hour for workers in the surrounding shops. The diner never lacked for customers.

This morning, however, the place felt strange. Elaine reached the counter and found herself facing Mavis, Maude's daughter, a virtual clone of her blunt and stocky mother.

Mavis took Elaine's insulated bottle without asking; it was a morning ritual. Then Elaine scanned the dining area and saw a few faces she didn't recognize.

When Mavis handed back the thermos, Elaine remarked, "Got some tourists, huh?"

Mavis snorted. "Don't know what they are. Sure ain't here for hunting or hiking. More like weirdos. But they ain't talking to me." She gave a harsh laugh. "Not sure I wanna hear nothing from them anyways."

Now Elaine's curiosity nagged full strength. She picked up her bottle, then headed toward the table with the four men and one woman she didn't recognize. The advantage of being a sheriff's deputy was that she could ask casual questions of strangers.

Before she reached the table, five sets of eyes turned her way. They knew she was headed for them, and swiftly exchanged looks. Something to hide?

"Howdy," she said pleasantly, putting a smile on her face. "You folks visiting us for a while?"

Looks were exchanged again. Then, silently, they appeared to have decided on a mouthpiece. The woman, with long dark hair caught in a ponytail, a woman who didn't look as if she'd even reached her midtwenties, spoke.

"Just a while," she answered.

"And you are?"

The woman's chin thrust forward a bit, as if she resented being questioned, but she didn't hesitate and didn't seem to have anything to hide. "I'm Lotte Berg. Who are you?"

Elaine's smile broadened. A young woman with spunk—she always liked seeing that. "I'm Deputy Elaine Paltier." She pointed to the embroidery on the front of her jacket. "And here's my badge number, if you feel like complaining because I asked for your name."

The entire group recoiled slightly at that, even the brave Lotte Berg. Apparently they didn't want that kind of encounter with a cop.

Elaine leaned back against the edge of a nearby booth. "We don't see many new faces around here. We get curious. So are you here for hunting? Wrong season, I'm afraid—but that would be true most places. Hiking?"

Now Lotte looked irritated. "We haven't done anything wrong, so it's none of your business."

One of the guys drew a sharp breath. Elaine set her bottle on the table in the booth behind her, pulled out an empty chair at the table where the group had gathered and sat with them.

"Well," she said slowly, looking at each face in turn, "it might could be my business. You go hiking up in the mountains or camping… Do you have any idea how fast the weather changes up there? We can get snow in July. Then there's rain. We're talking hypothermia here."

"So?" Lotte demanded.

"So you could die. You have any way of calling for help if somebody breaks an ankle? Or if you get lost? Cell phones don't work too good in the mountains. Any of you got a satellite phone? Regardless, it'd be wise to tell the forest service ranger where you want to hike and when you expect to be back."

Blank looks greeted her. Which told her instantly that these kids weren't at all familiar with the mountains. Great. Maybe it would be best if they bothered Lew Selvage after all.

Lotte suddenly looked a bit sullen. "We're not going into the mountains."

"Good," Elaine said amiably, getting ready to stand. "We don't like having to send out rescue parties for people who should know better." She paused. "If not the mountains, then what?"

No one answered. Looks passed around again.

Elaine stood, twisting a bit to grab her bottle. Then she looked down at them once more. "I don't know where you're from. But be careful of trespassing in these parts. You might find yourselves evicted at the end of a rifle or shotgun."

As she left, Mavis gave her a nod of approval. Elaine didn't feel she deserved it. She'd done what she could but figured it wasn't enough.

Driving out to the Selvage property gave her plenty of time to think. She scanned the roads, of course, looking for any kind of trouble. She laughed to herself. Trouble out here was likely to be a calf that had found its way past a fence and wandering in the road. Or a downed fence that created the possibility of a bigger problem.

Inevitably, her thoughts turned to Devlin. He really *was* a good houseguest. Yesterday—her second unexpected day off, brought about by the sheriff saying she looked tired—Devlin had limited himself to chatting with his mother and occasionally her. He'd even been respectful of Cassie's choice to be left alone. Unlike many people, he didn't press her to talk to him, or help himself to some of her crayons to prove he was a good guy who could color with her.

Elaine treasured her days off. She didn't have to "be on" for other people. No expectations, no duties—just time to be with Cassie. And with Lu, when her mother-in-law didn't take off to spend an afternoon with her friends.

Lu needed the breaks, too. Cassie wasn't troublesome, but she created a problem for those who loved her. Everyone wanted to help, but there seemed to be no way to open Cassie's world. She chose the people she would let in, the activities she preferred, and ignored the rest.

Elaine often tried not to think about the problems Cassie faced, because whenever she did, she grew so sad she wanted to cry.

So, for now, she dragged her thoughts away from Cassie and Devlin to wondering how Lew Selvage would react to all this. UFO hunters. For God's sake.

She knew people saw lights in the sky in the wide-open and scarcely occupied places out there, but most were shrugged off. Ranchers and farmers had more important issues to think about than wondering about some light, even though it might grow large. Elaine was sure most of these sightings were never mentioned or talked about.

Who'd want his neighbors to think he was crazy? It

was like Beggan Bixby. Those red lights had been there most of his life, and they didn't bother anything so he didn't worry about them.

What he was worried about were the trespassers—justifiably so.

Five of them in Maude's this morning. Were they the only ones? Were more coming?

"Ah, crap," she said to the interior of her vehicle. Five, maybe eight, could be handled; more than a dozen could become a serious problem. Larger groups were apt to be more defiant of land boundaries and a few cops.

Someone was going to get hurt. Maybe killed. And she didn't know what to do other than warn the UFO guys off.

At last the entrance to the Selvage ranch appeared to the right. Another mile and she'd be at the house. If Lew wasn't there, she'd have to call him on the sat phone, which wasn't going to make him happy if he was out on the range doing something.

Oh, well. He deserved a warning.

Lew *was* there, however. He came out onto his large porch to greet her as she approached. A short man, he was whipcord lean from a lot of hard work and owned a weathered face from years on the range. Anybody who thought raising cattle meant sitting on your duff until the time arrived to sell them at market ought to come out and try working with Lew or any other rancher.

He wore the standard uniform of jeans—nearly worn white in places—and a checked Western shirt beneath a shearling vest. He touched the brim of his black hat in greeting as she climbed out of her Suburban.

"Hey, what's up, Deputy?" he asked. "Don't recall having any problems."

Elaine shook her head as she approached, then shook

his calloused hand. "You may have one already. I'm not sure, but I know Mr. Bixby has a trespasser problem. We've warned them off, but I'm frankly not sure they'll stay away."

Lew waved her over to a wooden rocker. "I'll get us some coffee, then you can tell me about this gang."

Gang? Elaine didn't want anyone thinking of them that way. A desire to drive them off was one thing, but feeling free to shoot people who had been designated as criminals in many minds wouldn't be good at all.

Lew returned with two mugs and handed her one before settling in the other rocker. "So what's up with these trespassers that's got Bixby so mad? I swear, that man can explode about anything."

Remembering how Beggan Bixby had danced around with that shotgun and spat while ranting to her, Elaine privately agreed. "Well, he was angry, all right. Justifiably so, it seems. He's got those red lights. You've seen them?"

"Hell yeah. From one corner of my ranch. I don't like the way them damn things move around. But near as I can tell, they ain't doing any harm. Bixby's been seeing them for years. So what's the problem?"

Elaine couldn't quite suppress a grimace. "A bunch of people who think they're UFOs. Bothering Bixby's cattle. I don't know yet if they've crossed his fence, but he seems to think so." She tucked away the news that those lights moved around. As if that would help anything.

"Oh, hell," Lew said. He put his cup on a small wooden table between the two rockers. "That'd get him wound up. It'd get me wound up, too. I guess I need to have my ranch hands check the fence along Bixby's land. If someone has been cutting it…" He let the sentence trail off.

But Elaine didn't need him to finish it. She drained her

mug and stood. "Lew, you don't need me to tell you that you don't want the crime scene team all over your land because some idiot got shot."

Lew offered a crooked smile. "Trespassing," he said.

"I get it." Elaine shook her head and sighed. "But there would still have to be an investigation, trespassers or not, stand your ground or not."

She waved to him as she drove away, wondering where all this would lead.

No way to know.

DEVLIN TOOK THE afternoon to wander around Conard City. Some things had changed, he noticed, but not very many since he'd lived here the first couple decades of his life.

The school appeared to be the same except for a larger sports field. The hospital was bigger. The community college was probably the biggest change of all, as was a group of apartment buildings that seemed to be acting mostly as student housing. The park's trees and flowers had clearly become lusher with time. Familiar, yet a little unfamiliar.

He learned most about the changes from pausing to chat with people, some of whom remembered him. By and large, though, no one seemed reluctant to talk about the town.

He was a little annoyed he hadn't taken the time to walk around when he was here for his brother's funeral, renew some acquaintances. But then, he acknowledged, this no longer felt like home to him. Or like his hometown.

His job had taken him into a wider, different world. One that had changed him irrevocably. One that had moved him so far from Conard City and Conard County that he doubted either would ever feel like home again.

Honestly, though, he hadn't come back to this particular place to revive memories. He'd come to see his mother. To see his godchild, his niece. He'd been too absent to be a real uncle to the little girl. He even felt ashamed, knowing that Caleb would have expected better of him. Would have had every right to.

But his job hadn't given him a whole lot of leeway.

And that job had apparently caused someone to die. This had seemed like the safest place to come, his connections here so tenuous. A place to stay out of the way while his contacts were protected.

But the town seemed to have grown a whole new batch of strangers, from what little Elaine had said.

Knowing how little change this town was used to, a snort of laughter escaped him, drawing looks from passing pedestrians. He gave them a smile and a wave and kept walking.

Maude's, he decided. Instead of letting Lu cook yet again. He pulled his cell phone out of his pocket and called her. She sounded only too glad to have fried chicken, potato salad and fruit for dinner.

"Cassie loves fried chicken," Lu said.

"Well, I hope you do, too."

His mother laughed. "Of course I do. And Maude makes the best."

So he headed to Maude's, his personal list growing to include a pie. A peach pie. *Oh, yeah.*

Then he found himself facing Sheriff Gage Dalton on the sidewalk near Maude's. Gage looked pleasant enough—at least as pleasant as he could with half his face covered by a burn scar. A man who would forever limp because of a bomb that had killed his first family. A man who lived with constant pain.

Devlin remembered him from his youth here, back

when Gage had been known as Hell's Own Archangel as he walked off the agony of his losses at night on the streets of this small town. A face without expression, eyes black as midnight.

The man had changed over the years. He offered Devlin a half smile, the most his face could do anymore. "Nice to see you again."

"It's been a while," Devlin agreed. He wondered if he was about to get the third degree, considering how rarely he'd been in this town and how short his visits had been. A wedding and a funeral? Sounded like a bad joke.

"Staying a while?"

Devlin cracked his own smile, covering the darker thoughts that had haunted him for years. "About a month. Blame it on the bean counters. Apparently they don't want to pay me for unused vacation."

Gage lifted a brow. "But no other vacations in all these years?"

Devlin realized he'd walked into a trap he needed to ease his way out of. *All these years?* The subtler way of asking why he hadn't come back here much. Good question.

One he couldn't truthfully answer. But even while on vacation, he still needed to protect the people who worked for him, all of them out there in dangerous places, in danger of losing their lives if anyone found out their relationship with Devlin. That need usually didn't carry him far from headquarters, but this time, someone had died. He fought that memory back into the black box in his mind. "I'm a workaholic," he replied to Dalton. "The policy on vacations just changed."

Gage nodded, clearly only partially convinced.

Well, hell, what was he supposed to do about that? His life was already a mess of lies, and now he needed to add another. No, he decided. He would not. If Gage wanted to check him out, he'd get the official unshakable cover story. At least he and his colleagues thought it was unshakable.

Gage spoke after a few moments of studying him. "Enjoy your stay," he said and headed for the diner.

A second of indecision, then Devlin fell in beside him. "I told my mother I'd bring home some of Maude's fried chicken for dinner."

Gage smiled. "Best damn chicken I ever tasted. What about you? Being overseas all these years must have given you a taste for exotic foods."

Devlin had to laugh. "Sure, when I get out of the embassy. But our cafeteria makes a mean burger, too."

It was Gage's turn to laugh. "Hadn't thought about that."

Inside the diner, they parted ways, Gage heading over to a table to chat, Devlin going to the counter to order dinner.

When he stepped outside again, he felt uneasy. Looking around quickly, he saw nothing out of the ordinary, but the feeling didn't dissipate.

Hell. Once he rounded the corner, the sensation disappeared. He shook his head a little. Had he become paranoid because of that incident in Chechnya? Maybe so.

Another thing to work on. He seemed to have developed plenty of self-improvement projects over the years.

State Department. Ha!

Chapter Four

In the early evening, about to finish her shift, Elaine swung by the Bixby ranch. She could at least find out if there had been any more trouble since her fellow deputies had warned off the nuts.

It ought to make those trespassers more than a little uneasy that so many cops had an eye on them. Or that shooting them would be legal. Well, *might* be legal, although she wasn't about to tell those UFO guys it might not be. It was enough to let the ranchers know there'd be complications, an investigation regardless of their reasons. Nobody needed that.

Beggan Bixby was sitting on his front porch. His shotgun wasn't far away.

"Hey," Elaine said as she approached. "Still having trouble?"

"Not since those deputies came out here. Went out to check for myself."

She nodded, standing at the foot of the three steps that climbed to his porch. "So maybe it's settled."

Bixby snorted. "Like hell."

Elaine placed one hand on her hip, the side away from her holster. She'd been hoping that the peace, however temporary, would have calmed Bixby. Apparently it had not.

"Mr. Bixby, it's legally questionable if you shoot those trespassers."

"They're on my land!"

"You'd still wind up in the middle of a murder investigation. Maybe even wind up in court. You don't really need me to tell you that. But what good would it do your herd?"

That seemed to deprive him of speech. Finally, he said, "I can shoot trespassers. It's the *law*."

"Yup," she agreed. "Except a court is going to have to figure out the fine details of that law. Drive 'em off, but don't do it by pulling a trigger."

She left him with his mouth hanging open. Hardly surprising. A lot of folks thought they had rights they didn't. Like shooting people.

Well, she sure didn't like the way this might go. Lew Selvage, she trusted to be reasonable and deal with the problem in a way that wouldn't get him tangled up in some kind of legal mess. Bixby's fury might override any common sense he had.

She thought of those people she had warned at Maude's and decided she'd have to check tomorrow to see if they'd left town. Or if any more were arriving.

Because now that the Bixby spread was on the "UFO map," other seekers would probably show up, even for just a couple of red lights. Man!

When she got home, she was greeted by the mouthwatering aroma of fried chicken. Maude's. Nothing smelled quite like it.

Cassie emerged from the kitchen with a genuine smile. She wore her favorite outfit, pink leggings and a pink T-shirt with a sparkly butterfly on it. "Mommy," she said.

The sound of the word melted Elaine's heart. Cassie had started saying it only a month or so ago.

Elaine squatted, hoping against hope that Cassie would come to her for a hug. It didn't happen. It might never happen.

Instead, Cassie turned and went back to the kitchen.

"Food," she said.

Well, food was always a good thing. Especially when it smelled like that.

In short order, the four of them sat at the table with full plates.

WHILE EVERYONE TUCKED in and Elaine thanked Devlin for bringing dinner, he was looking at Cassie, thinking for the first time how hard this might be for his niece. Thinking for the first time that Caleb should be here to help her.

Like it had been Caleb's choice. He turned his thoughts away from that. He didn't need the guilt trip that was on the menu every time he thought of his brother and his brother's family. At least Elaine had Lu to help her. Even if Caleb's big brother was proving useless.

"How did your day go?" he asked Elaine.

"It was interesting, that's for sure." Her mouth tipped into a faint smile. "Nothing like UFOs to add a little excitement."

"UFOs? Really?"

Lu spoke. "Now this I wanna hear."

No reason to keep it secret. Protecting Beggan Bixby's privacy had probably long since gone by the wayside, given the speed of the local grapevine. Given the fact that, in his state of mind, Bixby had probably complained to everyone he knew. And why not?

The worst of it was, Elaine was sure he was probably

blaming the sheriff's department more than the invaders. Those complaints might give Gage Dalton trouble in the next election.

"Dang," she murmured to herself. This was hardly a political issue and, regardless, she was supposed to be worrying about the law, not the politics.

"What?" asked Lu.

"I just thought about how the politics of this whole situation might give Gage some trouble in the next election."

Lu snorted. "This county loves that man. Anyway, nobody's ever tried to stand against him. And what brought that on?"

"Beggan Bixby. UFOs. UFO hunters, I think they call themselves. And five or more strangers trespassing on Bixby's ranch to look at two red lights." She tilted her head. "I talked to five of them at Maude's, but I'm not sure they're the only ones going out at night to hunt those lights." She shook her head, thinking more detective work might be required, and returned her attention to the fried chicken.

Lu spoke, raising her eyebrows. "As often as those lights show up? God knows what they are, but is that worth traipsing out over rangeland in the middle of the night to take pictures?"

Elaine glanced at Devlin to find him smiling. Man, did he have a gorgeous smile. The kind that made a woman's heart skip a time or two.

"There are lots of believers," he said. "And judging by recent information, some of those UAPs can't be identified. Or brushed aside."

Elaine nodded. "You're right. Even so, now we have people driving Beggan Bixby crazy. They're trespassing and disturbing his cattle. Not a good thing when you consider how nervous cattle don't fatten as well."

"I didn't know that," Devlin remarked.

"You aren't here enough to know about such things," his mother answered tartly.

Elaine didn't miss the way Devlin looked down. Just briefly, just enough for her to realize that stung. So when it came to his mother, he could still feel scolded. That amused her but also made her like him more. The man who rarely revealed anything about himself, at least not during his brief visits, had just revealed quite a bit.

"So," he asked, "what can you do about these UFO hunters? If they're upsetting Bixby, then they should get off his land, right?"

"Exactly," Elaine said. "We warned them off. Unless they've left town, they'll be back out there soon. I need to check if they're still here. Or if more of them have come."

Lu spoke. "I can't believe all this fuss over a couple of red lights. Sure, they're weird, but who knows?"

"I haven't seen them before," Elaine said. "The other night, they were so big and orange I thought we had a range fire."

"Well, that's new," Lu answered before picking up a drumstick. "They were never that big when I saw them. Always thought they were lights on a tower or something."

"Well, they were big enough that I was in a real hurry to get the firefighters out there. Except, of course, my radio, cell and sat phone weren't working."

She shrugged.

Lu chuckled. "Never fails when you need 'em most."

"Anyway, Bixby was fit to be tied, mad at us because we haven't gotten rid of the trespassers and he pays taxes, too. Oh yeah, then there was the shotgun."

At that, Lu drew a sharp breath. "Elaine…"

"I wasn't really worried about him shooting me, Lu. He wanted to shoot some other people."

"Still…" Lu shook her head. "Your job isn't usually dangerous."

Elaine kept her lips sealed. She always tried to make it all seem safe for Lu and Cassie's sake, but it wasn't always. No cop's job could always be without threat.

Elaine looked at her daughter and saw she was picking at her food. Evidently, Cassie had eaten enough. "Time for a bath, Cassie?"

Cassie shook her head. "No!"

Another word her child had learned. Elaine stared at her, knowing they came to this sometimes, knowing it would only cause Cassie to totally withdraw if she pressed the issue. Or worse, cause a serious meltdown.

"Okay," she said after a moment. "We have to wash your hands and face, though. Greasy from the chicken." And everything else Cassie had eaten with her fingers.

After a few seconds, Cassie nodded. She'd tolerate the touching for that long.

DEVLIN WATCHED ELAINE coax Cassie to the bathroom, then helped Lu clean up the dinner mess. They chatted casually, and at some point, Devlin realized a gulf had grown between them over the years. This was not the kind of easy chatting that occurred between people who were close. They were two strangers working their way to some kind of relationship. It was a state he was familiar with in his job but uncomfortable with his own mother.

God, he'd been away too long.

Later, as night took over the world, he stepped outside

and stood in the near dark, arms folded and legs apart. He once again felt uneasy, as if the night held a threat.

It well might, he supposed. Intelligence sometimes had holes in it.

His bosses pretty much dismissed it, knowing the real threat was for Devlin's contacts overseas. And they were right. With a war going on over there, nobody would look for him any farther than the other side of the town.

But there was always a risk he might inadvertently reveal something that would give away another of his contacts.

So he'd come here, the most out-of-the-way place in his life. There was nothing he could do here that would expose anyone.

But the threat he felt was inchoate yet. It seemed to seep through the night with no focus. He'd felt that before in foreign lands, but his job always brought some danger with it. Always. This was different.

Just paranoia, he told himself. A learned response to constantly being a stranger in a strange land. Even here.

But it wasn't often that he suspected he might be a direct target. He thrust the paranoia onto a back burner but refused to douse it entirely. Fear, remaining alert, had been useful his entire adult life.

CONARD CITY WAS a small town. Not as small as some towns the foreign women were used to, but small enough that strangers might be noticed. They carefully stayed to the edges, watching the daily lives of the townspeople, trying to ascertain rhythms. To figure out under what circumstances they could risk being seen without being noticed.

To figure out how to pick out one man from the many,

a man whose face they didn't even know. A man whose name had never been given to them. The people who had sent them here either didn't know—which wouldn't be surprising when dealing with a spy—or didn't want them to know because it might reveal a secret.

Either way, the women weren't happy with any of it.

That would require talking to people, a dangerous thing to do when you only had questions that might arouse suspicions. When you had a foreign accent and a questionable command of English.

Maybe the man they wanted to find was a stranger here, too? Might he already stood out? But how would they tell the difference?

They found a spot in the woods near a trickling stream and made a rugged camp for themselves. Life had taught them to make do: a tent from their outer cloaks. Foraging for most of their food. Snaring a rabbit.

The number of animals surprised them. War, they surmised, hadn't decimated the wildlife here the way it had at home. But then, nothing around here had been turned into rubble by endless conflict.

Hunkering down, they tried to plan, only to realize that their original plan, the one that had brought them halfway around the world, had been incomplete. But how could it have been any better when they had no way of knowing what they might find once they arrived?

They ought to be pleased they had gotten this far, which was no mean task. It had taken a contact at their *own* consulate to point them this way. To arm them with a gun and poison. To tell them this much. They'd been fortunate in that because the woman had sympathized with their mission, hadn't demanded some form of bribe the way most men would have.

But she hadn't been able to identify the man they sought in any meaningful way. Evidently he hid behind a wall of secrets.

They'd also developed an uneasy appreciation for how much one side knew about the other. How could their consulate know where this man had gone to hide? Come to that, how could they know about this faceless, nameless monster at all?

Because of someone like their brother, someone who had been spying on this man? Perhaps someone who had betrayed their brother and not the American at all.

The awareness gave them shivers. This was a world they didn't know. They were used to an obvious war, actions in the open for the most part. Not secrets behind closed doors.

It also gave them plenty to wonder about. As they sat shivering around a tiny fire and the wind from the mountains blew an icy breath from the glaciers above, they had plenty to talk about and worry about.

Their brother had been betrayed. The man who had recruited Niko was responsible for his death; he must have somehow let it be known that Niko was informing. Directly or indirectly didn't matter.

That, they figured out without any trouble. But the woman at the consulate in Los Angeles gave them more reasons to fear. She had known where the American man had gone. How had she known? And now she knew that Zoe and Kalina had come after him. How could she be trusted not to reveal that to the people in the American Embassy that she must have talked to just to get this little bit of information?

The young women sat shivering, and their fear slowly deepened until it became almost as strong as their thirst for vengeance. Niko might not be the last one to be betrayed.

Miserably they realized they might have made some huge mistakes. They should run now. Right now.

But they refused to give up on their need for vengeance. They'd known from the start they could be killed.

They just hadn't suspected death might come from someone they had trusted.

And they still had to find a way to get into that town, to collect information without being obvious.

They'd never dreamed they would ever be aimed at like a bullet at a target.

THE NEXT DAY brought a powdering of snow, not unheard of even as the trees leafed out for the spring. The white dusting didn't last past the noonday sun, though, but the air remained invigoratingly crisp.

Lu insisted on making breakfast for the four of them even though Devlin offered to pick up food at Maude's or the truck stop.

"Don't deprive me," she said to Devlin. "For years and years, I enjoyed making breakfast for your dad. His favorite meal of the day."

Soon bacon sizzled in a large frying pan, eggs were beaten with a bit of milk and slices of bread were toasted and buttered. And Lu wanted no help, not even from Elaine.

Elaine's curiosity had been carefully tamped for days now, but it refused to be silenced permanently. She eyed Devlin over her coffee. "So what exactly do you do for the State Department?"

"A little of this and that."

She snorted. *"Right."* She drew the word out.

He laughed. "Yeah. I'm a foreign service officer. Depending on where I'm posted, I may be a diplomatic attaché."

"So more than one hat?"

He nodded, admiring the plate of food Lu placed in front of him. "Mom, that looks fabulous!"

"Told you I'm good at making breakfast. You ought to remember." She placed another plate in front of Elaine, then a small one in front of Cassie.

Cassie regarded her food with some interest, then pointed to the scrambled eggs. "Yellow." Another one of Cassie's very few words. The names of colors seemed to attract her, though.

Elaine braced herself. This might go badly. "Yes, the eggs are yellow."

Cassie shoved them off her plate and onto the table. Then she picked up a strip of bacon and began to eat.

Lu ignored the mess and sat with her own plate across from Elaine. "Oh, these yellow eggs are yummy," she said as she lifted a forkful.

"They sure are," Elaine replied, helping herself to her own. "I love yellow eggs."

No response from Cassie, who seemed quite content with bacon and toast.

After a minute, Elaine spoke again. "These yellow eggs are so good. Do you want to try just a little bit, Cassie?"

Cassie looked up from her bacon at the pile of scrambled eggs by the edge of her plate, which by now had to be cold. Not good. But still…

Elaine ate another mouthful of eggs, pretending to ignore Cassie, leaving her alone like she wanted.

But, causing Elaine's heart to leap, Cassie finally reached out a thumb and finger and pinched the tiniest bit of egg and carried it to her mouth.

Elaine reacted immediately with positive reinforce-
ment. "That was so brave of you, Cassie, to try the yellow eggs! I'm proud of you!"

Then she let it go.

DEVLIN, WATCHING ALL THIS, felt a strong pang for Elaine.
Over the last few days, he'd gotten a much clearer idea of
all she and her daughter were dealing with, and it definitely looked like an awful situation for Elaine.

He could see the pain in her eyes when she reached
out in some way to Cassie and she didn't respond. He
could read the yearning on her face for just one little hug
or touch.

He couldn't imagine how hard that had to be for Elaine.
Yet she always remained calm and patient with Cassie.
Always warm.

So did his mother. In just brief flashes, Lu was more
like a protective tiger, though. Protective of Cassie. Devlin wondered if Elaine showed that side, too, sometimes.
Probably.

Guilt speared him. What if he had quit his job and
stayed here to look after Cassie and Elaine after Caleb
died? Yet, looking at Cassie now, he wondered how he
could have made a difference. If Cassie wasn't connecting
with her mother in any deep emotional way, why would
she have connected with him?

He closed his eyes briefly, squashing a guilt that bor-
dered on the self-aggrandizing. No reason to think he'd
have had any more impact than anyone else.

Lu started clearing the table. Cassie's plate was mostly
empty of bacon and toast, but the eggs still lay on the
table. Most of them, anyway.

Cassie slid off her chair and got her crayons and coloring book from the counter. Lu moved quickly to clear away the eggs before anything landed on them.

Then Cassie started coloring her unicorn while her mom looked on sadly.

God, Devlin thought. Yet somehow sorrow didn't hang over this house. It didn't dog these two women's every waking moment, every step. They were remarkable.

"Sally's coming today, right?" Elaine asked.

"At eleven," his mother answered.

"Sally?" Devlin asked.

Elaine gave him a small smile. "Sally's helping Cassie. Right, Cassie?"

Cassie shrugged.

"Her support therapist," Elaine elaborated. "She helps all of us."

"But not today," Lu reminded her. "Today is Cassie's alone."

"That's right."

Lu tilted her head. "So find a reason to get out of here. Since you're not in uniform, I guess you have the day off. Go have a chilly picnic or something."

"That sounds like a great idea," Devlin said, rising, his determination growing. Elaine needed time that wasn't filled every single second with her job and Cassie. *Well, I ought to know something about that,* he thought wryly. He wasn't good at taking time for himself, either. "I wouldn't mind familiarizing myself with the area. I've been away so long I feel like a stranger." He looked at Elaine. "At least, if you don't mind the company."

Now she tilted her head back, looking up at him. "Sounds okay to me," she said after a barely perceptible hesitation.

So maybe okay, he thought. Fair enough.

Elaine told Cassie where she was going and offered her

an invitation to join them for the picnic. Cassie clearly wasn't interested, so Elaine slid off her chair, promising to return soon. Cassie remained superficially indifferent.

A trip to Maude's provided lunch and bottled water. Jackets on, the two headed out into the countryside in Elaine's official vehicle. It seemed, Devlin thought, that she was expected to use it all the time. Just as it seemed she had to strap on her pistol every time she stepped out her front door, even when in civvies, like now.

As the town dropped away behind them and the range began to spread openly over the rolling hills, he asked her about it.

"Are you on duty all the time?"

She glanced at him. "Why?"

"Because you're in your official vehicle and you're wearing your sidearm."

She laughed quietly. "Well…it creates a presence, and we're a small department. Add to that, that everyone around here is armed. Although you see little enough of it in town, it's not wise for a cop to ever be unarmed. We could need it at any moment—not that it happens often."

"I hope not. I don't remember this being the Wild West."

She laughed again. "Civilization arrived a long time ago. We're not having shoot-outs on Main Street."

Which wasn't true of a lot of the places where Devlin had been stationed over the years. He'd become used to an amazing level of violence and doubted anything in Conard County could hold a candle to any of his assignments.

He turned his attention to the passing countryside, trying to touch the boy and young man he'd been so long ago, the one who had grown up here, safer than he'd realized until much later.

"Whoa," Elaine said abruptly.

He looked forward and saw a small knot of people and three cars jammed onto the shoulder. The people appeared to be talking with one another.

"Campers," Elaine said. "Probably our UFO hunters."

Since she wasn't on duty, Devlin expected her to drive by, but instead she slowed to a stop. The group at the roadside had a variety of reactions and were quickly joined by four more.

"More of them have come," Elaine remarked. "I was afraid of that."

She put her vehicle in Park and climbed out. Devlin waited, reluctant to shove himself onto her turf. She didn't need *his* help to handle this. It was her job, after all. But he still itched to get involved and was glad she'd left her window half-open so he could at least hear.

"Howdy," she said, sounding friendly. "You folks doing all right?"

"We're just camping here," said one young man, who sounded more truculent than he probably should have. A greeting to anyone shouldn't sound like you were ready to start a fight, and certainly not with a cop.

Immediately, a young woman inserted herself between Elaine and the young man. *Smart,* Devlin thought.

"Honest," the woman said with a smile. "This is a public campsite, isn't it?"

Elaine nodded. "It sure is. There are turnouts in a lot of isolated places for just this very thing."

The young woman nodded. "I'm Doreen, by the way. This is Alex. We're probably responsible for making the locals crazy. Coming out here to see those lights was our idea."

"And now?"

Doreen raised her hands, open palmed. "We can see some of those lights from here. No problem for anyone, right?"

"Depends on where you watch from and what you're hoping to see. You think there's anything but those lights out there?"

"How would we know?" Doreen answered. "Just the lights are enough right now. Why don't you and your friend come and have some coffee with us? The fire's just back there."

"Thanks, but we're on our way down the road," Elaine said. "But what has you guys so fascinated out here? Just those couple of lights?" Elaine sounded as if she didn't quite believe it, but she kept that suggestion faint, easy not to hear.

"It's more than that," Alex answered, sounding less defensive. "Most people don't want to hear it, though."

"I would," Elaine countered. "Another time?"

"Sure," Doreen said brightly. "Some of us come into that café in town a couple of times a week. Tuesday?"

"Absolutely," Elaine agreed. "I'll see you then."

When she returned to the car and pulled away, Devlin remarked, "They seem inoffensive enough."

"So far. Especially if they stay off private land."

"I can see that." The temperature seemed to be dropping, so he rolled up his window. "So all of this is about some lights?"

"Evidently so. At least as far as I know. I'd like to hear what else they have to say about it."

"Then we should have stayed."

Elaine shook her head. "Before I talk to them again, I want to be sure they haven't gone back to trespassing."

"They've been warned off, haven't they? I don't get

why they'd go back." Not that he wasn't accustomed to people doing things they shouldn't. Part of his job.

"Me, neither, but there's a lot of things I don't get. I suppose I ought to do some research on UFO hunters."

He snorted. "That could get interesting."

"Yeah, and they probably come in more varieties than ice cream."

"Probably. What would you do if they say they've been abducted?"

Elaine let out a full-throated laugh. "Tell 'em aliens aren't in my jurisdiction."

ON THE WAY, although Elaine didn't figure they had a particular destination, she stopped at the Bixby spread. Bixby had rounded up most of his herd into a smaller area, apparently ready for a move.

"Gonna take 'em up to summer pasture," he remarked, punctuating his words with another spit of tobacco on the ground.

"Summer pasture?" Devlin asked.

Bixby eyed him. "Guess you're a greenhorn."

"These days," he admitted.

Bixby nodded, resettling his worn hat on his head. "Cattle need fattening. Land here's kinda dry. So we lease land up in the mountains where there's plenty of good grazing. Get 'em plumped up before selling 'em. Make sure the cows are fit to breed. Problem is, they don't eat as much when they get nervous, and near as I can tell, those damn trespassers are making 'em nervous. Better, now. Hope they keep away."

Elaine nodded. "You call if they don't."

"You betcha."

Back in the car, once again on the gravel county road, Devlin asked, "Do you think they'll stay away?"

"For now. They must feel like we're crawling all over them. First the trespass warning, then me questioning them at Maude's and now dropping by when they're camping?"

He chuckled. "*Definitely* all over them."

"The question is, how badly do they want to watch those damn lights?"

"Any idea what they might be?"

Elaine shook her head. "I thought they must be a fire the first time I saw them. The thing is, though, I've lived here my entire life, and I never heard anything about those lights before. Never saw them."

"So they've never caused any concern?"

"Not until these UFO hunters showed up."

"I guess that would do it." The same way the arrival of strangers could cause problems when he was on assignment overseas. Hostiles? Innocents who just happened to be there? Definitely people to be watched.

But UFO hunters hardly seemed like the biggest threat. More like nuisances.

Elaine chose another turnout, one surrounded by spring trees and firs that created a palette of greens beneath the blue sky.

A small, weathered picnic table sat beside a blackened firepit.

"This is kinda fancy for a simple turnout," he remarked.

"A lot of people have to travel long distances out here. These turnouts were probably used more often in the days when not everyone had a car, but they're still useful."

"It's a great idea." Welcoming, too. Boy, there was a lot he didn't know about the place where he'd grown up.

Maude had made their picnic easy to lay out: cardboard containers on the table, a couple of double-lined cardboard cups filled with lemonade, some plastic utensils.

"Maude's really moving into the environmentally friendly age," Elaine remarked. "Folks still want that foam, though."

"I remember when I was a kid and sometimes Mom would bring home dinner from Maude's. Man, did Caleb and I get excited at the sight of those foam containers."

Then he wondered if he'd made a mistake by mentioning Caleb. A shadow passed over Elaine's face, then vanished. "There's a whole lot I never learned about you guys growing up. Caleb wasn't one to talk, except about the present and maybe some about the future. Lu's told me more, but…" Elaine shrugged. "I guess your childhood doesn't matter that much."

An interesting thing to say, Devlin thought. "I don't think much about it," he admitted. "Not that it doesn't matter—only that most of it isn't relevant right now."

Elaine bit into her BLT and quickly dabbed at the tomato juice that ran down her chin. "I can see that," she said after she'd swallowed. "I'm not focused much on my childhood, either. It's just this feeling that I never got to know Caleb as well as I might have and then he was gone."

She looked away swiftly, hiding what he sensed was a sudden attack of grief. He let her have the space she needed and admired the woods once again as he ate his ham sandwich.

She was right about not knowing Caleb that well, he realized. Caleb had been his brother, yet over the past decades, they'd become virtual strangers, separated by their paths in life. Even as children, they'd pretty much had their own lives because of a five-year difference in their ages.

He felt his own sorrow, too, for a loss that couldn't be repaired. Brothers, yet not, separated by time and experience.

He looked at Elaine, who was continuing to eat her lunch. She'd gotten past her moment; now he had to get past his own.

"You need to ask Lu," he said.

Elaine looked up at him. "About what?"

"About Caleb. About the things you want to know about him. Nobody ever knew him better."

At that, Elaine smiled. "A mother is usually the best source."

"Up to a point," he agreed. "Right now I'm more interested in these UFO hunters of yours."

"Ah, don't blame *me* for them."

He laughed. "No such thought. No, I'm just curious about what makes people spend night after night watching the sky for something as weird as lights. I'd understand watching for artillery or some kind of air attack. Hell, I even understand plane spotters, those people who record tail numbers and can put together a plane's entire flight history. But watching a couple of lights?"

"I don't know." Elaine closed her container and pushed it to one side. "Maybe they expect something more to happen."

"Little green men?"

She grinned. "Or maybe something as simple as seeing more of them, or seeing them fly in ways that a regular plane couldn't? Some kind of proof that they're not from around here?"

"I'd go with the last one. It makes sense. Visitors from another world. Hey, that could actually be cool."

"It makes me think of those B movies from the fifties." She giggled. "Giant ants. Aliens in weird costumes. Queens who looked like they should have been in burlesque shows."

"Hey, I used to watch them when I was a kid. Mom liked to watch them with me. Man, did we laugh."

"Caleb didn't watch with you?"

Again he felt a pang. "Naw. He liked to read. Science fiction, for the most part."

"So not that far away from the movies you and your mom watched."

"Mentally, no. Except, as I learned over the years, the ideas in those books and in the magazines were far more intelligent than the movies."

"Where every problem could be caused or solved by a nuclear weapon."

"There was that."

They fell silent. A breeze began to rustle through the trees, lowering the temperature a bit but sounding almost happy. *Happy.* Something he hadn't felt in a long while. Elaine probably hadn't, either.

"What about *your* childhood?" he asked. A sister-in-law about whom he knew nothing. She must feel the same about him.

"Happy enough," she answered. "Friends, family. I had no idea that anything was wrong until my parents split and headed in opposite directions. Cassie can't travel, so they have to come visit us, but..." She shrugged. "New lives, new families for them."

Now *that* sounded sad—more like abandonment than anything else. "How old were you?"

"Fifteen. One of my teachers took me in." She smiled. "A long time ago, no permanent scars."

Maybe not. But nonetheless, he sensed something underlying that cheerful rendition. Of course, seeing past facades was an essential part of his job. Necessary to his survival and the survival of the people he worked with. Except for one serious misjudgment, for which he might never forgive himself.

"Which teacher?" he asked. "I'm testing my memory."

"Edith Jasper. The one with the Great Dane."

He nodded and smiled. "The dragon English teacher."

"That's her, all right."

"And Bailey? I always loved that dog."

Elaine shook her head. "Moved on, I'm afraid."

"Man, that must have been hard on Edith."

"I'm sure it was. She has a new dog, though. Harlowe. He's as big and gentle with her as Bailey was. It's a kick to see a woman that age walking a dog almost as tall as she is. But Edith likes to say that the dogs understand her limitations, and they sure seem to."

"Dogs are smart," he allowed. He'd seen strays using every wile they possessed to survive on the streets in places where they were despised.

Their lunch was coming to an end. Devlin took another look around—situational awareness, ingrained in him for years. Nothing here. But he still felt the faintest sense of threat.

Ridiculous, he told himself. A habit that just wouldn't quit.

But he still couldn't quite dismiss it.

As he wrapped up their leftovers and shoved them into the paper bag, he asked, "Mind if I come to the meeting with the UFO guys at Maude's on Tuesday?"

"No, it's not going to be official business. But why are you interested?"

He couldn't say that he wanted to get a feel for these people. A chance to see what might lie behind the apparently innocent UFO hunters. Because trust didn't come easily to him. No way.

"Just curious," he answered. "I probably won't ever see another UFO hunter again."

"I hope not," she said dryly. "I'm still waiting for the grapevine to pick this up. In a few days, we'll have little green men, werewolves and any other spooky things people can talk about."

He grinned. "What would all those have to do with UFOs?"

"Why would anyone think those red lights are UFOs? You want them to be UFOs, they need to do something."

"But what *are* they?" he asked as they strolled back to her vehicle.

"That's the question, isn't it? That's why they're here. I, for one, doubt the mystery will ever be solved."

But Devlin wasn't one to ignore a mystery. Mysteries were a big part of his life. They were just about more important things than some lights in the sky. Regardless, he'd always had trouble ignoring any mystery.

There probably wasn't a solution to this one, but he wouldn't give up until he'd checked out every avenue. At least it would give him something to do while he was riding out his enforced invisibility during his stay here.

"What exactly does Sally do for Cassie?" he asked as they drove back toward town.

Elaine compressed her lips.

"I'm sorry," he said immediately. "None of my business."

"Why not? You're her uncle."

He blew out a long breath. "I've been a lousy uncle."

"Trust me, I understand that your job keeps you away. Caleb's did, too, only he was closer and could come home for a few days at a time. You're oceans away. Nor are we very high on your radar. I'm sure you have a life of your own. Wife? Kids? People who need your attention."

Hardly, he thought. There was the job. Pretty much *all* there was, under the circumstances. "No wife. Not anymore," he said. "No kids." The only wife had taken a hike after one trip overseas with him. Not her taste at all, not even inside embassy walls.

He'd never wanted to attempt that one again. A woman could either travel with him—but only to safer places—or wait at home indefinitely. Not fair, no matter how he looked at it, and he certainly looked at it differently since his marriage blew up.

Other people managed to meld the job with a relationship, but most of them had married within the department. After his divorce, though, he'd never felt the urge to try again.

"Sally?" he repeated.

"She's a trained therapist for autistic children." Abruptly, Elaine pounded her hand on the steering wheel, astonishing Devlin. "I don't like those labels at all. What good do they do? Cassie's just Cassie. The way she is. Labels shouldn't define her, not to anyone."

He'd never thought about that, but he had an inkling of her frustration.

"It's pigeonholing," she said continued angrily. "Like it solves anything. Now they call it a 'spectrum.' *Where on the spectrum is your child?* What the hell does that help?"

"Maybe understanding from others?" he suggested cautiously.

"They don't understand regardless. It's just a label they can put on a kid, then not deal with it. Those of us who *are* dealing with it are dealing with individual children. Children who *are* individuals."

He waited, letting a mile or two pass by before he spoke again. "I take it Sally understands that?"

"Believe it. She tailors everything she does specifically to Cassie. Damn, I wouldn't let her near my daughter if I didn't believe that."

He absorbed her anger, understanding it the best he could. Since he couldn't really imagine how Cassie's condition affected her mother, his understanding was limited, other than sometimes seeing Elaine's pain.

But labels? He was aware of them, the dangers of relying on them. In his world, labels could cost lives. But was it the same with a medical condition? Labels might help there.

A spectrum, he thought. He'd heard that more than once, never much thought about it. But didn't the whole idea of a spectrum include Elaine's insistence that Cassie was an individual and needed to be treated as such? Maybe that was why the term had been created?

But it was still a kind of label, he supposed.

Then he stepped where only a brave man—or a fool— would go. "Will Cassie's condition change as she gets older?"

He anticipated an explosion, a justifiable one, but he needed an answer to assess the situation, and assessment was a part of his job that had been tattooed into his brain.

"I don't know," Elaine answered between her teeth. "No one can know. But that's what Sally is trying to help with."

Subject closed. He could hear it in her voice. Despite

being Cassie's uncle, he'd sacrificed his position in the family. He was entitled to nothing from Elaine, not even information about his goddaughter.

For the first time he could remember, he looked back over his life choices and wondered if he'd been a fool.

Devotion to country was one thing. Devotion to family was another, but maybe every bit as important. Maybe more important.

Chapter Five

The UFO hunters had proliferated almost as if by magic on the streets of Conard City. Elaine hooked her thumb into her gunbelt and just shook her head as she watched them. "This could get interesting," she said to her fellow officers.

Why wouldn't it? There were not only the groups who appeared to be "serious" about their hunt but also those who had come looking for some kind of party. Green alien heads dotted the landscape, along with other strange costumes. Their music was getting loud, too.

If she'd thought that first group was a small invasion, this crowd looked like the real thing. Not enough motel rooms, of course—not that that would have made much of a difference. Every road near the Bixby spread was filling with cars and tents. The hours were filled with excited voices. *Bixby must be ready to have a cow of his own,* Elaine thought, remembering that shotgun of his.

Gage had doubled the patrols outside town and increased coverage in Conard City itself. The force was stretched to breaking.

Then she headed out for her patrol along the ranch land, stopping by the house to ask Devlin if he wanted to ride along.

He did.

THE TWO WOMEN noticed the increasing numbers of UFO hunters in the city, and as the group had grown, it had become wilder and more fanciful. For Kalina and Zoe, the task of blending in had gotten easier. They eased their way into the fringes. No one even questioned their accents. In fact, the mob seemed delighted that others had come to view the lights.

"The more, the merrier," a guy wearing a mask with bug-like eyes had declared. He'd tried to give them cans of beer but they'd managed to slip away without offending him.

Which was fine with Zoe and Kalina. They were on a mission that had nothing to do with stupid lights in the sky.

According to Lance—the man who had seemed to have made himself the leader—more people were on the way. Nearly fifty, he judged, bragging to Zoe. She smiled and nodded appreciatively, aware that more people would make it easier to hide within the crowd.

For now, they had moved to a small campground near the base of a mountain, little more than a turnout from a gravel road, and were going out at night with others to try to see those lights and photograph them. Kalina and Zoe couldn't care less about all the fancy cameras or the lights, but they had to act excited themselves. Lance gave them meters to use since they had no useful equipment of their own except for a cheap camera. Meaningless meters, as far as Zoe and Kalina were concerned, but they pretended to be thrilled with them.

Who cared about infrared? So the lights were hot? Or they might have magnetic fields? The UFO hunters weren't getting any useful information out of those things, as far as the women could tell. The lights appeared to move just a little, sometimes fast and sometimes slow. Then they disappeared, winking out. And that was it.

Zoe and Kalina weren't amazed. They knew how things could appear to move because eyes jumped a little all the time. As for being impressed, they simply weren't. At all. Even when their new companions started whooping with glee because that infrared camera had caught a shape in the hot ball of light.

The lights posed no threat, so the women didn't care about them. They'd seen a lot of terrifying things in the sky at home, and these were a joke. Unfortunately, they felt they were wasting time on this game. Yet play it they must, because it afforded them a chance to go into town, to casually ask people about strangers.

This UFO thing was a stupid rich-man's game. They knew about life-and-death situations and were sure these people couldn't even imagine living that way.

But they remained stuck. They didn't know what the man they sought looked like. They'd expected to hear about strangers in such a small town, but the only strangers they'd found were the members of this group. And none of them could possibly be their target. It might have given the women ease of movement, but so far they'd learned nothing useful, unless one wanted an encyclopedia about orbs.

So they sat with the fools at night, a distance away from them, acting shy and modest, and whispered to each other. They were beginning to wonder if they'd been pointed to the wrong town.

All of a sudden, the task they'd set themselves seemed a whole lot bigger than when they'd left home.

But then, this country was overwhelmingly big. How

did you ever find a single person? It would have been hard enough in their own, smaller country.

Had they been directed here for some other purpose than the one they intended? But no, their informant could not have counted on this group of strange people seeming to come out of nowhere. Besides, she had helped them get the gun they carried. They trusted her because of that, mostly.

Glumly they watched those boring lights and tried to figure their way through all this. They'd had support at home, but they had no support here.

Two women, all alone. For the first time, they really felt it.

Then they scraped together some of the money they'd brought with them for a cheap used camera. That sealed their position in the group. It also made it possible for them to take pictures in town. That *could* be useful.

But they still couldn't believe how easy it was to get into this absurd group. Their first appearance had been received pleasantly enough, if a bit doubtfully. They could understand that, given the craziness these people were chasing.

But now, buying some camera equipment had gained them full membership. They no longer stuck out at all. Both thought their welcome had been too easy. They came from a world where trust had to be earned, not just given.

There was a disadvantage, however. It wasn't long before they realized the locals had begun to stare at the group as if they'd come from a different planet.

Which, in a way, Zoe and Kalina had. But apparently, united interests had allowed them to join the growing crowd of newcomers. And the bigger the crowd, the better the concealment.

Except it made it harder for them to pick out their target.

WHEN ELAINE ARRIVED back at the house, Sally had already departed, leaving behind a note with suggestions for Cassie. Lu had left another note saying she had taken Cassie for a walk.

The house was quiet, too quiet. Except for the virtual stranger who had walked into her life only a few days ago. He was a good-enough guest but still a guest. Still made her slightly uncomfortable, the way having company always did. Like you constantly had to be on your best behavior or something.

But when it came right down to it, Elaine decided he must be feeling much the same way. Not a single item of his had migrated from the office he was using as a bedroom. The one time she'd glanced in, she noticed all his clothes were still packed in his duffel, despite the closet with hangers in there.

She had no idea how long he'd be staying. Nor, she guessed, did he. He'd said something about being here for a while but still hadn't unpacked.

One thing was for sure—if he was going to hang around a few weeks, it'd be much more comfortable if they could get past the hostess-and-visitor stage.

"Thanks for dragging me around the county," Devlin said.

Amused in spite of herself, she answered, "Just one tiny little piece of it."

"True, but it reminded me of when I was a kid here. That was what I wanted."

"I'm going out on the porch. Join me?"

Together they went out front to sit on the wooden rocking chairs. One was small enough for Cassie.

Elaine spoke. "One of the things I love about these older houses is the way they have front porches. Newer houses focus on the backyard. Usually fenced. But these front porches—they're great if you want to see your neighbors, maybe chat a little."

"And pick up on the gossip," Devlin said wryly.

Elaine laughed. "Well, that, too."

"Any gossip about the UFO hunters?"

She shook her head. "It hasn't started to roll. Maybe so far, they're being viewed as transients."

"Or Bixby hasn't phoned everyone he knows about the kind of nuisances they are."

"That could be, too. But if all people see of them is when they show up at Maude's to eat, there's not going to be much to gab about, is there?"

His answer was dry. "Never knew that to stop a grapevine."

He had a point. "But the grapevine here isn't usually malicious or full of lies. Don't ask me why. You'd think the creation of something salacious would get everyone's interest. Ah, give it time. Those guys will start headlining out of sheer boredom, if nothing else."

"Some real information would be useful."

She looked at him, wondering at this trend in his thinking. "What 'real information'? They're a group of slightly wacky people. They probably believe in some conspiracy or other, most of which are basically harmless."

"Conspiracy theories aren't always harmless," he remarked. "Take a look sometime. Most are pretty much anti-government whether they have a good reason or not. Whether they seem threatening or not."

Elaine turned that around in her mind, considering the conspiracy theories she'd heard. "I guess you're right. No matter what they're about, they seem to claim the government is hiding something. Failing to do something. At least, the ones I know of."

He twisted in his seat, looking at her. "I'd be the last person to say that all governments are good, that they never do anything wrong. Of course they do. They're run by human beings. But to just theorize wrongdoing in the absence of real evidence, that could be dangerous. Anyway, in the course of things, I doubt alien conspiracies are a big problem."

Elaine nodded. "Well, other than some trespassing, I don't see this group causing any major trouble. They actually seem kind of harmless to me."

Then she saw Lu and Cassie walking down the street toward her, Cassie holding Lu's hand, one of those rare touches Cassie permitted. Her heart leaped as it always did when she saw her daughter. Cassie bounced a bit as she walked, but skipping was, as yet, beyond her. Lu waved cheerfully.

Did Cassie's step quicken? Oh, Elaine hoped so. Among her greatest joys in life were the moments that Cassie evinced even the smallest amount of happiness at seeing her. Or like the moment she had first said, "Mommy."

God, she wished she could lift her daughter into her arms and make all the bad things go away. She hated the feeling that her little girl was locked away somewhere inside a brain that couldn't share itself. A prisoner.

No, she couldn't afford to think like that. No way. Allowing sorrow to shadow her every day would do no one any good.

When Cassie and Lu reached the bottom of the porch steps, the girl's face brightened a little, and she said, "Mommy."

Oh, God. Elaine's heart squeezed with painful joy. "Hi, Cassie. Enjoy your walk with Grandma?"

Cassie didn't answer. Instead, she concentrated on climbing the steps.

"We had a lot of fun," Lu answered. "Squirrels are starting to run around with some spring fervor. An occasional brave soul of a bird singing its little heart out. Cassie loved the squirrels especially."

Cassie reached the top step and walked over to her mother—space between them as always, but only a couple of feet. Better than even six months ago.

"And a dog," Lu said, shaking her head slightly. "Read that list Sally left. I think she might have lost her mind."

Dog? In her heart of hearts, Elaine knew what was coming. Sally thought a puppy might draw out Cassie's responses. Well, if it would, then that was what was going to happen.

"I think I should talk to Sally first," Elaine said. "To make sure I do the right thing."

"Couldn't agree more. Training can be a lot of work."

Elaine thought of all that Lu already was doing for Cassie and her, and hated the idea of adding a dog to those burdens. "Unless I can get one already trained." As she spoke, she instantly remembered Cadell Marcus, who raised dogs for police K-9 work and trained service dogs as well.

With advice from Sally about what a dog would need to provide, Cadell would probably be able to come up with something appropriate for her daughter. A dog that already understood basic house rules. "I'll talk to Cadell," she said to Lu. "After I find out what Sally wants."

"Cadell would be a good idea," Lu agreed. "I'm capable of a whole lot, but running after a puppy might be beyond me now."

"It's practically beyond anyone," Devlin remarked.

Lu walked over to him for a hug. "I should have let you have that puppy you and Caleb wanted so badly."

"And you had a lot of good reasons for saying no. At the time it seemed unfair, but looking back I can see you were right." He smiled. "In terms of care and training, it would have become *your* puppy. Caleb and I were already a handful."

Lu laughed. "You sure were. Besides, I couldn't afford the expense."

Elaine hadn't thought about that. Just how expensive could a dog be? Food, yeah. Vet...but how often? Toys? Medicines? Shots?

Ohhhhh man. She needed to do some research on this subject.

A glance at Devlin told her he'd had the same thought. He just shook his head his head slightly, more a gesture of sympathy than anything else.

While Cassie enjoyed cookies and milk—leaving a lot of milk on the table as she dipped the cookies, then carried them to her mouth—Elaine reached for the note Sally had left on the refrigerator.

It was cheery as always, punctuated by Sally's balloon-style exclamation points. Sally loved exclamation points. But then, she lived her life that way, with a whole bunch of zest Elaine sometimes envied.

Today's note was full of positive descriptions of the minor ways in which Cassie had improved. Minor ways. Maybe sometimes undetectable when not looking very closely, not *watching* closely. Maybe infrequently enough that only an intensive therapy session could reveal them.

But that didn't matter to Elaine. Every small bit of improvement was like a warm ray of sunshine to her heart.

But then she came to the part about the dog in the note. Only it wasn't just the *idea* of a dog.

A dog might be good for Cassie, Sally had written. *The warm love always there is a good thing for anyone. It might slowly draw her out. On the other hand...*

Elaine almost stopped reading. That phrase rarely brought good news.

On the other hand, Sally's writing continued, *I think a cat might be better. A kitten, not too young. Cats have a way of remaining independent and often a bit aloof, which might be better for Cassie right now. Not overwhelming. Talk to Mike Windwalker about the personality differences. We can discuss it more later.*

Elaine looked up from the note. "You missed part of this, Lu."

Lu frowned faintly. "What?"

"Sally is also suggesting a cat because it might be more aloof. Which I guess I could see being better for Cassie right now."

"A cat, huh?" Lu didn't look very pleased.

"What's wrong with a cat?" Elaine asked.

"The way that they stare."

Elaine had to smile. "Like they know all the secrets of the universe? That's why the Egyptians thought they were gods."

Lu humphed. "Doesn't strike me that way." Then she sighed. "Whatever Cassie needs. I'll deal."

DEVLIN SAW ELAINE'S face droop at his mother's statement. She must worry that she was always imposing on Lu, but Devlin remembered his mother well enough to believe she'd moved in with Cassie because she was simply incapable of doing anything else. Lu had always wanted to be helpful. Of course, being helpful also gave her some control.

Stepping outside into the cooling afternoon, leaving the three inside to sort out whatever needed sorting, he realized his past had begun to haunt him. Mostly he kept it locked away, except for the lessons that had proved invaluable—ones he could never afford to unlearn.

But the emotional side of it? That was the part he needed to bury because no matter the purpose, he'd put peoples' lives at risk. His informants had a variety of reasons for working with him, and they all believed they'd never get caught, but sometimes they did. A personal nightmare he had to live with. A nightmare others had to live with, others such as their families and friends.

This last loss had cut him hard. Niko Stanovicz had been his informant for several years. A charming, fun-loving young man who concealed a strong devotion to one side of the war raging in his country. He might superficially act like it didn't matter, but it did. With every breath he drew, he wanted to make his family safe. At any cost.

Then someone had informed on Niko. This had resulted in not only Niko's torture and death but also the deaths of some of his closest friends. A stone running downhill, not caring what it killed in its path, and Devlin hadn't been able to do a damn thing to stop it.

Instead, he'd been yanked out before a mere conversation with him might put a target on anyone else. Because if Niko had been revealed, then likely so had Devlin. His entire informant network had to be rolled up and exfiltrated along with their families, forced to leave everything behind—but still alive.

He didn't like to think about all the lives ruined by one slipup.

One single slipup. But by whom? His bosses were looking into that, of course, but they might never figure it out. It might be as simple as one of Niko's friends having noticed something he considered suspicious.

There were places in this world where suspicion was a condition of life. Some of that had crept into Devlin as well. How could it not? In his life, trust wasn't easy to come by—it had to be earned.

The afternoon was waning into evening, but he felt no urge to return inside, even though the delicious aromas of dinner had begun to emanate through an open window.

He probably should go in and offer to help, but the size of that kitchen made it unlikely he could squeeze in or stay out of the way. Of course, he could sit at the table with Cassie. Maybe that wouldn't unnerve the child too much.

He wondered once again if it would have made much of a difference to have been here throughout Cassie's brief life. Then he thought of the distance the child kept between herself and her mother, and figured that even being here all along wouldn't have changed Cassie's problems.

Maybe he should do some research into Cassie's condition. Then again, that would probably only lead him into the thicket of labels that Elaine hated.

How would she react if he dropped one of those into the conversation? He couldn't begin to understand Cassie's challenges. All he could see was a terribly withdrawn child—but how withdrawn was she really? Was she more aware of all that went on around her than she let on? How did she fill up the inside of her head? Because he frankly couldn't imagine a brain ever going totally silent. So somewhere inside her were thoughts. Reactions. Feelings. Matters she couldn't share. How freaking lonely was that? Or was she possibly content being alone inside her own thoughts?

Crap. What did he know? How *could* he know anything? He suspected that Elaine was on a journey of discovery, too, watching the changes in her daughter, wondering what they might mean and if Cassie's situation might ever improve.

Tired of his thoughts and the pointless hamster wheel they were beginning to run around on, Devlin went back inside the house.

The kitchen smelled absolutely wonderful.

"Beef stew," Lu said over her shoulder as she stirred a huge pot.

"You always made the best."

"Still do," Lu laughed. "Cassie loves it, too."

Devlin pulled out a chair at the table and looked across at Cassie, who sat beside Elaine. For the first time, he noticed that Cassie's crayons were laid out in a neat row, all points upward. Similar colors next to each other. After each time the girl picked one up and used it on her new unicorn picture, she returned it carefully to the same place.

Devlin wondered how he might start a conversation without disturbing Cassie. What a curious thought to have. How could he have ever known that speaking might upset his niece?

"I guess Cassie loves unicorns," he remarked, then instantly wondered if Cassie might not like being talked about as if she weren't there. But how would anyone know?

"Right now." Elaine smiled. "Who knows what it will be next week."

"How can you find out?"

Lu turned from the stove, wiping her hands on a towel. "She'll just stop. Then we hunt through coloring books for something she *does* like."

Devlin nodded, then noticed something he hadn't really paid attention to before: Cassie was occasionally darting quick glances his way. He decided to address her directly. With no way to know if she was noticing, it seemed best to acknowledge her. It sure couldn't hurt anything. "That's a very complex figure you're filling in, Cassie."

"Adult coloring pages," Elaine said. "Fine detail. Cassie loves it. Don't you, sweetie?"

Cassie didn't answer. Her expression didn't even change.

"I'm thinking about getting her a set of coloring pencils. Better for detail. On the other hand, she might…reject them."

"Never know until you try," said Lu. "We got a ton of those coloring books on a shelf in her room. All we have to do is pull them out and see what she likes. Maybe the same for pencils."

How would they know what Cassie liked? Devlin wondered. Her face and expressions gave nothing away. But maybe all it took was Cassie starting to color one of the pictures. Right now she was all about unicorns. Next, maybe owls? Who knew.

In point of fact, though, he found he was genuinely enjoying watching her intense focus as she colored, the careful choices she made with the crayons. He was starting to develop a bit of intensity himself when it came to her drawing.

Cassie clearly didn't want to stop coloring to eat dinner. For a minute or so, it appeared she might have a meltdown, but it never came. Instead, she finally let Elaine move her picture and crayons to the sideboard, within her line of sight, and turned her focus to the bowl of stew placed in front of her.

She ate with the same intensity she had displayed when coloring.

Hyperfocus. That could be useful if it didn't dominate. He had a bit of it himself. Or maybe more than a bit of it.

Cassie fed herself, appearing indifferent but quite able to manage the small bites his mother had cut up for her.

"She's got some pretty good motor skills," Lu remarked. "Haven't you, Cassie? You worked hard at it."

"Yes, she did," Elaine said, a note of pride creeping into her voice. Then she looked at Devlin. "It wasn't easy."

Not easy for either his niece or his sister-in-law. A struggle for them both. He could almost imagine it. "How do you know what Cassie wants to do?"

Elaine shrugged. "She just won't do what she doesn't want to do. And pressing the issue tips her into anger. Into a meltdown. We try to avoid that."

"I imagine so." Because how could you comfort a child who wouldn't even accept a hug?

"So, a cat," Elaine said, returning to their earlier conversation. "I bet Mike Windwalker would have one with a calm temperament."

Devlin spoke, "It was interesting what you read from Sally's note. A cat would be more aloof?"

Elaine nodded. "That caught my attention, too. But a dog…well, dogs hate to be ignored. What if a puppy pushes Cassie too hard? Demands too much? I can see why Sally might be hesitant. I am, too."

She shook her head as Lu cleared Cassie's dish, then put the coloring supplies in front of the girl. Cassie dove right back into her picture.

Elaine left the table to help with the dishes. When Devlin expressed his desire to help, she waved him back to his seat.

"We got it," she said, smiling.

So he leaned back in his chair, wondering what the hell he was doing here. He hated not being busy, and right now he was anything but.

He also hated that his bosses had decided he needed to hide out in the hinterlands. Not that he wasn't glad to see his mother, and not that he wasn't grateful for this chance to renew his relationship with Elaine and finally spend time with his niece. Of course he was.

But that just wasn't keeping him focused and occupied to the extent he was used to. He closed his eyes, allowing the events of the past month to jam up behind his eyelids.

It had all happened so fast from the instant Niko had died. It hadn't taken long to learn that the young man had been exposed as an informant. And once they'd figured that out for certain, everything hit top speed. Getting Devlin out of there, checking to see if the info about Niko had traveled further. Then the roll-up of the entire network in that part of the world.

A great big hole in their global intelligence. A network that would take years to rebuild.

And the hunt for the informant. That was possibly the most important thing of all. Who had revealed Niko? And what if he or she had revealed others? They *had* to find the mole.

For his own part, Devlin thought his bosses were being hypercautious about *his* safety, though. He was probably at the least risk of anyone, because knocking off embassy attachés could bring a whole lot of unwanted attention, whereas Niko could have been killed for any number of reasons.

Hell.

AFTER DINNER, with the night growing chilly, Elaine joined Devlin on the front porch, in the rocking chairs that might have been there forever. They certainly had been there when she and Caleb had bought the house, dreaming of the evenings they could spend out here.

But she was troubled over Devlin. His continued presence, however good a roommate he was, bothered her. In all the years since she'd met Caleb, Devlin's visits had been few and short. Now he was talking about staying for a month?

As a cop, she'd long since lost any inhibitions when it came to asking personal questions. Well, except in situations where they might cause needless offense.

But being hesitant right now seemed ridiculous. "Devlin?"

He turned his head toward her. "Yeah?"

"Why did you come to visit?"

He didn't answer immediately. "To see Mom. And I thought it was time to get to know you and Cassie better."

She wasn't buying it. "How about right after Caleb died? Wouldn't that have been a better time? Your mom was all messed up. So were Cassie and I." Although it had been hard to tell exactly what Cassie felt, between her autism and her very young age. No, Elaine had just assumed the grief was there. She'd had to, in order to take care of her.

Devlin rubbed his chin. A neighbor and his dog were walking along the street, and Elaine waved, as did Devlin.

He was smooth, she realized. Very smooth. Easy with the social courtesies. Well, the State Department and all that.

He was also probably pretty good at lying. Wouldn't he have to be? How truthful could diplomats be, as a rule? They probably made a career out of skirting honesty.

But she was also pretty good at detecting lies, thanks to her law enforcement experience. She wasn't perfect at it—but then, most people weren't great at lying, either. Someone like Devlin would be, and she'd have to pay close attention. Very close.

Nor did it help that her attraction to him was steadily growing for some unknown reason. Good looking? Yeah. Attractive as hell? Oh, definitely. She hadn't reacted like this to any man since Caleb. But there had to be more than that, and right now she didn't fully trust Devlin. Simply showing up because he was Lu's son and Caleb's brother wasn't enough.

She sighed, thinking he was never going to *really* answer her question. That wouldn't help anything.

But then he spoke. Quietly, as if he didn't want to be heard by someone a few feet away. That quiet in his voice caused her skin to prickle with apprehension.

"I guess I owe you a little more," he said. "But I can't tell you much."

"Classified?" That wouldn't surprise her.

His turn to sigh. "Have you heard of classification of sources and methods?"

At that, her heart nearly stopped. She *had* heard of it, and she knew how closely guarded it was. Informants' lives depended on it. Intelligence gathering of any kind relied on the methods as well. A special place all its own in the layers of protection. "Then you can't tell me anything."

"I can tell you that somehow some of that information

leaked. But more than that? No. I probably shouldn't share even that much."

She looked at him, wishing the night illuminated more of him than just his eyes, but the shadows on the planes of his face, deeper in some places than others, revealed nothing.

"So you're here because…?"

"I needed to be out of the way until this gets sorted. That's all."

"Dear God," she said tautly. "Are you being hunted? Damn it!"

Without waiting for any response, she jumped up and stormed back into the house.

She didn't need a road map. If he was somehow involved in someone else's danger, then he might well be in danger, too.

And that could be dangerous for them all.

But as her fury eased, just a bit, another question struck her: Would his bosses have even let him come here if he was in any danger?

She heard his footsteps behind her.

"Elaine?"

"What?" She nearly snapped the word.

"I'm here so I don't inadvertently reveal someone else's identity. That's all."

"So you figure your own is already exposed?"

"Possibly. But right now no one knows."

She swung around, hardly caring at this point if Lu heard them. She'd probably be interested in all this, too.

"Then how is there no danger?"

He spread his hands. "In the first place, if anyone had thought I was personally at risk, I'd have been shipped to a safe house and cut off from everything. That didn't happen. I was told to take a vacation. That's it."

She nodded slowly, hearing but not believing. Not yet. The guy had to be a masterful liar.

He continued. "Additionally, given my position at the State Department, the bad guys don't want to screw with me. If they think they've got problems now, just let them take a shot at me. Not that anyone could track me here. Only my chief knows where I am."

She averted her gaze, thinking about it, trying to calm her racing heart and her fury. "So they just told you to get out of the way."

"Basically. For the safety of the people who work under me. I can't take the chance that I might slip in some way and reveal others. I have to stay way out of it."

It made sense, however twisted it might seem. And he'd probably just told her a hell of a lot more than he should have.

At last, her anger ebbed and common sense began to return. "Okay," she said. "But if you get one ping, one hint you might be in trouble, you get the hell out of here."

"I wouldn't dream of doing anything else." He lifted a hand as if he were going to touch her shoulder, then dropped it. Despite everything, despite her anger and the beginnings of a sense of betrayal, she was sorry his hand dropped away.

Then he said, "I'll leave in the morning."

The offer was tempting, until she thought of Lu. "You can't do that to your mother. Damn it, Devlin, she's seen so little of you. It's not right. You just practice your covert skills or whatever they are, and we'll get by just fine."

She started toward her bedroom, then paused to say one more thing. "And don't you dare stay away from Lu this long again."

Chapter Six

"Maybe being part of this crowd wasn't the best idea," Zoe murmured to Kalina in their native tongue.

"How else could we stay in this town without everyone staring at us and wondering?"

Zoe nodded, but she wasn't convinced—not anymore. As the group of outsiders had grown, so had the difficulty in picking out the stranger they needed to find. At first, it had seemed like there would be an easy way to blend in and look for this stranger, who didn't fit in with the small nutty group of people.

But now the crowd was truly large, with men of every age, so not even that would help, as they'd originally thought when the first people had appeared to be young. Almost as young as Niko, which made the women's hearts squeeze until it became hard to breathe.

And then there were all those people partying, wearing strange masks, which only confused the issue more.

Kalina spoke. "We may have a long wait."

"As long as it takes," Zoe said, her resolve in every word. "I'll wait forever to avenge Niko."

Kalina didn't disagree. If she did, she wouldn't be here.

But, Blessed Mother, she wished there were fewer people and fewer masks.

ELAINE CAME IN to the office early because downtown was becoming a problem for residents. Patrolling the roads had proved, so far, to be pretty tame.

Standing with her arms folded outside the station's door, she asked, "When are we going to limit the beer out there?"

"Can't do it," Stu reminded her. "Beer and wine are allowed in public, even with open containers. Just can't have 'em in the car."

Elaine shook her head. "This is madness, and it's getting worse. I don't think many people are enjoying this influx."

"It's not like Roswell," he agreed. "They make money off this kind of thing."

"These guys don't even think we have a crashed ship out here. What's with the lights? They aren't even interesting. They don't do anything."

Stu laughed. "Oh, listen to them now. Those lights are doing all kinds of things."

"I suppose. Somebody was talking about blue orbs yesterday."

"There you go. How long before we have little green men—"

"Gray," Elaine interjected dryly.

"Okay, the grays. And after that, we ought to be hearing about Bigfoot."

She turned to look at him. "What's *that* link?"

He shrugged. "I just heard that they come up together."

"That's all we need," Elaine said sourly. "And damn, I need to spend more time with my daughter. Makes me want to round up this whole crowd."

Stu raised an eyebrow. "And just where would we put them? You get on home and see Cassie. So far, these people don't look like they're going to create any real trouble. You can take a break."

"Except for annoying most of the local residents."

By this point, most of the in-town gathering had been occurring on the west end of the city, but a crowd kept congregating at Maude's diner, and she was getting truly frosted because they were getting in the way of her regular customers. Spending less, too. She'd probably be the next person to give Gage Dalton an earful.

Not many local residents wanted to breakfast with people who wore strange masks and costumes as if it were Halloween.

When she reached her own home, two blocks to the south of Front Street, where the big old mansions graced the road, the last of the revelers had disappeared. The usual quiet reigned.

To her surprise, however, as she pulled into her driveway, she saw both Devlin and Cassie sitting on the porch. *Cassie?*

It wasn't that her daughter didn't like sitting on the porch once in a while, but for her to be sitting with a relative stranger was quite something. A forward stride of some kind?

She approached slowly, not wanting to startle Cassie, who was totally absorbed in coloring. She sat in her yellow child-size rocker, with a small matching table in front of her. Just enough to hold her coloring sheet and her crayons.

Elaine's boots crunched on the gravel as she approached, and Cassie looked up with a small smile and said, "Mommy."

The word would forever cause Elaine's heart to squeeze. "Hi, sweetie," she said cheerfully. "I'm glad to see you decided to come outside." Then she looked at Devlin, who smiled at her.

"Cassie wanted to come out here and she's been happily coloring for the last hour."

"Did she follow you?" Elaine's heart skipped a beat with hope.

"You know, I couldn't tell you. Doesn't seem likely, though. I was out here for a while before Cassie showed up." His smile widened a shade. "So, how's the lunacy in town going?"

Elaine climbed the steps and sat in one of the other rockers. "It's going. A lot of these new folks seem to want a nonstop party, although I couldn't tell you why. The more serious UFO hunters—or researchers, I guess they're calling themselves—are parked up and down county roads, camping on the easement. The ones here in town..." She shrugged. "I can only say that the townspeople aren't thrilled by this."

He arched a brow. "Trouble?"

"Not yet. The revelers don't seem to be looking for any, at this point. Honestly, I'm not sure why they're here. It's not like we have some kind of history of this phenomenon. We're not on some kind of UFO map. No reason we should be. And all because of a couple of red lights that have apparently been here for years."

He tilted his head. "But no one knows what they are."

"Which means nothing." She shook her head. "Now, if we'd had a cattle mutilation or something like that, it'd be different. God save us from a cattle mutilation, though."

He rocked his chair slowly. It creaked a bit, but the sound was pleasant.

Looking down at the floorboards of the decking, Elaine saw another job that needed doing. The paint was peeling off. Maybe she should just scrape it all off and let the wood weather. She'd have to scrape it now anyway to apply a new coat.

Every time she turned around, she was aware of how little time she had to do things. How greatly some help would be appreciated.

Then she brushed the thought away. It would get done or it wouldn't. When she and Caleb had bought this house, they'd known it needed a lot of work. They had been excited about doing it, too. Except Cal was so often away, and Elaine's crazy hours didn't help much. Then Cassie…

She sighed quietly and looked at her daughter. She ought to be grateful, she supposed, that Cassie seemed so happy with her coloring. Or was she?

Questions like that would probably plague Elaine for years to come. Unless Cassie eventually learned to speak at least a bit about her feelings, they would always be a mystery.

Lu stepped out onto the porch. "I thought I heard you," she said to Elaine. "You're early!"

"Watching that crowd downtown didn't make me feel needed."

Lu sat on the last of the rockers and began rocking. "I'm glad they're not down this way. Nothing wrong with them, I suppose, but it feels strange to move through all those people, with their weird costumes. I'm just waiting for a bunch of new people to show up selling alien stuff, or whatever they call it."

"Now that would be a real headache," Elaine answered. Business licenses, shoplifting claims from kiosks that legally shouldn't even be there. No thanks.

"And what about drugs?" Lu demanded. "You know it can't be all beer and wine out there."

"Probably not." Elaine shook her head. "Unfortunately, unless we see something serious or smell something more than a little weed, we're going to have to let it go."

Lu made a sound of disgust.

"Look, Lu," she said, "us wading into that crowd because of a whiff of marijuana is going to cause a serious disturbance. How can we find the right perp to begin with? And if we start throwing our weight around trying to find out who has illegal drugs, we're going to have bigger trouble."

"I don't like it," Lu said.

"Nobody likes it, I'm sure," Devlin volunteered. "But why start a riot when it all still looks like a party."

That was a good way to put it, Elaine thought. Better than she had.

She looked at Cassie again and saw that the child had stopped coloring. Instead, she was looking at the adults. Nothing showed on her face, but she was clearly paying attention.

Another step forward? She hesitated, trying to figure out a way to encourage this change of focus without driving her daughter back into her shell.

After a minute, she stood. "I'm going to make some lemonade. Want to help me, Cassie?"

It was Cassie's turn to hesitate. She looked down at her picture and her crayons. Elaine held her breath.

"Cassie," Lu said, "if you want to go with your mommy, I can bring your crayons and picture inside for you."

A huge separation for Cassie. Allowing someone else to touch her beloved crayons and unicorn picture. Something she only allowed at bedtime. It wouldn't happen, Elaine thought. No way. Cassie would stay with her drawing and drink lemonade whenever it appeared in front of her.

But then, her heart climbed into her throat. Cassie stood, turned away from her drawing and walked toward Elaine. And ignored her crayons.

Elaine didn't touch her, fearing that might be too much, but Cassie followed right on her heels. A major breakthrough.

Everything else faded into the background—the UFO hunters, the weird party happening on the western side of town, the county road easements now full of people who wanted to see a couple of lights.

Cassie was taking a huge step. Nothing else mattered.

She looked at Lu and Devlin when they entered the kitchen. Cassie eagerly took her crayons back from Lu.

"Tomorrow," Elaine said, "if I can find the time, I want to take Cassie out to the veterinary clinic. Mike Windwalker must have cats for adoption."

A positive step forward. Maybe. It would all depend on Cassie.

Then, her decision made, she went to call Mike.

DEVLIN HONESTLY DIDN'T know how he was going to stand any more of this bucolic life. Hanging around here for the last week had only reminded him of why he'd left in the first place. He needed to feel more active. To feel that he was accomplishing something.

Elaine had her job, an important one. His mom seemed happy buzzing around the house and taking care of Cassie and getting out into the garden, little by little, in the burgeoning spring. Cassie seemed to like that, too, as much as one could tell what Cassie liked. She followed Lu outside, without her crayons, and sat watching.

Damn, he wished he could do something for that child. As for Elaine, she fascinated him. So strong. So powerful in her own right as a deputy. Seeming to need no one except help with Cassie. Probably explained how she'd endured Caleb's long absences when he was working a big construction job. Not as long as Devlin's absences, of course, but it was sometimes a month or more at a time with Caleb.

And Elaine had kept plugging along with her own life, her own activities.

But here he was, used to being involved and active damn near every hour of his days, sitting on a front porch, sometimes buying meals from Maude's and walking around a town that he knew but that would never be as familiar as during his youth.

Nope. Right now he fully understood the words *at loose ends.*

He hated it. Restlessness grew until he could barely hold still.

He wanted to call his chief but knew he shouldn't. You were hardly hiding if you started to call your contacts.

But the more he thought about this situation, the more he believed he'd been lied to. Sure, they wouldn't want him to have a high public profile, like that agent who'd been criminally outed all those years ago. That had put her entire network in danger and caused the agency to leap in and save everyone they could.

But there were also the innocent people, the ones who hadn't been her informants, people she had met in social situations. Had they been protected, too?

He had no idea.

That didn't keep him from feeling like he could have been more useful working on the problem of the leak than being here in the back of beyond, where he could do nothing at all.

The fact that that may have been the entire point didn't escape him, but he still loathed it.

Damn, he felt like a caged tiger.

Then a thought occurred to him. He could infiltrate those UFO nuts. A little research, a lot of practice from his career of blending in, and he could do it. He could find out what they were thinking and whether any of them posed a danger.

Not that he thought they did, but any one of them might. Some of them had to be truly unhinged. All it would take would be one.

He pulled his e-reader out of his duffel and went hunting for a few books, some more serious than others but quite a few on the edge of reality. They'd be the most enjoyable to read.

He loved to get into crackpot conspiracy theories. He'd even created a couple of them in his time.

Oh, they could be so useful in manipulation.

"WHAT ARE YOU READING?" Elaine asked later that night. "You've had your nose stuck in that reader for hours."

He looked up, half grinning. "I'm reading about UFOs."

"What?" She plopped down on the recliner and gaped at him. "You're not the type. Are you?"

He laughed. "No, not a bit. But…well, I thought I could understand some of what's going on out there."

She raised a brow. "Manipulate it, you mean."

He shook his head. "No. Wouldn't dream of it."

"Why not? Isn't that part of the reason you've been sent into hiding?"

He fell silent, compressing his lips. This woman was getting too close to a truth he didn't want to burden her with.

"What would you do with those silly people? Ramp

them up? Scare them? Make it all worse? Because you couldn't leave it alone, could you."

That last bit wasn't a question, and a coal of anger ignited in him. He set his reader aside on the end table. "I'm perfectly capable of leaving it alone. It's hardly my job."

"Then explain to me, Devlin. Just why do you want to read up on UFOs?"

"Are you aware that a few years ago, the federal government issued a report saying they were a number of cases for which they had no explanation? Cases with video and radar tracings?"

"I heard of it," she admitted. "They call them UAPs now, don't they?"

His reply was dry. "Only to dissociate the inevitable connection with aliens. There's absolutely no proof of anything like aliens."

"So you say."

His anger faded and he laughed. "And there it is. Whatever the government says must be one huge cover-up."

Elaine had to laugh, too. "I said that to get your goat."

"Didn't work. I'm used to that line."

She leaned back in the chair and curled her legs up beneath her. "So, why the reading?"

He leaned forward, placing his elbows on his knees. "Because almost invariably in any crowd, there's at least one person who's unhinged enough to cause serious trouble."

Elaine drew a breath. "A psychopath."

Devlin shrugged. "The word for it doesn't matter. The important thing is that some people get their thrills by causing trouble. Sometimes it's small problems, sometimes it's big ones."

"So what do you think you can do about it?"

"Join the party and listen."

Elaine stiffened. "You're going undercover with those guys? Are you kidding me?" Then she paused. "But that's what you do, isn't it?" She uncurled herself and stood up.

"I'm just going to listen," he said. And damn it, she *had* guessed more than he'd told her. She wasn't seeing him as some functionary on a purely diplomatic mission.

"You just be careful you don't draw the kind of attention that'll bring trouble back to Cassie."

Then she left the room. And Devlin once again considered moving to the motel. Except now it was overfull.

A sudden thought struck him: if any trouble came out of this invasion, he needed to be here to protect Cassie, his mother and Elaine.

That came first, before anything else.

He looked at his reader and wondered if he was being a plain fool to even think of infiltration.

ELAINE LOOKED IN on Cassie, as she did every night. The little girl was sound asleep, wrapped around a stuffed unicorn she'd had since infancy. The only stuffed animal she wanted. Elaine had no idea what she'd do when that cuddly doll could no longer be stitched together. Maybe a cat would help, but only tomorrow could solve that conundrum.

In the shower, she thought about Devlin. She'd detected the growing tension in him and felt that now she understood it. He wasn't good at sitting on his hands. Well, neither was she.

But to involve himself with that UFO crowd, especially the ones in town who took the alien ideas seriously? She supposed they should be expecting the media any day, the media with their cameras. And if this crowd hadn't bothered the locals sufficiently, an invasion of TV people would finish the job.

With a towel wrapped around her medium-length dark brown hair, she sat on the bench at the foot of her bed and began to apply skin cream. This was a dry climate, and cream, especially on her hands, was necessary. She had chosen the most odor-free she could find because she suspected a deputy running around smelling like roses or lavender wouldn't have the same authority.

She thought about Devlin again as she ran a brush through her hair. She was thinking entirely too much about him. Like she thought of Cassie. Not as much, of course, but too often. Cassie was her life. Devlin was a ship sailing through it, gone in a few weeks when he no longer needed this safe harbor.

Well, she hoped he left, because she kept sensing danger around him. It was a feeling she had so far mostly ignored, as if it weren't there, except for that one time when he'd said he would leave because she was angry with him.

Now this. In theory, this attempt of his shouldn't bring any danger to the rest of them. That group of people seemed pretty much harmless, if wacko. But as much as they irritated some of the locals, others seemed to be enjoying the show as if it were a big colorful parade.

Elaine wondered how long that would last. Or how long the crowd would stay out there. The fun had to wear off at some point. And some of them must have jobs to get back to.

Sliding into a nightgown and under her comforter, she stared into the night, her ears always on alert for Cassie.

But her mind roamed far afield, to what it must be like to work for the State Department, maybe to direct agents who persuaded people to inform for you, to keep intelligence flowing your way.

What it must be like to lose one of them.

Closing her eyes now, she thought of what Devlin might be feeling. He'd never expressed anything about it, but he wasn't a cold fish, as far as she could tell. So it had to be affecting him. Had to concern him that a man he had worked with had been betrayed. Who had betrayed him?

No wonder his bosses wanted him so far out of the way. If someone was leaking information, they might leak his whereabouts if they discovered them.

God, what a mess.

In the morning, as she was trying to persuade Cassie to pull on her jacket for a car ride, Elaine had another thought about Devlin.

Yeah, she was worried that his actions might draw trouble to this house, but she suddenly turned the thought around: she was a deputy watching over those partying alien fanatics. *She* could just as easily draw their attention. Maybe more easily than Devlin. She could be targeted simply because of her uniform and her role.

Then she shook her head. No reason to think anyone might do such a thing in that group of people, who seemed primarily interested in having a good time.

They were just having fun, and the two lights provided the excuse.

But why hadn't they gone to Roswell, the place where these things usually happened? Maybe they just wanted something different, some place that didn't already have diners playing up to them, or a museum of questionable artifacts, or places selling all kinds of kitsch.

In short, a fresh, untainted place to stamp a new mark.

God, she hoped this didn't become some kind of regular thing.

"Mind if I ride along?" Devlin asked as he emerged from his room.

"Let's see how Cassie reacts once I get her into the car."

"Fair enough."

At this stage, Cassie wasn't keen on leaving the house. She might occasionally take a walk with Lu or her mother, but she wouldn't go into the park or into a store, and she pulled away when people got too close.

But then Elaine found an amazing key. "Cassie, we're going to visit Dr. Windwalker so you can get a kitty, if you find one you like. A kitty for Cassie?"

Interest flickered in her daughter's blue eyes, and she stopped resisting the jacket she knew would take her from her beloved coloring.

In what seemed like no time at all, she was fastened into her car seat, an amazing thing all by itself since Cassie usually hated to be restrained. But she knew the car seat from doctor's visits, and while she sometimes might kick up a fuss about it, she still allowed herself to be strapped in.

Nor did she object when Devlin climbed into the front passenger seat. Lu waved them off with a smile. She had plans to spend this free time with her friends.

"I feel awful about Lu," Elaine remarked.

"Why?"

"Because she's given up everything to look after Cassie. Sure, I can take over when I'm not at work, but it still limits her. She's always been outgoing."

"And she's always been capable of saying no. She's also perfectly capable of saying she wants you to hire help."

Elaine nodded slowly. Lu had certainly moved *herself*

in to help Elaine and Cassie. She hadn't been asked, not that her decision had upset Elaine in the least. But it *had* been Lu's decision.

Cassie made some random noises from the back seat. Rare vocalization, but always welcome. Then there was "Mommy." A relatively new word. *Not often enough,* Elaine's heart said, even though her brain knew she ought to be grateful it was happening at all. There would be other words. There *had* to be.

"So," she asked Devlin as they drove from town toward the east, which spared them contact with the revelers, "what have you learned from your UFO research?"

A smothered laugh escaped him. "Plenty, little of it flattering. I was focusing mainly on what's been happening in Roswell, New Mexico. Conard City is a long way from having to face that."

"Are you sure?" she asked.

"What do you mean?"

"Wasn't there just one reported crash out there? And they're still partying after all these decades."

"Well, some think there was more than one crash. But apart from that, there's a conviction that alien bodies were found. Or that they're alive and were taken to Wright-Patterson Air Force Base."

Elaine spoke dryly. "And of course, there's the government cover-up theory."

"At least they've got some reason for that. Are you familiar with the story?"

"Not much."

"So, consider that news of the craft crashing was on the local radio station, along with an interview with a rancher who found the debris. I think it was the same morning that the local newspaper reported that the public information officer at the air base had announced the crash of a flying saucer and said they'd found debris."

Elaine felt like she should have been aware of this. It sounded major.

"Then, a day later, the air force debunked the whole thing by saying it was a weather balloon and showed pieces of wreckage. And that's why Roswell has never been forgotten."

"Wow," Elaine murmured. "But we don't have anything like that here. Just a couple of lights."

"And no cover-up yet."

"I'm not sure I like the way you said *yet*."

But before he could reply, she turned into the gravel road that led to Mike Windwalker's veterinary clinic and hospital. She'd barely parked before Mike appeared, smiling. He wore green scrubs, and his black hair was tied back out of the way.

He came round to Elaine's side of the car and bent to look into the window. "I understand this is a bit delicate. What do I need to do?"

Good question, Elaine thought. She hadn't walked through this mentally yet, hadn't made a plan. "I don't know, Mike. I could use an idea." Especially since she feared a major change could lead to a major meltdown, over which she had no control.

He nodded.

"I've got one," Devlin said.

Elaine looked at him, surprised. So far, he had done not one thing to insert himself into Cassie's care. "What's that?"

"How about you and I get out of the car. Then Mike gives you a kitten to hold, and you take it to Cassie. What do you think?"

Elaine nodded slowly, then decided it sounded like the best way to go at this. "I probably should have just brought the kitten home with me. Getting it from here to there might cause a crisis. Damn!" Trying to figure all this out sometimes overwhelmed her.

"I've got a cardboard box with holes in it," Mike said. "Cassie and the kitten will be able to see each other. But first…"

He straightened and headed for the front door of the clinic. "I've got two," he said over his shoulder. "We'll try the second one if it seems necessary."

Elaine looked at Devlin, and they both climbed out of the car to wait. Cassie looked around her but remained silent. She was definitely interested in the change, though.

At last, Mike emerged from the clinic with a small bundle of fur in his arms, a gray tabby with bright green eyes. "Let's see how we do with this little girl."

Elaine opened the back door of the car and leaned in, waiting for Cassie's gaze to settle on her. "Cassie, we have a present for you if you want it. A little kitten. Do you want to see it?"

Cassie's gaze immediately brightened. Hopeful now, Elaine turned to take the kitten from Mike's hands and gently hold it out to Cassie. Instead of pulling away, her daughter reached out a hand to the kitten.

"Do you want to keep her, Cassie? Take her home with us?"

Cassie didn't answer, but reached out her other hand. Gently, Elaine rested the kitten on Cassie. The kitten dug in, clinging with her little paws and resting her head on Cassie. Purring.

And for the first time, Elaine saw her daughter smile—

truly smile. Her hand came to rest on the kitten, and her fingers moved gently.

Then Cassie said a new word: "Soft."

Tears prickled in Elaine's eyes, and she drew a shaky breath. "Oh, wow," she breathed. "Oh, wow."

GETTING THE KITTEN home took some effort. Cassie had to be persuaded to let go of her. For the first time, Devlin stepped in, as did Mike. Mike explained that Cassie needed to keep the kitty safe on the way home. That was what the box was for.

Devlin added that he'd make sure the kitty arrived safely, and if Cassie wanted, he'd sit in the back seat to watch the box with her.

Cassie allowed it.

Then Mike loaded up the back end of Elaine's vehicle with a litter pan, a small bag of litter, some cans of soft food and a couple of small toys.

Elaine didn't realize how tense she'd been until they were halfway home. She glanced in her rearview mirror, liking what she saw in the back seat. "Thanks, Devlin."

"I didn't do much. Truth be told, I'm still astonished that Cassie will let me this close. It must be the kitten between us."

"Maybe." But Elaine didn't think so. Apparently Devlin had been around enough to win at least some of Cassie's trust.

The only question was whether that would prove to be good. Or very bad. Elaine frowned. She knew she could become a mama bear if needed. She didn't want to have to do that with Devlin.

At home, Cassie settled on the living room carpet, just watching the kitten with fascination. Occasionally the little bundle crawled up on her and clung, accepting a light stroke from Cassie's surprisingly gentle hands, then resumed its exploration.

Lu returned from her coffee klatch and regarded this development with a small amount of suspicion. "I really don't like cats," she said. "But…" Then she smiled. "Cassie sure likes it. Has it got a name?"

"Not yet," Elaine answered.

"Then you'd better pick one. Or we can just keep calling it Kittie."

Which wouldn't be bad at all, Elaine thought. Cassie sure wasn't going to come up with one.

But watching her daughter play with the kitten made everything worthwhile. Cassie wasn't devoting the same level of intense focus she gave her coloring, but her focus was strong. More importantly, it was on something else.

Thank you, Sally, she thought. Better than a puppy, too. A puppy might have been too rambunctious.

No, the kitten was just right.

CASSIE FORGOT ALL about her coloring. Elaine didn't know if that was good or bad. It would certainly be good if Cassie could have two things to focus on, but exchanging one for the other? She wasn't at all sure about that and wondered if she should call Sally.

But then came another moment, a huge moment. The kitten grew sleepy and curled up in a ball. Cassie looked almost panicked, and Elaine was quick to settle down with her and explain that Kittie needed to sleep just like Cassie and Mommy did. Then, almost holding her breath, she asked if Cassie thought the kitten needed a blanket.

Cassie held up both hands, so Elaine hurried to get an

old, fuzzy afghan she'd had for years, maybe since childhood. Didn't matter. The kitten would probably like it.

She spread it over the kitten, being careful not to cover its head. "See?" she said to Cassie. "All tucked in, but we don't want to cover her head." Although she doubted it would cause the kitten any problem. The blanket was porous.

"Okay? She'll wake up when she's ready."

Then she dared at last to go get herself a cup of coffee and return to her watch over Cassie. Devlin stood at the front window, and for the first time, she wondered why he'd been doing that since a while after they got home.

But she didn't dare ask when she looked again and saw that Cassie had pulled part of the worn blanket over herself and was sound asleep with Kittie.

Elaine's heart swelled as she smiled at her daughter sleeping with her new pet. Her daughter who had spoken a new word today: *soft.*

Then she realized what that said about her Cassie's development, no matter how hidden. And tears began to run down her cheeks.

DINNERTIME CAME, and Lu had to put up with a kitten roaming on top of the table.

"We can't keep that up," she told Elaine irritably. "But that's why I don't like cats. You can't train them."

"Sure you can," said Devlin. "I have a friend who has three cats, all very well trained about where they're allowed to go. It's okay. I'll get Kittie to stay off the table."

"But they like high places," Lu pointed out. "I know that much."

"Which is why I'll bring home a cat tree tomorrow.

Relax, Mom." Then he smiled. "Relax, *both* of you. Cassie will help me teach Kittie—won't you, Cassie?"

Cassie glanced at Devlin, amazing Elaine. Then she gave the smallest of nods.

Elaine looked at Lu, who had drawn a surprised breath. "Okay," Lu said, "that cat can dance on the table. For a while."

LATER, AFTER CASSIE'S BATH—with Kittie sitting on the edge of the tub—and after Cassie had gone to sleep with a cat curled up beside her, Elaine took her happiness to the living room, ready to share it, when she saw Devlin at the front window again. She could hear Lu in her bedroom, her TV turned on at low volume.

The night was once again filling with spring's seeping chill.

"What's wrong?" Elaine asked Devlin a bit querulously. "You've been staring out that window for hours."

He shrugged and turned to look at her. "Nothing," he answered.

"Sure, and I'm a werewolf."

At that, he smiled. "It's nothing, really. I saw a couple of those UFO types on this street earlier. They haven't come back."

Elaine turned her attention to the street, too. "Why are you waiting for them, then? You said they were basically harmless."

"I'm sure they are. But suspicion is practically engraved on my genes after all these years."

She had already gathered he was in some kind of secretive business, but the circumstances of everything he'd lived with hadn't occurred to her. No thought of what it might have meant for him. She edged toward the subject. "It must have been difficult, living overseas most of the time."

He didn't answer for a minute, maybe two. Then: "It had its good moments. Local people can be absolutely wonderful to nonresidents. Even Americans. In fact, I often think they have a better opinion of us than some of us do."

Elaine laughed quietly. "Why doesn't that surprise me?"

"The land of hopes and dreams," he remarked.

"And those weirdos you saw out there on the street? How are they being received?" Though she was wondering more about him than her neighbors.

"Probably my paranoia, like I said. Nobody else seemed bothered. Those two were likely just exploring for a change of pace. Although you'd think they'd take those masks off when they got too far from the crowd."

"You'd think." On that, she agreed with him. If they chose to look like something that might upset the locals, why leave the safety of the group? Why risk a bad reception from people?

But then, why not?

"We're a small town," she reminded him. "At least, small compared to other places—but a good place to get away in for a little while. You wouldn't have to go far."

"True. But I've been in smaller places. Much smaller."

She turned to face him again, deciding she'd tiptoed enough. Tiptoeing wasn't in her nature, certainly not as a cop. "Devlin? What the hell is going on? What has you on edge?"

Once again, he didn't answer, and this time his silence put *her* on edge. He was hiding something. He had to be. "Devlin?"

"Sorry," he said, wiping a hand over his face. "Like I said, bad habits. Learned responses. Nothing about right now."

She didn't believe him. She wondered if she should believe him at all, or if she'd ever be able to.

The thought made her feel ill. Devlin was her departed husband's brother. Lu's son. She shouldn't have to wonder about his honesty.

But now she did.

Turning, she went to knock on Lu's door. "I'm going to work for a while."

Lu answered groggily. "Okay, I've got the baby monitor on."

"Thanks."

In her own room, she put on her uniform and pulled her service pistol out of the gun safe.

As she passed through the living room, Devlin spoke. "I thought you had the night off."

"It's time to do some recon."

"I'll come with you."

She faced him once again. "I'm the cop, remember? I don't need your backup."

Walking out the door, she felt pretty good about herself. She'd just painted a necessary line and told him not to cross it.

Hell, she didn't need a man to protect her.

But the man came anyway, which irritated her. "I know you don't need me," he said. "You never have before, and there's no reason that should change. I'm just curious."

"Well, stay away from me," she said sharply. "You don't want to give the impression you're law enforcement."

"Nah, I'll take my own car."

As if he realized she could get into trouble if people

thought he was a deputy because he accompanied her. Maybe he did. Or maybe she'd pushed him away enough to make a point of his odd absence in his mother's life. His absence from Caleb's and Cassie's. It might have been his job, or it might have been self-absorption. How could she know? She just knew that her trust for him was shredding fast.

As he walked to his car, she said, "Watch yourself, Devlin. I don't want to have to rescue your butt."

Although she suspected he might be used to saving his own butt, probably by talking. Glib talking.

DEVLIN COULD FEEL Elaine pulling away from him. She'd never been in a hurry to get close, which he could understand, given his prodigal son routine over so many years. But now she was closing even that off.

He deserved it. He *didn't* deserve her trust. Trust needed to be earned, and God knew he'd done little about that.

He figured he was staying at her house only because of his mother, which was a sorry commentary on him. However, he needed to find a way to make at least some small amends.

As for the crowd downtown, he just wanted to see them. To take their temperature. On absolutely no mission he'd had overseas was a gathered crowd something to be ignored. Any group of people focused on a single thing was a fire waiting for a spark. Violence could break out at any time.

Even though these partiers seemed to be in good spirits and here just to have a good time, they were still a crowd.

He took his time driving to the center of town and

parked some distance away, taking care to approach at a casual walk.

He saw Elaine up ahead, talking to a small knot of people, making them laugh. She was good at this.

But he had a different perspective. She probably didn't see trouble, just a group who needed reminders to avoid any trouble.

Devlin saw trouble. In its nascent stages, to be sure, but still a huge potential for trouble.

And he didn't like the number of shopkeepers who stood outside their businesses with folded arms. None appeared to be carrying a weapon, but just because you couldn't see it didn't mean it wasn't there.

He turned to a couple of people in green outfits who were wearing the masks with big black eyes.

"Say," he said amiably, "is there somewhere I could get one of those masks? They're so cool!"

One of the aliens pulled back her mask. She was carrying a backpack, and she dropped it to the ground to paw through it. "I got some eyes in here. Best I can do, but nobody here is selling them. Not like Roswell."

He feigned something like excited interest. "You've been to *Roswell*? I've never been able to do that."

The young woman handed him a mask made mainly of cheap felt with two huge eyes. "You gotta find a way to get there. That party is a real trip. Every July, around the time the saucer crashed."

She gave him a wide smile. "It's not cheap. The place has really grown, hotels cost a lot—meals are cheap enough, though. If you go to the right places. If you come, find me. I'll show you around." Then she paused. "I guess I should tell you my name. Just look around for Alienne. Two *N*'s with an *E* at the end. Almost anybody knows me."

"That must be a lot of people."

She laughed. "The more, the merrier."

She and her silent companion were starting to move toward the center of the crowd, so he stopped her with a question. "What do you think about the crash?"

She shrugged. "Some of us believe it. Some of us think there are live aliens, some think there are bodies and pieces of a ship…" Then she laughed again. "Doesn't matter which story you want to believe. It's a great party."

Then she and her friend merged into the crowd. Devlin put on his mask and adjusted it so he could mostly see through the dark eyes, which were about like sunglasses.

Alienne, pronounced *alien*, amused him. A woman who believed very little about this whole issue but just enjoyed the partying. Not half-bad.

And about as fake as could be, given where she was. He would have expected some defense of one of the conspiracy theories. An impassioned one. Nope.

He turned a bit and picked her out of the crowd. Surprisingly easy, considering most of this motley crew were wearing similar costumes. She stood out anyway, being tall.

ELAINE BEGAN MOVING along the edges of the boisterous crowd so she could follow what was left of the sidewalk to talk to the shopkeepers.

Maude and Mavis were the first she met, and both of the large women looked as if murder wasn't far from their minds.

Maude spoke first. "There's gotta be a way to stop this, Elaine. Some way. I heard all that stuff about how it doesn't matter who shows up to eat, long as they all pay. 'Tain't true. I got regulars who can't get through my door.

Not as I blame 'em. But what's gonna happen if this keeps going on? Maybe they never come back."

Elaine honestly couldn't imagine that. Going to Maude's for a meal or just coffee was so ingrained in these parts that people were probably suffering from withdrawal.

Which meant what? That some people might try to take their town back? God, what a thought. Maude was right. They needed to find a way to stop this or at least shrink the numbers.

The UFO hunters out there along the roads seemed minimal by comparison. Although she wondered if Beggan Bixby would agree with that. So far, they hadn't gotten an annoyed call from Lew Selvage, though. If anything was happening on his ranch, it wasn't bothering him.

Or maybe he was burying the bodies.

The thought caught her by surprise, and she had to snort into her gloved hand. God, what a notion. On the other hand, Bixby...

"Damn," she nearly growled as she continued her stroll down the street, one eye on the crowd, the other on the annoyed shopkeepers. And more than one of them was able to justify his presence on the street.

But as the locals grew increasingly fatigued from protecting their property, trouble became more likely.

Chaz Rickard, who owned the organic-foods market, had a different take, though. He shrugged it off.

"Sure, I'll protect my windows, but they don't mean no harm, Elaine. Just an excuse for a party. Besides, I sometimes wonder about it myself, that spaceship crash near Roswell. Seems like the government changed its story in a whiplash."

There it was. The conspiracy. "I only heard a bit about that."

"Most people don't care. Why should they? Uncle Sam says it didn't happen, and that's all they need to make themselves happy."

"But you don't agree?"

Chaz shook his head. "Hard to, when they change the story. Now they released a report that said it was a weather balloon from some new program or other. Project Mogul, that's it. Anyway, records show they didn't launch any balloons for three days around that time. Hard to buy."

"It would be." She had to admit that much. Except where exactly was this info about there being no balloon launch coming from? A logbook of some kind? But those could be faked, too.

She suddenly wanted to laugh at herself. Now she was inventing her own conspiracy theory. Easy enough to do. Maybe some subjects just asked for them.

She turned around. Strangely shaped denizens of Zeta Reticuli, or some other planet, had disappeared. They were still clustering up near the center of town, which was no doubt making the sheriff's office unhappy. Maybe she should check in with her colleagues who were still working in town.

The remainder of the thinly spread force was trying to monitor the rest of the county.

Maude was right. In a lot of ways, this needed to stop. The city council was probably trying to write a new ordinance the sheriff could act on.

Yeah. First Amendment. Another laugh wanted to escape her. This entire situation was so ridiculous.

And so close to becoming a powder keg.

DEVLIN FOUND HER while she was still at the edge of the crowd. "Hey, Deputy. Recognize me?"

She looked into his green, bug-eyed face. "Gone over to the dark side?"

"Not exactly, but learning a lot."

"And?"

"They're mostly harmless. Mostly getting to the point of running out of money."

"Well, that's good news."

"Maybe. Some of 'em better consider transportation issues when they wanna leave. And of course, there are some hard-core types here. They honestly believe those lights are something from another planet."

Elaine bit her lip, then said, "So why aren't they out there with the other hunters?"

"I'm trying to find out. Probably nothing more important than that they really just want to have a party."

Which was entirely possible, he thought, scanning the crowd once again. The hard-core UFO types were camped all over the county watching a couple of lights. The rest here were mostly people who weren't hard-core but enjoyed the camaraderie.

Still, he remained uneasy, wondering what the hell was bugging him so much. There was nothing about this crowd that suggested they might be like the crowds he'd seen during his various assignments. Crowds full of anger, full of a desire for change no matter how bloody. Crowds just waiting for a match.

Which local governments gave them all too often. All it took was a bullet or two, or a bunch of soldiers marching in, to break it all up.

A lot of people lived on a hair trigger, often with some justification. But this group?

He shook his head. Maybe it was time to readjust his thinking. He was in a different world now.

"Is THAT HIM?" Kalina asked. Surrounded by loud, laughing voices, she had no need to keep quiet.

"I'm not sure," Zoe answered. "The informer said he was tall, but there are a lot of tall men around here."

It was true, Kalina thought, looking around. She and her sister were hardly bigger than children in this crowd. "How do they get so tall?" she wondered.

"Better food than we ate," Kalina said bitterly. "Better than Niko ever got."

Both women fell silent, recalling a past that goaded them, that angered them, that hurt them. Remembering parents who had tried so hard, only to be sacrificed on the altar of war.

Remembering Niko, who had somehow pulled the three of them to a better place, a place with a roof and regular food, however poor it might have been. Arranging for them to be protected when he was away.

A brother who had given them survival. Perhaps more than survival, because he had surrounded them with men who made sure nothing bad happened to them, surrounded them with women who had become mothers and sisters to them. People who had taught them how to take care of themselves.

Niko, who had never forgotten the importance of family. Niko, who had sacrificed himself, according to one of the men who looked after them. A man who got angry and shouted about Niko. A man they had feared until the day he looked at them and said, *Find the man who caused Niko to betray us. The devil who turned him into a* zradca. *The man who made us kill Niko.*

Two men? Or just one? When they had tried to find out, they'd been yelled at and told to find the American *diabol*. That it was their duty to their family. The only way to honor their brother. Their only way to pay their debt to those who had cared for them all these years. And the idea of vengeance was a good one.

The fear had followed the girls all the way across a war-torn country to an old man who drove them in a rackety truck to a border, where they boarded a fishing boat that carried them across an ocean. Then a much smaller boat sailed them along a misty coastline and dropped them on a ragged beach with only a map that had been rubbed almost to invisibility. By then, their fear had grown into fury.

They had no doubt that Niko had sold himself to save them. To keep them fed. To make life easier for the small community where they sheltered. But they could not escape the fact that whatever his purpose, he had stained their family.

Still, protected or not all these years, Zoe and Kalina had learned some things. They had learned to fight. They had learned to find their way along strange roads in unfamiliar lands. They had become warriors from necessity, because real protection didn't mean relying on others.

And for all these weeks, they had lived for a single purpose. To kill the man who had turned Niko into a traitor.

They'd had help getting close to him. It seemed the American *diabol* could be betrayed, too. And by one of his own.

A Slovak who for years had been working for the Americans, too, but in a regular job. A job where she got more information to pass the other way than Niko could ever have given the Americans.

The twisted story sometimes seemed impossible to the sisters, but they believed it anyway.

Now here they were, in a town that had suddenly turned stranger than they could believe.

And they had to become people who were very different from any they had known.

Americans had the security and the money to behave like this for fun? Or was it some kind of religious holiday they didn't understand?

MITCH CANTRELL, a highly successful rancher whose land abutted Bixby's, came to town a day later and entered the sheriff's office with a proposal.

"Just tell all those nuts outside town they can camp on my land. I got a parcel I'm not using this year just lying fallow, and it'll solve one problem. Folks are getting pretty annoyed out my way because the roads are being narrowed by all those campers. Can't get a good-sized truck and trailer through there, and we need to be moving cattle."

Gage Dalton liked the idea. "It would cut down on the number of people I need out there to keep an eye on things."

Mitch laughed. "Looks like you got enough trouble here in town. *You'll* need to move 'em, though. No way they'll listen to me."

ELAINE HAD BEGUN to grow seriously irritated. She ordinarily loved her job, and it usually offered her plenty of time to spend with Cassie, but these green, bug-eyed partiers were soaking up damn near all her time. Shifts were longer because they had a limited number of cops. Days off were canceled for the time being. Right then, the deputies were lucky to get a half day off.

Time with Cassie? Not enough of it.

Devlin joined her during the late afternoon as she was shoving some food in her mouth and changing her uniform shirt.

"I'd take the shift for you if I could."

She paused, her fingers on the buttons, and looked at him. Really looked at him for the first time in a couple of harried days. She didn't doubt him. Nor could she quite ignore the tingling attraction she felt for him. Caleb's brother? She was certain that would involve a guilt trip bigger than the state of Wyoming. "I'm sure you would."

Then, completely astonishing her, Devlin tugged her gently into a hug, his hands rubbing her back. "Elaine… No. Not now."

He stepped back. The loss of his embrace felt like her skin was being stripped away, more so because she knew exactly what he meant. Hunger, growing ferocious despite everything else going on. Damn, all she wanted was to fall into this man's arms and forget the whole world for an hour or two. Just shove everything away.

He was so good looking, so attractive, that she could barely withstand her own urge to pull him toward her, to demand he answer the needs that pounded through her body.

But he was right. Not now. She had a few minutes to spend with Cassie; then she had to get back to work.

"I hate this," she said suddenly, then turned away to go sit with Cassie and her kitten. Kittie was still commanding the kitchen table, curled up right beside Cassie while she colored.

Lu had given in, and there was no question that Cassie was looking happier.

Thank God for kittens.

Chapter Seven

When Elaine headed for the office the next morning, getting ready to organize the mass relocation of dozens of campers to isolated ranchland, Devlin insisted on riding along with her.

"You're going to need bodies," he said firmly. "All I have to do is stand behind you."

He has a point, she thought. He wasn't exactly the image of a guy who could be safely ignored.

"I won't interfere in any way," he added as they walked out to her patrol vehicle. "Your job. I'll be a fencepost."

Unless he decides something else is needed, she thought, but then she figured some ranchers were going to be out there, too. To *help* with the relocation.

She swore under her breath, considering all the trouble that could come from what had seemed like such a simple idea from Mitch Cantrell.

Yet the groups on the road hadn't seemed inclined to do much except try to sky watch. No parties, no drinking. A surprisingly sober group, unlike the crowd in town.

There was a lot of radio traffic as the deputies worked their way to the various groups. There were, as Elaine had worried, a lot of ranchers, too. Even those who weren't being hassled.

Radios continued to crackle as each deputy reached their appointed camp spot. A brilliant sky overhead made the day seem peaceful. Gentle, crisp spring air filled the whole area, dampened only by a few clouds of dust. Ranchers still arriving.

"This could get interesting," Devlin remarked.

"Maybe," Elaine answered. "On the other hand, the outsiders will be where they really want to be, and none of the ranchers should be bothered once they're on the Cantrell spread."

Devlin chuckled quietly. "That's the idea, anyway."

DEVLIN, FOR HIS PART, was pretty impressed by the calm with which Elaine approached this entire situation. Especially as they reached their appointed camp and five UFO hunters were facing three ranch-types. Hired hands? There couldn't be too many ranch owners out here. And if they were sending hired hands…

The back of Devlin's neck prickled. He had plenty of experience recognizing inflammatory situations.

Elaine climbed out, her gunbelt and baton in plain view despite her uniform jacket. In fact, she tucked her jacket behind the butt of her pistol. A subtle warning.

"Hey, folks," she said pleasantly, smiling. "What's up?"

Then she looked at the three guys in jeans, jackets and cowboy hats. "We're moving them. Isn't that what you want?"

Some mumbles greeted her.

"Exactly what I thought." She turned to the UFO people. "We're going to take you out to a place on the Cantrell ranch. It abuts the Bixby land you've been wanting to get onto. And you'll have a clear sky view, okay?"

One of the hired hands shifted. "No light out there for a fact."

The five UFO types exchanged looks. Elaine wished she could remember the names of the two of them she had talked to at Maude's, but they escaped her just then.

"Well," said the woman whom Elaine had believed was their leader, "that sounds good to me. We've got a lot of camping gear to pack up."

"We'll help," said one of the hands. "Them cars of yours ain't gonna get across the rough ground too well. You might need some help from our trucks."

Pickup trucks so old they looked like they might have been last painted fifty or so years ago. Plenty of dents, too.

But that didn't matter when the engines purred.

Devlin started helping fold up the camp and putting parts of tents, cookstoves and all the rest in the trunks of cars. To make it easier and quicker, some of the load went into the pickups.

What didn't leave the hands of the UFO hunters were their fancy cameras and other equipment. Devlin could understand that. A large chunk of someone's bank account had gone into the best money could buy, from cameras to special lenses to color filters. Then there were the magnetic field readers, and he thought he saw a Geiger counter.

The Geiger counter struck him as extreme, but he was prepared to shrug it off. After all, these people had come to the middle of nowhere because they'd heard of a couple of red lights.

Now *that* was extreme. Yeah, he was sure a lot of people wouldn't mind knowing what those lights were, but this kind of time and equipment devoted to trying to find an answer that would probably be mundane? If they even found one.

With the first group on their way down the road with the three cowboys, he and Elaine moved on to the next group. These people were feeling more threatened by the arrival of two cowboys.

Devlin could hardly blame them. These two cowboys looked a whole lot less friendly than the original three. Plus, this group of UFO hunters included four women.

He scanned them in the bright light of day, thinking he saw something vaguely familiar in one of the faces. He shook his head inwardly. At this point in his career, having seen so many thousands of faces, it might take only a single feature to cause a temporary misidentification. He always had to be wary of that.

Didn't stop the back of his neck from prickling once again, though.

This removal was a little more difficult than the first. These cowboys didn't feel like offering any help; they just made unflattering comments the whole time about the six people, mostly about the four women.

He could see Elaine gritting her teeth but not wanting to stir up trouble.

So he stepped in and started helping to break down the camp. As he did so, he remarked, "Just ignore them, ladies. Some guys just don't know any better."

He heard Elaine draw a breath. But the women relaxed a bit as they realized they weren't facing this alone. Then one of the boys with the UFO-hunters group said, "Yeah. I see it all the time at work. It's one way to get your jollies, I guess."

The guys getting their jollies looked pretty mad just

then, but a glance at Elaine in her uniform was enough to make them turn away.

"Tell the boss they's goin' away," one of them said as they climbed back into their rusty trucks. They jammed down hard on their accelerators, spraying gravel and dust everywhere.

"Well, that was pretty," Elaine remarked. "Thanks, Devlin." She offered thanks to the kid who'd spoken up, too.

The young man shrugged. "Easy to do when I had backup," he said, then laughed. "*Two* backups. I was just trying not to cause trouble."

A mature attitude, Devlin thought. *Very mature.*

"You know," that same young man said as they finished packing gear into trunks and car carriers, "we're moving. We got invited to a place to camp and keep looking at those lights. So why did those guys act like we were trouble? We're getting out of the way."

"Some people," Elaine remarked.

"Yeah, you'd know, wouldn't you?"

But Devlin noticed one thing. Two of the young women didn't look at all happy about going out to the ranch to camp, even though it would have to be better than camping by the roadside.

What troubled them? Feeling unprotected from all the guys who'd be out there, too? But there ought to be enough decent men to make sure nothing bad happened, and enough women to raise a ruckus if it did.

Bothered, he watched the crew depart, then looked at Elaine.

She'd sensed something, too. He could see it in the faint frown on her face. But then she tugged her hat to a more secure position on her head.

"Just one more group *we* have to move," she remarked. "The others must have moved their crowds by now."

"They've been springing up like weeds, huh?"

She grinned at him. "Maybe there's a shortage of spots for watching UFOs."

"Wouldn't surprise me, actually. But you're sure they know where they're going?"

"Yeah, they were already moving, which means Mitch Cantrell let 'em know where to go and probably has some hired help to guide across his ranch."

"Like a well-oiled machine."

She gave him another smile before they climbed into her Suburban. "Sometimes we get it right."

And sometimes people could get it very wrong. He slipped into the darkness inside himself, thinking of Niko, who'd only been trying to do what he believed best for his people. The kind of patriot one rarely met.

Too many of his assets had been interested only in money, a tidbit of info for some American dollars. Niko hadn't been like them. He'd brushed away the idea of money until Devlin had insisted he take at least some for the sake of his family.

Maybe the money had given him away, even though it had been in local currency. But a clue, perhaps, to the fact that Niko's family was living better than they had before.

God! What if his own insistence had brought Niko to the attention of the wrong people? It might well have, since the company still hadn't found a leak. Any leak.

Not that the CIA didn't have its share of them. Like in any huge organization, there were always people who saw a way for personal gain by sharing information, though usually not a lot of it and never revealing assets. Everyone, including the most venal, knew that assets were more than information sources. They were *lives*.

He felt gloomy anyway.

By the time they reached the entrance to the Cantrell ranch, a caravan was forming, ready to begin the trek to the land Mitch Cantrell had offered to let them use.

Cantrell stood on the bed of a pickup truck and whistled loudly to get everyone's attention. "Just a couple of things. I'm going to put a few of my men out there with you to keep an eye on some things. I don't want fires being accidentally started. Wildfires aren't a joke. You're going to clean up any litter. If you need bags, I'll provide them. And you cart your trash out with you? Got it?"

From the nods and murmurs, everyone got it, and most appeared to agree with the restrictions.

Mitch wasn't quite finished, though. "Livestock. Most of it is fenced elsewhere, but if cattle or sheep get through and come your way, just leave them alone. My guys will take care of it, and I don't want you scaring my animals."

Again, more nods. It appeared settled.

In fact, the groups were pulling together and talking in excited voices. A place to watch from. A place not polluted by light. A place where they didn't have to worry about being chased away by armed men.

Devlin looked at Elaine and saw her frown as she heard the group. "'Armed men'?" she repeatedly quietly. "Not here. Not yet."

"Well, there's Bixby."

At that, her frown vanished to be replaced by something approaching a grin. "He'd be the only one I'd worry about. Why do I get the feeling these people are talking about somewhere else?"

"Because they probably are. God knows how many UFO hunts some of them have been on."

They had begun their drive back to town, Elaine drumming her fingers on the steering wheel. "I never thought about those guys running all over to do this kind of watching. I also can't imagine what drives them."

Devlin gave it some thought as they turned onto a narrow paved road. The sun now came through the window on his side of the vehicle. Warm. Pleasant. A moment to be enjoyed, as so few were.

"I don't know," he said. "I probably should ask them. But I think they're hoping to see something that breaks all the rules. Something that hints at life beyond this planet."

Elaine sighed and shook her head. "Unless aliens want to land at the White House in front of all the TV cameras on the planet, I doubt we're ever going to have proof of that."

"Maybe not, but it's fuel for the imagination."

But there were limits to that, he knew. Limits to protect against very real dangers. Not on this alien-hunt thing. He didn't think those people were in any serious danger from UFOs or UAPs. The alien-abduction thing far exceeded his credulity.

The threat they faced more likely came from angry landowners than anything they might see in the sky.

But something was definitely wrong there. He'd felt it again, among those groups, though he couldn't localize it. Maybe someone in that crowd intended to do something that could bring trouble down on everyone's head.

Well, there was nothing he could do about it unless some information happened his way. And since he wasn't actively looking for it, wasn't actively trying to groom an asset, the chance that he'd hear something important was highly unlikely.

So he would relax and just enjoy the break from his duties.

Turning his head just a little, he filled his gaze with Elaine Paltier. His sister-in-law.

God, he ought to have guilt over his feelings. Ought to feel like he was betraying his brother.

But he didn't.

Sorry, Caleb, he thought. *She's alone now.*

More than alone. A single mom with a wonderful daughter who was going to need care for the rest of her life.

If Elaine thought about that, she must feel the weight of the future with Cassie. A weight that might become crushing, not because of needed care but because of emotional pain.

Because she loved Cassie and wanted a full life for her, and she might never see it. Or even most of one.

Devlin had missed Caleb many times over the years, and even more since his death because now there wasn't even a possibility of an email or a Skype conversation. All those avenues had been pruned.

But now he wished for Caleb for a new reason: for Cassie and Elaine. To provide the support they both needed, especially Elaine.

Because Devlin felt utterly inadequate in this situation.

ZOE AND KALINA sat around the small fire with other UFO hunters, eating small meat rolls from a tin and canned green beans.

"We need to be somewhere else," Kalina murmured to her sister, although she doubted anyone else was listening to them as the rest chatted noisily about past sightings and future hopes.

Hope, Zoe thought sourly. What did they know of hope? Pointless lights in the sky? Stupid people. Life was too easy for them. She looked at Kalina and saw at least some of her feelings reflected there.

"Niko," Kalina said, then looked down at the tin in her hand. "He would like these little sausages."

Zoe nodded her agreement and ate another one. "Majka made the best sausage."

But their mother was no longer with them. Too many people were no longer with them. Maybe that was what had driven their brother. Too many dead and a threat that wouldn't go away. But why had he thought the Americans would help? They did little enough, leaving it to the blue-hatted peacekeepers from the UN.

Who were little use at any time.

But Niko had never spoken about his choice or why he had made the decision. Never a word to anyone, which meant the Americans must be at fault for his exposure. His activities had been revealed only when he was discovered.

And the only American who could be blamed was the one Niko had spoken to.

The young women looked at each other, their faces perplexed and tired. They needed more information than they had been given. No way to identify this devil except…except how? Every man here seemed big. Or at least, most of them did.

"We have to go," Zoe said after a few minutes. "Back to town. We'll never find him here unless he's with this group."

A man who could not possibly be perverting anyone like Niko out here. Or anywhere at all in his own country.

But if he suspected he was being hunted, their task would become harder.

Kalina agreed. How were they ever going to identify this man?

Because now they had to be as careful as Niko had been for so long.

ELAINE WORKED THAT AFTERNOON. Devlin chose to spend time with his mother and Cassie.

"It's been too long," Lu said, for what must have been the fiftieth time since he'd arrived.

And he repeated, "I'm sorry. Work. I won't let it keep me away as long as it did before."

As if he had any choice about the matter. But he could certainly try. Over the years, there'd been an increase in his ranking, and thus his authority. But with both came greater responsibilities.

Cassie had once again returned to her coloring. Kittie now sat on her lap, and Cassie reached down occasionally to pet her gently. Gentleness seemed to be part of the child.

"Mom? Does Cassie enjoy anything else? Besides coloring, I mean."

"And the kitten," Lu said dryly. "Yeah. She likes walks. We go down by the park often, but she only watches. No interest in the equipment or other children. But Sally believes that will start to change with time. We hope so."

Devlin nodded, trying to imagine how Cassie might view the world and failing miserably.

"We try to introduce her to new things, but slowly," Lu said. "See what interests her and what she doesn't like."

"This must be hard on Elaine."

"Harder than hard," Lu said. "I don't think she ever

stops sweating it, except maybe when something big happens at work."

"I could see that." Then he reached across the table and touched his mother's hand. "What about you? This can't be easy for you, either."

Lu simply shook her head. "I'd do anything for that child. And I *do* have a life, Devlin. Friends. Places I go. It's not like I'm locked up." She pursed her lips, looking faintly amused. "I'm pretty happy with my life, if you're worried about that."

It wasn't something he'd worried about much, except for a period after his father died. But Caleb had been there.

Devil stared at the curly blond hair of his totally absorbed niece and thought about how selfish he'd been. His job was important, yeah. Essential, even. But did it really leave him no time at all?

Not much of it, but that could just be an excuse.

Hell, he thought. *What have I become?*

"I'd like to walk into town," he said. A walk to clear his head. "I don't suppose Cassie would come with me?"

Lu shook her head. "Not likely. Not yet. But go ahead and ask her."

About time he seriously talked to the girl beyond a simple greeting. "Cassie? Would you like to go for a walk with me?"

The child looked up, her hand tightening slightly on Kittie's fur. The look on her face said it all.

"I guess not," Devlin said. "Maybe another time."

Lu tipped her head. "Gotta go back for a look at those loonies, huh?"

Devlin had to laugh, even though she was right. Instincts, honed by long years, drove him to want to understand what made that crowd tick. "Anything you need while I'm out? Like dinner from Maude's?"

Lu laughed. "I won't say no. Just make sure there's some salad with it."

At least the current crop of partiers downtown seemed to be spending money locally, Devlin noticed as he approached the fringes, this time without his alien mask. A few merchants had set up small kiosks outside their stores to sell kitschy items and, like at Maude's, to sell coffee and tea with a visible menu of other quick foods.

The town was adapting to the invasion pretty quickly, Devlin thought. Making the best of it since they were stuck with it. He wondered how long it would be before the invaders moved on.

Not long, he hoped, for the sake of the people who actually lived here.

He slipped into the crowd, though, aware that deputies had formed a very loose cordon to prevent any trouble that might arise.

A number of beers went down throats, but at least the drinkers used the trash bins that seemed to have sprung up along the street, avoiding littering except for scraps of paper. More preparedness.

In all, he was pretty impressed with the general behavior on both sides of this divide.

But as he threaded himself into the crowd and tuned his ears to picking out individual words that might be of interest, he learned something about why this crowd was here: Roswell had become an expensive place to go. These people needed a cheaper place to gather.

Well, that meant certain sacrifices, as he overheard. Sleeping just outside of town in their vehicles because the single motel was overflowing. He also heard the beginnings of rumbles about leaving. Moving on. Maybe finding a better place.

Except for the red lights. The lights visible from the Bixby ranch seemed to have them stapled right here. Not that they expected to see anything from town, but because they hoped they'd be the first to hear the news from the serious hunters who camped out there.

A couple of red lights, for Pete's sake. By Bixby's report, they didn't even seem to move much, if at all. But where were they? If they'd been warning lights on a cell tower for air traffic, everyone should know that, shouldn't they?

His own curiosity was definitely growing. Everything had an explanation, one that didn't involve aliens.

So he did what he did on his job. He fell into conversation with one of them, a guy who wore no mask, just some bobbing green antenna on his head.

"What do you think those lights are?" he asked.

"UFOs," the guy answered promptly. "No reason for them to be there, not as far as we know."

The woman beside him disagreed. She wore the mask with the huge dark eyes, now pushed up on her forehead so she could see. "Sheesh, Jeff, we don't know *what* they are."

Jeff shook his head. "Never gonna know if we don't try to find out. And don't forget the Roswell crash."

"That *was* weird," the woman agreed. "Two different stories within forty-eight hours. Like it was and it wasn't. But whatever it is, I don't trust the government on this."

Devlin spoke. "It's hard, huh?"

"Really hard," Jeff agreed. "Always a pile of bull. At least now they're admitting they can't explain some of this stuff. That's a big step forward."

Devlin thought it was, too. He'd been interested in that UAP report himself. More intelligence. A reason to start looking at what might be a threat to the safety of the nation. A big reason not to dismiss the sightings and reports. His entire adult life had been devoted to the security of this nation, and now this was part of it.

He couldn't criticize these people for wanting to know. Not after they'd been dismissed as fools for seventy or more years.

"Ever seen one?" he asked Jeff, to keep the conversation going. To give himself a visible excuse to keep scanning the crowd.

"A UFO?" Jeff said. "Yeah. Really. Not the kind that makes headlines or anything like that. But I saw a plane, taking off at night, suddenly split into three pieces—red light going to the left, green light going to the right and white light continuing the climb. I thought it was gonna crash."

Devlin nodded, interested. "Did it?"

"Hell no. And when the paper arrived the next afternoon, I discovered I wasn't nuts. Over four thousand people in my area had seen it, too, and called in wanting to know what it was."

"That's a lot of people."

Jeff nodded, his fuzzy green antennae bobbing above his head. "But useless as a sighting."

"So these red lights won't be useful, either?"

Jeff laughed. "Probably not. Unless someone gets some good film of them performing aerobatics that are impossible for current technology. And who knows what current technology is, anyway?"

Devlin faced him. "Then what are you doing here?"

"It's fun. A great vacation. Spring break." Then Jeff

moved away to rejoin the woman, who'd drifted into the crowd.

Spring break, huh? Devlin started grinning himself. But he suspected Jeff's curiosity was strong after what he'd seen that time before. More than a spring trip.

Being faced with the unknown, something with no explanation, could make people devote their entire lives to seeking an answer.

He wondered how many people here were driven by the same unquenchable curiosity and how many had simply found a good reason to party. Lots of things like this pulled people together for good times.

He had just started walking back toward Elaine's house, crossing a residential street not far from downtown, when he heard an irritated man's voice say, "When are those jerks ever gonna leave? Blocking the street, dressed like they ought to be locked up, making life hell for everyone who lives here."

Devlin had no problem understanding the guy's point of view. But then, that kind of understanding had aided him for years.

He paused. The man sat on his front porch on a webbed lawn chair, a longneck in his hand. A birdlike woman, probably his wife, sat in a matching chair. She held no beverage.

Taking a step closer, but not too close, he said, "My name's Devlin. I'm staying with Elaine Paltier. Lu's my mother. You know them?"

The man nodded, as did his wife. "Good people," he said. "So, you finally come home, huh? Must make Lu happy. That child sure got problems, though."

His wife spoke. "Milt, don't be unkind."

He scowled. "I ain't being unkind. That child has problems. Damn shame. Anyhow, I'm more worried about these fruitcakes out there. Looks like a fire ready for a match. There's what? A hundred of 'em?"

A hundred was probably on the conservative side, but Devlin didn't say so. "Just a bunch of kids," he remarked.

"Kids get up to no good easy enough. Bet they got drugs out there." He shook his head. "Folks are getting mighty tired of them."

"Are they?" Devlin smiled and shook his head. "I thought people were being welcoming. At least from what I see."

"That welcome's gonna wear out," Milt said. "Mark my words. Business is all tied up in knots, people can't get to the simplest things. Hell, they got Freitag's department store blocked off."

True. Devlin couldn't argue that. "Well, it's got to end soon," he remarked. "They'll get bored. It's not like this town is set up for them, not like Roswell."

Milt snorted. "Never wanted to be like that place."

His wife spoke. "Bet Roswell makes money on it, though."

"There's more to life than making money."

Devlin had to conceal his amusement, as the woman very much looked like a little more money would be welcome in her life.

After another few casual words, he bade them farewell and moved on.

How many storekeepers were starting to get truly angry, despite the attempts from some of them to take advantage of the invasion? What he had viewed as friendly only a short time ago could take on a different character quite rapidly.

He'd seen it happen.

Then that sense of threat touched him again. Nothing in particular. No sense of being watched. Just something in the air like a faint breeze.

What the hell was going on?

Chapter Eight

Elaine returned from her shift for an evening with her family and arrived to find Devlin cleaning the litter box in the bathroom and Cassie standing nearby, watching intently.

All the while, Devlin spoke quietly about what he was doing and why. Kittie stayed close to Cassie's leg, seeming almost as absorbed in the process as Cassie.

Another step? Another interest? How long would it last?

Cassie turned her head, smiled and said, "Mommy," then returned to watching the litter box cleaning.

"I'm glad," Devlin said, "that Mike Windwalker gave us the dust-free litter. I hate to imagine the cloud otherwise."

Certainly something Elaine wouldn't want Cassie breathing.

As soon as the box was cleaned and the cover back in place, Kittie decided to inaugurate it, which made a tiny laugh escape Cassie. Miracle indeed.

Lu called from the kitchen. "Wash up, folks. I'm about to heat up dinner!"

Risking it, Elaine touched Cassie's shoulder quickly, lightly. Before Cassie could pull away or otherwise react, she headed for her bedroom to ditch her uniform.

Little bits of hope, like that quick touch, every single one as welcome as a miracle.

As soon as she had changed, she found that Cassie had already made her way to the kitchen table, awaiting her dinner with Kittie on her lap.

Devlin had seated himself at the far end of the table and started to rise when Elaine entered the room. God, she'd thought those manners had died years ago. Unnecessary, too, as far as she was concerned, but it was hardly something to turn into an issue.

Lu had already moved place settings and serving dishes to the table, and mouthwatering aromas filled the air.

"It all smells too good," Elaine said. "I think I should thank you, Devlin?"

"Absolutely," Lu said. "I didn't exactly waste my time in raising him."

Devlin laughed. "No, Mom, you didn't."

Cassie continued to pet Kittie but simply stared at the food on her plate.

After a minute or so, Elaine asked, "Aren't you hungry, sweetie? I see french fries and salad. You usually like them both."

But Cassie continued to stare without eating until Elaine began to wonder if her daughter was ill. "Upset tummy, Cassie?" Sometimes that got a nod. God, it was frustrating to have a nonverbal child. Sally felt that would ease with time, that speaking later in childhood wasn't uncommon for autistic children. In the meantime, Elaine spent a whole lot of time wondering about matters such as whether Cassie was ill.

But after what seemed entirely too long, Cassie reached for a cherry tomato, lifting it with delicate fingers to pop it into her mouth.

Elaine released a breath she hadn't realized she was holding and looked away to find Devlin staring at her with sympathy. As if he understood. Maybe he did.

"So," she said, hunting for a safe topic, "what did you learn from your expedition among the weirdos?"

He smiled, shaking his head. "That most of them are here because it's a cheaper place to party than Roswell. Not that I'm sure quite a few of them won't make it to the main event in July."

"Around the time of the supposed saucer crash?"

Devlin nodded. "It's an interesting mix of people who just want to have fun and people who want to be present if the hunters get any information at all. Like the lights moving."

Elaine ate salad and a few fries before she spoke again. To her relief, Cassie was still eating. Kittie didn't seem much interested in a piece of fry, though. Elaine wondered how far she'd get explaining that it wasn't good for a cat to eat human food.

Instead, she gave her attention to Devlin. "How did your intelligence run go otherwise?"

Lu turned her head to look at her son. "'Intelligence'? Why would you do that *here*?"

"Just taking the temperature of the crowd out there. Crowds always make me a little nervous."

"You know," Lu said, "it would be nice if someday you could tell me a little about what you've been doing that's changed you this way."

Elaine expected Devlin to ask what his mother meant by him changing, but he didn't. As if he knew he didn't need to explain. Or couldn't explain.

She kept her attention on Cassie and the kitten throughout the meal, only half paying attention to the desultory conversation between Devlin and Lu.

But Lu's question had raised some questions in her own mind. He'd been off doing something these nearly twenty years. Traveling the world, she gathered, from what little he'd said. But what kind of world traveler came home without a hundred stories to share? Descriptions of sights seen and memorable places visited? Hadn't there at least been some historic monument in all his travels?

It seemed Devlin had erased a huge chunk of his past. Or locked it in a safe that required a combination to open.

That wasn't fair, though, she thought later, as she led Cassie to her bath and bed. Not fair at all.

Devlin could probably open that past any time he wanted. Or any time he needed. Well, clearly he didn't feel the need here, and his desire to had gone only as far as collecting some intelligence from that off-the-wall crowd in town.

As she sat on the rocker beside Cassie's bed, reading a Dr. Seuss book that always brought a tiny smile to Cassie's face, Elaine thought about Devlin, about his evident heap of secrets, and decided she shouldn't trust him.

A man without a past, her husband's brother or not, had plenty to conceal.

Too bad he was so attractive.

But that was unfortunate, too. Caleb's brother. Maybe time to move on, if she felt like she was cheating. But would she be, really? She doubted Caleb would ever have wanted her to spend the rest of her life alone.

And of course, there was Cassie. She had to be extremely careful about whom she let into her daughter's life. Stories about stepfathers—mostly unfair, she supposed—still concerned her.

Cassie had slipped off into her dreams, so Elaine closed the thin book and set it on the night table. A night table that had never been allowed to hold anything but a small lamp, a tiny stuffed unicorn and the book. One of the ways Cassie was particular.

Then Elaine sat there, the room illuminated now only by a night-light, and stared into the gloom.

She didn't want to return to her living room. Didn't want to see Devlin again, not right now.

She couldn't trust him, but he was living with her.

Nice.

Especially when she acknowledged a growing desire for him. It was just an inkling, but it wouldn't go away.

DEVLIN NOTICED ELAINE'S ABSENCE, hoping that Cassie wasn't having a problem. But his mother seemed undisturbed as they sat talking over coffee. They were both the kind of people who could drink coffee right up until bedtime and still sleep without a problem.

Caleb hadn't been like that.

A sigh escaped him as he thought of his brother. They'd made lots of good memories together in their younger days, some of them that had made Gage Dalton frown. A frown you very much didn't want to be on the receiving end of.

Gage had made no secret that he thought teenage boys had no sense of judgment or consequences, and he preferred to teach those things with a frown and a good lecture. Gage possessed a scowl that would scare the willies out of you.

But he also didn't like to arrest kids or teach them a lesson overnight in one of those cells above his office. So it all depended on just how bad you were. And Gage was the judge and jury for that, unless he decided the transgression was serious enough to have Judge Wyatt Carter look down at them from his bench.

The magistrate usually handled those minor problems, but there were times when Gage determined something more was required. Thus, the judge.

Devlin grinned, and Lu caught sight of it. "What's so funny?"

"Just remembering some of the hijinks Caleb and I got up to."

Lu snorted. "Plenty of those, as I recall. You weren't very good at keeping secrets back then."

"Not with everybody from the principal to half the town willing to tattle."

Lu laughed. "Never did learn."

"Hell no. Too much fun."

Fun, he realized, was very much a thing of his past. At least the wild, cutting-loose kind of fun he and Caleb and their friends had gotten into.

Was that just growing up? Or did life change some people, like him, from the carefree idiots they'd once been?

What did it matter? He was the man he was now. Couldn't flip that overnight, nor did he think he wanted to.

Finally, Elaine emerged from Cassie's room. Her uniform had given way to jeans and a denim shirt. She'd knotted the tails around her waist, showing just a finger's width of skin. He'd always liked that look, although it was not often seen anymore. Probably because of those crop tops.

Man, was he thinking about women's fashion? He was losing it in more ways than one.

"I'm thinking," he said when it was clear that no conversation was in the offing, "of driving out and taking a look at those lights myself."

Elaine plopped down in the chair facing him. "Why? I thought we already saw them."

He shook his head. "Curiosity," he said. "It's bugging me."

"Well, nobody's apparently ever figured them out. Beggan Bixby says he's been seeing them his whole life. Near as I can tell, nobody ever paid them any mind until this lot turned up. What do you possibly think you can learn?"

"How about," he suggested, "that it's going to drive me to the edge if I can't figure something out."

Elaine laughed. "Good luck, Devlin. But tell you what, I'll ride along. Lu? Is that okay?"

Lu, holding her reader in her lap, waved them on. "Get out of here so I can read my book without red lights in the sky."

Elaine and Devlin laughed quietly as they left the house.

DEVLIN HAD RENTED a Jeep for driving out here—he apparently remembered that much about the terrain—and they took his vehicle. Elaine liked that because in his car, without her uniform, she didn't feel even remotely like she was on duty.

Although she carried her pistol on her hip. Required, even off duty. But in the Jeep, she could ignore it. No crackling radios, no computer screen flashing information, no extra dash controls and no shotgun racked upright and locked between the two front seats.

She was able to relax, to allow her head to sag back against the headrest, to allow her entire body to unwind. For a while, it was plenty to have the window cracked just enough for a chilly breeze to blow gently on her face. She just pulled her jacket closer and inhaled the fresh, sage-scented night.

"You and Caleb ever get out here?" Elaine asked a while later. "Or were you town guys?"

"We had friends who lived on the ranches out here. Plenty of long weekends, even a couple of summer camping trips. Then when we got older, we had some summer jobs."

"A broad experience, then?"

"Oh, definitely. The hard labor was good, although I'm sure we were never as good as an experienced hand could be." He snorted. "We *did* spend some work time cutting up."

"Irresistible."

"Seemed to be. But we didn't get in any trouble for it. Our friends' dads seemed to be understanding, although from time to time, they'd remind us we were *working*."

A small laugh escaped Elaine. "You were lucky."

"We sure were. Good people who made allowances for us. What about you? Townie?"

"Yeah, almost all the time. A different kind of experience, but the nice thing was that my friends were all nearby and it was easy to get together."

"You still have any of those friends?"

Again, Elaine laughed. "I've still got most of my friends but we've developed different interests. You?"

"I doubt it. Just absence. Gone. Probably forgotten by now."

Elaine nodded slowly. That was kind of sad.

"My choice," Devlin said. "They were all my choices."

But he didn't sound as if he thought that was such a

good thing. Maybe coming home had changed his perspective.

The way she had been changed by Caleb's death. The way she had been changed by the growing understanding of Cassie's problems.

Life could do that to you. A single thing could change, and nothing ever looked the same again.

ELAINE POINTED OUT to Devlin the spot along the road where she'd first seen the red whatevers that had made her think there might be a range fire.

Devlin pulled over immediately and asked her to point as best she could. "I don't see them now, though."

"Me, either. How big were they?"

"Not very. Just big enough to catch my eye and make me worry about fire."

He stirred in his seat, making the leather creak. "Did they get bigger as you approached Bixby's place?"

Elaine thought back to that night. "I think so. I know I was getting pretty wound up about the possibility of a range fire by the time I reached him. Yeah, they seemed to be getting bigger, or I wouldn't have thought the fire could be spreading."

"Okay." Another few minutes, then Devlin said, "Exactly for how long did you see them?"

"I saw them all the way to Bixby's place from here up the road to his house, and then after I left, they were visible for a short while until they winked out. All told, maybe a half hour, tops."

She could feel him looking at her.

"They winked out?"

"No better way to describe it."

"Okay, that's weird. Had to be mechanical, don't you think?"

At that, a laugh began in her belly and rolled out of her. Damn, it felt good. "You ask me if that's weird when we've got a whole bunch of green-costumed people partying in the street and a somewhat more sensible group camped out here hoping to see some *lights*?"

"Well, when you put it that way…" He started to laugh, too. "So I'm on this wild goose chase because…"

"You need a concrete answer," she finished for him. "I'd like one, too, but I'm not holding my breath. Bixby says they've been there off and on his entire life. So maybe it's the aurora. Once in a while we see it down here."

"At least the aurora would be a logical explanation."

"Yeah, I could live with that. But I don't think the aurora would make two defined spots like that."

He laughed again. "Don't crush my hopes."

They drove another mile, closer to Beggan Bixby's ranch, when Elaine suddenly said, "There!" She pointed.

Devlin wheeled the Jeep onto the shoulder without going far enough to tip them into a drainage ditch. He switched off the car and lights; then they jumped out to look.

There they were—two red lights, brighter than Elaine had recalled, and certainly bigger.

"Wow," she breathed. She hadn't expected *this*.

"It's like my mind made them smaller," he said. "It turned those two red orbs into the kind of pinpricks you'd see from the top of a cell phone tower."

"They've grown," Elaine said. "A whole lot."

"Well, that should make the UFO hunters happy."

"Yeah, but probably not Bixby. Or Lew Selvage. He said they could camp on his property."

"That group is about to grow."

Where would that lead, Elaine wondered. It wasn't as if she could just sit back and enjoy the show. She thought of calling Lew Selvage to ask how the hunters he'd allowed on his property were behaving, whether they were giving him trouble.

Then she remembered they were in a communication dead zone. Still hard to believe, even after all this time, that even a sat phone wouldn't work out here.

She guessed she'd have to wait until she got back to town.

Devlin surprised her by going to the rear of the Jeep and returning with a rather impressive pair of binoculars. "Boy, do you come prepared."

His smile was hard to see in the darkness of the night, but she caught a glimpse of it anyway.

"You got a good sporting-goods store in town. Jackson was kind enough to rent them to me."

"Well, it would be hard to get them any bigger. At least around here."

He put them to his eyes, gave them a bit of adjustment and focused toward the lights.

After a minute, she asked impatiently, "Well?"

"Two orange-ish red lights. Nothing else. Wanna look?" He started to pass the binoculars to her, but she waved them away.

"Just lights?" she asked.

"Just lights. Of course, these binoculars only see in the visible spectra. I wonder if your UFO hunters are better equipped."

"They're not *my* hunters, and you'll have to ask them."

He laughed. "Point taken. Well, as far as visible light

goes, that's all they are. Lights. But I can't figure out what they're doing there."

"I sure couldn't. Nobody seems to know, but then nobody's been paying much attention all these years. So I suggest we drive on a little farther. Maybe you'll see them wink out the way I did."

"Which will create another mystery. They shouldn't be there, but if they are, then why do they turn off? It's got to be mechanical. With some kind of timer."

Elaine had to agree with that. Nothing else made any sense.

"Devlin," she said as she thought about what they were doing, "you're so bored that you're trying to go down the rabbit hole."

He chuckled but shook his head. "I just like to solve problems. And this is the problem *du jour.*"

PROBLEM OR NOT, Devlin thought as they began driving again, the main thing was enjoying this time with Elaine. Seeing her relax this way. No worries for just a couple of hours.

He just wished he didn't find her so attractive. Life would have been easier without feeling such a strong physical tug toward her. Apart from her having been Caleb's wife, which was enough to swamp him with shame if he let it, she had more important matters to occupy her. Like Cassie. Elaine couldn't seem to find much time in her life for anything but work and her daughter.

That was something he actually understood, having been guilty of something similar most of his adult life. A life he needed to remember that he'd return to, leaving nothing for anyone else behind him.

That would be cruel, even assuming Elaine wanted to

fit a new relationship into her life. Building a decent relationship took a lot of time and effort. He'd never been able to stay around long enough for most of the effort part.

For once, he cursed the skills that made him such a good covert operative. He could read people. He could assess their motivations fairly well. Judge the shortages and weaknesses in their lives.

Right now he saw an Elaine whose life was too full to make room for anything else. Apart from her job, she lived with constant emotional worry. He doubted she forgot Cassie often, even when at work.

But none of that kept him from wanting her, from wanting to feel her curves pressed against him, her warm smooth skin beneath his hands, the warm hot depths of her surrounding him.

Oh, man. Stop now.

Think of Cassie instead. He was coming to love that little girl, and experiencing the first glimmers of frustration and fear that Elaine must feel on an almost constant basis. Was that an improvement? Was it real? How much? Would it remain? Would it expand?

God. He thought of Cassie's wonderful gentleness with the kitten and decided her therapist, Sally, was brilliant for thinking of it. When he'd first met Cassie and begun to realize the extent of her problems, he'd never have thought of her being able to take care of a pet.

Yet there she was. A step to bigger things? Did it matter, when Cassie's love for the kitten was so evident?

And then it happened. A strong sense of connection with Elaine slammed into him. As if for an instant their hearts connected. A feeling so strong that he almost missed the instant when the lights in the sky winked out.

"Oh, for the love of heaven," he said in exasperation.

Growing distracted was an unfamiliar experience for him. Not one he could afford. That's what Elaine did to him.

"What?" Elaine demanded.

"I almost missed the lights winking out. And what the hell made them turn off like that?"

"Well, you saw it happen, for what that's worth."

"Yeah, but now it's too late to chase. I want to come out here tomorrow night and try to triangulate them."

Elaine erupted into a full-throated laugh. "Oh, God, Devlin, I never thought I'd see you turn into one of *them*."

She might have a point, he thought, and he joined in her laughter.

"It's different," he protested.

"Right. And Mitch has part of his pasture full of people who think there must be something *real* in those lights. People who may even be trying to triangulate them. People who think they're just a mystery to be solved."

"Dang, Elaine." But he had to laugh anyway. "Nailed it."

"I like it," she said. "Makes you seem more human."

Oh, now he needed to seem human? What the hell was he acting like? Had he become as reserved as some kind of robot?

Questions that were suddenly more important than some lights in the sky.

Who had Devlin Paltier become?

WHEN THEY REACHED the house, Lu was already sound asleep in her bed, the baby monitor on the night table near her head.

Devlin and Elaine walked quietly, trying not to disturb Lu or Cassie, and made their way to the kitchen, where Elaine decided to make some hot chocolate.

A small sound caught her attention, and she looked down to see that Kittie had abandoned Cassie's bed and was looking up with sleepy eyes.

"Aw, sweetie," she said quietly, then lifted the kitten into her arms. The cat snuggled in and began to purr. "This cat has the right idea," she remarked. "Just enjoy everything in life."

"Yeah. Good lesson. Let me make the hot chocolate."

She stepped away from the stove and took a seat at the table. "I hope Cassie doesn't wake up looking for her." That concerned her.

"I think Cassie knows her way out here. This would be the first place she'd look, don't you think?"

"Maybe." Looking down at the purring kitten in her arms, Elaine decided this was one thing she just couldn't worry about. Somehow Cassie would have to get used to the fact that the kitten couldn't spend its entire life on her lap or beside her arm at the table.

She looked at Devlin, who was stirring the cocoa. "I need to start playing with Kittie. A cat needs playtime, and maybe Cassie will pick it up."

Another hope. Always another hope, too often followed by a crash. But she let herself have those moments anyway. Every once in a while, Cassie shattered those disappointments with a big step. Like calling her *Mommy.*

And while Cassie didn't like hugs, generally didn't like to be touched, she allowed Elaine to bathe her and dress her. Even pull her covers up. Good things.

There'd be more. She had to believe it. Sally certainly thought so. And look at this lovely kitten. A huge step, a beautiful one.

She smiled as Devlin placed a mug of hot chocolate in front of her. Kittie chose that moment to jump down and head out of the kitchen door, her tail raised high like a flag with a crook at the very top.

"I guess she's claimed her home here," Devlin remarked. "At least, I've heard that about cats' tails."

"Me, too."

A minute later, they heard scratching from the area of the cat box. When Kittie didn't reappear, Elaine assumed she'd returned to bed with Cassie. At least, she hoped she had. She didn't want to imagine Cassie's upset if the cat was gone in the morning.

Because Cassie, who appeared to be a placid child with serious limits on how she could be treated, was capable of having memorable meltdowns when seriously bothered. The worst part of those meltdowns for Elaine was that she couldn't, and never had, found a way to calm Cassie. Those spells just had to burn themselves out.

They were based entirely in sensory overload, though, and sometimes there was just no way to predict where an overload could come from. Looking for Kittie and not finding her might spark one.

Elaine, however, resisted the urge to go make sure Kittie had returned to Cassie's bed. As far as she knew, it was hard to make a cat do anything it didn't want to do.

DEVLIN WATCHED THE play of emotions over Elaine's face and wished he could help. But how? Cassie was, justifiably, the center of Elaine's life, and nothing was going to change that. Not now, not ever. Nor should it.

He looked down at the cooling mug of cocoa in front of him so that she wouldn't feel like she was being stared at, even though he was getting to the point where he never wanted to look away.

A bad place to be, when he had nothing to offer and a

job that would take him away again. A month? Was that all he had to offer?

He stifled a sigh and tried not to analyze himself too hard. He had always believed in what he was doing, the importance of it.

Now he was looking at something that in its own way could be every bit as important. The job had also twisted him in ways he didn't want to think about. When lying came as easily as breathing when you needed it, what did that make a person?

That he could still tell the difference was probably his only saving grace.

Elaine rose, dumping her remaining cocoa in the sink. "I have an early morning, so I'll turn in."

He watched her go and had the worst feeling that her absence was cutting a hole in him.

Then he told himself not to be ridiculous. People came and went from his life. That was the nature of the beast.

He had a couple of friends, colleagues who had become more than people he just worked with. But only a couple. Getting too close was dangerous in his line of work.

It could also be dangerous to Elaine, he reminded himself. Not just over a few weeks, but if the relationship extended longer? If she became more important to him?

There might also be a danger to Lu and Cassie.

Given his recent experience with Niko, he didn't exactly trust all his coworkers. Someone had talked. What if they learned enough to talk about his family?

Another week. He'd get out of here soon.

ELAINE COULDN'T HELP HERSELF. She peeked into Cassie's bedroom, the door never closed all the way, and saw Kittie curled up once again on the bed, near Cassie's head. For now, that was okay.

But after she finished her shower and climbed into her flannel pajamas, she stretched out on her bed and didn't sleep.

Sleep eluded her primarily because she couldn't stop thinking about Devlin. Sadly enough, she knew his visit was short. His job had kept him away for years and absolutely no reason to think that might change.

She also had a strong suspicion embassy duties barely covered what he was up to. Having to get away? Having to go to the ends of the earth for a "vacation"? She wasn't buying it. There were other things, too. Hints.

Even so. She rolled over and hugged her pillow, wishing it were Devlin. Silly, she told herself. Attraction to a man who'd be gone so soon? Her husband's brother?

Yet that guilt didn't plague her as much as she would have expected. Caleb and Devlin were different in so many ways. Maybe because they'd spent the last years so far apart, pursuing such different jobs. It wasn't as if she were attracted to Caleb's clone.

Yeah, that would explain it.

But a pillow, even a firm body pillow, couldn't make the bed less empty. Couldn't replace the warmth of Caleb's muscular body beside hers. How she had teased him about being a heat engine. The way she could tuck her feet between his legs and they'd never get cold.

That had always amused Caleb, but he'd never once complained. He'd retorted that she was his summer air conditioner, so it was all fair.

Except it wasn't fair that he wasn't there right now. Even after two years, she felt the emptiness in that big bed. Often thought of exchanging it for a smaller one so maybe it wouldn't feel so empty.

But she couldn't let go of the bed she and Caleb had chosen together. It was nothing fancy because it'd had to fit their budget, but it had a wooden carved headboard. No footboard because Caleb was too tall and would have shoved it away and broken the bed. Not that Elaine cared about a footboard.

She cared about little in this room except the way it made her stomach feel hollow.

At last, sleep slipping away and coming no closer, she pulled on her gray robe, pulled her hair into a ponytail and headed for the kitchen. It was the one room in the house where if she made a little noise, it wouldn't be heard in all the bedrooms.

To her surprise, she found Devlin sitting there with what smelled like fresh coffee. He wore a chambray shirt that stretched across his broad shoulders, jeans and a pair of socks. His dark hair was tousled.

"Can't sleep?" he asked.

"No. What about you?"

"Way different time zone. I'm still trying to adjust."

Way different from where? Certainly farther than the East Coast, if he was still adjusting.

"Fresh coffee," he said, pointing with his mug. "Unless it'll keep you awake even more."

"I'm one of the lucky ones. Doesn't do that to me."

She sat facing him, then looked down at her coffee and the table, unable to think of a thing to say. Although, at this time of night, maybe conversation wasn't necessary.

Devlin didn't seem to think so. Except for the faint occasional sound of his sips and the cup coming to rest on the table, he might not have been there.

Then Kittie arrived, jumping up on the table with amazing grace. Devlin reached out to pet her gently. Kittie rubbed her head against his palm and began to purr.

"You wouldn't think," Elaine said, "that such a small cat could purr so loudly."

"Kind of amazing," he agreed. "But I shouldn't pet her. She needs to attach to Cassie, not to me."

"You may be right." Which didn't make the kitten any easier to resist. Still, Devlin dropped his hand, leaving it on the table. Kittie rubbed against it a couple of times; then, evidently realizing it wasn't going to rub back, she jumped down and disappeared.

Another cup of coffee later, with sleep still stubbornly eluding Elaine, he spoke again. "Is Gage getting uneasy about the green party with the bouncy eyes?"

She snorted. "Probably, but he's not saying anything. Yet."

"All that drinking in the streets. I'm not used to it."

That might have revealed more than he realized, Elaine thought. Had he been somewhere alcohol wasn't allowed?

Then he half dashed her speculation. "Funny, I don't remember open-container being legal here. It's not most other places."

"It's always been legal here in public spaces. Better not drive under the influence, though. Or operate a vehicle with an open container that's in reach of the driver. There *are* limits."

He nodded and leaned back in his chair. "That party could turn into mayhem easily enough. Put enough beer in 'em and look out."

"That's always a risk. We're forever having to break up brawls at Mahoney's or one of the roadhouses out in

the county. Most excitement we usually get around here."
Thank God.

"Not always, though?"

"Not always." She shook her head, simply not wanting to talk about the downsides of her job. Of course worse things than drunken brawls happened. People lived here, and people weren't perfect. Everything from spousal abuse to the occasional murder happened around here. Even one kidnapping.

Which, as the previous sheriff would have groused, meant the county was going to hell in a handbasket. Elaine had always loved that phrase but doubted it was true. More likely an expression of frustration when things *did* go wrong.

Her cell phone buzzed suddenly, and a quick glance at the screen told her it was the office. Kind of them not to set off the much louder satellite phone.

She picked it up. "Paltier." Then she listened a moment, and said, "You've got to be kidding me! I'll be there."

She jumped up, heading for her bedroom and her uniform. Before she got out the kitchen door to head for the hallway, Devlin's voice halted her briefly. "What's wrong?"

"Cattle mutilation," she said between her teeth. "And I'm sure it didn't involve any little green men!"

Chapter Nine

Elaine didn't argue when Devlin climbed into her Suburban beside her. She was past arguing about anything. She was exhausted from lack of sleep, seriously bothered that she'd had to wake Lu to tell her she was going on duty. Worse, she was frankly furious that she'd miss breakfast with Cassie, something she tried strenuously never to do.

A mutilated cow? Seriously? She'd heard about such things but was inclined to believe they were some kind of misdiagnosed predation. Especially since it was her understanding that veterinarians didn't even want to look at a "mutilated" carcass anymore.

"Cattle mutilation?" Devlin said as they raced through the night. "I thought that had been debunked."

"It has been. I heard a few ranchers lost a lot of cattle somewhere or other, and in a case or two they lost their entire ranches because of it, but if it were me, I'd be getting all my neighbors together to start hunting for big cats. Bobcats. Cougars. Whatever."

"Aren't they leaving meat behind, or something?"

She shook her head. "I don't know. I gather, in these cases, they leave a lot behind, which I would think is unusual, but big cats wouldn't be the first animals that took to killing just because they like it. Packs of wild dogs will do that."

"Like *us*," he remarked.

She nearly snorted. "Too much so, sometimes."

He fell silent as the miles sped away, often with the sound of gravel hitting the rear of her vehicle. His silence was fine, although she was a little surprised that he had so much knowledge about cattle mutilations tucked away.

What the hell did he do for a living?

"Now," she muttered as she turned onto Mitch Cantrell's road. The man was a wealthy cattle rancher who also took care of a large flock of sheep for his bride, Grace. He could withstand the loss of one or two head of cattle, but he'd still be furious. Maybe want to toss those nuts off his land.

She shook her head, thinking about the mess. They'd have to figure out who'd killed the cow and made it look like a mutilation, if it even really was. Well, obviously a suspect could come from the UFO crowd, who stood to gain from such a story. Which wasn't a good thing, given those fools were hanging around all over the place now, annoying the locals. More people than Mitch were going to be angry about this.

So they had this crowd they'd have to both protect and get out of town while hunting for whoever had pulled this ugly stunt. Because she seriously doubted one person could do this. Damn calf was probably pushing six hundred pounds, if not more.

Poison, maybe? Well, the state lab could check for that. Among a million other things, she supposed.

As they drove up Cantrell's road, her hands tightened on her steering wheel until they ached. At the ranch house, one of Mitch's cowboys was waiting for them. "Out that way," he said, pointing with a powerful flashlight. "You won't get far before you'll see a whole bunch of these lights. You won't see any of your own floodlights out there yet. I suppose they're coming."

"I'm sure they'll come. How's the crowd?"

The cowboy shook his head. "We been keeping an eye on 'em. They didn't get anywhere near that damn calf, not since one of 'em found it. Tripped on it, actually. Kid was screaming his fool head off."

Elaine thanked him and rolled up her window. "Well, hot damn," she said irritably. "This is going to be fun."

Devlin didn't say a word.

ZOE AND KALINA knew they had to get away the instant one of the ranch guys watching the group had started cussing about a dead cow.

The ranch hands who watched the group had changed out during the day, but always at least two of them kept an eye on the group.

Come sunset, the telescopes and cameras always got set up. A couple of those telescopes watched all day, but as far as Kalina and Zoe could tell, they never saw anything. Or at least, no one let on to any excitement.

But then those lights at night. The two women admitted to each other that the sight of the lights unnerved them. Not rockets. Not helicopters, not even the threatening drones that had hovered over their people too often. Just red lights hanging there, almost like a demon's eyes.

Children of their own culture, demons were part of the lore they had learned while growing up. They were just stories for children, of course, but some of their elders had nonetheless believed them, and Zoe and Kalina couldn't quite shake them.

They slipped down into a drainage ditch, easing themselves away from the crowd that had provided protection, and leaned back against the side, ignoring the prickly dry grass.

"We've got to leave," Kalina said.

"Yes. That man is going to make noise about the cow, and others will come." It was not like at home, where people who raised livestock had no way to complain if some were killed.

"Police. I don't want to talk to police."

Neither did Zoe. She knew she and her sister had unmistakable accents and while these bizarre skywatchers might not notice or care, neither of the women trusted police to ignore it. They knew too much about police, none of it good.

In fact, they were terrified of just about anyone in uniforms of any kind. With good reason.

They huddled together against the deepening chill of the spring night and listened as the crowds grew, as the huge lights pierced the night. Their shadowed space seemed to shrink. The pistol was nestled in one of Zoe's pockets, while additional bullets were in another. A small bottle of poison filled a space in Kalina's pocket. They never talked about the instruments of death. As if they didn't exist. Until tonight.

Now they knew they'd made a mistake poisoning that cow. Yes, it had been a distraction. Yes, the cow had started to die elsewhere, leaving most of its blood behind before it got here. Informative for their possible future plan. But it had drawn too much attention, and the small dogs that had torn at it briefly after it fell had only made it worse, judging by the excited conversation around them.

"We shouldn't have been sent," Kalina said suddenly,

although quietly. "There are others better suited than us." Others who wouldn't make such foolish mistakes.

"But it was explained to us," Zoe said. "Most people don't expect women to come seeking vengeance."

"Perhaps in this part of the world." Kalina shook her head, now unable to accept the whole idea of this mission. In her heart of hearts, she believed Niko wouldn't want his sisters taking on this risk. He had tried so hard to protect his family.

She also knew that she had agreed to carry vengeance across the world. The poison had worked on the cow, she reassured herself. It would work on the man, too. But they still hadn't found a way to get close enough to give him the poison. Or even shoot him.

They had begun to think they knew who he was, though. A local man who'd surprised the town by returning recently.

Still, she and her sister weren't the best choice for this job.

But family honor needed to be avenged, too. Niko had been an informant, had possibly betrayed his own people.

Neither Zoe nor Kalina truly believed he would have betrayed them or their parents, or even his friends. If he was passing information, it must have been about the other side.

But they had no proof. Judgment on Niko had been rendered, and he had died. All that was left was vengeance.

And two Eastern European women were far less likely to draw attention in this country than two men.

Not that there was a lot to choose between men's and women's roles anymore. Not with endless war. Sooner or later, everyone became a combatant.

But thinking about this whole situation wasn't helping

them complete their mission. They had to find a way back to town for a longer time than the few short trips they'd taken with members of this group. Into town, where it was likelier they could reach their target.

And those red lights kept staring balefully at them.

ELAINE AND DEVLIN hadn't arrived much sooner than the crime scene unit. It wasn't the biggest unit, Devlin noticed. Probably didn't have much call for them around here.

But there was no mistaking the mutilated calf lying on the ground. Elaine's estimate of six hundred pounds might have been on the low side.

The first thing he noticed was lack of visible blood. Now, you couldn't just butcher an animal this size and have no blood. There should have been at least some on the hide around the wounds. He could envision most of it soaking away or staying inside the animal, but...

It was a head-scratcher, one he would have to think about. Everything had a reason.

"Damn," said one deputy, a young guy with glasses. "That's what those folks talk about! No blood!"

"Easy," said an older deputy with long gray hair. Micah Parish, Devlin seemed to recall. A Cherokee who'd caused some ripples in this town when he arrived, a place that was probably still not very friendly to Indigenous people. They'd sure eventually made an exception for Micah, though, and a few others.

"Easy?" the young man said, his voice rising. "Tell me where the blood is."

Micah's jaw set. "Where are you expecting to find it, son? That calf's been lying on the ground for a while. It's night. It could have all soaked into the earth right there under the animal, and we wouldn't see it. There's probably a whole lot of it inside that calf. Now, calm down or go back to the office. We don't need panic."

"But the cuts…" The young man trailed off as Micah turned to face him directly.

"Back to the office," Micah said flatly. "Don't make me tell you again."

The youngster skedaddled. Micah returned his attention to the calf, and Elaine went to stand beside him. Devlin wasn't far behind.

"Luminol," Elaine said.

Devlin was familiar with the substance and how it made blood glow under UV light. "Too soon?" he asked.

Elaine glanced at him. "Definitely too soon. The techs need to finish their other tasks." She looked at Micah. "What do you think? Back everyone away behind a cordon?"

"Yeah, we don't need a lot of chin-wagging, and there's been enough trampling by us guys. Tell Sampson to get the tape up. Then choose four people to go interview that group over there. The hired hands who were watching them say none of them went near that calf."

He rocked on his heels.

"But someone did," Elaine remarked.

"Hell yeah," Devlin agreed. "Diversion."

Both Micah and Elaine looked at him. "Diversion from what?" Micah asked.

"Damned if I know. But it's so out of place it's like a neon sign in the middle of a dark, empty road."

"Well, hell," Micah said, and squatted beside the carcass, now awash in the growing number of floodlights. "Well, hell."

THE CORDONED-OFF area and brilliant lights didn't draw a crowd, thank goodness. Too far out on ranchland to get any lookie-loos at this time of night. Remaining were the crime scene unit along with six deputies, two ranch hands, an annoyed Mitch Cantrell and a huddled group of UFO hunters who weren't even pretending to watch those lights in the sky.

Then, at last, after a million photographs and some poking and prodding from the coroner, the luminol was sprayed in a wide area. The UV light turned on.

And almost nothing glowed.

Silence fell, no one making a single sound. No one moving.

Finally, Elaine whispered, "Impossible." She looked at Devlin and saw that his face had hardened into a granite frown.

"Nothing's impossible," he said roughly. *"Nothing."*

But like the rest of them, he felt as if he stood there looking at the impossible.

SOME OF THE UFO hunters had lost their taste for being out on the empty land in the dead of night after the cow's death, and climbed into their cars as soon as they were allowed to leave. Kalina and Zoe managed to hitch a ride with two of the guys.

The men were talking excitedly about the dead cow, their voices loud with adrenaline as they pored over every idea they'd ever heard about mutilations and talked about official positions and ever more about cover-ups.

"We saw it, dude!" said the passenger in the front seat. "We *saw* it. Not just a picture in a book or on TV, but the real thing. And we never saw nothing come near it. Not even a helicopter!"

"Yeah." The driver was slightly less excited, his mind apparently already moving ahead. "How do you think they'll explain it away? They always do, don't they?"

At that, the passenger fell silent. Zoe and Kalina exchanged looks, suspecting that the excitement in the front seat was slowly calming into something else. Maybe something darker.

"They can't hide all those pictures they took out there," the passenger said.

"Wanna bet? They got full control of them. They can bury them and replace them with something else. How you gonna prove it?"

Sadly, Zoe and Kalina were used to seeing things that had no rational explanation, at least to their minds. Things that were often covered up with amazing speed until you thought you'd imagined all the horror. But this time there was a rational explanation. Neither allowed themselves to even think about it.

Was believing something was imagined any better than knowing it was real? The young women had decided that, although they sometimes talked about it, testing one sister's sanity against the other's.

Now they listened to these young men talk about the very same questions that had plagued them for years. Was it real? Would it be hidden?

"Maybe we should have stayed," said the driver. "So they couldn't hide anything."

"What good would that do?" his passenger scoffed. "They've published photographs of mutilations for years and almost nobody believes it anyway. Veterinarians don't even believe it."

"They're part of the conspiracy," said the driver. "They'd lose their licenses if they told the truth."

"Well, I say we go back tomorrow by daylight and see if we can get our *own* photos."

The driver remained silent. In gratitude, Zoe and Kalina soaked up the car's interior heat and fell asleep for the rest of the drive.

Their nightmares followed them, as always.

AT THE RANCH, HOWEVER, little had quieted. Mitch Cantrell, a levelheaded man, had left his anger behind and now studied the remains along with the crime scene folks, the coroner and the remaining cops.

"It's a puzzle," Mitch said eventually. "Honestly never seen a cow dead like this. Usually predators do a good job of cleaning it up, leaving bits for smaller hunters. This was a wasteful kill."

He walked over to stand by Gage Dalton, who'd arrived fifteen minutes ago. "Maybe those UFO guys scared a predator off."

"Or they did it," Gage said. "If that calf needed moving from the kill site, it'd have taken more than one man to do it." He looked at Elaine. "What do you think?"

"How should I know? I'm not a ranch girl. But as for the UFO hunters scaring something off…" She shrugged. "If that group was scary enough to do that, then a predator wouldn't have come round, would he?"

Devlin eyed her, one corner of his mouth lifting. "What are you suggesting? Little green men?"

He was glad to hear her laugh. "Of course not. It's a puzzle, like Mitch said, but we'll get to the bottom of it."

Mitch pointed. "Something had to drag that calf here. Be easier to tell in the morning light."

Eventually a big truck pulled in, and a backhoe lifted the cow into the bed.

The evidence was carted away for a necropsy.

Elaine stared at the ground, troubled.

Devlin looked at Mitch. "You gonna hunt?"

"Believe it," Mitch said. "A bobcat. A pack of wolves… Yeah, we're gonna hunt, starting at dawn. But it's still weird." Then he looked over his shoulder. "It's kinda obvious to me that those two guys couldn't have been keeping watch like they were supposed to, or this couldn't have happened. Somebody's lying about something."

Devlin nodded. "Never saw so many remains left behind, though."

"Or so little blood." But then Mitch laughed. "Well, this'll fuel the party in town."

"Don't remind me," Gage groused.

Elaine looked at him. "You mean you're not enjoying the invasion?"

Gage scowled at her, then grinned. "It sure as hell is different. Nothing like it in this county's entire history."

Gage was right. Despite the area's long history, some of it quite violent, this was still a first, all right.

"But it's probably wild animals," Elaine remarked without preamble as she and Devlin drove back into town.

"Had to be." But his suspicions ran in a different direction. The killing had been achieved with those UFO hunters nearby. That didn't sound like animals at all. Attacked animals screamed or made some kind of noise, no matter how silent a predator might be. Someone should have heard something if that calf had died right there.

No, his thoughts ran to poison. But then, who had cut the animal like that? Someone must have moved it there. Sure as hell someone should have seen something.

AT HOME, Elaine confessed her exhaustion, and without any apology, she headed for her bed. Cassie and Lu still slept, leaving Devlin in a silent house, which he kept mostly darkened. A pot of coffee was his only self-indulgence.

Plenty to think about, and he didn't see any good purpose in entirely adjusting his biological rhythm to Wyoming. He'd be headed back out into the field somewhere soon enough. Somewhere the time difference would be large enough to require adjustment again. The less adjustment, the better. He preferred to have a clear mind, not a sleep-fogged one, no matter where in the world he was, no matter the kind of assignment.

Although this time he figured they'd keep him low-visibility, with few demands. At least for a while.

And he'd sure love to know who had squealed about Niko. He didn't care if it had been inadvertent, because it had cost Niko his life, and Devlin feared that the dominoes of that revelation hadn't yet quit tumbling. Not only was he at risk, but his entire circle of assets might now be at risk, too.

Ripples. Always ripples. Pretty on a pond, hellish in real life.

Despite his other concerns, he had plenty of time in the predawn darkness to think about Elaine, Cassie, his mother. About a dead calf that needed some explaining.

He slapped a salami sandwich together, remembering only at the last moment to squirt it with some mustard. Then, sitting at the table again with fresh coffee, he ruminated, turning things around in his mind in whatever order they showed up. That mental Ferris wheel had always served him well, moving, moving, moving until bits and pieces started to make sense. Sometimes giving him a bird's-eye view of his own rambling thoughts.

Until, little by little, the randomness would begin to

yield a bit of order, like a thousand-piece puzzle without a picture on the box to guide him.

Some colors would grow brighter. Others would fade a bit. All of them mattered, but how they meshed was the important first step or two.

But tonight his thoughts weren't handing him much as a guide. The dead calf really troubled him. A threat? A strange place to make one, so far away from anything. Yet the lack of blood couldn't be accidental. How could either an animal or a human have killed and mutilated that cow while no one noticed?

Mitch was right: that calf had to have been dragged there. Without anyone from that UFO group noticing a thing? Hell, not even one of those aliens could manage that. Just think of the Travis Walton story. A bunch of his friends had seen him disappear into a beam of light. No, every UFO story he could think of had been witnessed somehow, or there'd have been no story to tell. Except the supposed mutilations, which made them even more problematic.

Not that he was any expert. A boundless curiosity led him to dip into a bunch of things, but not necessarily deeply. Aliens and UFOs had never seemed like something worth a whole lot of his time, even with the AATIP report from the Pentagon that said some of the sightings couldn't be explained.

Well, a whole lot of things in life would never be explained.

But Devlin liked finding explanations, and that damn calf sure deserved one. Especially considering the people who had descended on this town. Odd to have a cattle mutilation when all these weirdos had turned up for a party and to watch a couple of lights in the sky. So far, he'd found the costumed group in town to be amusing. No real trouble, just a group having a lot of fun among themselves. He found it hard to believe that any of them would have killed and mutilated a calf for entertainment or excitement. Although he knew people well enough to realize that they could astonish him.

He had to admit, the lights troubled him, the way no one knew what they were and all the years they'd been there. Until the past few days, no one had seen them move. But they didn't trouble Devlin enough to spend countless nights out there trying to get some tidbit of information about them.

They certainly didn't occupy his thoughts the way Elaine, Cassie and Lu did. He'd gone from being a man without a family to one who very definitely had a family. Ready made. All he'd needed to do was step into the waiting shoes.

An act that was beginning to prove remarkably easy. Even his guilt over Elaine being his brother's wife seemed to be fading.

But what wasn't fading was the idea that he'd have to leave for long spells, maybe years at a time, and he might well be in danger.

How could he possibly inflict that on Cassie or Elaine? Elaine had certainly been through enough with Caleb.

Then another thought crept into his mind, totally unwanted: he didn't have to be a field operative. No, he could work from a desk.

He brushed the idea away. It didn't suit him at all.

Even if thoughts of Elaine slipped into every corner of his mind, a tempting wraith.

Chapter Ten

The rising sun brought no answers about anything. Devlin showed off his cooking skills, such as they were, by making eggs, toast and bacon.

"You learned something," his mother said.

"Well, sometimes I *do* have to feed myself without a restaurant handy."

It pleased him to hear Elaine chuckle. Cassie managed her bacon easily. He'd made her egg over hard, so once Elaine cut it into manageable pieces, Cassie handled them well. He realized he might have been thinking the child was more disabled than she was.

Maybe he should start paying attention to what Cassie did for herself. Like giving Kittie, who was on her lap, tiny pieces of egg white. Kittie kept lifting her head; Devlin suspected the cat would prefer the bacon. Hardly surprising. He preferred it himself.

Elaine looked well rested and more relaxed this morning. Whatever had disturbed her about the calf mutilation and the alien-party invasion, she seemed to have let go for now.

"Are you working today?" he asked.

She shook her head. "Since I was out so late last night, Gage told me to relax today."

He had to grin. "So you might relax until what? Midday?"

She responded with a sly smile. "Are you reading me, Mr. Foreign Officer?"

"Learning you. I wish I was psychic." That would have avoided a whole lot of problems in life, and he wouldn't have needed to use assets like Niko.

Elaine looked at Cassie. "I'd like to be psychic, too."

He bet she would. The lack of communication must be one of the most frustrating parts of Cassie's condition. There had to be other frustrations, too. He'd noticed that the only time Cassie would allow her mother to touch her was bath and bedtime, and maybe dressing her. He certainly hadn't seen any hugs, and Elaine didn't strike him at all as a cold person.

"Is anything going to be done about that calf?" If anyone had discussed it, he hadn't heard. Hardly surprising, when he'd busied himself with other things.

"A necropsy. Mitch apparently isn't going to be satisfied with the idea of a predator. I don't think he really wants to have a necropsy, either."

"How come?"

"Because some of his neighbors are going to wonder if he's lost his marbles. Cattle mutilations don't happen around here, and the general attitude is that people are mistaking normal predation for something else."

He finished wiping egg from his plate with toast. "What do *you* think?"

She shook her head. "I have no real information. A dead calf. Looks weird, but maybe it's not. I'm going to trust Mitch's eventual estimation, though. He knows a whole lot more about cattle and predators than I ever will."

WHEN SALLY ARRIVED late in the morning to work with Cassie, Devlin and Elaine set out for Maude's to find something for dinner so Lu wouldn't have to cook.

"I should go grocery shopping for the clan, carry my weight," Devlin remarked.

"Your mom seems to enjoy doing it. Probably because it's a chance for her to change scenery and people." Elaine sighed. "I don't know how or why she keeps helping this way. Yeah, Cassie's her granddaughter, but nearly full-time childcare? Especially with a kid who's autistic? That's a whole lot."

"Well then, I'll give her money for groceries. Hell, she's the one who taught me to pay my way."

Elaine laughed but found herself wondering why he hadn't responded to what she had said about his mom dealing with an autistic granddaughter. The question nagged at her. Did he disapprove?

At Maude's, while standing at the counter waiting for takeout and a couple of lattes, Elaine scanned the room. Scanning rooms like this came with her job. She always took in the people around, looking for any kind of trouble.

But then she noticed two young women sitting in one of the booths. They had cheap plastic alien masks on the table between them and salads in front of them.

They stared at Devlin, then quickly looked away when they saw her looking at them. Something about that struck her as furtive. Were they just curious? But why? Those women were the strangers in town.

Or maybe… She was smiling as they walked out the door with food bags and the cups of hot coffee in their hands.

"I think you've got admirers," she told Devlin.

"Huh? Why?" He looked as if he didn't realize that was possible.

"Two young women in the café. They were eyeballing you. Then, when they knew I saw them, they looked away. They appeared embarrassed." She laughed. "If you were wondering if you still have it…"

But he responded oddly. "Yeah?" he said quietly, thoughtfully. "I'll catch up in a minute. I meant to get a slice of peach pie."

He turned around and strode back into Maude's.

And Elaine was too much of a cop to believe he was going back for pie. So two women admiring him was enough to get him to go back to check it out?

Not Devlin, not for a couple of women. He wasn't the type, as far as she could tell. Too mature for that kind of reaction, probably.

So what the hell was going on?

She kept walking, but slowly, waiting for him as she took some sips of her coffee. Maybe she could find out something when he rejoined her.

But that was another thing about Devlin she'd figured out. He kept a lot to himself. She was sure he wasn't even being totally forthcoming about his work.

Nope. She hated it. The cop in her hated it. She needed her answers.

DEVLIN WALKED BACK into Maude's and went up to the counter to get that peach pie, his cover story. Then he looked around the café as he waited and saw the two young women Elaine must have been referring to.

He caught them looking at him, then turn away as if embarrassed. He'd seen that reaction from women before during his career. Shyness, or culture?

Something about them… They reminded him of someone, although he couldn't say who. He just knew that he'd never set eyes on the two of them. He had a great memory for faces.

After paying for the pie, he walked out to catch up with Elaine.

Something troubled him about those women. But what? Why? God, he had become far too paranoid. On the job was one thing. In normal life, it had no place.

Maybe.

WHEN THEY GOT back to the house, Sally was working with Cassie. She was thrilled with Cassie's reaction to the kitten and the way she was taking care of it.

"This is good," she said with a smile. "Another step for Cassie. Her progress between this visit and the last is great, Elaine. It's great. If she's ready to accept the kitten into her personal space, she'll accept something else, probably not too far down the road."

Elaine started smiling.

At the door, Sally looked back. "She's begun to expand her world, and this was a big step in that direction."

Devlin saw Elaine gaze at Cassie, who sat on the living room rug with her kitten, and caught the sheen of tears in her eyes. The expression of hope.

Without giving any thought, or at least not enough thought, he reached out to lay his arm across Elaine's shoulders and give her a gentle squeeze.

She glanced at him and smiled.

And she didn't move away.

ELAINE WAS OVERJOYED. She'd thought she'd seen improvement in Cassie, but Sally had just confirmed it. The cat had been such a wonderful idea, and now she was wondering what next. What else might she do to encourage a reaction like this?

But she knew better than to press it. Baby steps, at least for now. Although Kittie was proving to be more than a baby step.

She was acutely aware of Devlin's arm around her shoulders. In the midst of her joy, she needed to share this moment, to savor the warmth of being held, however loosely. To feel a man wrapped around her, holding the joy in and offering more of it.

At last, she tore her gaze from Cassie and smiled at him. It was okay, right? Cassie's uncle and godfather, her brother-in-law. Family.

Except, for just a few seconds, she didn't think of him that way at all. She saw him as a man who could easily walk away with her heart. Dangerous.

Just then, Lu emerged from the back of the house, running her fingers through her hair and yawning. "Wow, did I fall asleep! With Sally here, I just kinda let go, I guess. How's Cassie?"

"Sally thinks she made a huge step with the kitten. We can talk about it when you have a chance to wake up."

Lu's laugh was self-deprecating as she passed them to go into the kitchen.

Cassie continued to sit on the floor, cat in her lap, watching the adults.

"Kittie," she said, pointing to the kitten in her lap.

Elaine's heart stopped; then she could hold back the tears no longer. "Yes, Cassie, I see Kittie. She's beautiful and loves you."

Then her daughter's gaze wandered down to the cat, and the moment broke.

Well, not entirely. Elaine turned into Devlin's embrace, his arms closing around her, welcoming her. God, it felt so good.

"I WANT TO go to the office," Elaine announced after an easy lunch of ham sandwiches. "I need to catch up about last night. Is that okay, Lu?"

"It's always okay. Now, scat. Cassie and I will play with the cat or color unicorns."

"I need to take a walk," Devlin said.

They both stepped outside, Elaine to get into her patrol vehicle and Devlin to start striding into town.

He was troubled by the sense of familiarity he'd detected about those two young women. Nagged at him too much to ignore. In his job, he rarely ignored it when something nagged him.

He needed to figure out what had caught his attention. Or just to see if he reacted the same way. If not, it had been some kind of mental mistake. Unfortunately, mistakes happened.

ELAINE FOUND THE office buzzing. Those who weren't out on patrol gabbed about last night. They also still gabbed about the crowd down the street. A crowd that didn't seem to be diminishing. A crowd that was starting to become a nuisance, filling the street, lining the roads just outside town with camping gear.

Had those people come prepared to camp? She suspected at Roswell they had hotels and motels to house the crowd. Could all these people have come here without checking the accommodations?

Well, of course they must have checked, or there wouldn't be so much camping gear. Regardless, they still seemed to be having a rollicking time. Sharing UFO stories, arguing finer points of the theories that seemed to have sprung up like weeds. All in fun. So far.

Dang, something was making her thoughts scatter. Red lights? An alien invasion? Devlin? She almost laughed at herself as she entered the office.

Connie Parish was seated at one of the desks, and when she saw Elaine, she waved her over. Kerri Canady sat nearby with her Snowy.

"We're just discussing the messes," Connie said. "Or should I just call it the alien invasion? All of it, including the dead calf."

Kerri spoke. "The street party is going to become a serious problem before much longer. People found it kind of fun and funny when it first started. They were even making money off it. But now?" She shrugged.

"Well," Elaine said dryly, "we don't live in a time when the sheriff could strap on his six-gun and throw people out of town."

Connie grinned. "I wish. I bet the city council is going to want to do something about it if this goes on much longer."

"Agreed," said Kerri.

"At least they're not causing trouble," Elaine remarked. "So far."

"Probably because they're smoking instead of drinking," Connie said.

Elaine joined her laughter.

Kerri spoke. "You could get high walking past them."

Elaine snorted. "No kidding."

Guy Redwing joined them. He'd taken to letting his hair grow longer, part of his Native American heritage. As a detective, he wore plain clothes. "We could start arresting them for the pot," he said. "That ought to make most of them head out of town. Or we could have a riot."

"Yeah," Kerri said. "There's that. I'll skip the riot."

Elaine grinned, enjoying herself. "Don't they outnumber us now?" Then her enjoyment slipped away. "Hey, you heard anything about Mitch Cantrell's calf?"

"I just heard," Guy answered. "He's firing two ranch hands. They were supposed to be keeping an eye on things last night and it seems they wandered away. Quite a way, given the calf."

Elaine shook her head. "Not good. But it still doesn't give us an answer unless those guys mutilated the calf themselves."

Humor vanished. All of them were troubled.

AROUND THE PARTIERS hung a cloud of marijuana smoke, an easily identifiable aroma. Devlin figured half the people here could get high without smoking anything. He smiled and looked around.

Some "aliens" draped themselves against lampposts. Long lines of them sat on the curbs. Others, heedless of traffic, stood in the streets, talking and laughing. Some even danced. Music played from several different locations. Yeah, a party.

A big, funny-looking party of green and silver and black. A lot of bug-eyed masks and one stand-out who had managed to make himself over into a praying mantis. How did mantises get into the alien world? He guessed his education was lacking. Though he had no intention of expanding it.

A surprising number of people actually talked about their reasons for being here, and it wasn't just for a party with like-minded others. They were quite serious about the Roswell crash, about Area 51, about the hangar at Wright-Patterson AFB that supposedly housed alien bodies. Or even live aliens. That, Devlin discovered, was quite an argument among these believers.

He found others recounting tales of crash retrievals, insisting there were many of them. Some said modern technology sprang from the crashed spaceships.

Then there was the abduction argument. Were they or weren't they? The cattle-mutilation discussion, which, surprisingly, varied between only two opinions: government or aliens. That was when he became certain that some of the conversations were being exaggerated by illicit substances.

A group of five was having a heated argument about whether these aliens came from the future, creatures that had evolved from humans a million years in the future or from a different planet. That group laid out plenty of reasons for their opinions, reasons that might have been fun for Devlin to listen to at a different time.

If he got that Vulcan peace sign one more time, though, he might growl.

But while he measured the crowd, his own passport of a green bug-eyed mask on the back of his head, he sought anything that might keep alerting him about being watched.

It was an odd sensation. It didn't feel like a hard focus but rather a blurry one, as if something hadn't yet clicked for the watcher.

But concern for Elaine, Cassie and his mother kept him moving among the people, stopping occasionally to throw a word or two into a conversation. He had to appear to belong with this group to avoid drawing the wrong kind of attention. Standard operating procedure.

The crowd could provide cover for anyone, himself included, and it would be hard to pick anyone out in this crazily dressed mob. He had to content himself with watching people's actions. Interpreting their meaning even though not always clear, but that was apparently his only tool here.

Still, the feeling of being watched wouldn't go away, whether strong or weak. And he was getting past the point of telling himself that his job had made him too paranoid.

The huge question looming in his mind, one that he'd been unable to resolve, was *who* in this place would be watching him and *why*.

He'd been away from this town for over fifteen years. Nobody held a grudge for that long, not that he could remember having left any grudges behind him.

So what and why? And only one answer came to him: his job in intelligence. Being a field officer running assets. He'd done that in more than one location in his career, but the risks were always the same. If the bad guys found out you were the officer running assets, your life became a target. *You* became a target.

Even so, why the hell would anyone have followed him here, of all places? And how would they have managed that since his own office had clamped a lid on his whereabouts.

He closed his eyes, gritted his teeth and faced it directly. Someone had leaked information about him. Maybe the same someone who had leaked Niko's identity.

A rats' nest that needed rooting out.

Then he heard a quiet voice that came from somewhere in the crowd, not too close, standing out only because of the accent.

His eyes popped open, and he looked around. He knew that accent.

Just as he had thought he recognized the two women at Maude's.

No reason that any person from that part of the world should be here.

And no reason they should not. This UFO crowd appeared to be pretty international in its membership.

But those few words in that accent stuck with him. A woman. Maybe. Replaying that snatch of conversation in his head, he realized he couldn't be *sure* if it had been a man or a woman. Too little of it. Voices varied in both genders, making it impossible to judge gender with surety.

Instead of going home to check on his family like he wanted, he kept circulating, listening for that accent, but he didn't hear it again.

Damn!

"I THOUGHT I told you to take the day off," Gage Dalton said to Elaine as he entered the office. "You've been working more hours than you realize."

"So has everyone else," Elaine answered, bridling a bit even though she truly liked Gage and didn't usually mind his fatherly concern.

"I've been giving people comp time as I can. This is yours. I don't even know why you came in today."

"To catch up on the scuttlebutt."

Gage laughed, the sound raspy. "I'll tell you when the necropsy reports come in. Or if Mitch figures it all out. You won't be out of the loop just because you're not here."

So she snatched up her light uniform jacket and headed out to her vehicle. The extra time with Cassie would certainly be welcome. Gage was right. She should never have gone in. She should have stayed home with her daughter.

So what had gotten into her? Sharing a house with a man who had begun to make her nerves tingle with a yearning she didn't want?

Yeah, probably. But he was going to be here awhile, from what he'd said and was entitled to visit his mother. End of subject.

Her guilt was ebbing, though. Slowly settling into her heart like a warm touch, she felt Caleb close to her. Felt that Caleb would want her to get on with her life and wouldn't mind if she had a thing with his brother.

Caleb had been rough around the edges, the result, no doubt, of the construction work he did and the people he was around all the time. But he'd never lost a heart as big as the whole outdoors.

No, he would want her to be happy in whatever package that happiness came.

She'd known that all along, of course, but she hadn't *felt* it. Now she was beginning to.

Still, a sexual relationship with a guy who'd be leaving soon and most likely permanently, given his past?

No way. She wasn't the type for flings and didn't want any more heartache. Nor did she want to expose Cassie to any fleeting relationships.

Having settled that in her mind, she came home to a potential crisis. Cassie was sitting on the living room floor, cat in her arms, looking mulish. Lu sat on the couch, perplexed. Elaine's mother radar immediately started pinging.

"What's wrong, Lu?"

Lu sighed. "I don't think it's major, but when I wanted Cassie to come for a walk with me or even sit on the porch, she wouldn't because she doesn't want to be separated from the kitten."

"Oh, man." Elaine dropped onto one of the recliners and regarded her daughter. There was nothing in the world as immovable as Cassie when she got stubborn. So what now? She knew what that kitten would do if allowed outside. It would go exploring, and judging by her bouts of hyperactivity indoors, Kittie would get distracted by something and be off like a shot.

Just as she was thinking that, Kittie stood, stretched, then dashed off Cassie's lap, running around the living room, climbing the back of the couch and just otherwise being exuberant.

"I see a cat tree coming," Elaine remarked.

Lu nodded. "Might be a good idea. I'll remind Devlin he said he'd get one."

Cassie was watching her cat's antics with obvious delight. Okay, then.

Rising, Elaine said, "I'm going to change, Lu. Then I'll rummage through the things that Mike Windwalker sent home with us. Maybe I'll find something there. I know he sent toys I need to get out."

"Good idea," Lu said.

"And if I don't find a solution there, I'll call Mike. We can't let Cassie become a recluse because of Kittie."

MIKE HAD INDEED sent them home with a great deal more than a litter box and litter. Elaine felt silly for not having looked through the bag earlier, but it had become an ingrained habit not to introduce too much to Cassie at once. The cat had seemed enough for a beginning. And what a beginning!

Opening the bag at last, she found a collection of toys.

Some were balls, soft and fuzzy or with shiny fringe, toys that bounced on strings at the end of wands. One of them looked like a praying mantis, of all things.

But at the very bottom, she found something that looked like a harness. Pulling it out, she studied it, figuring out how to use it and wondering if it might be too soon for some of this, even though the kitten needed play.

God, did most parents have to make these kinds of decisions all the time? Maybe. On the spectrum or not, kids depended on parents to take care of them.

The harness, she decided. Cassie needed to be able to go outside, and for now she refused to be separated from Kittie.

How much would the cat struggle against this? Elaine snorted. What were a few scratches?

She checked once again to make sure she understood how it should fit, to minimize disturbance or fear for the cat. To limit it for Cassie's benefit as well.

Out in the living room, Cassie was still watching Kittie play rock climber on the curtains, climbing up and down as fast as her little paws would carry her. Cassie, wonder of wonders, was grinning.

Elaine sat cross-legged across from her daughter and held up the bright pink harness. Cassie dragged her gaze from the cat to the harness and then to her mother's face. Her expression had begun to darken.

Lu called from the kitchen. "I was bad and made us cinnamon rolls. You want some coffee?"

"Love some in a few minutes."

Cassie still regarded that harness with suspicion.

"Honey," Elaine said quietly, "this is for kittens. It's like a dog's leash. It won't hurt her."

Cassie tightened her lips. Elaine tensed inside. Was this about to go seriously bad?

"Just think. If she wears this, she can go outside with you. Sit on the porch. Go for walks with Grandma Lu. Maybe even chase butterflies in the park. But she won't get lost. She'll always stay with you."

Elaine sat quietly, waiting, wondering how much had truly gotten through or if Cassie had stopped listening before the explanation was complete.

Cassie had a bulldog determination about some things, but others, if they lost her interest, couldn't get past some kind of internal resistance.

Finally, however, Cassie's face smoothed over. Not by any means did she offer agreement, but the resistance was clearly gone.

Rising, Elaine went to pry Kittie from the curtains. As soon as she was cradled in Elaine's arm, the cat grew still and began to purr. A good temperament.

Then, sitting facing Cassie again, Elaine slipped her forearm forward between the cat's four paws and beneath her chin.

It turned out to be easier than she had anticipated to slip the harness over Kittie's head, down around her chest and midsection, then gently tighten it until it fit. Just like that.

Someone with experience had created that design.

Then Kittie leaped easily into Cassie's lap and began to purr up a storm.

"Kittie," her daughter said, and began to pet her new best friend.

Elaine's throat tightened, and she had to hold back tears. Such a good thing for Cassie. A friend. A companion she didn't fear. Warm and cuddly, the only kind of cuddle Cassie had so far accepted.

That cat was a miracle.

Elaine rose from the floor and went to the kitchen to join Lu. For the first time, she realized how tense she had been because her knees started to feel a bit shaky. So afraid, she guessed, that something might have gone badly wrong. The only thing in the world that could make her this fearful anymore was Cassie. Every single step was fraught with danger for Cassie. Never, ever did she want to set her daughter back.

It might be the biggest fear of her life.

"I watched," Lu said quietly. "That was brilliant."

"It was also scary."

Lou poured coffee into the mug in front of Elaine. "I was holding *my* breath. You were good, though. Calm and gentle but kinda firm, too. I think Cassie's responding better, Elaine."

Elaine nodded, cupping her mug in both hands. "I hope so. The cat has been a boon, for sure."

Lu laughed quietly. "I never thought I'd have been so glad to see an animal on my kitchen table."

That drew a laugh from Elaine, too. "Listen, I'm going to try putting the leash on Kittie and see if I can get them onto the porch. Gently."

No pushing it. Quiet, careful suggestions.

Sitting on the floor once again in front of her daughter, who watched the hijinks of a kitten who wanted to explore and climb everything in the room, Elaine made her suggestion.

Keeping her voice quiet and cheerful, she said, "Do you want to take Kittie onto the porch? She might like a little sunshine. I know *you* would. What do you think?"

Cassie gazed at her from a smooth face. Okay, no objection, then.

Rising, she went to get Cassie's jacket and the leash, then pulled on her own jacket.

"Lu? Cassie's going to take her kitten outside."

"Lord," she heard Lu say from the kitchen. One word that conveyed hope and trepidation.

Elaine knelt, speaking to Cassie to explain what she was doing. "See? This is how the leash clips into the harness. None of this will hurt Kittie, but it means she can come everywhere with you now."

Cassie seemed to like that idea. She stood up, but when Elaine offered her the end of the leash, she didn't take it.

Okay, small steps. Or huge ones, now that she'd gotten the kitten harnessed and her daughter willing to make a trip out front with it. All this was a wonderful leap that had been very much needed. Maybe more leaps were around the corner.

So she opened the front door and led Kittie by the leash onto the porch. The kitten balked a little at first, but it didn't take her long to figure out that if she went forward a whole new world of scents and sounds existed. Curiosity had won the day.

Outside the late afternoon had begun to blow a slightly chilly breeze off the mountains, but it hadn't become cold. Elaine gave Kittie her head, letting her roam the whole porch while Cassie sat on her little chair, watching. Then Kittie jumped up on the porch rail, and Cassie shrieked a delighted laugh.

Elaine's heart nearly stopped. She wanted to hear that sound from her solemn daughter again and again.

Then Cassie reached a hand out to Elaine. Understanding, her heart beating happily, she turned the end of the leash over to her daughter. "Just make sure not to let it drop. Kittie will run off to explore everything, and that's not safe for her, okay?"

Cassie responded in no way other than tightening her hand around the pink loop of the leash.

Elaine sat on one of the lawn chairs and watched every single second. One cat. One little girl stepping a tiny bit out of her shell. Was there anything more beautiful?

She could have stayed there the rest of the day watching, but after about fifteen minutes, Kittie landed back in Cassie's lap. Cassie stood, cradling her furry friend, and turned toward the door.

Time to go inside.

Inside, Elaine took the leash off Kittie but left the harness on so the kitten could get used to it.

Elaine released a long breath, letting go of the tension that had been stretching every nerve. She'd passed through hidden dangers without once upsetting Cassie.

DEVLIN DIDN'T RETURN to the house immediately. He was troubled by the accent he'd heard. Troubled by the increasing feeling that someone in his group might have betrayed him, a sensation that made his skin crawl. Everyone in field operations depended on secrecy for their lives. What if someone had failed him?

Not that anyone should. But then, the whole world had heard about the name of a female operative who had been publicly exposed for no better reason than vengeance. That's all it took to violate national security and throw agents and assets to the wolves. One man's need for power and his hatred of being proved wrong. Other than that, the woman's exposure had benefited not a single soul but may have cost lives.

What made him certain he wasn't in the same boat?

The fact that they'd yanked him home so swiftly after Niko's cover had been blown? That he'd been instantly protected?

But only one person was needed who liked to flaunt his or her knowledge just to display importance.

Devlin didn't often lose his cool. His career had long since taught him that was the most dangerous thing he could do. But he wanted to lose his cool just then.

Had he been deluding himself? Had he believed he was protected by his colleagues more than he was? Had he exposed his entire family to danger? Had he, God forbid, trusted too much?

The idea made him want to smash something. Then he felt sickened. If you couldn't trust your own people charged with your protection, the ones who worked closely with you and knew most of your secrets, who *could* you trust?

Nobody. Maybe he ought to just pack up and get out of here. If someone was following him, they could follow him to somewhere else, away from the people he cared about.

The more he thought about it, the less he wanted to go back to the house, exposing his mother, his sister-in-law, his niece to whatever might be chasing him. Uncaring that he might be exposing his back, he strode out of town, then a short way down the state highway, hearing and feeling the blast of air as the big trucks raced past him in the dimming late-afternoon light.

A huge problem gnawed at him, though. If someone had followed him here—and the tingling sensation at the base of his skull argued that they had—then his leaving might not help at all.

He cursed in several languages and walked faster. He hated that he might have been playing the fool all along.

Confident in his colleagues and allies at the agency. God, a damn clerk could have become a serious problem.

Realizing he was far enough out of town now to have a conversation that couldn't be heard, he pulled his satellite phone from his pocket, pressed the button to encode his conversation and then dialed a memorized number.

As he listened to the connection click through, he turned and saw those two baleful red lights. Wondered again what they could be, made a silent promise to himself to check them out soon, ignoring the fact that he should be long gone before he had the chance.

"Hi, John."

"Hey, Dev," said a familiar voice at the other end. "I thought you were taking a vacation. What's up?"

"Am I being followed?"

Silence greeted him. Then: "Why the hell would you think that?"

"A feeling. An accent I heard. If I am, just say so and I'll get the hell out of here now."

"How about I don't know where *here* is?" John fell silent. Then: "Seriously, Dev?"

"Unless I've gone off the deep end and started to imagine things, yeah. I'm being watched."

John cussed vociferously. "A feeling? Hell, man, I know that feeling. Maybe you should just get the hell out of wherever you are now."

Devlin hesitated, then took the dangerous step of revelation, trusting John because they'd been friends throughout his entire career. Because he had to trust *someone*. "Biggest mistake I made was coming home to visit. I clear out, fine, but what if someone thinks my family knows where the hell I've gone?"

A long silence from John. Devlin could imagine his

surprise at learning that Devlin had a family. Another closely guarded secret, although easy to keep when he never came home.

Then John offered, "We're still looking for the leak that betrayed your asset. That info had to have come from here. We'll find whoever it is."

"Small help now. Whoever betrayed him might well know where I am to judge by the way I'm feeling now."

"Your location is being protected. Hardly anyone should know where you are."

"Who should have known about Niko? You know they had to identify him through me. That's why I was pulled out. Come on, John." But now a new kind of tension was creeping along his spine. This conversation was beginning to make him wonder if he could trust John.

John paused again. "I'll speed up the search for the traitor on our end. Clearly this can't drag out. But you get the hell out of there if you can. As soon as you can."

"John." Not a question but a warning.

"Yeah?"

"Be careful. Someone can't be trusted." And if it was John, the man's tracks would be buried so deep they might never find him. And now John knew too much. Or maybe he'd known too much all along. He'd said he didn't know where Devlin was, but that might be bull. Devlin cussed again, silently.

John answered, "Hell, man. You think I'm too dense to figure that out?"

After completing the call, Devlin shoved the sat phone into his jacket pocket and turned, heading home. Now he had a bushel of new worries. But no, it couldn't have been John. John had no irons in the fire when it came to Eastern Europe.

But secretaries and others were damn-near invisible and almost always around. Just one example of people who could learn things they weren't supposed to know. Locals who had security clearances, which made too many people lax with secrets.

He thought about Cassie, that sweet child, and Elaine and his mother. About three people he needed to protect somehow. About how he might have brought a threat to their door.

God, he hated himself. And hated himself even more because deep inside, he knew part of the reason he didn't want to leave: he had come to crave Elaine with a deep, piercing ache. A need so strong it could have brought him to his knees.

ONCE DEVLIN RETURNED, Lu heated up dinner. It was kind of late for Cassie, but Elaine didn't want to complain about that, especially since Cassie seemed quite content with Kittie.

It was usually bad to disrupt the schedule, but this time Cassie didn't appear at all disturbed by the change. Another bit of progress? Or was it just temporary because Cassie was distracted?

Elaine sighed quietly, accepting that she would never know until someday when Cassie chose to talk. If she ever did.

It felt good to have Devlin home, though. He stayed in the kitchen, helping his mother as much as he could, a solid and somehow reassuring presence.

Even so, Elaine felt a subdued tension in him, and she didn't like it. Had something bad happened? Damn, she was beginning to think that Devlin shared about as much as Cassie did.

So different from his brother. Caleb had always seemed so open, so ready to talk about things in his life or in Elaine's life. Considering how far away Caleb often worked, video calls hadn't been enough. Certainly hadn't been intimate enough. But once he came home, intimacy thrived in every sense.

And yes, very different from Devlin, who sometimes struck her as a locked box of secrets.

After dinner, a bit restless, she stepped outside onto the porch, wrapping a sweater around herself to withstand the spring chill in the air. In another hour or so, it would be too cold out here without a winter jacket. A single spring day sometimes ran through all four seasons.

The breeze, stirred by the changing temperature between land and mountains, was gentle. Later it would grow stronger, icier, but right now it was a soft caress with chilly fingers.

Before long, however, she felt something besides the breeze's touch. She felt something far more, something that made her feel downright creepy. Part of her was afraid to look, a ridiculous reaction for someone who lived life in law enforcement with each day bringing the possibility of true danger.

Annoyed with herself, she turned slowly, trying to penetrate the nocturnal spaces, the dark holes amid tree branches, the shadowy places created by the deepening night.

Of course she saw nothing, no matter how often she peered into the night. Vision was odd in the darkness, though. Things seemed to move even when they didn't. The brain tried to turn amorphous shapes into something familiar.

It was a waste of time to stand here like this.

Just as she was about to give in to this uncharacteristic feeling and go indoors, Devlin joined her. The springs on the storm door creaked.

At first, he didn't say anything as he came to stand beside her. Then, a minute or so later, he asked, "Are you okay?"

"Why wouldn't I be?" she answered, reluctant to reveal the crazy sensation of being watched. Even though she'd learned it was rarely imagination. But who the hell would be watching?

"I dunno. It's just that since I got here, you've never come out to stand alone here in the dark."

"And that's such a long time," she answered, a trifle tartly, forcing herself to shed the uneasy feeling.

He chuckled quietly.

Then, astonishing her, he drew her into a snug embrace. Elaine wanted to melt. Wanted to give in to the softening he caused inside her. Never wanted to move away.

KALINA AND ZOE watched from the bushes, looking through the night at the porch, where their target stood with a woman.

Zoe sighed. "He never goes anywhere we can use the poison."

"Never. It's going to have to be messy." The gun. She wasn't afraid of it. She'd had to kill before. But this was different. One man, not a mob or part of a so-called army. They had always fought to protect others.

But even the need for vengeance didn't make this feel right. Anger had subsided. Now Kalina had begun to wonder why they'd been sent to kill one man. Did they think he knew too much? That he still had contacts like Niko?

She and her sister had been led here, pushed here, driven here. All to kill one man.

She had begun to view the mission in a very different way. Very. "Zoe? Has this mission begun to feel wrong somehow?"

Zoe didn't answer immediately. When she did, her answer remained firm. "Maybe we don't know everything. But we know what we need to do. For Niko. Maybe for something bigger."

"I don't think we were sent for Niko. A life for a life?" That kind of measurement had always struck her as distasteful.

Again, Zoe fell silent for a minute or two. "Maybe not."

But they knew they'd been ordered to complete this task. Failure to do so would cost them everything. As it had cost Niko.

Kalina stuck her hand in her pocket and felt the pistol. Was it time to load it?

Then Zoe surprised her. "We have to take care not to kill the two women and the child."

"I know." That kind of killing was the reason they had fought at home. To end it.

But how could they possibly succeed?

Chapter Eleven

In the living room, after Lu had gone to bed, Elaine and Devlin sat quietly in the two recliners, an end table between them. One table lamp cast a golden glow. The heat kicked on, first blowing cold, then warm air into the room.

Peaceful. Except it wasn't peaceful to Elaine because she sensed that Devlin was tightly coiled. What was he tense about? Damn it, she was getting tired of wondering and never learning much about him. He was here in the house with her daughter. Her initial instinct was that he was part of the family, that she could probably trust him. But shouldn't she know more? Especially when he seemed unable to relax himself?

Almost as if reading her mind, Devlin spoke. "I'm going to tell you about my situation. Then I'd like you to tell me whether you think it's better for me to remain or go."

"Why is there a decision?" Now tension creeped along her own nerve endings. A *decision*?

"Each has its advantages, but let me tell you a bit about myself and why I'm here."

"So it's not just for your mom." Elaine snorted. "I didn't think so. After all these years? Right. So dump. I want to know everything." Not that she believed she'd get everything from him. Box of secrets.

"I know I said I work for the State Department. I actually work for the CIA. As a field operative."

"What's that?" Then Elaine shook her head. "That State Department claim must be wearing thin after all this time."

"Not really. I doubt you have any idea how many people work at most embassies or consulates."

She sighed, wishing he'd come to the point. "Probably not."

"It's a lot of people. Everyone knows there are intelligence operations everywhere, including foreign agencies, but pointing out the officers is hard in the crowd."

"Okay." She waited, holding on to her patience, which was growing thinner as he moved through all these details.

"Long story short," he said, "as a field operative, I worked overseas out of embassies over the years. It was my job to recruit assets. Local people who could provide important intelligence. One of my assets was exposed and killed. I was yanked out immediately for fear that the asset had been exposed because *my* cover was blown, and they didn't want more of my assets to be exposed. Hell, that was the last thing *I* wanted. I had to get lost until they could find the leak."

"So you thought you could get lost by coming *home*?" Anger began to replace her tension. "Devlin... Oh, man." She couldn't even finish.

"I thought no one would think of my hometown because I'd hardly visited in so many years."

"Not since Cassie's baptism," she snapped. "Which wasn't that long ago."

"I never revealed I was coming here. Habit after all these years."

"Oh, God, Devlin." Elaine jumped up from her chair and started pacing. "What you're telling me is somebody knows you're here and it might be dangerous. How could you?"

She turned, putting her hands on her hips and glaring. "How am I supposed to protect Cassie from whatever you've dragged to my doorstep?"

"That's what I want to talk to you about."

"A bit late, isn't it? Let me wrap my mind around this before we discuss protecting Cassie and your mom. God, Devlin," she repeated and resumed pacing. Fury had overtaken her, and she needed to get a grip before it screwed up her ability to think. She'd controlled anger many times in her job, but not rage like this. A whole new level. So much anger that she couldn't even face the anguish of betrayal buried somewhere in this mess.

Two circuits around the room and she spoke again. "Somebody had to know you were here."

"Nobody should."

She paced some more, then faced him again, jabbing her finger at him. "So you're being protected by a sieve?"

She heard his voice grow tight with anger. "So it would seem."

"God, I can't believe this. I'm not going to drive you out of here right this instant only because I believe that *you* believed no one would find you."

She dropped onto the edge of the recliner seat. "Damn it, Devlin, what about Cassie?"

THAT WAS THE QUESTION, Devlin thought as he watched Elaine react, felt her reaction to his very core. Fury fulminated in him, fueled by betrayal, fear for his family and a need to take this assassin out of the picture permanently.

How could anyone have found him here in this out-of-the-way two-stoplight town?

He had records at the company, of course. Impossible not to. But the only place this town should have been mentioned was when he applied for this job and his security clearance. And once he was vetted, that info was classified and locked away.

"I've been trying to figure out how anyone could have found me here. Anything mentioning this place ought to be buried almost as deep as nuclear secrets. As for me being linked to my asset? That's truly a big worry."

She looked at him, still angry, but a hint of sorrow was forming in her expression. She'd lost trust in him. He couldn't blame her.

"Leaving isn't good," she said. "If they lose track of you, they might come looking for information from us." Then she shook her head. "And if you stay…" She didn't complete the thought.

His heart squeezed from the pain he'd brought her. "I've been having the same thoughts. That's why I wanted to talk to you about the choices. I don't give a damn about myself. The family here, that's all that matters. You're the one with skin in this game. I can be gone by morning."

She sat for a long time, thinking. So long that he started to wonder if she was thinking about more than this situation.

When at last she got around to speaking, she astonished him. "We've got to get rid of this assassin, Devlin. You can't have him chasing you all over the place and I refuse to have to worry indefinitely about Cassie and Lu. So we need to make a plan. Capture or kill. And I'm not apologizing for threatening to kill. Not under these circumstances."

He'd brought her to that. He hated himself. *Loathed* himself.

She stood. "Let's make coffee and start talking about how to deal with this mess."

No, he hadn't expected her to take on this problem. He'd thought she'd want him to leave as quickly as possible to draw the threat away from Cassie and Lu.

But she was a law enforcement officer. Of course. She wasn't designed to run from anything.

KALINA AND ZOE spent a cold night in dark spaces created by trees and shrubbery not far down the street from the house where the man stayed. They tried to take turns sleeping, but the chill prevented it.

It had to be something more than the weather, Zoe thought. At home, they'd spent more than one freezing night in the mountains and had managed to gather some sleep.

So it was nerves, she decided. She and Kalina were experiencing the kind of fear they'd felt when they faced a battle. One man was not a battle. Except that this had become a battle, an internal one.

This man, too, was a soldier, an enemy soldier. But his family wasn't.

She understood the turmoil that afflicted Kalina. Life hadn't prepared them for this kind of mission.

Assassin. The word floated into her mind for the first time and remained, leaving a sour taste in her mouth. Leaving her stomach twisting with nausea.

Who had sent them and why?

She turned to look at her sister and saw the same question reflected in Kalina's face. *Were they being used?*

BEFORE DAWN, Elaine's phone rang. The department. She listened, murmuring some answers, then hung up. She looked at Devlin.

"And thus, the mystery of mutilated calf is solved. It apparently died from a sudden pneumonia and a couple of dogs had apparently chewed on it. Two of Mitch Cantrell's range hands found the carcass, drained it, cut it up some, then delivered it to the spot near the UFO hunters. They thought it was funny."

All Devlin could do was shake his head.

"Yeah," Elaine said. "They've been fired. Anyway, it's time to wake everyone up."

LU WANTED ANSWERS before she would pack up Cassie and head for her sister's house in Glenwood Springs. Devlin decided to leave the answers to Elaine, primarily because Cassie was involved. It went without saying that Elaine was a better judge of how Cassie might perceive this sudden move.

Although, how that could be smoothed over, Devlin had no idea.

"It's a special trip." A simple explanation, offered in a steely tone to Lu, shorter than Devlin would have offered. But then, he'd become pretty good over the years at spinning a longer yarn.

Lu looked worriedly at him but he kept his lips zipped. Elaine's tone and his silence apparently told Lu quite enough. Her lips tightened, her eyes darkened. When she spoke her voice, much like Elaine's, was threaded with steel.

"I don't know what's going on, and I'm sure I probably don't want to know. We'll pack up right now, and I'll call Suze on the road."

She turned sharply on her heel and marched toward the hallway. "And, damn it, make breakfast for Cassie. Now. At least some cereal."

"And a thermos of coffee for Lu," Devlin added quietly. He headed straight for the pot.

Outside, dawn had just started to break, washing the world in that odd blue color that came before the reddish-orange brilliance of the rising sun, flattening the light until shadows could hardly be seen. Concealing more than Devlin would like.

But Elaine managed to impress him yet again. She encouraged a sleepy Cassie to eat while telling her that she and Grandma were going to Aunt Suze's house for a visit. The child visibly brightened, but said only one word: "Kittie."

"Yes, Kittie will go with you."

Lu snorted. "Yeah, a litter box in the car. Suze is going to love me."

Because of the cat, the trip involved more than strapping in a young child and a tote full of clothes. There was a carrying box. The litter box. The box of canned cat food. A bucket of cat litter. Cat toys.

Cassie only took her coloring book and crayons for herself.

"This *could* be amusing," Devlin remarked as he helped load the trunk of his mother's car with all the cat supplies.

Elaine just looked at it and shook her head. "We need a whole troop movement now. No cat sitter for that girl."

"Doesn't look like it," he agreed.

Casual conversation when he was sure neither of them

felt in the least casual. His neck was creeping again. A glance at Elaine suggested she detected it, too.

At last, they sent Lu, Cassie and Kittie on their way. The sun had risen above the eastern mountains, casting a golden glow over land that hadn't quite reached the fullness of spring yet.

The sight carried Devlin back to a place he didn't want to see ever again. Not since Niko had died. Not since he had been forced to face just how much of a danger he could be to those who helped him. Sure, the possibility was always there, but usually those assets were never revealed unless they did something to reveal themselves. Niko had done nothing. Of that his colleagues had been sure, hence yanking Devlin back to the United States.

No, the leak had come from within the protected walls of the intelligence service. A place where even a small leak could be deadly. And the people he had to rely on to locate it…well, one of them might be the leak.

Hellacious situation. He looked at Elaine as she watched the car carry her daughter away.

"This is going to be hard on Cassie," she remarked, her voice level. "Suze always comes *here* to visit."

"So this is really going to throw her out of her comfort zone?"

"Badly." She faced him then, anger glimmering in her eyes. "I'm going to get ready for work."

Part of the plan. Her putting on her uniform and making it look as if she went to work, and Devlin was alone. Except Elaine would be out there, watching.

However many days and nights it took.

Just one big lousy assumption on his part, and he'd come here to wreck everyone's life.

But he hadn't been alone in that assumption. Everyone

had assumed the leak had come from within the consulate itself, probably from one of the local employees who had tipped somehow to the information. No one had initially suspected that it could have come from higher up the food chain.

Nobody except the traitor, anyway. And if he or she was hunting for the leak, intent on concealing it, they could be in even deeper trouble. They'd have someone who didn't observe the guardrails, who couldn't be found. Yeah, they'd be in some deep dung.

So could all his assets and the assets of other field operatives.

He watched Lu's car turn the corner to head toward the state highway. At least those two were out of it.

He heard Elaine go into the house. She was now up to her neck in his problem.

Remove the assassin even if she had to kill him? That she had announced her willingness to do that sent a deep chill down his spine. God forbid he turn her into a killer.

ZOE AND KALINA saw the older woman and the very young child leave the house, drive away. Judging by the amount of things they had stacked in the trunk, it was going to be a long trip.

This gave the sisters a large dose of relief. Then the deputy had left the house in her official car and wearing her uniform.

Their target was alone. A clean kill.

But neither of them moved immediately. Throughout the night, questions had begun to seethe in them.

"Why couldn't they give us his name?" Zoe asked.

"So we couldn't tell it if we got caught before we killed him?" Kalina suggested.

They pondered that for a while. Then Kalina spoke again. "Why would they worry about that? We're not doing anything except traveling. We even have passports. Nobody will stop us."

"Until we kill him. Then everyone will know who our target was. It won't need to be secret anymore."

"But we're going to get away."

Zoe stared another question in the eye. "So why didn't they give us instructions like when we got here? Why don't they tell us where to go after this?"

Kalina offered no answer, but there didn't appear to be one. Fired up by the idea of avenging Niko, they hadn't asked enough questions, or so it now seemed. Not that they had been given an opportunity to question their mission.

The questions held them still as the morning brightened. They'd have to move before the cop came back from duty, but they still had time.

Time to wonder exactly what they'd been sent to do.

ELAINE CLIMBED AN evergreen tree in front of one of the older houses on the street. The height of her position gave her a nearly uninterrupted view of her house through binoculars.

She saw Devlin settle on the porch with a cup of coffee and wondered how he could possibly think that made him a target, out there in public in the bright light of day.

Any assassin would be wary of that setup. But then, coffee finished, he went inside the house, where contradictorily he made himself a better target. Concealed from any watchers who happened along the street.

But then there were the close quarters of the house. God, Elaine wished for a clearer picture of what might happen. How could she possibly know that the assassin wouldn't look like one of the town's residents, strolling along the sidewalk? Slipping into the house from the back.

Or maybe the guy wouldn't care, he'd take his shot while Devlin was outside then flee before anyone could react. A silencer. Yeah, it might conceal the sound of the gunshot enough that she could come home tonight and find Devlin dead.

Thoughts swirled in her mind, not making perfect sense as they turned one way and then another. Focus. She had to focus.

Then, making her heart nearly stop, she saw Devlin emerge from the house and start walking toward the edge of town. Where he'd be fully exposed. He was nuts.

Or very smart. Because then she saw two figures trying to move surreptitiously around bushes, right behind him. He was drawing them out.

She scrambled down from the tree as fast as she could, stripping her gloves when she reached the bottom because they were sticky with sap.

Unsnapping her holster. Getting ready.

Two of them? God, somebody definitely wanted to get rid of Devlin.

Then she began her own surreptitious tracking of those two figures. What if Devlin had no idea they were behind him?

DEVLIN WAS SURE the assassin was following him. That was the whole point of this little stroll of his. He'd often felt the guy watching him and had no reason to think he'd taken his eyes off his target.

No, he'd come. The only question was how Devlin

proposed to handle it. The guy probably meant to shoot him. So Devlin's entire life might depend on hearing the sound of a gun cock, not the noisiest sound in the world. As if the world wasn't full of many other sounds as the morning grew busier.

There was Elaine, of course. She'd gone to watch for exactly this. If she moved in time, they might be able to round the guy up before he took his shot.

But Devlin was really past caring. If he died, oh well. The important thing was to remove this threat from his family. His death would be a small price.

Although he would have liked to know who had betrayed him.

He kept marching along, moving at a casual speed as if suspecting nothing at all.

"SOMEONE'S FOLLOWING US," Zoe said. War had taught them to be hyperalert when necessary.

"Yes. I think it must be that woman cop."

"So today we die." They weren't afraid of that, either. They'd looked death in the face too many times. They just needed to know that they'd died for something important.

And right now, feeling that Niko's death might have been used to manipulate them, they weren't all that certain what they might be dying for.

They weren't far away from their target now. Zoe pulled out the gun.

Then Kalina said, "I can't."

Just as a woman on the right said, "Drop that gun now."

Turning their heads, they looked straight into the barrel of that cop's gun.

Without hesitation, Zoe dropped her pistol. They'd failed. The worst of it was that she didn't feel like a failure.

Then the two women dropped to their knees. Kalina started crying.

As their target approached them, Zoe looked at him and said, "I'm sorry." Then she closed her eyes, expecting to die.

IT ALL RESEMBLED a strange dream to Elaine. Weird. Hard to make sense of. Two women, one pointing a pistol at Devlin, then giving up instantly and dropping to their knees. One saying she was sorry and crying. The other simply looking resigned with her eyes closed.

My God, they thought they were going to die!

Galvanized, Elaine hurried over to them and kicked the pistol away. She knew she needed to cuff them, but a strong part of her rebelled for some reason. They had been about to murder a man. She shouldn't even hesitate.

Devlin came to stand about six feet in front of them. "You look familiar," he said quietly.

The woman who wasn't crying opened her eyes and said, "Niko."

Devlin swore, but it was a quiet sound. Full of sorrow.

Then he looked at Elaine. "Do you have to take them right in?"

Her heart was warring with the cop. Her heart won. "We can get coffee and some breakfast first."

It somehow felt like the right thing to do. She patted them down anyway.

THE HOUSE WAS eerily quiet without Lu, Cassie and Kittie. No movement. No little sounds. No greeting from the kitchen from Lu. Empty.

Elaine definitely didn't like the emptiness. Except it wasn't really. Not with Devlin and the two women here.

Order of priorities, maybe? Or just emotional attachments?

Didn't matter. Still armed, she went to make coffee.

Devlin and the two women sat at the kitchen table, he on the side facing them. While brewing the drip pot, she heard the first word. It came from Devlin.

"Niko," he said. Just one word.

She turned, folding her arms, listening. Those women shivered and looked hopeless. She almost felt sorry for them, except they had tried to kill Devlin.

One of them spoke, her words heavily accented. The one who had dropped the gun. "Niko was our brother."

A silence as heavy as lead settled in the room. Devlin didn't move a muscle. Both women looked at him with a glimmer of hatred but far more despair.

Finally, he said, "Kalina and Zoe."

The women looked startled, their gazes leaping first to him, then to each other.

"I am Zoe," said the one who'd held the gun. "How do you know?"

"Because Niko talked about you a few times. I know he was proud of you."

The other woman, who must be Kalina, looked down. "He betrayed us. You betrayed *him*."

Devlin drummed his fingers on the table, his face as dark as a midsummer storm. "Niko didn't betray you. Never once. He was working to help make you safe."

"But he…"

Devlin cut right through the protest. "Not everyone you trust is trustworthy. Do you understand me? There are some people you think are working with you who are working against you. Niko was hunting them. Yes, for me as well as you. So we could find out how bad it was, maybe find a way to stop it. But he never, *never* betrayed you."

Kalina drew a deep, shaky breath. "You betrayed Niko."

"Somebody betrayed *me*. That's how Niko was found."

Both women's heads snapped up. Then they faced each other, their expressions growing angry.

Zoe spoke. "We have been used." Then she looked at Devlin. "Do you know much about them?"

"Some. I was working on getting closer to uncovering them."

Kalina nodded. "They fear you. They feared Niko. And they must be the ones who sent us."

Zoe, frowning until the corners of her mouth nearly reached her chin, nodded as well. "We began to fear…" Then she shook her head. "Niko. They used Niko against us. To get you."

Then they put their heads on the table, buried on their arms. Quiet tears could be heard.

Elaine had made the coffee strong and poured cups full for everyone, and her overriding sense was sympathy for these women. She couldn't begin to imagine their heartbreak, having already been surrounded by so much loss and betrayal.

And she had no idea how she was going to put these two in a cell. There had to be some other way. As far as she could tell they'd been through enough hell and weren't likely to go around attempting to murder anyone else.

A few minutes passed; then Zoe and Kalina sat up, wiping their faces on their sleeves. Their expressions had turned solemn.

"We are soldiers," Kalina said. "You will punish us for what we have done. It will be just."

Just? Elaine was having a problem with that. She looked

at Devlin. "You're the diplomat. Find me a way around arresting them for attempted murder. If you want to."

A slow smile appeared on his face. "How about we just report them as illegals so they can go home? If that's what they want." Then he looked at them. "How did you get into this country?"

"Consul in San Francisco."

Devlin shook his head. "Well, they can't go there. Don't know how much of a vipers' nest that might be. In fact, this whole situation may have put Kalina and Zoe in a great deal of danger from more than one direction."

He leaned back, clearly thinking. "I need to call someone."

Then he left the house.

Ten minutes later, he returned. "I'm taking Zoe and Kalina with me. I've arranged protection."

Elaine gave him a cockeyed smile. "I hope it's better than the protection *you* got."

He gave her a wider smile. "It will be. They've caught the leak. A clerk on this end fell in love with a clerk on the other end, and the one on the other end liked to use pillow talk for a little intelligence gathering. That's being cleaned up right now."

He shook his head. "Love. It can cause a brain amputation sometimes."

What the hell was that supposed to mean? Elaine wondered.

But as she watched them drive away in Devlin's rental, she was sure she'd never see him again. Always passing through briefly on the rare occasions he showed at all. Now he was going back to work.

No, they wouldn't see him again for years.

Chapter Twelve

A couple of months had passed since Devlin had left. They'd been good months for the most part. The party of alien watchers had moved on, leaving the streets once again to the locals. The red lights overlooking Beggan Bixby's ranch still hung there most nights but had become so boring nobody bothered to watch them anymore, or even to wonder.

But the exciting news was within the walls of Elaine's house. Kittie had proved to be a miracle. Cassie had spoken a few words to the cat, adding to her repertoire of "Mommy." Then, for the first time ever, she held her arms up for a hug. Not just to be carried to bath and bed but now just for hugs. Once, when Kittie crawled into Elaine's lap, Cassie had followed her.

Huge strides. *Huge.* All because of a little kitten who wasn't quite so little any longer.

Lu's gaze sometimes grew distant, though, as she sat in the evenings in the living room. Elaine suspected she was thinking of Devlin. Wondering how long it would be before she saw him again.

Elaine was more than a little irritated at Devlin for that. It hadn't seemed like such a big thing before, not when it was the usual, not when Caleb was still alive. For some reason, her feelings about that had changed.

What she didn't want to do was admit to herself how much she missed him. How she missed crazy things like the sound of his voice, the fresh, soapy smell of him out of the shower. The way he sometimes looked at her.

The way it had felt the couple of times he'd held her.

Aw, man, she didn't need any complications. She had her job, her daughter. Mostly her daughter, who was at last blossoming a bit and such a joy to be with. Cassie needed every bit of time Elaine could give her. No room for anyone else.

Except she didn't quite believe that no matter how many times she scolded herself about it.

Eventually, though, the silence ended. Without warning at nearly eleven at night. A night when she wasn't on shift. A night when she sat curled up on a chair alone in her living room, an ebook beside her, a glass of white wine beside it.

The knock on the door was quiet. She straightened immediately but before she could rise to answer, the door swung open. In the dim light of the one end-table lamp, she made out the figure of Devlin. She could hardly believe she hadn't fallen asleep into a dream.

"Sorry to come so late."

That was his voice all right. No dream. She pulled her legs from beneath herself and said in a hushed voice, "Devlin?"

"Yeah, the bad penny and all that. Mind?"

He closed the door behind him, though, as if he knew she wouldn't tell him to get lost. Although maybe she should after a couple of months without even a phone call.

He took the recliner across from her. "The two women? We've got them protected in the U.S. until we can figure out how to give them a life back. Thanks for not arresting them."

"Best failure of duty I've ever committed," she said. Her heart was beginning to hammer in her chest. Her mouth began to grow dry. He hadn't come here just to say that. A phone call would have done.

"How's Cassie?" he asked.

"Wonderful. Making great strides. That cat is a miracle."

He smiled. "I am so glad to hear that. And my mother?"

"I think Lu was wondering if you were going to come back. I should go wake her."

He shook his head. "No need. I'll be here in the morning. I'm here to see *you*."

He was? Her heart began to rise into her throat. Breathing grew more difficult, as if the air had been sucked from the room. In a whisper she could barely manage, she said, "Devlin?"

"Well, you probably don't want to hear this, but I've got to say it anyway. While I was gone I realized just how much I missed you. Everything about you. You're strong, stronger than almost anyone I've known. You're a good cop but you've got an even bigger heart. It's just that I missed you. But more than that, I realized I love you. I don't want to be without you.

"So if you can at least give it a little thought, I'd be grateful. And I can promise you I wouldn't be going overseas. Desk job from here on out."

Wow. Just wow. Elaine tried to absorb it all even as her heart lifted with joy. For the first time she faced the feelings that had been developing in her, too. Feelings she'd forced herself to bury beneath guilt, beneath obligation.

Feelings that erupted without hesitation. "I love you, too."

He rose and came over to kneel before her, sliding himself between her legs, wrapping his arms around her waist, encouraging her to rest her head on his shoulder.

"I've never felt this way about anyone," he murmured. "Never, ever. And I don't want to lose you ever. Just say you'll marry me."

"I will." That proved to be the easiest statement in her life.

And it only got better a few minutes later, when Cassie came stumbling down the hallway, rubbing her eyes, Kittie at her side. She stopped and looked at the two of them.

"Devlin," she said, as clear as a bell. Then she walked over and joined the hug.

Elaine thought her heart would stop and never start again. Never had there been a moment more perfect.

* * * * *

Colorado Kidnapping

Cindi Myers

MILLS & BOON

Cindi Myers is the author of more than seventy-five novels. When she's not plotting new romance storylines, she enjoys skiing, gardening, cooking, crafting and daydreaming. A lover of small-town life, she lives with her husband and two spoiled dogs in the Colorado mountains.

Visit the Author Profile page
at millsandboon.com.au.

CAST OF CHARACTERS

Ryker Vernon—Rayford County's newest sheriff's deputy has returned to his hometown as a single dad to raise his daughter and make a fresh start. But the past won't leave him alone.

Charlotte Vernon—The happy four-year-old has weathered the storms of her parents' divorce well and is the focus of Ryker's energy.

Harper Stanick—Ryker's high school sweetheart secretly mourns the loss of her first love, but she's not sure the unhappiness of their past relationship bodes well for the future.

Kim Vernon Davis—Ryker married Kim because she was pregnant, but she proved unfaithful and unwilling to stay to be a mother to Charlotte.

Micky Davis—Kim's second husband is an ex-con and drifter whom Ryker wants to keep far away from the ones he loves.

Chapter One

The little girl squealed with delight as she ran across the playground, blond hair flying out behind her. When she stumbled and fell she popped up immediately, still laughing, and resumed her race with her companions. Sheriff's deputy Ryker Vernon, standing just on the other side of the playground fence, swallowed past the catch in his throat and marveled at his daughter's—Charlotte's—sunny disposition. Where did she get that from? Not from her mother. Kim had a decidedly darker outlook on life, one that had led her to eventually leave him and her daughter behind.

Charlotte didn't get her happy personality from Ryker, either. Five years as a law enforcement officer had shown him too much of the bad side of people to make him inclined toward lightheartedness. Yet here was Charlotte, bubbly personality intact despite her mother's desertion and their recent relocation back to his hometown of Eagle Mountain, Colorado.

Charlotte reached the apple tree that apparently marked the finish line of the race and stopped, puffing for breath, her round cheeks bright pink, deep dimples on either side of her smiling lips. She turned and caught sight of Ryker and all but jumped for joy. "Daddy!" she shouted, and took off toward him.

Her teacher, Sheila Lindstrom, caught up with her just as Charlotte raced past the boundary of the fence and, also spotting Ryker, accompanied the child to meet him. He was glad to see the teacher was so diligent. "Hello, Deputy Vernon," Sheila said as Charlotte threw her arms around Ryker's legs. "I didn't know you were picking up Charlotte this afternoon." She tucked a strand of hair a shade paler than Charlotte's behind one ear and smiled up at him in a way that reminded him he was a single man in a small town where the dating pool might be thought of as limited.

He didn't return the smile, and took a step back, hoping to give the impression that he wasn't interested. Not that Sheila wasn't a perfectly nice woman, but he was juggling enough right now, with a new job, a new home and a little girl to raise. He didn't need the complications that came with a relationship. "Charlotte's grandmother will be picking her up, as usual," he said. "I just started my shift and since Charlotte will be in bed by the time I'm back home, I swung by to say hello." He rested his hand on the little girl's head as she beamed up at him.

"That's so sweet," Sheila said, and tilted her head to one side, blue eyes still fixed on him as if he was some delectable treat.

"Ryker! What are you doing here? Is everything all right?"

He and Sheila and Charlotte all turned to see Ryker's mother, Wanda Vernon, hurrying up the sidewalk toward them. Slender and athletic, with dark curls past her shoulders, Wanda Vernon looked younger than her fifty years, but right now worry lines creased her normally smooth forehead.

"Nothing's wrong, Mom," Ryker reassured her. "I just stopped by to say hello to Charlotte."

"Grammie, I found a horny toad at recess this morning, but teacher made me put it back," Charlotte announced.

"You know our wild friends are happier remaining in the wild," Sheila said.

"I know," Charlotte said. "But he was so pretty. He had gold eyes and a gold and brown body with bumps on it. Amy thought he was icky, but I thought he was beautiful."

Ryker hid his smile behind his hand. That was his daughter. She had never met an insect or amphibian or item from nature that frightened or repelled her.

"Horned toads are very interesting," Wanda said. "But it's always best to just look at them, and not touch. You wouldn't want to accidentally hurt one."

"Oh, I would never do that!" Charlotte looked offended at the idea.

Ryker's shoulder-mounted radio crackled, and the dispatcher's voice came through clearly. "Unit five, report to Dixon Pass, mile marker 97, to assist at accident site. EMS and SAR on the way."

Ryker keyed the mike, aware that everyone within earshot had turned to stare. "Unit five responding. I'm on my way." He squatted down until he was eye level with his daughter. "I have to go now, honey," he said. "Can I have a kiss goodbye?"

She responded by throwing her arms around him and kissing his cheek. "Be careful, Daddy," she said.

"I always am, sweetheart. You be a good girl for Grammie and Grandpa."

"I always am!" she echoed.

"Be careful," his mother and Sheila said in unison as he nodded goodbye, then jogged toward his sheriff's department SUV.

He turned the vehicle toward the highway and switched

on lights and sirens to cut a clear path toward the accident. As he passed the preschool he caught a glimpse of Charlotte with his mother on the sidewalk. The little girl was smiling and waving. Some of the heaviness in his heart lifted, as it always did when he was with her. Through all the upheaval in her young life, Charlotte was resilient.

Ryker was trying to follow her example, to roll with the punches life threw at him, or at least do a better job of hiding his bruises.

"It looks like the vehicle rolled several times before it came to land on that ledge." Eagle Mountain Search and Rescue Captain Danny Irwin stood with the cluster of volunteers on the side of the highway as they peered over the side at the battered silver sedan wedged between a boulder and the cliff approximately one hundred yards below. "You can see pieces of the car that broke off every time the car bounced."

Harper Stanick, a search and rescue rookie, winced as she took in the trail of debris and the battered vehicle. It looked like this was going to be her first body recovery. She had been warned this was part of search and rescue and told herself she was prepared, but still. What would a person look like after enduring that kind of trauma?

"I saw movement!" Paramedic Hannah Richards, who had arrived with the ambulance but joined her fellow SAR volunteers in surveying the scene, pointed at the vehicle. "There's someone alive in there!"

Her exclamation prodded them into action. Danny directed volunteers Eldon Ramsey and Tony Meissner to rig ropes for a rappel onto the ledge beside the car. Harper joined fellow trainees Grace Wilcox, Anna Trent and veteran Christine Mercer in gathering helmets, harnesses, a litter and other gear they would need to stabilize the injured survivor and get them to safety above. Danny radioed to have a medical helicopter land two miles away at the soccer fields in town to meet the ambulance and transport the injured person or persons to the hospital in Junction.

"What can I do to help?"

At the sound of the man's voice, deep and slightly hoarse, Harper fumbled the safety helmets she had been charged with, and had to juggle to keep from losing one. "Careful," Christine said.

"Close the highway, if you haven't already," Danny said. "Clear space on the side of the highway for us to go down and keep everyone back from the edge. We don't want anyone else falling in, or kicking rocks down on top of us as we work."

Harper turned to see who Danny was talking to and this time she did drop the helmets. Seven years since she had laid eyes on Ryker Vernon and she might have thought she was hallucinating him now, except that it made perfect sense for him to be here. Ryker was from Eagle Mountain, just like her. The first thing she had done when she moved back was to snoop around, long enough to determine he had left town, but apparently he had returned. Just like her.

What didn't make sense was that Ryker was now apparently a cop. No mistaking that khaki uniform or the gun on his hip. Ryker, a cop? The motorcycle-riding bad boy who had practically sent her mother into a faint the first time he showed up at their house to pick Harper up for a date was a law enforcement officer?

And damned if he didn't look just as good in that uniform as he had in his motorcycle leathers all those years ago. Better even, his chest a little broader, his jaw firmer. The Ryker she had known had been barely eighteen, still with a bit of the boy about him. This version of him was harder. A man.

"Hey, earth to Harper. Are you okay?" Christine followed Harper's gaze toward the officer who stood with Danny and she grinned. "I take it this is your first encounter with the newest addition to the sheriff's department," she said. "He's pretty easy on the eyes, isn't he?" She nudged Harper with her elbow. "I hear he's a single dad. Maybe when we're done here you can introduce yourself."

The bottom dropped out of Harper's stomach at the word *dad*. Ryker was a father? When? Who?

"Pull your eyes back in your head and focus on the job," Christine said, her voice firm. "You can chase after the cop later."

Harper turned her back on Ryker. "I'm not going to chase after him," she said. "I was just surprised. He reminds me of someone I used to know."

"Must have been a pretty special someone," Christine said. "The way you were staring at him. Like one of those cartoons, where the air fills with hearts."

"Not like that at all," Harper said, and gathered up the helmets she had dropped. Maybe at one time she was that gaga about Ryker Vernon, but those days were long past.

DESPITE HOW FAR the vehicle had rolled and the shape the car was in, three people emerged alive. Ryker watched from a distance as search and rescue volunteers descended on ropes to the ledge and worked to stabilize the vehicle, then cut most of the rest of the car away to reach the passengers trapped inside.

First up was an infant, a living testament to the effectiveness of child safety seats, as he sustained nothing more than a minor cut on his forehead from broken glass. Volunteer Eldon Ramsey carried the baby, still secured in his seat, up to the road, where the paramedics pronounced him perfectly okay then reluctantly turned him over to the Victim Services volunteer, who was tasked with locating a relative or temporary foster parent to care for him until his parents were released from the hospital.

Said parents also both survived, with several broken bones between them. They were brought up one at a time strapped into litters. The technical aspects of the maneuvers required to bring them to safety fascinated Ryker, who would admit to being nervous about heights.

"That was amazing," he said to SAR Captain Danny Irwin after the injured had been transported to the waiting helicopter and the road had been reopened. Accident investigators from Colorado State Patrol had arrived on the scene and were taking photographs and measuring skid marks for their reports, so Ryker had turned to helping the search and rescue volunteers with their gear.

"We're always looking for more volunteers," Danny said. "Deputy Jake Gwynn is on the team."

"Yeah, I hear he loves it," Ryker said. "Unfortunately, I can't commit that much time. I need to be with my daughter when I have time off."

"How old is she?" Danny asked.

"Four. It's just the two of us. And my parents. They're a big help."

Danny nodded. "My fiancée has two kids. They're a little older but I get what you mean about wanting to be there for them. They won't be little forever."

"Hey there! I heard you were back in town." Ryker turned to find Hannah Richards grinning up at him. The two of them had been in the same grade at Eagle Mountain High School way back when.

"Hi, Hannah. It's good to see you. I've only been back a couple of weeks. I'm still getting settled."

"Jake told me you signed on with the sheriff's department," she said. She held up one hand to reveal a modest diamond. "He's my fiancé, in case you haven't heard."

"He's mentioned the amazing woman he's engaged to, but I had no idea that was you."

She punched his shoulder and he pretended to recoil in pain, both of them laughing. "Hey, there's someone else here you need to see," Hannah said. She turned and waved. "Harper. Come over and see who the cat dragged in."

The name itself was enough to set Ryker's heart hammering, but seeing the woman herself made his world tilt for a moment. If anything, she was more beautiful than he remembered—her curly brown hair escaping from a twist at the back of her head, her green-hazel eyes fringed with dark lashes. Kim, to whom Ryker had confided the whole story of his and Harper's ill-fated romance, had prickled at what she interpreted as his too-fond descriptions of his teenage girlfriend. "No one is that perfect," she had protested.

But to him, Harper had been perfect. And she had reminded him of how imperfect he was. "Hello, Harper," he said, surprised at how calm and even his voice sounded. "It's good to see you again."

"Hello, Ryker. I heard you'd left town."

He had heard the same about her. "I just moved back," he said.

She was looking at him, but at the uniform, not into his eyes. "I can't believe you're a sheriff's deputy."

"Neither can I, some days." He was trying to make a joke, but the words came off flat. Hannah was watching them, her face full of questions. Did she remember that he and Harper had dated in high school?

Maybe she hadn't known. Harper's rich parents had pitched such a fit about their adored daughter seeing a guy whose father worked at the town's sewage treatment plant that he and Harper had to sneak around in order to see each other.

He had a hundred questions he wanted to ask her: What was she doing back in Eagle Mountain? What kind of work did she do? How had she ended up volunteering with search and rescue?

Was she okay? Could she ever forgive him?

"I have to go," Harper said, and turned away.

"See you around, Ryker," Hannah said. "Jake and I will have you over for dinner sometime."

"Yeah, that would be great," Ryker said, with less enthusiasm than he probably should have. He stared after Harper. She was still beautiful, all shiny hair and soft curves, but more defined now, the blurred edges of youth replaced by the firm lines of maturity. Not that she was old, but she had been through a lot in the past few years.

She had been through a lot, and he hadn't been there with her. One more failure he was having a hard time getting past.

Chapter Two

"I just found out Ryker Vernon is back in town."

Harper was still nursing her first cup of coffee the next morning when her mother called to share the news. Harper frowned, even though her mother couldn't see her. Someone had told her people could tell when you were smiling into the phone, so maybe Valerie Stanick would sense that Harper wasn't pleased about starting her day with this conversation. "Yes, I knew Ryker is in town." She took a sip of coffee. "He's a sheriff's deputy."

Valerie sniffed. "They must be desperate for officers to hire him."

"Mom!"

"Don't *mom* me. After what happened with that little boy, I'm surprised Ryker would show his face around here."

Harper's stomach knotted at the memory. "Mom! Ryker had nothing to do with Aiden Phillips's disappearance and you know it. He was completely cleared of all wrongdoing."

"But Ryker was babysitting the boy when he went missing. And they never found who killed him."

"It wasn't Ryker." Her fresh anger over this old hurt surprised Harper—anger on Ryker's behalf, but also anger that her mother was still holding that old tragedy against him. Aiden, Ryker's six-year-old cousin, had been taken from his bedroom while Ryker watched TV in the next room. "I don't need you to lecture me about Ryker Vernon. If that's why you called, I'm going to hang up now."

"I only called to warn you. I didn't want you to be upset if you ran into him accidentally."

Too late, Harper thought. "I need to go, Mom. I'm going to be late for work." She had half an hour before she had to report for work at Taylor Geographic, a company that produced detailed maps of all kinds.

"I wanted to know if you've made another date with Stan Carmichael," Valerie said. "His mother told me that he told her the two of you had a terrific time the other night."

That makes one of us, Harper thought, though she was smart enough not to say the words out loud. Barbie Carmichael was president of the Woman's Club and she and Valerie had been trying to match Harper and Stan since high school. Dinner the other night was the third time in those years that Harper had allowed herself to be pressured into going out with Stan, and the results were no better than the previous two evenings. Stan was sweet and earnest and painfully besotted with her. She had felt like a bug under a microscope throughout the entire date. Not only did he stare at her and hang on her every word, but when he touched her, his hands were always clammy. She didn't hate him, but she wasn't the least bit attracted to him. "Stan is not the man for me, Mom," she said.

"He's not a macho jerk who's going to treat you badly like Frank or Ryker." Valerie's voice rose with indignation. "I don't understand why you wouldn't want to be with a *nice* man. And Stan is a doctor! He makes a very good living."

Stan was a proctologist. She didn't want to think about how he made his living. "*Franco* did not treat me badly," she said. If anything, she had been the one to blame for their brief, failed marriage. "I never should have married him, but that was my fault. And Ryker never mistreated me, either." Not really. He had been as much a victim of circumstances as she had.

"All I can say is you didn't get this self-destructive tendency from me," Valerie said. "One of these days you're going to wake up and realize I was right."

"I really do have to go now, Mom. Talk to you soon." She ended the call, then stared into her now-cold coffee and thought about Ryker. Why had she been so unfriendly to him yesterday? He probably thought she hated him, and that wasn't it at all. As often as she had thought about what it would be like to see him again, she hadn't counted on that heart-pounding, bone-melting sense of equal parts longing and panic that had swamped her.

There was simply too much history between them. Mistakes that could never be undone.

She glanced at the clock and a different kind of panic jolted her out of her chair. She had to leave now or she would be late. Considering how few jobs in this town allowed her to employ her graphic arts degree, she didn't want to screw up and lose this one. Not when she had only been hired two months ago.

Thank goodness for work, she thought an hour later as she focused on a new trail map for a ski resort on the other side of the state. She could lose herself in a project like this and think of nothing else for the next few hours. By the time everyone else starting filing out of the office at five, her neck and back ached and her fingers were cramped around her computer mouse, but she had completed a rough outline of the map that she was proud of. She would spend the rest of the week refining the details before turning it over to another artist on staff for the colorwork.

She was gathering her belongings when her phone pinged with a text from Hannah, in the group chat they were part of with Christine and Grace. She had known Hannah since high school, but the others she was just getting to know through search and rescue. Meet us at Mo's? Hannah had typed.

Harper smiled and hit the button to reply. On my way.

Mo's Pub was packed with the usual mix of after-work locals and tourists looking for a drink or a quick meal. Harper spotted Hannah and the others at a booth near the back and pushed her way through the crowd to join them. "It looks busier than usual tonight," Harper said as she scooted into the booth next to Grace.

"It's five-dollar burger night," Christine said. "That and two-dollar draft beer pulls in a crowd."

"If there's a rescue call, we can leave from here," Grace said. "Half the team is here." She waved across the room to where Ryan Welch, Caleb Garrison and Eldon Ramsey sat side by side at the bar.

"Where's Jake tonight?" Harper asked as she helped herself from the pitcher of beer on the table. Hannah's fiancé was a SAR volunteer, too.

"He's on duty," Hannah said.

"Him and Declan." Grace made a sad face.

"Declan Owen is with the sheriff's department, too," Hannah explained in answer to Harper's confused look.

"Are there a lot of SAR volunteers dating law enforcement?" Harper asked.

"Sheri's husband is with the Colorado Bureau of Investigation," Hannah said. "And Anne is seeing Lucas Malone, with the Mesa County Sheriff's Department." She laughed. "Don't look so horrified. We work with law enforcement at a lot of accident scenes. And if anyone is going to understand the need to drop everything and rush out to an emergency, it's another first responder."

Harper nodded. Did this mean she was going to have to get used to seeing Ryker more than she had planned? Eagle Mountain was a small town, but she had really hoped to avoid him as much as possible. Things were just too awkward between them.

The server arrived and they ordered the burger special, then she excused herself to visit the ladies' room. She was washing her hands and studying her face in the mirror, wondering if she should bother to touch up her makeup when she felt a tug on her trousers. She looked down to see an adorable little blonde girl looking up at her. "Can you lift me up so I can wash my hands?" the girl asked.

"Well, sure." Harper dried her own hands, then grasped the child around the waist and boosted her up until she could reach the sink. "Do you need help turning on the water?" she asked, though how she was going to manage while she was holding the child, she couldn't imagine.

"I can do it," the little girl said, and twisted the handle of the faucet. She pumped soap, then scrubbed vigorously, a look of deep concentration on her face.

"You're doing a great job," Harper said. Such tiny hands, though she was a sturdy child, heavier than Harper might have thought, dressed in a pink ruffled dress and jeans with a hole in one knee, a pink ribbon coming loose from her hair. She leaned closer and caught a whiff of strawberry shampoo. A rush of tenderness almost overwhelmed her.

"Okay, I'm ready to dry now."

Harper set the child on her feet and handed her a paper towel from the dispenser on the wall. The girl very carefully dried each finger, then crumpled the paper towel and deposited it in the trash.

"Is there anyone named Charlotte in here?" a woman called from the door.

"That's me!" The little girl stuck up her hand as if she'd been called on in class.

The woman smiled. "Your dad asked me to check on you," she said. "He's getting a little nervous out here."

"Okay." Charlotte turned to Harper. "You need to come meet my dad."

Who was Harper to argue with a command like this? Curious, she followed her new friend into the hallway outside the restrooms.

And stopped. Because of course, she should have known this was coming. If she had learned nothing else the past few years, it was that the universe had a definite sense of irony. "This lady helped me wash my hands," Charlotte was saying, holding up both hands as if for inspection.

"Hello again, Ryker," Harper said

"Hello, Harper." He had exchanged his uniform for jeans and a T-shirt that did a good job of showing off his chest and biceps. The Ryker she had known before had definitely not been this pumped. "Thanks for helping my girl."

My girl. The affection behind the words brought a lump to her throat. He rested one hand on Charlotte's shoulder as she leaned back against his legs, her gaze shifting between them, bright and expectant. "I was happy to help."

"This is Charlotte," he said. "In case she didn't introduce herself."

Harper forced her attention to the child. She could see a little of Ryker in the broad forehead and something about the eyes. But the rest of her must take after her mother. Christine had said Ryker was a single dad, so what had happened to Charlotte's mother? "It's nice to meet you," she said. "I'm Harper."

"I never knew anyone named Harper before," Charlotte said. She grabbed Ryker's hand and swung on it. "Can we eat pizza now?"

"Would you like to join us?" he asked.

Was that hope she saw in his eyes? Or was he merely being polite? "I'm with friends," she said. "And I already ordered."

"Sure." He took a step back, his expression unreadable. "I'll let you get to it."

Maybe some other time, she should have said. Or even *I'd love to catch up with you.*

Oh, what was the point? She and Ryker were over and done with and had been for years. The sooner she accepted that, the better.

She headed back toward her booth but hadn't gone far before someone grabbed her arm. Startled, she found herself face-to-face with a petite woman with a halo of messy blond hair. The woman's long nails dug into the skin of Harper's forearm. "What were you doing with that little girl?" the woman demanded. She had very blue eyes, fringed with long false lashes, and her gaze bored into Harper.

Harper wrenched away from her. "Who are you?" she asked.

"I saw you in the ladies' room with that little girl. What were you doing with her?"

"I was taking her to her father. Her father, the sheriff's deputy."

Harper had hoped the mention of a cop would make the woman back off, but she only laughed. "I know all about Ryker," she said. "He should keep a better eye on his kid." She turned and walked away, leaving by the fire door at the end of the hallway.

Harper stared after her. Should she say something to

Ryker about the strange woman? But what would she say? Some nosy woman thinks you shouldn't let your little girl go to the bathroom by herself? He had stood outside the door waiting for Charlotte, and even sent someone in to check on her. What else could a dad do?

She moved to the fire door and pushed it open enough to look out. No sign of the woman. She was probably just a local busybody. Better to leave it.

"I was beginning to think we were going to have to send out a search party," Christine said when Harper returned to their booth. "Your burger is getting cold."

"I ran into someone who wanted to talk." She popped a french fry into her mouth, hoping to forestall conversation.

"Is that a bruise on your arm?"

Harper followed Grace's gaze to the four round dark spots forming on her arm. She could still feel that woman's fingers digging into her, her gaze searing. But she didn't want to talk about that. Because talking about the woman would mean talking about Ryker, and she wasn't ready for that. Not yet. "I wonder how that happened," she said, and went back to eating her burger.

THE NEXT MORNING, Ryker reported to the sheriff's department for a mandatory meeting of all personnel. He filled his coffee cup from the carafe at the back of the conference room and greeted some of his fellow officers, then took a seat along one side of the long table. It had felt strange at first, being in this place that held no good memories for him. He had had pretty much zero interactions with law enforcement until Aiden had been kidnapped. Then they had questioned him repeatedly, making it clear he was their chief suspect. Even though they had eventually cleared him, his life hadn't been the same since. Back then he never would have dreamed he would end up on this side of the law.

A lot had changed in the seven years since his arrest. Sheriff Travis Walker, only in his early thirties but recently reelected—having run unopposed—sat at the head of the table, flanked by his brother Sergeant Gage Walker on one side, and Deputy Dwight Prentice on the other.

Ryker looked around the table at his fellow officers, some he knew better than others. They were a fairly young lot, typical of a small department. Many of them, like him, had young children. Travis had nine-month-old twins— a boy and a girl—while Gage had a six-month-old baby girl as well as a seven-year-old daughter. Jamie Douglas, the only female deputy, had a three-month-old daughter. Dwight Prentice and his wife had no children. Declan Owen had been the newest recruit until Ryker was hired, though he had more experience than most of them, having worked for the US Marshals Service. Shane Ellis, Chris DelRay and Wes Landry rounded out the force, along with a few reserve officers who filled in during vacations, illnesses or emergencies.

"Let's get started," Travis said, and the hum of conversation died down. "We've had a string of vandalism incidents in the high country. Someone stole some metal roofing the Historical Society had purchased to stabilize the old mine boarding house up at the Mary Simmons Mine. Maybe the same person or persons took a dozen two-by-fours the owners of a mining claim off Iron Springs Road had purchased to build a storage shed on the property."

"Dale Perkins stopped me last week to complain about people camping illegally at his place," Dwight said. "I told them if he caught them in the act we could charge them with trespassing, but he said since he doesn't live up there, that's hard to do. He was most upset about all the trash they leave behind."

"Illegal camping increases the danger of a campfire getting out of hand," Jamie said. "People who ignore private property signs won't necessarily comply with fire regulations, either."

"It might be transients," Gage said.

"Whoever this is doesn't seem to be moving on," Travis said. "Keep your eyes and ears open around town, and if you get a chance to patrol some of the roads leading into the high country, do so."

The meeting moved on to cover the need for traffic control during a Jeep rally in the town park the upcoming weekend, preparations for Independence Day celebrations the next month, a firearms training session in two weeks and a reminder to turn in reports on time. "Adelaide says if she gets any incomplete reports, she will come looking for you," Travis said.

Nervous laughter circled the table. Ryker had already learned that Office Manager Adelaide Kinkaid was not someone he wanted to cross. She didn't have to raise her voice to make him feel like an errant schoolboy.

The meeting broke up and Ryker gathered his belongings. He had a few free hours until he reported for his shift at three. "How's it going, Ryker?" Gage asked.

Travis's younger brother was more outgoing than his sibling and served as a de facto training officer for the new recruits. Even though Ryker wasn't a true rookie, having worked four and a half years with the police department in Longmont, Colorado, he was still settling into the routine here in Eagle Mountain. "It's going well," Ryker said. When he had interviewed for the job here, he had been upfront about his past experiences with the department. Having grown up in Eagle Mountain, Travis and Gage knew Aiden's case, and made it clear they considered it irrelevant to Ryker's hiring. Which it was. He tossed his coffee cup into the trash.

"How's Charlotte doing at Robin's Nest Day Care?" Gage asked.

"She's doing well. She likes her teacher and is making friends." Not that Charlotte ever had problems making friends.

Gage leaned back against the counter beside the coffee machine. "Maya and I are thinking about enrolling our youngest there in a few months when Maya goes back to teaching school," he said.

"If we all keep having more babies, we could open a department day care." Jamie squeezed past Ryker to refill her travel mug with coffee.

"Who's watching your little one?" Gage asked.

"My neighbor. She's helped with Donna for years, and she seemed thrilled to add a baby to the mix." She glanced at Ryker. "Donna is my sister. She has Down's and is pretty independent, but it's good to have someone around she can call on when Nate or I are working."

"Nate's a ranger with the forest service," Gage said, filling in yet another detail to help Ryker form a complete picture of his coworkers.

"Thank goodness he works a set schedule," Jamie said. "That makes it a lot easier to manage care."

"My mom and dad are a big help with Charlotte," Ryker said. "It's the main reason I moved back to Eagle Mountain. I don't know how I'd look after her without them."

"This is a great place to raise a family," Gage said.

"Says the man who's never lived anywhere else," Jamie said.

"Doesn't make it any less true." Gage turned back to

Ryker. "If you need anything, let one of us know. On or off the job. That's what we're here for."

"Thanks." But Ryker was unlikely to ask. It had been hard enough turning to his parents for help after Kim left.

He was halfway across the parking lot to his car when his phone rang. "Hey, Mom," he answered, as he hit the key fob to unlock the door.

"Ryker, is Charlotte with you?"

The panic in his mother's voice stopped Ryker cold. "Charlotte is at day care. I dropped her off this morning before my meeting."

"She was there, but she isn't now. The director just called to ask if one of us had checked her out without telling anyone. I told her we would never do that."

"What do they mean, she isn't there? She couldn't have disappeared." His heart beat painfully and he fought a wave of nausea.

"She went out with the other kids in her class for morning playtime. The teachers were with them—two of them." His mother sounded more in control. She had always been good in a crisis. "A little boy fell and they thought he had broken his arm. They were tending to him and when they called everyone to come back inside, Charlotte wasn't there. Sheila Lindstrom said she looked everywhere. They even checked the houses near the day care, thinking Charlotte might have gone to visit someone there. You know how friendly she is. But she wasn't there. Ryker, what are we going to do?"

His first instinct was to go to the day care center—to tear the place apart if he had to, looking for his daughter. Maybe she was hiding, and she had fallen asleep. Or they had overlooked her somehow.

But the cold black knot in the center of his chest told

him that hadn't happened. Sheila and the others would have thought of those things. "Just sit tight, Mom," he said. "I'll take care of it." He pocketed his phone and hurried back into the sheriff's department. This couldn't be happening again. Not his little girl.

A group of deputies were gathered around Gage and Travis outside the conference room. They looked up as he burst inside. "My daughter is missing," he announced. "Someone's taken Charlotte."

Chapter Three

Harper had just settled into lettering the ski trail map when Devlin Anderson, a talented young artist who had a penchant for vintage menswear, swept into the studio. Today he wore the pants and vest from a brown plaid suit, with brown wing tips and a brown bow tie. But his normally neat hair was ruffled, and he was red in the face, as if he'd been running. "I was down the street getting a latte when I heard there's a little girl missing," he said. "They're asking for volunteers to help with the search."

Chairs scraped and paper rustled as people rose from their worktables. "Who's missing?"

"When?"

"From where?"

The owner of the business, Patterson Taylor, emerged from his office. "What's going on?"

"There's a little girl missing," Devlin said. "We need to help look."

"Who is she?" Harper asked.

"All I know is her name is Charlotte," Devlin said. "She's four years old with long blond hair. She's wearing a pink-checked sundress and she disappeared from Robin's Nest Day Care. You know, that cute little house over on Second Street."

"Charlotte Vernon?" Harper didn't know her voice could squeak like that.

"Do you know her?" Another coworker, Lisa, rushed over to take Harper's arm. "You'd better sit down. You look like you're going to faint."

Harper straightened and forced herself to breathe deeply. "I'm okay," she said. "But I need to go help." Poor Charlotte. Poor Ryker! He must be frantic.

"They're asking volunteers to assemble in front of the sheriff's department," Devlin said. "They'll give us instructions."

Harper's text alert sounded and she studied the message. "You sure you're okay?" Lisa asked.

Harper nodded. "It's search and rescue. They're asking for search volunteers also."

The office emptied out as everyone hurried two blocks over to the sheriff's department. The sidewalks were filled with others headed in the same direction. Harper spotted SAR volunteer Carrie Andrews, an architect whose office was nearby and moved to join her. Hannah Richards and her mother, Brit, from the Alpiner Inn several streets over, soon gathered with them.

Sheriff Travis Walker asked for silence, then read out Charlotte's description. Four years old. Thirty-eight inches tall. Thirty-eight pounds. Blond hair, blue eyes. Pink sundress and shorts. Pink sneakers. "She's been missing less than an hour," he said. "Sheriff's deputies will search nearby homes. I'm asking civilian volunteers to search alleys, backyards, vacant lots. Look anywhere a small child might hide. It's possible she fell asleep or was hurt. Behind dumpsters, in tall grass—look everywhere. If you find anything, call for help and wait for others to assist."

Harper studied the faces of the deputies gathered around the sheriff, their expressions grim. She didn't see Ryker. Was he inside the station? Or somewhere else, already searching for his daughter?

Wherever he was, he was probably beside himself. In the few moments she had seen them together, there had been no mistaking the love he had for his daughter. And after what he had been through when Aiden was taken—people had said some terrible things, and even after it was proven he couldn't have been the one to hurt the boy, there were still whispers. Harper's parents had been quick to condemn him, and they hadn't been alone.

Search and rescue volunteers split into two teams, assigned to search a condo development under construction a few blocks from the day care. The site was full of potential hazards for a small child, from broken glass and jagged nails to an open basement. Upon hearing the situation, the construction workers pitched in to help. They formed a line to move through the site, turning over sheets of plywood and peering into any cavity. No one said anything, but Harper sensed that, like her, they were steeling themselves for the sight of a small body, injured in a fall or crushed by a piece of lumber. There were so many ways a small child was vulnerable, and she could see how a place like this might be tempting for an adventurous little girl.

Charlotte had struck her as the curious type, her big blue eyes looking into Harper's without fear. Harper remembered the weight of her as she lifted her to the sink, and the strawberry scent of her hair, so sweet and innocent. Obviously Charlotte wasn't the first little girl she had encountered in the past seven years. But she was the first who had affected her so viscerally.

Because she was Ryker's. Because she made Harper think of their little girl. Would she have been like Charlotte if she had lived?

Seven years ago

"CAN'T I STAY up and watch TV with you?"

"Sorry, bud. Your mom was really clear that your bedtime is eight." Ryker patted his little cousin's shoulder. Aiden was small for his age, with a cowlick that stuck up at the back of his head no matter how much his mother, Melissa, tried to plaster it down. He had recently lost a tooth and the gap gave him a particularly rascally look when he grinned, as he did a lot. He was a happy kid, and even though he whined about having to go to bed, he obediently climbed under the sheets. "Did you brush your teeth?" Ryker asked.

"Yeah." Aiden looked toward the window beside his bed. "Can you leave the blinds up? I like to look out until I get sleepy."

"Okay. I'll be just down the hall if you need anything."

Ryker shut the bedroom door and walked down the hall to the living room. He turned the television on, keeping the sound low, and flipped through the channels, looking for something to hold his interest. He thought about calling Harper, but her parents didn't let her have her own phone, so he would have to call their home phone, and her mom was liable to answer. Mrs. Stanick had made it clear she didn't like Ryker, though he couldn't figure out why. Yes, he had a motorcycle, but that didn't mean he was dangerous or anything.

He settled on an episode of *Deadwood* and lay back on the sofa, a pillow under his head. He had gotten up early to finish an essay for English class and found himself drifting off.

When he woke, the show was over and it was dark outside. He sat up and checked the time. Nine o'clock. He went to the bathroom, then moved to the end of the hall and eased open the door to Aiden's room. He expected to find the little guy sleeping, but instead the bed was empty, the covers thrown back, half-trailing on the floor.

"Aiden?" Ryker stepped into the room. He looked around the small space and started toward the closet, but a rattling noise stopped him. The window was wide open, a breeze knocking the top of the blinds against the frame.

"Aiden!" Ryker rushed to the window. The screen was missing. He stuck his head out and could just make it out, lying on the ground. "Aiden!" He stared down at the screen—six feet down. A long way for a little boy to drop. And there was no sign of the boy anywhere.

Heart pounding, he raced outside. "Aiden!" he shouted. "Aiden, where are you?"

He ran around to the side of the house. No sign of the boy. No sign of anyone.

"Ryker? Is everything okay?"

He turned and saw Mrs. Kenner, a retired teacher who lived across the street, on her front porch. He jogged toward her. "Have you seen Aiden?" he asked.

She frowned, and pulled her robe—faded pink and quilted—more closely around her. "No, I haven't seen Aiden. Isn't it a little late for him to be out?"

"I put him to bed at eight and when I went to check on him just now, he wasn't there." He looked back toward the house, hoping to see the little boy pop out from behind the shrubbery or a dark corner of the yard. "His window is open and he isn't there."

"Where could he have gone?" Mrs. Kenner didn't look upset, merely puzzled. "Do you think he's hiding from you?"

"I don't know," Ryker said. "He's just...gone."

Mrs. Kenner put her hand on his arm. "Then maybe you'd better call someone."

He nodded, and groped in the pocket of his jeans for his phone. He stared at it for a long moment, wondering who to call. Not Aiden's mom. Melissa would faint if she thought something happened to her little boy. Aiden's dad was at work, and Ryker didn't know that number. He dialed a number he knew by heart. His father answered on the second ring. "Ryker? Is everything okay?"

"Aiden is missing," he said. "I went to check his bedroom and he's just...gone." He felt cold all over, and started to shake.

"Can you think of any place Charlotte might have gone to? A friend she might have decided to visit? A store she liked and wanted to see again?" Declan Owen sat with Ryker in the sheriff's office, conducting what passed for a formal interview. Ryker wondered if the sheriff had assigned Declan this duty because, like Ryker, he was new to the department. Or because of his experience with the US Marshals Service. Or maybe it was because Declan didn't have children of his own. It didn't take a particularly perceptive person to see how Charlotte's disappearance had hit hard among the many officers in the department who were parents of young children.

"I don't think she wandered off from the day care," Ryker said. "She wouldn't have any reason to do that. I think someone took her." He closed his eyes, willing himself to keep it together. Charlotte wasn't Aiden. What had happened to him wouldn't necessarily happen to her.

"Why do you think that?" Declan asked. "You've taught her not to go with strangers, right?"

That was basic parenting 101, especially for a cop. Despite the way Charlotte had apparently enlisted Harper, a stranger to her, for help in the ladies' room, he didn't think his little girl would let someone she didn't know talk her into leaving the day care. They had even playacted scenarios where someone tried to tell Charlotte her daddy was hurt or they had a puppy they needed her to see. Charlotte had practiced saying *no* and going to get an adult for help. "This wouldn't have been a stranger," he said, and the certainty behind those words edged out some of the stark fear.

Declan leaned toward him. "Who do you think took her?" he asked.

"Her mother. My ex-wife." Was he saying that because he believed it to be true, or merely because he wanted it to be true? He wet his lips and said, "Charlotte wouldn't go with a stranger, but she would probably go with her mother. Even though she hasn't seen Kim in years, she has a picture of her mother in her room and she talks about her."

Declan nodded. He would be familiar with the same statistics as Ryker—the vast majority of kidnapped children were taken by a relative, often the noncustodial parent. "Has your ex-wife threatened to take Charlotte with her? Have the two of you argued over custody?"

"Kim hasn't seen Charlotte in three years," Ryker said. "Not since she packed up and moved out of the house to live with another man. When I filed for divorce and asked for full custody, she didn't argue. She's never even attempted to visit Charlotte."

"Then why do you think she would take her now?" Declan asked.

How to explain how Kim's mind worked? Not that Ryker

would ever be an expert, but two years of living with her had lent him insights he didn't necessarily want. "Kim is impulsive. And self-centered. When she wants something, she wants it now and will run over anyone who tries to keep her from getting her way. She was also very influenced by her boyfriend. If he decided he wanted them to have Charlotte, Kim wouldn't bother with petitioning for custody through the courts. She would storm in and take what she wanted—her daughter. I think that's what she's done now." His stomach churned at the idea, but he could so clearly see it happening. Charlotte hadn't seen her mother since she was thirteen months old, but she had never forgotten her. In the beginning, Ryker had believed that Kim would change her mind and want to see her little girl, so he had kept pictures of Kim and Charlotte together, and when Charlotte asked questions about her mother, he tried to answer honestly, without making Charlotte feel that her mother's abandonment was in any way her fault.

So Charlotte would probably have recognized Kim if she approached. And if Kim had urged Charlotte to come with her, she probably would have obeyed. What little girl wouldn't want to go with her mother? Especially when her mother was beautiful and petite, and bore a more than passing resemblance to the fairy godmothers in the picture books Charlotte loved.

"Have you had any contact with your ex-wife in the past few months?" Declan asked. "Do you know where she's been living?"

"The last I heard, she was still with Mick and they were living out east of Denver, in Gilcrest." He shifted in the chair. "I haven't spoken to Kim in more than three years. The divorce was negotiated through our lawyers and we were never in the same room after she packed up and moved out. But I've kept tabs on her over the years." Given Mick's criminal history, Ryker had felt safer knowing what he and Kim were up to.

"Do you think she's still with the man she left with?" Declan asked.

"I don't know for sure. Maybe." He shifted, uncomfortable. If Kim was still with Mick, she had stayed with him almost twice as long as she had been with Ryker. But he could see it. Kim hadn't just loved Mick, she had been enthralled with him. Under his sway.

"What's this man's name?"

"Michael Davis. He goes by Mick. If you look him up, you'll see he has a record."

One of Declan's eyebrows twitched, but it was the only tell that this surprised him. "Has he served time?" he asked. "For what crimes?"

"Drugs. Extortion. Fraud. Theft."

"Nice guy."

"Oh yeah." He blew out a breath. "Kim said she wanted someone who wasn't like me. I took it as a compliment."

"I'll pull his record, see if I can get a recent photo," Declan said. "Does your ex have any priors?"

"Not unless they've happened since the divorce. When I met her she was squeaky clean. I made the mistake of believing she was ordinary."

Declan stood and rested a hand on his shoulder. "We'll put out an APB on your ex. We've already issued an Amber Alert for Charlotte. We're knocking on doors around the day care, trying to find anyone who might have seen someone talking to Charlotte. And most of the town is out looking for her."

He left the room and Ryker collapsed forward, elbows on his knees, head in his hands, fighting back tears and a terror that threatened to overwhelm him. Charlotte had to be all right. His beautiful girl had to be all right. He prayed she was with Kim. The woman might be irresponsible and misguided and a hundred other adjectives that added up to someone he could never trust. But she wouldn't hurt her child. She wouldn't let Mick hurt her child.

She wouldn't. He had to hold on to that belief.

THE SEARCH FOR Charlotte Vernon ceased when it became too dark to see. By that time more than two hundred people had combed every inch of the town and found no sign of the little girl. Too upset to go home to an empty apartment, Harper gathered with her fellow search and rescue volunteers at their headquarters, where they sat at the long tables used for training and watched television reports about the missing girl, her picture filling the screen, sometimes alone, sometimes with her father.

"I feel so sorry for Ryker," Hannah said. "Jake says he's holding up okay, and they're all rallying around to support him and his parents, but I just know he's sick about this."

"Shh. Who's that?" The question, from someone at the other end of the table, directed their attention to the television. A different picture filled the screen, of a woman with abundant blond hair and blue eyes.

A second picture took its place—Ryker and the woman together, the woman holding a baby. "Kimberley 'Kim' Rhodes Vernon, who may also be going by the name Kim Davis, is wanted for questioning in the disappearance of her daughter, Charlotte Vernon. A woman who was passing the day care facility about the time of Charlotte's disappearance reported seeing a blond woman—who may have been Kim Vernon—with the girl on the sidewalk in front of the day care."

The image on the screen changed to one of a man, thinning blond hair in a single braid, heavy eyebrows and a blond moustache, a flag tattoo on one bare arm, an eagle on the front of the T-shirt. "Ms. Vernon may be in the company of this man, Michael or Mick Davis. If you see either of these people, especially in the company of a little girl, please notify the police."

Harper shoved back her chair and stood. Hannah stared up at her. "Are you okay?"

"I need to talk to the sheriff," she said. "I saw that woman."

"When?"

"Today?"

"Where did you see her?" The questions came from all sides. Harper shook her head. "She was at Mo's last night. I need to tell the sheriff."

No one tried to stop her as she hurried outside to her car. She forced herself to slow down and pay attention to the road as she drove to the sheriff's department.

The parking lot at the sheriff's department was full and at least a dozen people milled about outside, from curious locals and tourists to a few reporters. Harper pushed through the door and found the lobby even more crowded. She made her way to the desk at the back of the room, where an older woman with purple-framed bifocals regarded her with tired eyes. Her name tag read Adelaide. "May I help you?"

"I need to see the sheriff," Harper said. She lowered her voice, not wanting any reporters nearby to hear. "I saw Kim Vernon. Yesterday, at Mo's."

Adelaide stood. "Come with me."

Harper followed the older woman through a door and down a long hallway to a cramped office. Sheriff Walker stood when they entered the room. Ryker, slumped in a chair in front of the sheriff's desk, looked up at her with red-rimmed eyes. "This woman says she saw Kim Vernon yesterday," Adelaide announced.

Ryker shot out of his chair. "Where did you see her?" he asked. "Was she alone? Are you sure it was her?"

"Sit down, please. Harper, isn't it?" asked the sheriff.

She sat on a folding chair and scooted it closer to the desk, within inches of Ryker. He sat down and stared at her, hands gripping his knees. "Harper Stanick," she said.

The sheriff pulled a yellow legal pad toward him and took a pen from a cup on his desk. "Tell me what you saw."

She told him about her conversation with the woman she was sure was Kim Vernon, outside the restroom at Mo's Pub the night before. "She said I should keep a better eye on my kid?" Ryker's deep voice held even more gravel than usual. "Why didn't you tell me about this?"

"I didn't think it meant anything," Harper protested. "She was just some nosy woman."

"You say she left out the fire door?" Travis prompted.

"Yes. There's a door at the end of the hallway that goes out into the parking lot."

"Did you see what kind of vehicle she was driving?" Ryker asked. "Was she with anyone else?"

"No. I didn't see into the parking lot." She turned to Ryker. "I'm so sorry about Charlotte. But if she was taken by her mother, surely she wouldn't hurt her."

The tight lines around his eyes didn't ease, but he nodded. "No, I don't think she would hurt her."

"Thank you for coming forward with this information," Travis said. "We appreciate it."

She stood, and was surprised when Ryker rose also. "I'll walk you out," he said.

In the hallway, he touched her arm. "Let's go out the

back," he said, and pointed down the hall. "Less likely to see reporters."

She waited while he badged through the door lock, and they stepped out into what was apparently the employee lot, black-and-white sheriff's department SUVs interspersed with other vehicles. Moths flitted around the security lights, but beyond where they stood, all was dark and quiet. The chill common to nights in the mountains, even in summer, had also descended, and Harper tried not to think about Charlotte without a sweater in the cold.

"How are your parents doing?" she asked. She didn't know Wanda and Steve Vernon very well, but she remembered them being nice people. Much nicer to her than her parents had been to Ryker.

"They're taking it hard. Especially my mom. She's spent a lot of time with Charlotte since we moved here." He sighed. "I was floundering on my own, trying to work shifts at the police department and find childcare. When my mom suggested I move back home I resisted the idea at first, but it ended up being a lifesaver. I think it's better for Charlotte, too, having my folks around."

"I'm glad you have their support now, too," she said.

"I didn't mean to jump down your throat just now," Ryker said, not looking at her. "There was no reason you should have mentioned seeing Kim to me. You didn't know her, and it's not like she really did or said anything threatening."

"How long were you married?" She wanted to take the question back as soon as she said it. Of all the things to ask at a time like this, that wasn't one of them. It was none of her business anyway.

"Less than two years," he said. "It was a bad idea from the start but we had only been dating about six weeks when she found out she was pregnant, and I wanted to do the right thing." He did look at her then, eyes dark and shadowed. "I would have married you, you know."

"I know." She blew out a deep breath. "But my parents were right. I mean, about us being too young. That wouldn't have been a good way to start out." She had been seventeen. He had just turned eighteen, in their senior year of high school.

"Would you have waited for me?" he asked.

"Yes." She didn't have to think about the answer.

"Then I'm sorry I didn't wait for you. I figured you felt the same way about me your parents did."

When Harper's parents had learned she was pregnant, and that Ryker was the father, they had been beyond furious. When Aiden had disappeared only a few days later, they had been even more set against him. They sent Harper to Florida, where she was to live with her mother's sister, Florence, until she delivered the baby.

"You know they sent me to Florida, right?" she said. "They took away my computer and my phone. My aunt wouldn't let me out of her sight. It was like being in prison." A posh prison, with its own pool and beach access. But she had been miserable without him.

"I didn't know about that until later. You had just vanished." He glanced at her again. "I even had some wild idea they might have harmed you. Your mother was so furious, the one time I tried to talk to her."

"You talked to her?" Harper felt her eyes go wide at the idea.

"Yeah. She told me she wasn't going to see her only child's life ruined and while you were upset with her now, you would thank her later for preventing you from making a huge mistake. Awful as they were, her words gave me hope. Leaving hadn't been your idea."

She pictured him, trying to be a tough guy, but really still a boy. Hurt and probably angry and more than a little lost. She had felt all those things, too. "I'm sorry," she said. "I wish I could have at least said goodbye to you, and explained what was going on."

"It was a long time before I found out you lost the baby," he said. "A friend of yours told me. I don't think she knew I was the father."

She stared at him. "I wrote you a letter," she said. "You didn't get it?"

"No. But I moved away the week after graduation." He stared off across the parking lot.

"What a mess we both were."

"Yeah, well. I met Kim three years later and we got involved and that was a mess, too. Except for Charlotte. It was all worth it for her."

She did what she had been wanting to do all night then, and tucked her hand into the crook of his arm and leaned against him. "You're going to find her," she said. "You've got so many people looking for her and Kim—she's a striking-looking woman, isn't she? The kind who stands out. And Charlotte is such a beautiful kid. People will notice her, too."

He didn't say anything. Maybe he didn't believe the words. As a cop, he had probably seen and heard all kinds of horrible things that happened to missing kids. And then there was Aiden. His killer had never been found. She was grateful she didn't have those things in her head. "Thanks for your help tonight," he said. "And I know you and the other search and rescue volunteers looked for her today."

"She's a terrific kid," Harper said. "She won me over right away."

"She does that. I don't know where she gets it from." He unwound her hand from his arm and took a step away. "I'd better get back in there," he said. "Thanks again."

I'm not going to cry, she told herself as she walked around to the front of the building where she had left her car. She had spent so many years imagining what their reunion might be like—how they would exchange their stories and maybe laugh at the mistakes they had made. In her imagination it had never been like this—the facts laid out but so much left unsaid. And the heavy weight of sadness over his missing child threatening to pull them under.

She got into her car and started it, but sat for a long moment, the tears in her eyes blurring the world around her like raindrops on a window.

Chapter Four

Ryker left the sheriff's department an hour after Harper. The search for Charlotte was paused until first light, and while the sheriff had sent another bulletin alerting all law enforcement agencies to be on the lookout for Kim, there was little hope of a response until the next day. Wherever Kim and Charlotte were, they were probably sleeping.

He was walking toward his truck when a man on the sidewalk called his name. He looked up and was surprised to see a gray-haired man hobbling toward him. The man moved quickly, despite the fact that one shoulder was hunched and he moved with an awkward, sideways gait. He stopped in front of Ryker and a nearby streetlight illuminated a weathered, deeply lined face. "Any news about your little girl?" the man asked.

Ryker shook his head. The man didn't look like a reporter. He wore dirty jeans and a red-checked flannel shirt with a rip in one sleeve. "I was one of the searchers today," the man said. "I wanted to do what I could to help."

"Thank you," Ryker said. "I appreciate it."

The man looked around them, at the deserted street, lined with silent and closed businesses. "It seems strange to be out here doing this again. I helped looked for your cousin, too."

Ryker stared. "What is your name?"

"Gary. Gary Langley." He held up a hand, the fingers knotted and twisted. "I'd offer to shake hands but I can't anymore. I had an accident at work just about a year after your cousin went missing, caused a lot of neurological damage. I've been on full disability ever since. But something like this, I like to get out and do what I can."

"Thanks." Ryker took a step back. "Is there something in particular you wanted?"

"No. I was just hoping for news. I hope you find her soon. It's terrible the things that can happen to a child these days."

He turned and shuffled away. Ryker stared after him. Had the man reminded him about Aiden on purpose, perhaps with the goal of unsettling him? If so, he had succeeded. Not that Aiden's disappearance and death had been far from his mind all day.

He shook his head and continued walking to his truck and drove home. His mother met him at the back door, eyes full of unasked questions. He shook his head. "No news."

"Nothing?" Wanda followed him into the kitchen. The room smelled of coffee and lemon dish detergent, the black granite countertops reflecting pools of overhead light. "I can't believe no one has seen her," Wanda said.

"I'm sure she's with Kim," Ryker said. "Harper Stanick came in and said she ran into a woman who fit Kim's description at Mo's last night. Kim had seen Harper with Charlotte in the ladies' room and asked what she was doing with her."

"Harper was with Charlotte in the ladies' room?" Wanda looked puzzled.

"I had to send Charlotte into the ladies' room by herself. She won't go into the men's room with me anymore, and it's not really appropriate, anyway. She couldn't reach the sink to wash her hands, so she asked Harper for help."

"We've told her not to talk to strangers."

"We've also told her how important it is to wash her hands. Anyway, I guess she figured Harper was trustworthy. And Harper brought her right out to me."

"How is Harper? I didn't know she was back in town." Unlike the Stanicks, Wanda had welcomed Harper into her home. While she hadn't been happy about the news that her son's not-yet-eighteen-year-old girlfriend was going to have a baby, she had adopted a positive attitude and promised to help as much as possible. When Harper had disappeared from their lives, Ryker had come to believe his mother had mourned almost as much as he had. After all, Harper's baby would have been her first grandchild.

"She's okay, I guess," he said. "She looks good. She's volunteering with search and rescue. I ran into her when I worked that accident Tuesday—the one with the baby in the car seat." Was that really only two days ago? It seemed a lifetime.

"You didn't say."

"Yeah, well." There were a lot of things he didn't tell his mom.

"What did Kim say to Harper?" Wanda asked.

"She wanted to know what she was doing with Charlotte. Then she said…she said I needed to do a better job of watching my kid." His voice cracked and he had to turn away. He didn't want to break down. Not just because he didn't want his mother to see him that way, but because he was afraid if he started sobbing, he wouldn't be able to stop. He had to keep it together. His parents needed him to do that. And Charlotte needed him, too. When she was found—and he had to believe she would be found—he was going to be there, not in a heap somewhere crying.

He felt something warm on his back. His mother's hand rubbing up and down, the way she had when he was a boy. "You're a good father," she said. "The best. Charlotte knows that. You didn't do anything wrong. This is all on Kim. To be honest, I'm relieved to know Kim is probably with her, instead of some stranger who might harm her."

He nodded. Instead of some stranger like the one who had harmed Aiden. He turned to face her again. Maybe the best way to get through this horror was to shift into cop mode. Focus on the job. "We put out an APB for Kim and Mick, and we're trying to find any vehicles registered to them. Maybe somebody will spot them."

"Somebody will spot them," his mother echoed. She stepped back. "I saved dinner for you. It's chicken soup. I thought that might be easiest to get down."

He shook his head. "I couldn't eat."

She opened her mouth and he knew she was going to urge him to eat, but she apparently thought better of it. "Then try to get some sleep," she said. "Tomorrow is going to be another long day."

RYKER SPENT A restless night, drifting to sleep, then waking to the remembrance that Charlotte was gone. He fought back thoughts of all the worst things that could happen to her, managing to doze again, only to come fully awake just after six to pale light showing behind the bedroom shades. He stared at that light and wondered if Charlotte was seeing it, too. Where was she? She was such a part of him now—how could he not know where she was?

But she wasn't in control of where she went—Kim and Mick were. And they were unknown to him. He tried to think of everything Kim had told him about Mick that might be relevant. When she left it had been all about Mick and what Mick wanted, and he didn't think that would change. Mick wanted to be free. He wanted to live by his own rules. He wanted to go somewhere and live off the land and look after himself. Kim was all in. They were going to create their own little paradise together.

And what about Charlotte? Kim had fallen silent for a long minute when Ryker had asked this question. "Once Mick and I get our place built, she can come see us," she said. "Until then, she might as well stay with you. We're probably going to be traveling around for a while, looking for the right place, and that's hard with a little kid."

"You would just abandon your daughter this way?" Ryker asked.

"I'm not abandoning her. I'll be back when I have a place for her."

"That's not going to happen," Ryker said. "If you turn your back on her now, she will never live with you again. I'll see to it."

He wanted to frighten her into doing the right thing. Not that he wanted her to stay with them. He had known months before this moment that their marriage was over. But Charlotte adored her mother, and she deserved to have two loving parents. He wasn't going to let Kim hurt their daughter this way.

But Kim wasn't frightened. She even had the nerve to smile. "Oh Ryker, I'm her mother," she said. "Of course she'll live with me again, when the time is right."

He had to leave the room then. The urge to lash out at Kim was so strong it frightened him. He went into Charlotte's nursery and held the baby until he heard Kim and Mick drive away.

Kim didn't contest the divorce or the custody arrangement. He lost touch with her and after a couple of years, he had begun to believe she was out of their lives for good.

But somehow she had found them here in Eagle Mountain. Did that mean she and Mick had established their homestead and she was claiming what she thought of as hers? Never mind that she was a stranger to Charlotte and didn't know anything about her, from what she liked to eat to her favorite books and what childhood illnesses she had suffered. What Kim wanted, Kim took.

He showered and shaved, and dressed in his uniform. Travis had told him he was on family leave until Charlotte was found but if he was going to spend the day at the sheriff's department, he wanted to look like he belonged there.

He was drinking his first cup of coffee when his phone rang. When he saw the sheriff's name on the screen, he scrambled to answer, his hands shaking. "The FBI is coming in this morning to interview you," Travis said. "They say they have some information but they wouldn't tell me on the phone what it was."

Right. It made sense to call in the feds for a child abduction. "I'll be right there," Ryker said.

His mother didn't say anything when he told her he had to go to a meeting at the sheriff's department, but she shoved a travel cup into his hand. "It's a smoothie with protein powder," she said. "Drink it even if you don't want to. You're no good to anyone if you don't eat."

He felt better after he drank the smoothie. Strong enough to face the feds, anyway. Travis was waiting in his office, pressed and polished as ever, though the shadows under his eyes suggested he hadn't slept much better than Ryker. Was he thinking about what it would be like to have one of his children taken?

Special Agents Guy Cussler and Adam Reno shook hands with Ryker when Travis introduced them, then the four men gathered around the conference table. "We've had a report of a couple with a little girl matching the descriptions of your daughter and Kimberly and Mick Davis at a campground just outside of Utah last night," Agent Cussler said. "Unfortunately, by the time authorities arrived at the campground this morning, they were gone. But we now know they've traveled into Utah, so we'll be pursuing the case from there."

"Do you know of any connection they have to anyone in Utah?" Agent Reno asked. "Relatives or friends?"

"Kim's mother is in Oregon and her father is dead," Ryker said. "She never mentioned siblings and I don't know her friends." He tried to rein in his frustration that law enforcement had been so close to apprehending Mick and Kim but hadn't been able to get to them in time. "I haven't seen Kim in three years. And I never knew Mick well. I met him exactly once, when he came to help my wife move out of our home. We didn't have much to say to each other." Only later had he run Mick's name through the police department database and seen his rap sheet. Knowing Kim had chosen a man like that over him had been one more knife to the gut.

"And you're absolutely sure you had no idea this was coming?" Agent Cussler asked. "Your wife hadn't made threats to you, or talked about regaining custody of your daughter?" Cussler sounded as if he couldn't believe this was even possible.

"I had not heard one word from my *ex-wife* in three years," Ryker said, struggling to keep his voice even. "Neither had Charlotte."

"So your ex-wife hadn't called or written to your daughter, maybe without your knowing?" Cussler continued.

"Charlotte is four," Ryker said. "She can't read yet, and she doesn't have a phone."

"The preschool said they never heard from Ms. Vernon," Agent Reno said. "They never saw anyone matching her description near the day care, either."

"We have a witness who saw a woman she believes was Kim Vernon at a local bar the night before Charlotte disappeared," Travis said.

"Yes, we read your report," Cussler said. "Are you sure of this witness's identification?"

"The description she gave sounded like Kim to me," Ryker said.

"People sometimes give reports like this in order to insert themselves into a case and gain a little of the spotlight," Cussler said.

"I know this woman and she's not like that," Ryker said. Or, he had known Harper once. She couldn't have changed that much.

Cussler nodded and made a check mark in his notebook. Did he have an actual to-do list in there?

"Are you sure about the identification from the witness in Utah?" Ryker asked.

"The description the man gave fit the one broadcast for your daughter, your ex-wife and her paramour," Cussler said. "Why? Do you think they wouldn't go to Utah?"

Ryker tried to recall if he had ever heard anyone use the word *paramour* before, then forced himself to address the question. He might not like Agent Cussler, but the man had a job to do and Ryker needed to help him do it. "They might go to Utah," he conceded. He glanced at the sheriff. "Kim said she and Mick wanted to move somewhere away from people and live off the land."

"There are people who come to Utah looking for a place like that," Reno said.

Ryker nodded. "But people try to do that here, too. You can still buy mining claims cheap. Or maybe they decided to just squat on a piece of land they thought was vacant and scrounge for what they needed to build a place."

"We've recently had an uptick in vandalism in the high country," Travis said. "Someone has been stealing building materials."

Ryker swiveled toward him. "Mick strikes me as the type who would think he shouldn't have to pay for building materials if people were careless enough to just leave them lying around. And maybe once they got here, and Kim realized how close she was to Charlotte, she decided to just…take her."

"An impulsive move," Travis said.

"Right. Because Kim was impulsive. She never liked to wait for anything she wanted."

Agents Cussler and Reno shook their heads. "It doesn't make sense for them to kidnap a child and then stay here," Cussler said.

"If they are here, why not just drive up there and arrest them?" Reno asked.

"Because there are thousands of acres of unoccupied wilderness in this county alone," Ryker said.

"There are a lot of places to hide," Travis added.

"Utah makes more sense." Cussler closed his notebook. "We'll be in touch if we have any more information."

Travis escorted the agents from the room, but he returned a few minutes later. "Do you really think your ex and her boyfriend are up there on some abandoned mining claim?" Travis asked.

"I don't know. It just…feels right." He forced himself to

meet the sheriff's gaze. Travis had a reputation as a hard man, but all Ryker saw now was compassion. "I need to look for them," he said. "I'll take time off work to do it, if you want."

"You don't have to take time off," Travis said. "And we'll look with you. We know this county better than the feds, anyway. But I wasn't exaggerating when I said there are a lot of places to hide. It could take a while to find them."

Ryker stood, feeling stronger than he had in the last twenty-four hours. "I'll spend as long as it takes."

Chapter Five

"Harper, I have a new project I want you and Devlin to work on." Patterson approached Harper's drawing table, a sheaf of rolled papers in his hand. In his forties, Patterson kept his head shaved smooth and wore his usual uniform of jeans and a denim shirt with the sleeves rolled up. She suspected he had a closet full of the exact same shirt. Devlin moved in beside them as Patterson unrolled the papers and began pinning them to the table's surface. Today Devlin sported black trousers, a white short-sleeved shirt, suspenders and a string tie. Harper, whose approach to getting ready for work was to pull the first thing from her closet—today it was a navy sheath dress and flats—wondered how either of the men had arrived at their sense of style. Would it be liberating or confining to be so committed to a single way of dressing?

"This resort development in California wants us to update their maps," Patterson said. "There are five sections." He indicated the five 11-by-14-inch sheets tacked to the work table. "The place has been around since the 1980s. These maps were done in 2000, but obviously, there's been lots of changes. They're sending files with aerial views of the entire place which I need you two to incorporate into updated maps of each section. They want something artistic, in keeping with their current style. You'll get a feel for that on their website. They want to frame the maps in their office and common areas and have smaller versions to hand out to interested members, visitors and potential buyers."

"Looks like fun," Devlin said. He leaned over the drawing table and squinted at one of the maps. "Looks like they've got stables and riding trails, and a golf course." He grinned at Harper. "Think we could talk them into comping us a visit? Strictly for research purposes, of course."

Harper returned the smile. Though visiting a resort by herself—or even with Dev for company—didn't sound as much fun as going with a romantic partner.

With Ryker.

She pushed the thought away. She was sure the last thing on Ryker's mind right now was romance. "Has anyone heard anything more about the search for Charlotte Vernon?" she asked.

"I haven't," Patterson said.

Devlin shook his head. "That poor kid. And poor dad." He began untacking two of the maps. "I'll start matching these up with the aerial photos. You take two others and we'll work on the fifth together when these are done."

"Sounds good." She moved to her computer and downloaded the aerial files, then searched for the resort website. But she couldn't focus on the photos of smiling couples on the golf course and trails, and the upbeat prose about the benefits of life with every amenity right outside the front door. Her thoughts continually shifted to Charlotte and Ryker. Where was that dear child, and how was Ryker enduring the torture of not knowing?

"Harper?"

The familiar, low voice made her jump and she looked up to see Ryker himself, in his sheriff's department uniform, walking toward her desk. "Ryker, how are you?" She rose and started to give him a hug, then thought better of it, aware of Devlin and her other coworkers in the open-plan office watching.

Ryker looked around the space, which featured large windows on three sides and drawing tables and desks, as well as long counters for spreading out large-format pieces scattered throughout. Everything was white and pale blue and filled with light. Finally, his gaze came to rest on her once more. He looked tired, but determined. "I need your help," he said.

"Anything."

"Someone at the county clerk's office told me this office has maps of all the mining claims in the high country. She said you actually drew the maps the county has, and can produce them in a larger format than she had available, with more detail."

"Yes, we do." She moved to the far corner of the room, to the large, flat file drawers that held copies of all the work they had done. "If we don't have what you need here, we can print them for you."

He came to stand beside her, close enough that she could hear the clink of the various implements on his duty belt each time he moved, and the low hiss of static from his shoulder-mounted radio. "What exactly are you looking for?" she asked.

"Mining claims above ten-thousand-feet elevation," he said. "Above that point, county building codes don't allow for permanent residences, but people buy the places to camp in the summer or because they want to reopen the mines."

"Are you thinking they would be good places to hide?" she asked.

He moved closer and lowered his voice. "I think Kim and her boyfriend might be camping or in some kind of makeshift shelter on one of those claims. When we split up, she talked about wanting to live somewhere off-grid and said when she did she would take Charlotte to live with her. I used to worry she was serious, and I told her she would never get custody. Maybe that was a mistake. Rather than go through legal channels, I believe she decided to just take Charlotte."

Harper studied the labels on the drawers, then opened one. "The maps are organized by mining districts," she said. "We don't have information about who owns each claim. You'd have to get that from the county."

"Do you have topographical maps?" he asked. "I'm trying to get an idea of the terrain."

"We can do better than that," she said. "On our computers, we'll have the aerial photographs and even satellite imagery we used to compile the maps."

"That's exactly what I need."

She pulled out half a dozen large maps, then led him into a separate workroom with a long table and a fifty-inch monitor. "It's going to take me a minute to find the photographs," she said. "But you can study the maps while I'm looking." While she waited for the computer to boot up, she swiveled her chair to watch him. He bent over the table, studying one of the unrolled maps. "How are you going to narrow down where to look for them?" she asked.

"I'll start by looking for places accessible by roads. Mick has a Jeep registered in his name. Anything with a structure on it would be good. There are a lot of those claims that have been abandoned and ownership has gone back to the county because of unpaid taxes. If I was going to squat on a property, I would choose one of those."

"Maybe they bought one of the claims," she said.

"I checked with the county and there's no record of that. Since neither of them have held any kind of regular job for the past three years that I can determine, I don't think that's likely."

"How do they support themselves?" she asked.

"They work off the books. Odd jobs. Mick has been convicted twice of fraud, so maybe he's got a new swindle police haven't learned about yet. And there's old-fashioned theft. He's been convicted of that, too."

She turned back to the computer. "Kim was a law-abiding citizen when I met her," he said, as if he had read her thoughts. "I guess she was looking for someone who was my exact opposite when she got together with Mick."

"Your marriage lasted longer than mine," she said as she began to scroll through the list of photographic files. "Franco and I only made it thirteen months, but we managed to part as friends."

"Oh." So much emotion behind that one word. "I didn't know you'd been married."

She shrugged. "I was lonely. I thought getting married would fix that, but I was wrong."

"Yeah. I was lonely when I met Kim, too."

"At least you ended up with Charlotte."

"I would have been reasonable, open to some kind of visitation arrangement, but that wasn't good enough for Kim and Mick. Now she's going to find out how unreasonable I can be."

She smiled in spite of herself. That was the Ryker she had fallen so hard for when she was seventeen. He had been full of righteous anger and tough-guy swagger, with a black leather jacket, a motorcycle and an attitude. And tender as a marshmallow inside, though most people didn't get to see that side. They had judged him so harshly when Aiden was taken. She had believed they were wrong, but her parents had whisked her away before she had the chance to tell him.

"What do you have for me to look at?" He was back to business. Maybe now wasn't the time to bring up that old hurt.

"I have the set of aerial photos pulled up that corresponds to the Galloway Basin district," she said. "You're welcome to look at them here, but I can also load them and the others onto a flash drive for you to review at the sheriff's department."

"I'd like the files to take with me, but I'd also like to study them here," he said. "We don't have a monitor like this available at the sheriff's department."

"You're welcome to do that." She brought up the first photo, an aerial view showing a narrow dirt road running alongside a section of land with few trees, and a half-collapsed structure of rusting metal and silvery wood. "You can zoom in, scan out, and even highlight a section to print if you like," she said, demonstrating these functions. "Let me know if you need anything."

She slid out of the chair and he took her place, already focused on the screen.

"Can I get you some coffee?" she asked.

"What? Oh, no thanks."

She stood behind him for a moment, watching as he guided the cursor across the photo, zooming in on the ruins, then backing out and switching to the next photograph. What, exactly, was he looking for? Was there any way she could help him?

If he wanted more help, he would ask, she told herself. And she had work to do.

She left the room quietly and returned to her desk. Devlin looked up from his computer. "Everything okay?"

"He's looking at maps that might help with the search for his daughter."

Three hours later, she was debating suggesting Ryker take a break for lunch when he emerged from the back room. "Did you find anything useful?" she asked.

"I think so." He stopped beside her desk. "Thanks."

"If there's anything I can do to help, just ask," she said. "I could help with the search. Everyone here would."

He shook his head. "We can't risk civilians running around those old mines. Though if we narrow the search area, we might call on search and rescue."

"If that happens, I'll be there." She looked down at her desk, suddenly feeling awkward. "And if you ever just want to talk, I'm here for that, too."

"Thanks." He covered her hand with his, and she felt the shock of that contact, and looked into his eyes. She saw the same awareness there—a connection she had thought long-severed flickering to life. Then he pulled his hand away. "I'd better go."

"Poor guy," Devlin said after the door shut behind Ryker. "Being a cop he's probably tortured by all the horrible things that might have happened to his daughter."

She wanted to tell him that Charlotte was going to be all right, that she'd been kidnapped by her mother. But she didn't know anything about Kim or her boyfriend, did she? Maybe Charlotte wouldn't be all right with them. The thought made her sick. She wanted to do something to help, to comfort Ryker and his family. But she wasn't really part of his life anymore.

BACK AT THE sheriff's department, Ryker showed Travis and Declan the maps and aerial photography he had collected. He unrolled one of the maps on the table in the conference room and the three men bent over it. "We could start by comparing what's in these photos to existing structures,"

Ryker said. "We can drive up and take a closer look at any new or altered structures."

"Best to do that from the air," Declan said. "Maybe we can find someone to fly us over. We might even be able to hitch a ride in a fire-spotter plane. They're making regular patrols in the area this time of year."

"I think that would be safer than approaching on foot or even in a department vehicle," Travis said. "Declan, make some calls and see what you can arrange. In the meantime, have you seen this?"

He slipped a folded newspaper from beneath his arm and offered it to Ryker. Ryker opened the paper and stared at the article filling the bottom of the page:

Search for Missing Girl Focuses on Utah

The search for missing toddler Charlotte Vernon, who disappeared from her day care in the western mountain community of Eagle Mountain on Wednesday, is now focused in Utah, after what FBI officials have termed a credible sighting of the little girl with a couple at a campground outside Moab on Thursday.

The woman the child was seen with matches the description of her estranged mother, twenty-nine-year-old Kimberley "Kim" Vernon, who is suspected of kidnapping the child. Since her divorce from Charlotte's father, Rayford County sheriff's deputy Ryker Vernon three years ago, Ms. Vernon has reportedly had no contact with her daughter. Mr. Ryker was awarded sole custody of the child as part of the divorce proceedings.

Mother and daughter are alleged to be in the company of Michael "Mick" Davis, described as a thirty-five-year-old drifter with a criminal record for theft, assault, fraud and a number of other offenses. If you see the trio, do not attempt to approach, but contact law enforcement immediately.

The article was accompanied by photos of Charlotte, Kim and Mick. Mick's picture was clearly a mug shot. Ryker didn't know where Kim's photo had come from, though it looked as if it had been enlarged from a snapshot, one taken outdoors in the summer, Kim squinting into the camera, a breeze pushing her hair to one side.

Charlotte's image was the recent school photo Ryker had provided that was printed on posters all over the county. Her big smile showed off a row of pearly baby teeth and the deep dimples on either side of her mouth. Her blue eyes shone with excitement. He laid the paper aside. "Have there been any more sightings?" he asked.

"Not that we've heard," Travis said. "Not here or in Utah."

"I could be wrong about them still being here," Ryker said. "I could be wasting our time, but I don't think so." He stared at the map showing the winding mountain roads, timber-framed adits and weathered ruins of the Galloway Basin mining district. "This is something I think Kim would do."

"Fleeing to Utah would make it harder for you to find her," Declan said.

"I don't think she would see it that way." He hesitated, trying to find the words to explain the puzzling woman he had married. "She liked to taunt people. She believed she was better than anyone else—that her ideas, or Mick's ideas that she adopted, were better. She's probably convinced herself that whatever she had planned for this off-grid life-style is so superior to the way everyone else is living that

Charlotte will naturally want to stay with her, whether I ever find her or not."

"What about Mick?" Travis asked. "Any insight into how he thinks?"

Ryker shook his head. "I don't know much more about him than you do. I've studied his criminal record. As a felon, he's not supposed to own firearms, but he probably does. Kim probably bought them for him. Or he stole them. She said living off-grid was his idea, but she was all for it."

"Having a base of operations near but out of reach of a lot of people in a generally well-off town like Eagle Mountain might be tempting," Declan said. "Lots of summer homes and vacation properties to rob when they're unoccupied. Lots of tourists to rip off. A relatively small sheriff's department Davis probably believes he can outwit."

"It's worth looking into more closely," Travis said. He nodded to the maps. "Give us some places to focus on. Declan, see about that plane. I'll get in touch with the FBI and see if they have anything else to tell us."

When he was alone in the room, Ryker bent over the maps. Given free rein, his mind would have focused on Charlotte. Was she afraid? Tired and dirty? Hungry? Did she miss him?

He didn't have the luxury of indulging in such thoughts. The only way to get through this was to keep moving forward. To do whatever he could to find his daughter. He pulled out a notebook and pen and focused on the maps. He needed to come up with a plan.

Chapter Six

Friday afternoon, Harper's mother called and invited her to dinner, so Harper headed there after work. Her parents' two-story, cedar-sided home was in a neighborhood of similar homes built in the mid-to-late-1990s, showing its age but still well-cared for. Harper parked in the driveway in front of the garage and—as she always did when she visited—looked up to the right front bedroom, which had been hers for most of her life. She had last checked the bedroom about ten days ago, and it had been exactly as she left it, as if her parents were expecting her to move back in any moment.

She knocked, then let herself in the front door. "I'm in the kitchen!" her mother shouted. Harper headed in that direction, but stopped in the living room to say hello to her father, who was watching a World War II documentary on television. Tom Stanick was a self-employed financial advisor. For as long as Harper could remember, he had rented an office above the local bank. Time had added silver to his still-thick hair, and more lines around his eyes and mouth, but he was still a handsome man. "Hello, sweetie," he said. "What a nice surprise."

"Mom called and invited me to dinner."

"That's nice, but you know you don't have to wait for an invitation. You can stop by anytime."

"I know, Dad." He, especially, seemed to miss having her in the house. She was an only child, which meant they had no one else to focus on. It had taken her a long time to forgive them after the way they had acted over her pregnancy, but her ire had gradually faded. They had wanted the best for her, and after her miscarriage they had been gentle with her, welcoming her back home and encouraging her to think of the future and her education.

Ryker was gone by the time she'd returned to Eagle Mountain, and she didn't stay long either, moving that fall to Ohio, where she had enrolled in a small arts college and pursued a degree in graphic arts.

Tension between her and her mother had increased after she had eloped with Franco, a Bronx-born musician who her mother, especially, hadn't approved of. But Valerie had gritted her teeth and tried to be welcoming. "I'm sure we'll feel more comfortable with him once we know him better," she had said after meeting him for the first time at their wedding.

But he and Harper had been together such a short time that a second meeting had never happened.

Harper had been determined to build a new life on her own in Ohio after the divorce, but the company she worked for folded and she had been unable to find a new job. When her dad contacted her about an opening at Taylor Geographic, she had resisted the idea. But of course, the job was perfect, and her parents had welcomed her back with open arms. She had lived with them for six weeks before finding her own apartment in Eagle Mountain, but in that time they had settled into a new peace. She was ready to move on with her life, and that meant letting go of her resentment over how things had worked out with Ryker, and their role in that.

"Hi, Mom." Harper hugged her mom around the shoulders, and snatched a piece of carrot she was chopping for salad.

"Hello, Harper. You can set the table. Dinner is almost ready."

While Harper set the table, her dad came in and filled water glasses, so that when her mother carried the steaming platter of spaghetti and meatballs to the table, all was ready. This was how so many evenings in her life had started— the three of them gathered at this same oak table, chatting about their day or the latest happenings in town. The very sameness of these moments over the years comforted her. She hoped one day she would have a family that could build this kind of tradition.

"I just saw a news bulletin about that missing child," her dad said as he scooped salad onto his plate. "They think the couple suspected of taking her are driving a white Jeep."

"Well, I hope they find her soon," her mom said. "You can't go anywhere without seeing that poor child's face on a poster."

"Apparently, they suspect Ryker's ex-wife of kidnapping her and taking her to Utah," her dad said.

Her mom shook a bottle of salad dressing. "I don't know how a man like Ryker ended up with sole custody of a little girl," she said.

Harper tried to let a lot of things her mother said to annoy her slide, but this wasn't going to be one of them. "Ryker is a wonderful father and he's sick about Charlotte being gone," she said. "And the reason he ended up with sole custody is because her mother abandoned her."

Her mom froze and fixed her daughter with a gaze sharper than the knife she was using to slice into a meatball. "How do you know this?" she demanded. "Have you talked to him?"

"Yes, I've talked to him. Ryker is my friend, and he's going through something terrible right now."

The meatball was too tender to require the ferocity with which her mother was attacking it. "I don't like the idea of you seeing him again," she said.

"This isn't about what you like, Mother." Harper forced herself to pause and breathe deeply. She wasn't a sullen teenager anymore. They could discuss this like adults. "And I'm not seeing him. He came by the office today to get some maps. For the sheriff's department."

"Ryker has done well for himself, getting that job as a sheriff's deputy," her dad said.

Harper sent her father a grateful smile, but she didn't keep the expression long, as her mother said, "I'm surprised he was able to become a law enforcement officer, considering his past."

"He didn't do anything wrong." Harper laid down her fork, her appetite vanished. "He was cleared of all charges."

Her mother looked away. "I'm entitled to my opinion. And you can't say Ryker was good to you. As soon as you were out of sight, he left town and ended up married to an awful woman who has now kidnapped his child."

"You kept us apart," Harper said. "He probably thinks I left him. And he certainly had no idea his ex-wife would kidnap Charlotte. That's a terrible thing to say."

"I stand by my opinion."

Her father sent Harper a look that told her not to waste her time arguing with her mother. She focused on her food, though she scarcely tasted the meal as she ate. This wasn't a new conversation for them, but her mother's refusal to see Ryker in any other light frustrated her almost beyond bearing.

When dinner was over, she thanked her mom and prepared to leave, but her father said, "Harper and I will do the dishes, dear."

"Thanks for not arguing with your mother," her dad said when he and Harper were scraping plates and loading the dishwasher. "I know it's not always easy."

"Why is she so set against Ryker? He didn't do anything wrong."

"I'm not trying to justify her feelings, but losing a child is every parent's worst nightmare. When Aiden disappeared, your mother was so upset. And when they accused Ryker of being involved, all she could see was that her only child was in danger. She can't let go of that feeling."

Harper slid a handful of silverware into the basket on the door of the machine. "It's ridiculous. The Vernons are very nice and Ryker is a good man. And from what I've seen, he's a great father, and he's worried sick about Charlotte."

"You're not a teenager anymore. You get to decide who you want as a friend. And for what it's worth, I don't think Ryker would be a bad choice."

"Thanks, Dad. That means a lot."

"Your mother loves you and she doesn't want to see you hurt, but that doesn't mean she's right about everything."

There were plenty of days when Harper thought she herself might be wrong about everything. Acknowledging that made it a little easier to forgive others' mistaken opinions. She had certainly thought she had been wrong about Ryker in those lonely days after her miscarriage, when he never responded to the letter she had written, giving him the news. But in her heart, she had never believed he would be so cold. When he told her he never received her letter, she felt the truth of his words, and that particular wound, at least, was less painful.

"Search and rescue may go to search for Charlotte again soon," she said.

"Good luck. And be careful."

"I always am." At least with her physical body. With her heart…maybe not so much.

STRAPPED INTO THE passenger seat in the cockpit of the small fixed-wing aircraft—which was parked at the airfield in Delta—on Saturday morning, Ryker tried to pay attention to the safety briefing the pilot was giving him. Alissa Mayfield had short, sandy hair and freckles and said she had been flying planes for twenty years. Ryker studied the array of dials, gauges, switches and lights in front of her and thought brain surgery might be easier than sorting out all of that. Alissa followed his gaze and laughed. "It's not as complicated as it looks," she said. "Trust me, I know what I'm doing." She handed him a headset. "It gets really noisy in the air. This will protect your ears, and there's a speaker and microphone so we can communicate."

He donned the headset and heard her voice in his ear. "You want to take a look at Galloway Basin and the Camp Frederick area, is that right?" she asked.

"Right. I want to look at the undeveloped mining claims in the area for any signs of new or updated construction. And any vehicles parked on any of the claims." Or a little girl who might run out to wave at a plane. If that happened, it was going to take everything in him not to insist they land immediately.

"Got it. I can fly pretty low with this in most areas, but let me know if there's anything you want to take a better look at." The engine started and the roar—even muffled by the headset—vibrated through him.

The plane taxied down the runway and he gripped the

seat. He wasn't a fan of heights when he was standing still, but this sensation of rushing down the runway, then rising into the air made his palms sweat and his breath come in gasps.

But then they were soaring, the ground falling away quickly. "It's a good day for flying," Alissa said. "Nice and calm."

He couldn't help but think of the aerial photography he had been poring over the previous day. They followed the silver ribbon of the highway over Dixon Pass for a while, then angled west, soaring over dense stands of fir and spruce, the roofs of luxury homes set among the trees. Then the trees grew less prominent, and the landscape was dominated by rock in sunset shades from yellow and orange to a red so deep it was almost purple. "This is the Galloway Basin area," she said. "I think most of the mining claims you're looking at are above tree line."

"That's right." Forgetting his fear of heights, he leaned forward to peer out the side window, past the wing of the plane to the scenery below. He was reminded of the train sets he had seen set up in museums. There were no trains here, only the scars of dirt roads winding among old tree stumps that were once evergreens cut for their timber for the mines over a century ago. Colorful spills of mine waste flowed like melted candle wax down the sides of the mountains, and piles of gray rock marked the openings where trams had once been loaded with ore to be transported to stamp mills. The rusted, bent tram rails stitched across the landscape in places, along with snarls of cables from the old overhead trams. Clusters of gray lumber were all that remained of the buildings that had once housed hundreds of miners and support staff, while isolated cabins marked the smaller claims, where one or two people had tried to wrest riches from the mountains.

They flew over an expanse of treeless green—startling in its emerald lushness—through patches of orangey-brown, like stains on velvet, that marked clumps of beetle-killed timber. "That's the old Alexander mine." Alissa pointed to their right. "Those grass berms and holding ponds are part of the mitigation process to leach the arsenic, magnesium and other hazardous metals from the water before it empties into the river or soaks into the soil."

They flew on. Ryker spotted a cow moose and her calf, a trio of backpack-laden hikers climbing up a trail leading to the top of a peak, and clusters of Jeeps on the backroads like the toy cars he had played with on the living room rug as a boy. But no one who looked out of place. And no sign of life on any of the claims.

"We need to head back now," Alissa said after a while.

"Okay," he answered.

He was too distracted by thoughts of Charlotte to even be nervous about the landing. When they were on the ground and the plane was silent, they removed their headsets and he unbuckled his seat belt. "Thanks for taking me up," he said.

"I'll go out with you again, whenever you want," she said. "I've got two kids of my own."

"Thanks. I may take you up on that."

He returned to the sheriff's department to pore over more maps and photographs, hoping to spot some clue that would lead him to the right place. The alternative was to go home and do nothing, and he couldn't bear that. But all these mining claims were beginning to look alike, and there were a lot of trees obscuring some claims. It would be so easy to overlook the very place Kim and Mick were hiding.

The door opened and Gage stood there. "I thought I saw

the light on," he said. "You look like you've been here a while."

"What time is it?" Ryker stretched, his neck popping loudly as he did so.

"After seven." Gage moved into the room. "I heard you went up in a plane today."

"I did. But I didn't see anything."

"There's a lot of territory to cover."

"Yeah. And maybe the feds are right and they're in Utah."

Gage rested one hip in the table and crossed his arms. "Four years ago, my little girl Casey disappeared," he said. "She wasn't kidnapped, she was lost, up on Dakota Ridge."

"I didn't know that. How long was she missing?"

"Three days, but it seemed like a lot longer. She wasn't my daughter then, I was just a deputy on the scene, but I was still worried sick. My wife, Maya, was Casey's aunt. Casey's parents—Maya's brother and his wife—were murdered. Casey got away and was hiding in the woods, afraid to come out. She was only five, and she's hard of hearing. The search for her is how I met Maya. We ended up adopting Casey. Anyway, that's all to say I know a little of what you're going through and I hope you have the same good outcome."

"How's Casey doing?"

"She had nightmares for a while. And sometimes she misses her parents. But overall, she's doing good." He smiled. "She's crazy about the baby, so that's good. I hope they'll be close."

"Thanks for telling me."

"Yeah, well, what you're going through has me and Maya reliving all of that."

He nodded. "I keep thinking about my cousin, Aiden."

"I remember when that happened," Gage said.

"People thought I was responsible."

"But you weren't."

"No. But they never found his killer. Some people still aren't convinced of my innocence."

"You can't worry about them." He stood. "Focus on the people who are supporting you. Anything you need at all, just ask."

"Thanks." But what he needed was his daughter. Kim was the only person who could give her back and right now that wasn't happening.

Seven years ago

"YOU HAVE THE right to remain silent. Anything you say can and will be used against you in a court of law."

"But I haven't done anything wrong," Ryker interrupted the beefy, blond sheriff's deputy who stood in front of him.

"You have the right to an attorney…" The deputy droned on with the rest of the warning Ryker had only heard previously on TV shows. He didn't look up from the card in his hand until he had read it all. "Do you understand what I just read you?" he asked.

"Yes," Ryker said. "Yes, sir."

"Sit down." The deputy indicated a wooden, straight-backed chair in the small, brightly lit room. "We have some questions for you."

"You said I didn't have to say anything," Ryker said.

"That's right." The deputy—his name tag said Rollins—crossed his arms over his barrel chest. He had thinning blond hair, the pink scalp showing through at the back. "But if you didn't do anything wrong cooperating with us will have you out of here sooner rather than later."

"Okay." He definitely wanted out of here. The deputy

had driven him away from his cousin's house before his parents arrived. Did they even know where he was?

"Tell us what happened with the little boy, Aiden."

Ryker related the same story he had told multiple times by now—how he had put Aiden to bed at eight, fallen asleep while watching TV, checked on the boy about nine and found the window open, the screen off and the boy gone.

"So you're saying someone removed the screen, climbed in that window and took the little boy out of bed while you were in the next room and you never heard a thing?" Deputy Rollins squinted as if trying to make out something in the distance.

"Yes, sir. And I wasn't in the next room, I was down the hall." Still, why hadn't he heard anything? Surely, Aiden would have cried out.

"I find that hard to believe." Rollins leaned across the table toward him. "What I believe is that maybe the little boy was fussy, giving you a hard time. Maybe you lost your temper and hit him. An accident. Maybe he fell and hit his head and wouldn't wake up. It scared you, so you decided to hide the body and fake a kidnapping."

Ryker stared. "No! Aiden's a good kid. And he's just a kid. I'd never hurt him."

Rollins slammed his fist down on the table, making Ryker jump. "You need to tell us the truth, so we can find the boy. His poor parents are wrecks, wondering what happened to him. You're the only one who can help them."

"I don't know where he is," Ryker said. "You need to find him."

"You listen to me, kid." Rollins put his face so close to Ryker's he could smell onions on his breath. "I know nobody took that boy but you. You need to tell the truth."

A loud knock sounded on the door. Rollins looked up. "Who is it?"

"Carson Shay. I'm Mr. Vernon's attorney."

Ryker thought for a moment that Rollins wasn't going to answer, but after a moment, he straightened and went to the door. "Vernon hasn't asked for an attorney," he said.

"His father called me." He looked past Rollins to Ryker. "Hello, son. How are you doing?"

Not so good, Ryker thought. "I'm glad to see you," he said.

"Mr. Vernon won't be answering any more questions tonight," Shay said. He moved past the cop into the room. Rollins glared at them both, then left them alone. After the door shut, Ryker clenched his hands into fists, trying to stop himself from shaking.

"I didn't do anything wrong," he said. "I don't know where Aiden is. Why aren't they looking for him?"

"There are people looking." Shay stood in the same place Rollins had stood. He was probably in his late-thirties, with black, curly hair and black-rimmed glasses. He wore khakis and a dress shirt, but no tie, and was freshly shaven, even though it had to be after eleven at night. "I know you've probably gone over this a lot already, but I need you to tell me again what happened."

So once again, Ryker told his story and relived the horror of finding Aiden's bed empty and the window open. Shay made notes and nodded. When Ryker fell silent, Shay said, "They don't have enough evidence to charge you, so I'm going to take you home. But they will probably question you again. Tell them you won't talk without your attorney present. Then call me."

"Why do they think I did it?"

"You were right there in front of them. They came up with a story they thought fit. It's a lazy approach, but it happens. They'll try to find evidence to fit their story. My job is to hold their feet to the fire and insist they look at everything, not just the parts that make their job easy." He clapped his hand on Ryker's shoulder. "Let's get you home."

"Do other people think I hurt Aiden?" Ryker asked.

The fine lines around Shay's eyes deepened. "Some people will. You'll find out who your real friends are."

Harper, Ryker thought. *I have to talk to Harper.* "What time is it?" he asked.

Shay checked his watch. "It's ten minutes to one."

He couldn't call Harper now. She'd be asleep. He would call her tomorrow. She was going to have his baby. She needed to know he was innocent.

Except when he did finally call her, she was already gone.

Chapter Seven

Harper was sleeping in on Sunday when her text alert sounded. Groggy, she groped for the phone on her bedside table and squinted at the message. One man and dog fallen down mine shaft, Ida B Mine, off Stoney Gulch Jeep trail.

Fully awake now, she sat up and texted that she was on her way. Ten minutes later, she was dressed and headed out the door. She gathered with seven other volunteers at search and rescue headquarters. Ryan and Eldon were out of town on a climbing trip, Hannah and Jake were both working, and several other volunteers were unavailable for one reason or another. That left Danny, Tony, Caleb, Christine, Sheri, Carrie and Harper to load gear into the rescue vehicle and head into the mountains.

"I don't think I've ever been to the Ida B Mine," Harper said as Caleb guided the specially outfitted Jeep up a steep and rocky trail scarcely wide enough for the vehicle.

"There's not much up there," Christine said. "But it's near enough the trail into Crystal Basin that some people detour to poke around among the ruins."

"And apparently, fall down mine shafts," Danny said.

Half a mile farther on, a woman waved them down. She wore a red fleece top and gray hiking pants, her dark hair in a long braid down her back. "I'm the one who called in the emergency," she said. "My boyfriend and my dog are stuck down in this mine shaft."

"How much farther can we drive?" Caleb asked.

"Maybe another hundred yards? There's kind of a flat spot at the end of the road where you can park."

They proceeded slowly, the woman, Rachel, walking alongside them. From her they learned that the man and the dog—a golden retriever—were mostly unhurt, but the man might have sprained his ankle. Neither of them were able to climb out of the shaft, which was about a hundred feet deep. Caleb parked on a level gravel strip at the end of the road and Danny and Sheri hiked ahead with Rachel, while the others unloaded anything they thought they might need for the retrieval, including ropes, helmets, first aid gear and a special harness designed for dogs.

By the time they were finished, Danny and Sheri returned. "The guy's name is Scott," Danny said. "Twenty-something, in good physical shape, no medications or health conditions. His dog, Ginger, was chasing a pika in some rock rubble and suddenly disappeared. Scott could hear her barking and went in search of her. He found her at the bottom of the shaft and thought he could get to her and bring her back up, but it was a lot farther than he estimated and he ended up slipping and falling and hurting his ankle. He says he doesn't think it's broken, but it's swollen and he can't put much weight on it. The dog is fine, but they're both stuck down there. Luckily his girlfriend, Rachel, was able to get a phone signal and call for help. She even tossed a pack with some water and snacks down to him so he's been fine, just ready to get out of there."

"So this shaft opening was hidden by the rocks?" Caleb asked.

"Yeah, you can't see it until you're right up on it," Danny

said. "We flagged it with a stick and a red bandana so none of us accidentally fall in."

"I thought there was a law that open shafts had to be covered," Christina said.

"There's some concrete and iron strapping around this one, like it might have been covered at one time, but that's gone now," Sheri said. She picked up a coil of rope. "I'm going to go down in the shaft and get the dog in the harness to haul up, then I'll send the guy up and we'll see to his foot. It looks like there's only room for one person at a time down there."

She led the way back to the shaft. The others followed, each carrying gear. Harper carried the dog sling and a safety helmet. By the time she reached the group around the shaft, Tony and Caleb where already setting anchors and arranging ropes to allow them to haul Scott and Ginger to the surface. Rachel sat cross-legged beside the shaft, relaying instructions to Scott. Occasionally, the dog barked.

Harper listened to Tony's instructions about setting the ropes, then stood back while Sheri, wearing a safety helmet, harness, and a pack, climbed down into the shaft. The dog's barking increased, amplified by the rocky sides of the shaft.

Less than ten minutes later, Tony and Danny began hauling on the ropes. They had fashioned a pulley over the center of the shaft in order to raise the dog without scraping her against the shaft walls. She rose into the air, looking confused, but remaining still until she spotted Rachel, then she began wagging her tail wildly. She greeted her rescuers with enthusiastic whimpers and wet kisses as they unfastened the harness. "Let me get the leash on her before you let her go," Rachel said. "I don't want her falling back down there."

Raising Scott took longer, and required the strength of

Tony, Danny and Caleb, but he also rode a sling to the top. He was able to sit on the side of the shaft and swing his legs over until he was clear of the opening. While he was still in the harness and wearing the helmet, Danny, a registered nurse, tended to his swollen ankle.

Sheri emerged shortly after, quickly scaling the shaft with little assistance. Scott insisted he could walk to the search and rescue vehicle with a little support, so with Caleb on one side and Tony on the other, he started down the trail, Rachel and Ginger right behind them.

The others began gathering the rope and other scattered equipment. One of the helmets rolled down an incline and Harper ran to retrieve it, almost tripping over a piece of rusty metal as she did so. She stopped to examine it. "Hey!" she called to the others. "Come look at this."

Christine was the first to respond to her cry, followed by Carrie and Sheri. "What is it?" Sheri asked.

"I think it's the cover that's supposed to be on top of that shaft." Harper bent and tugged at the metal strap fastened to the edge of a square iron grate.

Christine and Sheri helped her drag the heavy grate from the rocks that half-covered it. Harper studied the edges of the strapping. "This didn't rust away," she said. "Someone deliberately cut it."

"Why would they do that?" Christine asked.

"Maybe they thought there was gold in the mine and wanted to get down in it?" Carrie suggested.

"It hasn't been here that long," Sheri said. "There's not much dirt on it, and no plants growing up through it. It's almost like someone tried to hide it under the rocks."

"Let's drag it back over the opening so no one else falls in," Harper said.

The women managed to lift the heavy grate and walk it

over to the shaft, where they positioned it over the opening. It fit perfectly. They piled rocks around the edges to further secure it.

Harper walked back over to where the grate had been hidden. "What are you looking for?" Christine called.

"I don't know," she admitted. "I'm just trying to figure out why someone would do that." A flash of bright pink in the rocks a few feet away drew her attention and she picked her way toward it. At first, she thought it was surveyor's tape, the kind used to mark property boundaries. Maybe it had originally been tied to the grate to make it more visible. But when she knelt and pulled the pink strip from the rocks, she was startled to find herself holding a length of satin ribbon.

"What have you got?" Christine asked, coming up behind her.

Harper stared at the ribbon, stomach churning. "It's a ribbon," she said. "A little girl's hair ribbon."

"That's Charlotte's hair ribbon, I'm sure of it." Ryker stared at the once-bright pink ribbon, now dirty and frayed. Half an inch wide and about a foot long, the ribbon still bore the creases from where it had been tied into a bow. He remembered watching his mother make that bow one morning earlier that week. He looked up at Harper, who had walked into the sheriff's department three minutes before, ribbon in hand. "Where, exactly, did you find it?"

"At the Ida B Mine, off Stoney Gulch Road. Search and rescue were called up there this morning to retrieve a man and a dog from a mine shaft they had fallen into." She glanced over at Travis and Gage Walker, who stood to her left, both in identical postures, arms crossed over their chests. "Someone had removed the grating that was supposed to be covering the shaft and tried to hide it under some rocks. You could see where someone cut the strapping that held the grating to some concrete poured around the shaft. I was looking around in the rocks to see if I could spot any more strapping, or even what it had been cut with, when I saw this." She looked back at Ryker. "I thought at first it was surveyor's tape, but when I realized it was a ribbon, I remembered that Charlotte had a pink ribbon in her hair Tuesday night at Mo's."

"The description you gave us didn't say anything about a pink ribbon," Travis said. He picked up a flyer from the corner of the table that held the stacks of maps. "This says Charlotte was last seen wearing a pink-checked sundress and pink sneakers."

Ryker frowned. "Right. She was wearing the pink ribbon the day before." He rubbed the side of his face. He was so tired he could scarcely feel his skin. "We need to ask my mom. She helps Charlotte with her clothes, though mostly Charlotte dresses herself."

Gage straightened. "I'll call her." He left the room.

Travis turned to Harper. "Did you see anything else suspicious or out of place at the mine? Any vehicles, or campfires, or signs that anyone had been there?"

She shook her head. "No. But I didn't go much farther than the mine shaft. I didn't explore the other ruins on the site."

Gage returned. "I talked to your mom," he told Ryker. "She's on her way over."

Wanda, dressed for church in a skirt and blouse and low heels, raced into the office five minutes later, her face flushed. She stopped short when she saw Harper. "Hello, Harper," she said.

"Hello, Wanda." Harper moved farther back in the room, clearing the space between Ryker and his mother.

Wanda turned to Ryker, her expression pleading. "They said you have something of Charlotte's you need me to identify."

"We need you to tell us if this really belongs to Charlotte," Gage said. He nodded to the ribbon on the table. "That."

Wanda walked over to the ribbon and started to pick it up, but Travis put out a hand to stop her. "It would be better if you didn't touch it," he said.

She nodded, and stared at the ribbon. "Yes, that's Charlotte's," she said after a moment. "I'm sure."

"When did she wear it last?" Gage asked.

"She wore it Tuesday. She had on a pink outfit that day." Her eyes grew shiny with unshed tears. "She wanted to wear it Thursday, too, but I told her it was wrinkled. I wanted to iron it before she wore it again." Her voice broke and she covered her mouth with her hand.

Ryker wanted to go to her, to put his arm around her and try to comfort her. But he couldn't really comfort her, and she was strong enough to get through this. So he sat, his hands clenched into fists, and suffered along with her. "I'll need you to check and see if the ribbon you remember is at your house," Travis said.

"It isn't." Wanda straightened her shoulders. "Thursday, after…after Charlotte went missing, I decided to iron the ribbon. So it would be ready when…when she gets back to us." She closed her eyes and breathed deeply. When she opened them again, her voice was steadier. "I thought I must have misplaced it. I've been so scattered. But now I wonder…" She stared at the ribbon. "Maybe Charlotte took it. She might have put it in her pocket, to show to a friend, or to wear later." She looked at Ryker. "You know how stubborn she can be about getting her way."

He nodded. "Yes. She's stubborn."

"Harper, why are you here?" Wanda had noticed Harper again.

"I found the ribbon," Harper said. "On a search and rescue call in the mountains."

"In the mountains? Where?"

"I'll explain later, Mom," Ryker said.

Gage stepped forward and placed the ribbon in a plastic evidence bag. "Did anyone besides you touch this at the scene?" he asked Harper.

She shook her head. "I put the ribbon in my jeans pocket to bring back down here. Do you think I destroyed evidence?"

"It's doubtful anything useful survived after being out in the elements for a few days, but we'll test it anyway," he said.

"We'll get a team up there to examine the area and see if we find anything else," Travis said.

Ryker stood. "Charlotte was up there," he said. "I'm right about Kim and Mick taking her into the mining district. They didn't go to Utah."

"If this ribbon really does belong to Charlotte, then yes, you could be right," Travis said.

Ryker knew the sheriff was being cautious. It didn't pay to jump to conclusions in criminal investigations. But he couldn't help feeling the sheriff was doubting him. "It's Charlotte's ribbon," he said again, proving his daughter wasn't the only one in the family who was stubborn.

Gage and the sheriff left the room. Wanda moved over to hug her son. "That ribbon is Charlotte's," she said. "We both know it."

He patted her back. "It is."

Then Wanda turned and embraced Harper. "Thank you

for bringing that to us. Anything of Charlotte's is precious to us."

Harper awkwardly returned the embrace. "I hope it helps," she said.

Wanda backed away. "I'd better go home," she said, and turned and all but ran from the room. Ryker suspected she would go off and cry somewhere where no one would see her.

"Your mother is such a nice person," Harper said.

"Yeah, she is. Charlotte being gone is killing her."

"It's awful for all of you. And I'm sure Charlotte misses you terribly. I could see how much she adores you."

He looked away, jaw clenched. Sometimes the only way he knew to cope was to think about anything but his little girl—what she must be doing right now. What she must be feeling. When he felt more in control, he turned back to her. "Will you take me to the place where you found the ribbon?" he asked. "After the crime scene investigators have done their work. Don't tell anyone. I'm probably not supposed to be up there, but I have to go."

"Of course you do. I'll go with you any time you're ready." Her eyes met his, such tenderness there that he felt the protective wall he was building around his emotions threaten to crack. She had always had a knack for seeing past any screen he tried to hide behind.

Chapter Eight

"I borrowed this Jeep from my folks," Ryker said when he picked up Harper for their drive to the Ida B Mine Monday afternoon in a red Rubicon. He had called midmorning to tell her the sheriff's department had found nothing of significance in their investigation of the site, and they were free to make their own visit. She had rushed to her apartment over her lunch hour and grabbed a change of clothes and a daypack. At the end of the day, she changed out of her dress and heels into jeans and hiking boots in the ladies' room at the office minutes before Ryker arrived. "I didn't think my car would make it up Stoney Gulch Road."

"It wouldn't," Harper said. "We barely got up it in the Beast—that's what we call the search and rescue vehicle. It has four-wheel drive and can go a lot of places regular cars can't go, but that road is really narrow. I was glad I was sitting in the back and couldn't see everything we had to navigate."

"Feel free to close your eyes on the way up," he said.

"I didn't used to be so nervous on those Jeep roads," she said. "But I've attended a few accidents now and heard enough stories about others that I know all the ways people get into trouble when they're just trying to have fun."

"How did you get involved with search and rescue?" he asked as they headed up the highway leading from town.

"I was living in Ohio and the company I worked for folded and I was out of a job. I was having a hard time finding a new one and my dad told me Taylor Geographic was looking for someone. I didn't want to have to depend on my parents for help, but I was getting desperate, so I interviewed for the job and was hired. I lived with my folks for six weeks until I got my own place, but in those six weeks I was restless and looking for excuses to get out of the house." She shook her head. "It's silly, I guess. But being back home, in the room I had since I was a little girl, unemployed and newly divorced—I felt like such a failure."

"I felt the same way when I moved back home with Charlotte," he said. "I needed help with her, but I felt like I was right back where I started. I'm starting to get over that. It would help if I had my own place, but you know what housing is like around here, and being in the same house with Mom and Dad really works better with Charlotte. Anyway, I didn't mean to interrupt. Tell me about search and rescue."

"The second week I was back I ran into Hannah Richards and she told me about volunteering with search and rescue and it sounded so, well, *important*. Not the sort of thing someone who was a failure would do. She invited me to an orientation class for new recruits and I liked what I heard. And it turns out, I'm pretty good at it. I don't panic and I'm good at pitching in to do whatever needs doing. And I really like helping others."

"That's great. It really is important work."

She angled toward him. "Now I want to know how you ended up as a cop."

"Don't sound so shocked. It's not like I was a juvenile delinquent."

"I would have thought after the way you were treated

following Aiden's disappearance, you wouldn't be the biggest fan of law enforcement."

"I mainly wanted to avoid cops," he said. "I got a degree in computer science but had a hard time finding a job after I graduated. Then my girlfriend, Kim, got pregnant and I had to find a way to support a family. The Fort Collins Police Department had a hiring fair and I picked up an application. The officer I talked to seemed like a good guy. The job had decent pay and benefits, so I decided to apply. I was shocked when they called to tell me to report to the police officer training academy." He frowned. "Kim laughed when I told her. She said she didn't know if she could stand being married to a cop."

"So you took the job because you didn't see another choice," she said.

"I thought so, but I ended up really liking the work." He slowed, searching for the turnoff to Stoney Gulch Road. "A patrol officer works alone much of the time. I had to learn to think on my feet, to act in a way that protected myself but also protected those around me. And even though I was working alone, I was part of a team of good officers who banded together to keep people safe and to prevent or solve crimes. There's a lot of variety. A lot to learn, too. And the paperwork is a pain. But I guess, like you with search and rescue, I discovered I'm good at the job. And I like making a difference."

"I wouldn't have laughed at you," she said.

"I know." He had spent too much of his marriage to Kim comparing her to Harper, or at least the ideal of Harper that he carried around in his head.

"I didn't leave because of what happened with Aiden," she said. "Or at least, that was one of the reasons my parents sent me away, but I never believed you had anything to do with his kidnapping."

He glanced at her, then back at the road. "I wondered. My lawyer told me I would find out who my friends really were, and when you left and I didn't hear from you…"

"My parents didn't give me a choice. I tried to get in touch with you, but my parents took my phone away, and my aunt didn't give me access to a phone or computer."

"I hoped that was the case," he said. "But it's good to hear you say it, even after all this time."

"I hated that I couldn't be there for you. And I hated more that you didn't know how much I believed in you."

"You're here now. That means a lot."

He made the turnoff onto Stoney Gulch Road and they immediately began to climb. The farther up they traveled, the narrower and rougher the road became, until he had slowed to five miles an hour, inching the Jeep over or around rocks and through deep ruts. "How much farther do you think it is?" he asked Harper, trying to gauge how many hours of daylight they had left. He didn't relish coming back down this road in the dark.

"Not much farther," she said. "The road ends at the mine and there's a flat space where you can turn around and park."

Fifteen minutes later he spotted the gravel apron that marked the end of the road. He parked and they got out. "That path leads to the mine." Harper pointed to an obvious trail as she slipped on a daypack.

He grabbed his own pack, locked the Jeep and they set out, Harper in the lead. The place was typical of other mountain mines he had visited, gray and red rock scraped bare of all but the most stunted vegetation, piles of waste rock and gravel spread around, bits of dried-up timbers, scraps of rusting metal, and the occasional old can or bottle the only testaments to what had once been a source of hope for the people who dug the shafts and searched for precious metals. Despite the barren landscape, the vividly blue sky and expansive views leant a wild beauty to the scene.

"The shaft is over here." Harper picked her way through loose rock to a metal grate approximately three feet square. Looking through the metal mesh, he could just make out the rocky sides of a shaft that extended into darkness. "Somebody said it was probably an air shaft, not an actual mine entrance," Harper said.

"Gage Walker said the mine entrance is a few hundred yards from here, and it's covered with an iron gate with a big padlock," Ryker said. "He said it didn't look like it had been disturbed." He nudged the grate with his toe and it shifted. "Why would someone cut off this grate?"

"I don't know." She turned to look along the small ridge they stood upon. "I found the ribbon over here."

He followed her to what looked like another pile of rock. "The grate was there." She pointed to a spot. "And the ribbon was about here." She looked down at their feet.

Ryker knelt and studied the ground. He didn't know what he had hoped to find that his fellow deputies or Harper hadn't already noted. There were no footprints. No blond hairs caught in the rock, nothing else to indicate a person had ever been here.

He rose again. "That ribbon couldn't have gotten up here unless Charlotte was here," he said. "Kim and Mick must have been here."

"It's a pretty desolate place to try to live," Harper said. "Let's take a look around."

They followed a faint path away from the shaft, slightly downhill to the wooden frame and metal gate that marked the mine entrance. Peering inside, he could see a narrow hallway, not tall enough for him to walk upright, leading into the side of the hill. "Hello!" he shouted.

Only silence answered him. He examined the lock and his hand came away covered in orange rust. The lock, and the gate itself, looked as if they had been in place a long time.

They found a few old boards, some rusted cans and a no-trespassing sign full of bullet holes, but nothing to indicate Kim and Mick had spent any time here.

"There are a couple of other mines near here," Ryker said. "Let's see if we turn up anything there."

They walked back to the Jeep in silence. He tried to shrug off the heavy disappointment. It wasn't reasonable to expect to find anything where so many others had already looked. "I wonder," Harper said when they reached the vehicle. "Do you think Charlotte dropped that ribbon on purpose? As a clue, maybe?"

He stared. "What makes you think that?"

"You've read her stories, right? Little Red Riding Hood, leaving a trail of breadcrumbs in the woods?"

"I have. And we've gone hiking since she was a baby. I used to carry her in a pack on my back. I taught her to look for blazes on the trees to find the trail. We made a game of it and she loved spotting them before I did."

"You taught her a lot of useful skills she can use now," Harper said. "And she knows you're looking for her. I have no doubt of that."

"I hope she knows."

"You're a good dad," Harper said.

"I try. I read books and stuff, before she was born, but there's so much no one talks about. How the responsibility of having someone who depends on you totally is so heavy." He fit the key into the ignition but didn't start the Jeep. "I used to think about the baby you and I almost had. Would I have had any idea how to take care of him—or her—when I was so young?"

"She was a girl," Harper said.

An image of Charlotte as a newborn flashed into his mind. So tiny and fragile and utterly amazing. "I'm sorry I wasn't there for you," he said. "I should have—"

"Don't! Don't beat yourself up. We both did the best we could."

He started the Jeep. She was right. But that didn't really make him feel better.

He eased the Jeep back down Stoney Gulch Road to the highway, then turned off again a few miles farther on. The route here was not as rough, and led to a popular hiking trail. But before the trailhead was an unmarked turnout across bare rock to a claim that had been marked on the map as Sharp #8.

Long shadows stretched across the landscape by the time Ryker parked in front of what was left of the mine. "We can't spend much time here," he said. "But I'd like to look around."

"Sure." Harper turned in a half-circle, taking in the site, which had a few more trees than the Ida B Mine, stunted piñons bent by harsh winds and broken by heavy snow. A cabin formed of unchinked logs, silvered and hardened by a century or more of exposure to the elements, sat in the shadow of a hill, an orange-and-black no-trespassing sign affixed to the wall beside the opening for the door.

Ryker walked to the opening and peered in. The sharp, acrid tang of woodsmoke hit him. As his eyes adjusted to the dimness, he could just make out the remains of a campfire in the center of the room. "Someone has been here," he said as Harper moved up beside him.

He stepped over the threshold and pulled a small flashlight from his pocket and trained its beam on the fire ring. Someone had pulled a trio of stumps around a circle of rocks that formed the fire ring. He held his hand over the charred wood. It was cold. It could have been lit days or even weeks ago.

Harper moved slowly about the small room, examining the dried leaves, shells of piñon nuts, and other debris that littered the floor. She returned to Ryker's side with the wrapper from a stick of beef jerky and a crushed soda can. "I found these."

They were probably left by hikers who had stopped there for lunch, but he stuffed them in an evidence bag he had brought along just in case. He conducted his own survey of the little cabin, but found nothing.

When he and Harper stepped outside again, most of the daylight had faded. Ryker played the beam of the flashlight over the ground around the cabin and they walked as far as the mine opening, sealed by a metal gate. As they stood there, a trio of bats exited, and Harper jumped back with a squeak. "They startled me," she said, watching them flutter away.

"We'd better go," he said.

The Jeep bounced back down the narrow trail to the intersection of the Jeep road. He was preparing to turn when a vehicle sped past him, headed uphill at a reckless rate of speed. He braked hard to avoid being hit and stared after a white Jeep, its back end splattered with mud.

"There was a little girl in the back seat," Harper said. "A blonde. And a blonde woman in the passenger seat."

Ryker didn't hesitate, but turned to follow the other Jeep. The road quickly deteriorated, and they jounced over deep ruts and he jerked the wheel to avoid boulders that could have wrecked the vehicle. He gritted his teeth to keep them from slamming together at each jolt, and Harper clung to the dash with one hand and the strap hanging from the roof with the other. But no matter how fast he drove, the other Jeep was getting farther and farther away. He could barely make out the glow of its taillights in the distance.

They came to a section of road lined with three-foot boulders. He had to slow to a crawl to navigate through them. He could no longer see the other vehicle ahead. "I don't know how they're driving so fast," Harper said.

"They either know the road or they're being reckless," he said. "Probably a little of both."

"Where does this road go?"

"I think it ends at a trailhead, but I'm not sure. I've never driven it." Why hadn't he brought the maps with him? He had thought he could remember all he needed to know.

"If it ends, they'll have to stop and we can catch up with them then," she said.

They could, and what then? If the driver really was Mick, he was likely armed. Would Kim put Charlotte in danger? The thought made him cold all over, but it also made him keep driving. If the girl Harper had seen really was Charlotte, Ryker couldn't leave her with Kim and Mick.

He kept his speed down as the road climbed steadily. The moon rose, its light faint at first, then brighter. It painted the rocks in pewter shades. Some creature, dark and sleek, darted across the road in front of them and up into the rocks.

"There's the trailhead," Harper said.

A brown wooden sign listed the trails accessible from this parking area. A pit toilet sat at the far end of the lot, which was otherwise empty. "Where did they go?" Harper asked.

Ryker put the Jeep in Park, but didn't shut off the engine. He got out of the vehicle and turned to look in every direction. Was the other Jeep here, parked behind a boulder or an outcropping of rock? Moonlight drenched the landscape. Surely a white vehicle would stand out in all that light?

"I don't see anything," Harper said.

He walked to the edge of the parking lot. The ground dropped off sharply in a jagged cliff. No one had driven down there.

He moved to the trail. It was narrow, winding between boulders. No vehicle had passed this way, either.

He returned to the Jeep. "Let's go back the way we came," he said. "Maybe there's a turnoff we missed."

He found the turnoff a half mile back the way they had come. The narrow track was almost hidden by a rock outcrop, and was even rougher than the road they had traveled so far, carpeted with fist-size chunks of granite. Two hundred yards on, Ryker had to stop the car. "You wait here and I'll go ahead on foot," he said.

"Oh no you don't," she said. "The first rule of wilderness survival is 'don't separate from the group.' I'm coming with you."

He didn't argue, merely set out up the road, her walking behind. He had no trouble seeing the way in the moonlight, but he was also aware that they would be visible a long way before they approached wherever the Jeep had parked. They were taking a big risk, but the only alternative was leaving his daughter behind, and he couldn't do that.

"Look to your left," Harper whispered behind him. "There's something white behind those trees."

He slowly scanned to the left and spotted what she was talking about—a flash of something pale among the trees. "I've got to get closer to get a better look," he said. "But we need to pretend we haven't seen it, in case someone is watching."

"I'll follow you," she said.

He turned, and led the way back down the trail, as if they were returning to their Jeep. When they were out of sight of the clump of trees, he veered off into a boulder field. Trying to keep the largest rocks between him and the trees, he set an oblique, meandering path toward the spot.

They moved slowly, partly to avoid making noise and partly to keep from falling in the uneven terrain. He estimated it took the better part of an hour to circle around and come up on the other side of the trees. The pale object Harper had spotted was more visible now. It wasn't, as he had thought, the Jeep, but a tent. His heart beat faster as he realized he may have found what he was looking for—the place where Kim, Mick and—most important to him—Charlotte were staying.

"Wait here while I move closer," he whispered to Harper. "If anything happens to me, run back to the Jeep." He pressed the keys into her hand.

She nodded, eyes wide in the moonlight.

He crept forward, moving from bush to boulder, until he was on the edge of the clearing that contained the tent, a stack of firewood and a firepit lined with chunks of rock the same sandy red as the surrounding terrain. He paused, listening for any signs of movement inside the tent—the whisper of fabric as a body shifted in a sleeping bag, or the soft snoring of someone deep in slumber.

But the silence was absolute. It bothered him that he didn't know where the Jeep was. If they had followed the trail farther, maybe they would have found its parking place, but he would have felt better about approaching the tent and whoever was inside if he could have been sure of the vehicle's location.

He bent and scooped a handful of gravel from the ground at his feet, then straightened and hurled it toward the tent. It hit the side with a series of staccato patters.

No response. He repeated the gesture three times, waiting a full minute between each barrage, but no one stirred inside the tent. No one called out and no one emerged.

He took a step into the clearing, then another. He moved quickly after that, to the back of the tent. He drew out a knife and plunged it into the taut nylon fabric. The cut easily widened into an opening large enough for him to peer through.

The tent was a large cabin model, maybe eight feet square. Inside were three cots and several duffel bags, clothing spilling out of each. He played the beam of the flashlight over all of it, sorting out items suitable for a man, a woman and a little girl.

He stepped into the tent and went to the child's clothing. It was a smaller pile than the rest, only half a dozen items—shirts and pants and socks and underwear, all in Charlotte's favorite pink and purple. At the bottom of the pile was a pair of shoes. Pink tennis shoes with flowers stitched on the toes. The shoes Charlotte had been wearing the day she disappeared.

Chapter Nine

Harper waited in the dark for Ryker, focused on his silhouette moving around the campsite. What if whoever was in the tent pulled out a gun and shot him? What if it wasn't Kim and Mick at all, but someone else who didn't like someone creeping up on them in the middle of the night?

What if she was wrong and the little girl she thought she had glimpsed in the back of the white Jeep wasn't Charlotte at all? What if it was a little boy, or a dog, or a figment of her imagination, conjured up because she wanted so badly for Charlotte to be found?

But no, she had seen the girl. And she had definitely seen a blonde woman who could have been Kim. And the other vehicle had run away from them, as if wanting to escape.

She was sure she had never been anywhere so quiet. She sat on the ground behind a boulder the size of a compact car and the silence rang in her ears. She breathed in the aroma of sun-warmed rock and piñon and wondered what Ryker was doing right now.

The crunch of gravel set her heart to pounding, and she strained her eyes to see across the expanse of ground between here and the trees where the tent was staked. The moonlight washed everything into shades of gray and blurred the outlines like a monochrome impressionistic landscape.

Someone was coming. Someone tall and broad-shouldered, moving quickly and with confidence through the scattered rock. She relaxed and stood to meet Ryker as he drew near.

"They're gone," he said. "But they were here. I found Charlotte's shoes."

She wanted to cry out in frustration that they had been so close to the little girl, yet she had vanished again. "Where did they go?" she asked. "We were right behind them."

"We drove past this turnoff to the end of the road. They knew we were following them, so they probably waited until they were sure we were past and turned around and went back to the highway."

"Do you think they'll come back?" Harper asked.

"Probably not." He put his arm around her. "Come on. Let's go. As soon as we have a phone signal, I'll call the sheriff and let him know what I found. They can get someone up here to watch in case anyone returns. But my guess is they've moved on."

They trudged back to the Jeep, the walk seeming to take much longer now. Harper's feet dragged and her stomach growled. She wished she was home with her feet up, eating dinner and binging some mystery show on television, rather than being caught in the middle of a real-life mystery.

But then she focused on Ryker's broad back and felt guilty for those thoughts. When she left him, she could go back to her normal life, but he could never escape the reality that his daughter was missing.

They reached the Jeep and had to endure the slow, rough drive back to the county road, and another five miles on that road before they had a cell-phone signal. At last, Ryker pulled over at a scenic overlook and punched in a number. "Sheriff, this is Ryker. I've found where Kim and Mick were camping. They got away in a white Jeep. They covered the license plate with mud, so I couldn't read it. Charlotte is definitely with them. I found some clothes and a pair of her shoes at their camp."

He listened for a long moment, then gave directions to the camp. Then he hung up and turned to Harper. "If you want, you can call someone to pick you up. But I have to stay and take the sheriff and the crime-scene crew back to the campsite."

"I'll stay." Her stomach growled. "At least for a little while."

He leaned over the seat and pulled out a backpack. "I've got some protein bars and nuts in here."

"I've got a couple of apples."

They divided the food between them and ate. It wasn't the worst dinner she had ever had, and when she was done she was no longer hungry. In between bites, Ryker told her what he had seen at the campsite. "They had bought Charlotte some new clothes," he said. "And she had her own cot."

"So they're taking care of her."

"They're dragging her with them all over the mountains," he said.

She said nothing. Taking care of the child wasn't the same as doing what was best for her.

"The tent and all the camping equipment looked new," Ryker continued. "Which makes me wonder if they really planned this, or if it was a last-minute decision."

"If they didn't plan ahead, that could make it harder for them," she said.

"Harder for Charlotte, too."

"She knows you're looking for her."

"Does she? She's only four. What if they told her I wanted her to go with them?"

Harper didn't know what to say. He knew his daughter

better than she did. But she had been a little girl once, and he hadn't. "When I was Charlotte's age, I thought my father could do anything," she said. "He could climb mountains and fix cars and make pancakes and tell silly jokes, and he knew the names of the stars and the names of all our neighbors. If I had been lost or afraid or homesick, I would have believed he would come for me."

A vehicle approached and slowed. A black-and-white sheriff's department SUV pulled in behind the Jeep and stopped. Ryker switched on the Jeep's interior lights, then stepped out where he could be better seen. Harper lowered the window and waved. Sheriff Travis Walker got out of the SUV and moved toward the Jeep as a second sheriff's department vehicle turned in and parked. Seconds later, Gage Walker joined his brother and Ryker. "Three more deputies are on the way," the sheriff said. "Where is the campsite you saw?"

"I marked the mileage on our way out," Ryker said. "In three quarters of a mile, take a left onto the Jeep road that leads to a trailhead. Travel two point seven miles on that road. You'll see a big boulder on the left, and directly behind that boulder is a narrow dirt track. It's hard to see coming from this direction. That track ends at a clump of trees and in those trees is the campsite."

Travis looked past Ryker to Harper. If he was surprised to see her here, he gave no indication. "Did you see the camp, too?" he asked.

"I saw the trees and part of the tent, but I waited behind while Ryker went to investigate." She swallowed, suddenly nervous. "But I saw the white Jeep with Charlotte in the back seat, and Kim in the passenger seat."

"We'll need a statement from you later," Travis said. He returned his attention to Ryker. "Ride with me up to the camp so I can take a look. Then I'll bring you back here and the deputies will take over from there. You and Harper can come to the station tomorrow to give your statements."

Ryker turned to her. "I'm sorry you'll have to wait a little longer."

"It's okay." She took out her phone. "I've got a book on here I can read." She almost joked that she had been waiting for him for so many years, what was a few more minutes or hours? But she wasn't ready to admit that truth out loud. For so long she had told herself she was fine without Ryker in her life.

Until he was with her, and she realized she wasn't.

WHEN RYKER FINALLY returned home, he spent another restless night, anxious to know what evidence the deputies had found at the camp. Travis had ordered him not to return to the scene after he took Harper back to her place, so he had no choice but to go home and pretend nothing had happened. He was apparently a lousy actor, because his mother asked him what had happened to make him so agitated. He ended up telling her and his dad the whole story, meaning all three of them had slept little that night.

The next morning, he showered, shaved and put on his uniform, as he had been doing all week. Though he arrived at the sheriff's office before first shift began, Travis was already there. "What happened last night after I left?" Ryker asked.

"We took everything inside the tent for evidence," Travis said. "We left the tent in place and Declan is watching to see if they come back for their belongings. Wes will take over at nine."

"I can take a shift watching the tent," Ryker said.

"No you cannot. You're too involved already."

"You don't think I can remain professional?" Ryker asked.

"I'm not sure I could, if my kid was involved." Travis's tone softened. "I can tell by looking at you you've hardly slept since Charlotte disappeared. You're not in any shape to be out there in the field. I'm fine with you being here. I get it, you don't want to sit at home doing nothing. But you have to let the rest of us handle this."

He knew the sheriff was right. He also knew that Travis could have ordered him to go home and wait for them to call, and he appreciated that he hadn't done so. "All right," he said. "Thanks."

He returned to the conference room and the maps laid out on the table. He called up the aerial views of the terrain around the trailhead where they had turned around the night before, and found the little clearing where the tent had been. There was nothing there when these photos had been taken over a year ago, but he would have expected that. He looked through other photos and studied other maps, but his heart wasn't in the work anymore. Now that he knew Kim and Mick and Charlotte were close to Eagle Mountain, he wanted to be out there actively hunting them, not sitting here, helpless.

At noon Adelaide knocked on the door, then entered the room. She set a brown paper bag in front of him. "I made you a sandwich," she said. "I know you probably don't feel like eating, but think of it as something to do."

She left before he could even say *thank you*.

The sandwich was good, and she had included an apple and cookies she had probably made herself. He was reminded of the lunches his mother had packed for him when he was a child. The lunches she packed now for Charlotte.

As if summoned by the memory, he thought he heard his mother's voice down the hall. "I need to see Ryker. Please, where is he?"

"Mom?" He went to the door and was startled to see Wanda hurrying toward him, an envelope clutched in her hand. Gage followed her. She shoved the envelope at Ryker, her hands visibly shaking. "I went home at lunch and this was in the mailbox."

He took the letter, handling it by the corners, though it was already wrinkled where she had clutched it so tightly in her hand. It was addressed to him in a loopy cursive writing, with no return address. His stomach dropped. "It's from Kim," he said.

"I recognized her writing," Wanda said. "I remembered it from the wedding invitation she sent."

Gage inserted himself between them. He had slipped on a pair of latex gloves. "Let me open it," he said.

Ryker let Gage take the letter, and he and Wanda followed the sergeant into the conference room, where Gage shoved aside the stack of maps and dropped the envelope onto the flat surface. He teased open the flap of the envelope with a penknife and carefully removed the single folded sheet of notepaper inside. Ryker stared at the words Kim had written, confused.

Dear Ryker,
Charlotte is my daughter and you have no right to keep her from me. We're going to take good care of her. You need to stop looking for us. Mick will be a good father and he'll do whatever it takes to protect her, so don't mess with us.
Kim

Gage flipped over the envelope and examined it. "The postmark is Green River, Utah," he said.

"We know they're not in Utah," Ryker said. "They were here, just outside of Eagle Mountain last night."

"Are you sure? How good a look did you get at them?"

"I never saw them," he admitted. "I saw the backs of the heads of two people in a white Jeep, driving in front of me. But Harper saw them. She said she was sure there was a little girl who looked like Charlotte in the back seat of the Jeep, and a woman who looked like Kim in the front passenger seat. And Charlotte's clothes were in that tent."

"You said the clothes were new," Gage said. "That Kim probably bought them for Charlotte. Maybe they belonged to some other little girl."

"The shoes were Charlotte's. They were the pink ones with flowers on the toes that she was wearing when they kidnapped her."

Gage's expression was pained. "We checked and those shoes are really common. They're sold in discount stores all over Colorado."

"Sergeant, don't you think it would be an amazing co-incidence that a little girl who wore the same size clothing as my granddaughter, who owned the same shoes she was known to be wearing when she disappeared, who even fa-vored the same colors as her, was at that remote camp in the mountains? Especially when Harper Stanick is sure she saw Charlotte in that car."

"Coincidences happen." Gage rubbed his jaw. "I'm not saying you're not right about your ex and her boyfriend being here last night. But if that's the case, who sent this letter from Utah?"

"Green River is less than three hours from here," Ryker said. "They could have driven there to mail the letter, then come back. They've probably seen the news reports about the FBI looking for them in Utah and figured this was a good way to keep them on the wrong track."

"And you're sure this is Kim's handwriting?" Gage asked.

"Yes," they both answered at once.

"I'll need to show this to the FBI," Gage said. "They're going to say it supports their theory."

"You'll give the information about the camp I found, too," Ryker said.

"I will. But they might insist on taking over the investigation."

"I don't care who's in charge, I just want somebody to find Charlotte," Wanda said.

Gage nodded. "That's what we all want." He took out an evidence bag and eased the letter inside, then put the envelope in a second bag. "Let us know if you get any more letters. And we'll contact the post office in Green River and see if they know anything about who mailed the letter, though likely it was dropped in a mailbox somewhere."

He left the room and Wanda dropped into a chair. "I can't stand this," she said.

Ryker rested a hand on her shoulder, but said nothing. She looked up at him, eyes red, her mascara running. "When you were a teenager and you told us Harper was pregnant, I was so upset. Not only were you too young to be a father, I thought I was too young to be a grandmother. But over the next few weeks, I grew used to the idea, and I even felt a little excited. Then Harper left and we didn't know where she was, and later we found out she had lost the baby…" She shook her head. "What I'm trying to say is that by the time you told us Kim was pregnant, I was in a completely different place. I was over the moon, and I hated that the two of you didn't live closer so I could be more involved. I don't know if I've ever been as happy as I was the first time I held Charlotte. As much as I love you and your sister, I was even happier about Charlotte. You know I was never that wild about Kim, but I was determined to love her because she gave me that beautiful granddaughter." She covered his hand with her own. "Having the two of you here, living in the house with us, has been the best thing I could have imagined. I know one day you'll probably move away. I hope you find someone who can make you happy and be the mother Charlotte needs." She gave a hiccupy laugh. "I have so many dreams. But you know that now, don't you? It's what parents do."

"I know," he said. He had found himself imagining what Charlotte might be as she grew up, what great things she might accomplish.

"But right now all I want is for her to be safe and home again with us," Wanda said.

"We're going to find her," Ryker said. "We're going to bring her home."

Chapter Ten

Harper and Devlin were comparing notes about the resort project on Wednesday when Jacy, the receptionist, came in looking flustered. She hurried to Harper. "There are two men here who say they need to talk to you." She lowered her voice to a whisper. "They showed me identification that says they're with the FBI."

Devlin's eyes widened. "What have you done to have the FBI after you?" he asked.

Jacy scowled at him. "I don't think that's very funny. I put them in the client interview room next to Patterson's office," she said.

Harper followed her to the comfortably furnished lounge where clients could review the work the company had done for them or discuss new projects. "Are you Harper Stanick?" a craggy-faced man with very black hair and olive skin asked.

"Yes."

"Special Agent Cussler and Special Agent Reno."

"May I see some identification?"

They each displayed badges and ID. "Sit down." Cussler motioned to the sofa. "We have a few questions to ask you."

She sat, perched on the very edge of the sofa, in danger of sliding back on the marshmallow-soft cushions.

"We've received a report from the local sheriff's department about an incident in which you reported seeing Charlotte Vernon and her suspected kidnappers in a car near here," Cussler said.

"That's right."

"Could you describe the incident again for us, please," Agent Reno said. He smiled, while Agent Cussler's expression remained stern.

Harper described that evening again, until the point where Sheriff Walker and his deputies arrived. "Are you sure you saw Charlotte Vernon in that car?" Cussler asked.

"I saw a child with long blond hair who looked to be about Charlotte's age. And the woman in the front seat definitely looked like Kim Vernon."

"You know Kim Vernon?"

"I met her the night before Charlotte disappeared and spoke to her briefly. She's a very striking woman, not one I would forget."

"What about Charlotte Vernon? How well do you know her?"

"I met her that same night. She asked for my help washing her hands in the ladies' room. She is a very friendly, beautiful child."

"What is your relationship with Ryker Vernon?" Cussler asked.

The shift in the conversation startled her. "Ryker and I are friends."

"You're friends, but you only met his daughter for the first time the night before she disappeared?" Reno posed this question.

"I've only recently returned to town after living out of state," she said, determined to remain composed despite their firing questions at her. "Ryker and I ran into each other the day before—Tuesday. He was working an accident scene and I was part of the search and rescue crew called to help rescue the accident victims. Before then, we hadn't spoken in more than seven years."

"But you knew each other before?" Reno asked.

"Yes. We went to school together."

"So the two of you met at this accident and you saw him again the next night at Mo's Pub, is that the name of the place?" Cussler took over again.

"Yes. I was there with some friends and he was there with his daughter."

"So you didn't arrange to meet?" Cussler asked.

"No."

"You didn't think it was strange, seeing him again so soon?" Reno again.

"This is a very small town. It's not unusual to see people you know."

"Back to Monday afternoon," Cussler said. "This car drove past and you recognized Charlotte and Kim. Where was this exactly?"

"We were stopped at the end of a dirt road in the mountains, about to turn left onto another dirt road that leads back to the highway. We hadn't seen any other traffic all afternoon, but Ryker had to stop to wait for this car to go past."

"What kind of car?" Cussler asked.

"A white Jeep. I don't know what model. I don't know cars."

"How fast would you estimate it was going?" Cussler asked.

"Fast for travel on those rough roads, but not that fast overall. Maybe twenty-five miles an hour."

"What time of day was this?"

"About seven o'clock."

"Wasn't it too dark to see much in the car?" Reno spoke up again.

"It passed very close by. And there was plenty of light to see. It was dusk, not yet dark."

"Is it possible you saw someone else?" Reno asked. "Or imagined the child?"

"No. Why don't you believe me?"

Cussler moved closer. He was a tall man, looming over her. "Maybe you said you saw Charlotte because you wanted Ryker to like you better."

"I wanted… What are you talking about?"

"You say Ryker Vernon is your friend," Cussler said. "Why were you with him that afternoon?"

"I already told you I volunteer with search and rescue. While on a rescue call, I found a pink hair ribbon that belonged to his daughter. He wanted me to show him the place where I found the ribbon."

"Did you go with him to the campsite?" Cussler asked.

"Yes."

"Did you see the items he found in the tent—the child's clothing and shoes?"

"No. I waited outside the camp while he went to investigate."

"So you don't know if the items were there or if he put them there," Cussler said.

"Why would he put them there? And he wasn't carrying anything when he went up to the camp."

"He had a backpack, didn't he?"

"Yes, but it didn't have his daughter's clothing in it."

"How do you know?" Reno asked. "Did you look inside?"

She glared at both men. Before, she had been annoyed. Now she was getting angry. "Are you accusing Ryker of something?"

"We're not accusing anyone. But we have to consider all possibilities. What was his relationship with his ex-wife?"

"I don't think they had a relationship. He hadn't seen her since they divorced three years ago."

"You knew that or he told you that?" Cussler asked.

"He told me that but I've never known Ryker to lie."

"He didn't move to Eagle Mountain to get away from her?"

"He moved to Eagle Mountain so that his parents could help him care for his daughter. Why are you asking me all these questions about Ryker?"

"Why are you so upset?"

"I'm upset because a little girl is missing and you don't seem to be doing anything to find her."

Cussler stepped back. "That's all the questions we have for now. We may want to talk to you again. You can go now."

She was shaking as she walked out of the room and decided that instead of going back to her desk, she needed to get some fresh air and try to calm down. She crossed the street and walked two blocks to the park. The day was sunny and mild, a soft breeze stirring the broad leaves of the cottonwoods that towered over the park. A group of toddlers swarmed the playground in one corner, and a man played fetch with his dog on the grassy stretch in front of the stage where there were sometimes concerts in the summer.

She hadn't walked far before she saw a familiar figure ahead. "Ryker!" she called, and jogged to catch up with him.

He stopped and waited for her, hands in the pockets of his khaki uniform pants. "What are you doing here this time of day?" he asked.

"I needed some fresh air."

"Me too." A shriek went up from the playground and they

both looked over as a little boy slid down the slide, laughing all the way. "I never really noticed how many children are around, everywhere," he said.

"The FBI came to my office to interview me," she blurted. "They were horrible."

He stopped. "What did they do?"

"They practically accused you of having something to do with Charlotte's disappearance. They suggested you planted her clothing in that tent."

The lines around his mouth and eyes tightened. "I guess I shouldn't be surprised," he said. "They probably read about Aiden's case and the accusations against me."

"I told them you didn't have anything to do with Charlotte's disappearance."

They started walking again in silence. "I'm sorry I got you all tied up in this," he said after a moment.

"I'm not. I want to help."

"It helps just being with you. It was always like that, from when we first met."

"I was a little nervous about you at first." She smiled, remembering that first date. He took her to the local drive-in, having borrowed his father's car for the evening. "I didn't think you'd want to mess your hair up on a motorcycle," he had told her, and she had been both touched and disappointed. She had liked the idea of pressing up close to him, hanging on for dear life on the back of his motorcycle.

"Why were you nervous?" he asked.

She laughed. "Are you kidding? You were the cutest guy in our class. And you had that bad boy reputation."

"I thought you were the prettiest girl." He took her hand. "I still think you are."

She squeezed his hand, afraid to speak and break this spell. Then her phone buzzed. She sighed. "I'd better check that text," she said, and disengaged her hand from his. "It might be search and rescue."

It wasn't search and rescue, but Devlin. You okay?

I'm good, she replied. *I just had to get some fresh air.*

Good...bring me a latte when you come back?

She laughed, then showed the screen to Ryker. "I'd better get back to work," she said. "But I'm feeling better now."

"Me too."

She set off across the park toward her office, but at the street she stopped and looked back. He was still there, watching her. She waved and he lifted his hand in return. Of all the awful circumstances in which to fall in love with a guy, this had to be the worst, but then, she had always had a terrible sense of timing, from getting pregnant at seventeen to marrying a man she had known all of six weeks, to having to move back in with her parents at twenty-four.

What if Charlotte was never found? Or she was found and needed all of her father's attention to recover from her ordeal? Harper didn't see where she could fit in that scenario.

"Be careful," she whispered. She didn't want history to repeat itself. She had had more than enough of being hurt by Ryker Vernon.

RYKER WASN'T SURPRISED to find agents Reno and Cussler waiting to interview him when he returned to the sheriff's department after talking with Harper. "We have some questions about your alleged sighting of Kim Vernon and Mick Davis," said Cussler when the three of them were alone in one of the interview rooms. He was the older of the two agents and had the demeanor of someone in charge.

"All right." He reminded himself these men had the same goal he did—to find Charlotte and bring her home safely.

Cussler pulled out a chair and sat, while Reno stationed himself by the door. "How good a look did you get at the people in that Jeep you followed?" he asked.

"Not a very good look," he admitted. "The woman with me—Harper Stanick, I believe you've already spoken to her—told me she saw a child with long blond hair and a woman who looked like Kim in the vehicle."

Cussler's right eye twitched at the mention of Harper, or maybe it was the idea that Ryker already knew the feds had interviewed her, but he let the moment pass. "So it might not have been your daughter and your ex-wife in that car," he said. "It might have been two ordinary tourists."

"Except that we tracked them to a campsite with a tent that contained items I know belonged to my daughter."

"How do you know the clothing belonged to your daughter?" Cussler asked, his gaze drilling into Ryker, as if daring him to lie.

"I know my daughter's clothing."

"Do you?" Reno spoke for the first time. "I don't know mine. Except she has a lot of it."

"You probably have a wife to dress her," Ryker said. "I don't."

"You have a mother, though," Cussler said. "Isn't that why you moved here—so your mother could take care of your daughter?"

"I moved here so my parents could *help* care for my daughter. Especially when I have to be away at work. That doesn't mean I'm not the person primarily responsible for her." He leaned forward, his voice harder. "It's not a burden. I like spending time with her." If either of these men took this as a dig against their own parenting styles, so be it.

"Tell me more about the letter you received from your ex-wife," Cussler said.

Abrupt change of subject. A classic interviewing technique, designed to throw the suspect off guard. Was that how they saw him—as a suspect in his own daughter's abduction? "It was delivered to my parents' home yesterday," he said. "My mother found it and brought it to me here, at the sheriff's department."

"You recognized the handwriting?" Cussler asked.

"Yes. The handwriting looks how I remember Kim's. Though I haven't seen anything she's written in three years."

"The letter was postmarked from Utah," Cussler said.

"Yes. About a three-hour drive from here."

"So you think she drove all the way to Utah to mail a letter, then returned here?"

"Why not? She's probably heard the news reports that you guys think she and Mick and Charlotte are in Utah."

No eye twitch this time, but he gave Ryker a hard stare. "We'll be investigating this thoroughly."

"Did you check the items from the tent for fingerprints?" Ryker asked. "I know Mick's are on file."

"We know how to do our job, Deputy."

Ryker nodded. He wanted to believe this, but part of him couldn't help insisting that no one would work as hard to find Charlotte as he would.

"Tell us about Aiden Phillips," Cussler said.

Ryker had expected this, but the words still sent a chill through him. "Aiden was my cousin. I was babysitting him when he was taken from his room. His body was found two days later. I didn't have anything to do with his murder. I was cleared as a suspect."

"Because a neighbor provided a statement that the motorcycle you rode never left the front of the house the night Aiden disappeared," Reno said. "And you didn't have access to another vehicle."

"And my DNA wasn't a match for that found on Aiden's body."

Reno looked away. Cussler shifted, the chair creaking beneath his weight. They would have known the facts in Aiden's case before they brought it up. They were purposely trying to unsettle him. "You said you haven't spoken to your ex-wife in three years," Reno said. "She had no contact with you or with your daughter in that time?"

"No."

"Why do you think she came to Eagle Mountain now? Why take your daughter?"

He had lain awake nights thinking about this question. "I don't know," Ryker said. "But when Kim left she said that once she and Mick were 'settled' she would come back for Charlotte."

"What was your response to that?" Reno asked.

"I didn't say anything," he said. "I intended to ask for sole custody of Charlotte—I didn't want a felon like Mick Davis to have anything to do with her. But I was also hoping Kim and I could work out some sort of visitation arrangement so that Charlotte could still see her mother."

"That seems very generous, seeing she abandoned you both," Cussler said.

"I would have been fine with never seeing her again," Ryker said. "But I had divorced friends who used their children to get back at their exes. It was ugly and I'm convinced it hurt the children. I had other friends who worked things out amicably and I saw how much better that was for the children. I wanted to do what was best for Charlotte."

"But Kim never took you up on the offer of visitation?" Cussler asked.

"She never contacted me again," he said. "I had to hire

a private detective to track her down to deliver the divorce papers, and even then she didn't ask about Charlotte."

"Did that surprise you?" Cussler asked.

"Yes and no. For all her faults, I thought she was a good mother. But she was also…unpredictable. And once she and Mick started seeing each other, it was like she was obsessed. She didn't want to have anything to do with anyone but him."

"Do you believe he manipulated her?" Cussler asked. "Do you think he's behind the abduction?"

"I don't know. I probably haven't spoken ten words to him in my life. Though I can't say he ever showed any particular interest in Charlotte before. And Kim told me once that he didn't want children. I always believed that was why she hadn't tried to be involved with Charlotte's life."

"I wonder what changed," Reno said.

"I don't know." Ryker looked at the younger agent. "You probably know more about Mick than I do. I've read his rap sheet, but that's it. Is there something I should know?"

The look that passed between the two agents sent an icy surge up Ryker's spine. "What?" He leaned forward. "What aren't you telling me?"

"You don't need to be concerned," Cussler said, but while he was probably practiced at deceiving suspects, Ryker immediately knew he was lying.

"You need to tell me," Ryker said, barely managing to keep his voice even. "We're talking about my daughter."

Cussler wouldn't meet his gaze. He pushed back his chair and stood. "You're free to go now. We'll be in touch if we need anything else."

Ryker stood also, hands in fists at his sides. He wanted to grab the man across from him and shake him—to force him to reveal whatever he knew about Mick Davis. But that wouldn't get him anywhere, except perhaps arrested.

He left the room and stood in the hallway for a long moment, trying to slow his breathing and calm his racing heart. He tried to think of who might help him. Sheriff Walker had been sympathetic—a man with two young children of his own. But the sheriff was also a man who played by the rules. He had taken over a department that had a history of scandal and made sure there was nothing like that associated with his watch.

He headed for the office across the hall from the sheriff's. Gage Walker looked up from his desk. "Finished with the feds?" he asked.

Ryker stepped inside and closed the door. "I need a favor," he said.

"Let's hear it."

"The feds know something about Mick Davis that they won't tell me. I think maybe something to do with his history with children, a crime involving a child, something like that. They know I can find anything on his rap sheet, but maybe he's a suspect in some crime involving a child—something I can't uncover. They didn't come right out and say it, but they implied that he might be the one behind Charlotte's kidnapping, not Kim."

"And you want me to see what I can find out," Gage said.

"Yes."

"If it's not good, it's only going to make you feel worse," Gage said. "It's not going to make him easier to find."

"No. But my daughter is with him. I need to know."

Gage looked as if he wanted to dispute this. "If it was your daughter, wouldn't you want to know?" Ryker asked.

Gage blew out a breath. "Yeah." He looked at his computer. "I'll do some digging, let you know what I find."

"One more thing." Ryker didn't wait for Gage to answer, but pushed forward. "I want to see the file on Aiden Phillips's disappearance."

"Do you think Mick Davis had something to do with that?"

"No. But I want to see what evidence investigators collected at the time. Maybe I'll spot something they overlooked, or a new lead to follow."

"You were a suspect in that case."

"But I was cleared. My DNA wasn't a match."

"Do you really think you'll find anything?" Gage asked.

"Probably not. But I want to try. Even though my DNA wasn't a match, there are still people who believe I had something to do with Aiden's death. Those people aren't going to be satisfied until someone else is proven guilty." At Gage's doubtful look, he added, "I'm officially on leave and I can't drive around searching for Charlotte twenty-four hours a day. Going over Aiden's case will give me something else to focus on."

"I'll have to dig it up out of the archives," Gage said.

Ryker stood. "Thanks. I'm going to go home now. You can contact me there."

"Just one thing," Gage said. "Whatever I find out about Davis, you have to promise me you won't do anything rash. It won't help Charlotte and it will only hurt you."

Ryker nodded. His head knew this was true. His heart, on the other hand, wasn't so sure. If Mick or anyone else hurt Charlotte, he didn't know what he might do. He was her father. His job was to protect her. If he couldn't do that, did anything else really matter?

Chapter Eleven

Seven years ago.

Ryker hesitated when he stepped out of his house, a deputy on either side. He had known a crowd had gathered outside his parents' home, but he hadn't been prepared for the number of people who suddenly crowded around him, or their animosity. Some shouted his name as the deputies hurried him toward the black-and-white cruiser waiting at the curb, while others yelled accusations and questions. "What did you do to Aiden?"

"Where is Aiden?" Others carried homemade signs with words like *Murderer!* or *Confess!* The sight shook him.

His father and the lawyer, Mr. Shay, walked behind him. His mother had stayed behind, barely keeping it together.

"Don't look," Shay said when Ryker started to turn his head toward the crowd.

One deputy put a hand on top of Ryker's head and pushed down, guiding him into the back seat of the cop car. They hadn't cuffed him. "You're not under arrest," one deputy had said, but they hadn't said coming to the station and answering more questions was optional, either.

At the sheriff's department, more people had gathered. Reporters, too. They pushed forward with microphones, cameras flashing, and shouted more questions—at him, at his father and at the deputies. No one said anything, their expressions stony.

Except Ryker. Later, when the pictures ran in the paper and on television, everyone could see how frightened he was. He was eighteen, but he looked younger.

They led him to the same room where they had questioned him before. His lawyer sat beside him. Ryker retold the story of everything that had happened that night, just as he had before.

"Tell us what you did with Aiden," the sheriff demanded. "Tell us where he is."

"I don't know where he is," Ryker answered. "I didn't do anything to him."

The sheriff, a craggy-faced man with a gray buzz cut who smelled of cigarette smoke, stalked back and forth in front of Ryker. "We know you killed him," he growled. "When we find his body, we're going to find the evidence that you did this."

A knock on the door interrupted them. Urgent whispering, then the sheriff and the two deputies left. Ryker looked at Shay. "They don't believe me," he said. "I would never hurt Aiden. He's a great kid."

Shay squeezed his hand. "I know this is hard," he said. "Just hang in there. They're trying to frighten you. They don't have any evidence."

The door opened and the sheriff returned. "We found Aiden," he said.

Hope flared in Ryker's chest. "Is he alive?"

"You know he isn't. We found his body where you left him. You should make it easy on yourself and tell us what happened right now. We're going to get DNA evidence from the scene. It's going to be a match. Then it's going to be all over for you."

"My client doesn't have anything more to say," Shay said. "He's already told you everything he knows."

The sheriff's face grew redder. He shook his head and left the room. Shay stood. "Come on, Ryker. Let's get you home."

Ryker glanced at the deputies. One was looking at the wall, but the other glared at him. *He really thinks I'm a murderer*, he thought.

Shay put a hand on his arm and Ryker stood and followed him out of the room. No one tried to stop them.

Ryker's dad joined them. He hugged Ryker. "They found Aiden," Steve said.

"I know." Ryker tried to swallow tears, but the knot in his throat wouldn't go down. His voice broke. "They said he's dead."

Steve nodded. Tears streamed down his face and seeing that made Ryker cry, too. Shay led them outside to the car. Inside, away from the reporters and the shouting people, Ryker pulled himself together. "What's going to happen now?" he asked.

"We'll wait for the DNA to come back," Shay said. "That will point to Aiden's real killer."

"Who would want to hurt him?" Ryker asked. "He was a great kid. I thought that night—I just found out my girlfriend is pregnant. I thought how great it would be to have a little boy like Aiden as my son."

Steve put an arm around Ryker's shoulders and pulled him close. Neither of them spoke—they didn't have to.

It took three weeks for the DNA results to come back. Three weeks of crowds in front of the house, shouting and waving their signs. Someone at the sheriff's department had told a reporter that Ryker was the only suspect. His mom had to take a leave of absence from her job after someone called her boss and berated her for keeping a murderer's mother on staff. Someone keyed his father's truck and wrote an obscenity on the window.

Aiden's parents asked the family not to attend Aiden's funeral, as it would be too upsetting.

When the sheriff called a press conference to announce the DNA found on Aiden's body was not a match to any known person, most of the attention died down. But Harper didn't return to town, and people still stared and whispered when Ryker walked by. As soon as he graduated, his parents suggested he visit his cousins in Texas. Ryker left, though he felt like he was running away. He left because it would be easier on his parents. He thought he would stay away until they found Aiden's killer. Except they never did.

HARPER HAD POURED her first cup of coffee Thursday morning when she received a text from search and rescue. All available volunteers report to Ruby Falls to search for missing child. Her breath caught as an eerie sensation of déjà vu swept over her. Another missing child? Or had Charlotte been spotted in the Ruby Falls area, triggering this new search?

She finished dressing, then left a message for her boss that she had been called out on a search. As she headed for her car, she dialed Hannah Richards. "Who is the missing child?" she asked as soon as her friend answered the phone.

"I don't know any more than you do," Hannah said. "I guess we'll find out when we get there."

The summons had brought out the full contingent of SAR volunteers, veterans and trainees alike. Harper followed a line of familiar vehicles up Dixon Pass, toward a section of red rock cliffs that flanked the highway. The steep cliffs were prone to avalanches after heavy snows, but this time of year they were merely one more section of stunning scenery along the winding mountain road.

She parked behind Christine Mercer's blue RAV4 at a trailhead a few hundred feet from the falls, just behind a trio of yellow-and-black barriers that closed the road to traffic. Beyond the barriers, lights from several law enforcement SUVs, a wrecker, and an ambulance strobed off the cliff walls. A dark gray SUV was snugged up against the rocks, its front end smashed in, all four doors open. Paramedics were transferring someone to a litter as Harper joined the others around Captain Danny Irwin.

Danny hoisted his lanky frame atop a square of granite that had fallen from the cliffs years ago and now served to mark the edge of the narrow shoulder where some of the emergency vehicles were parked. He surveyed the gathered volunteers, who fell silent, waiting to learn the details of their mission.

"We're searching for a five-year-old boy, Noah," Danny said. "He and his parents were in that vehicle when someone ran them off the road and they crashed into the cliffs."

They all looked toward the smashed-up SUV. "His mother, the driver, sustained injuries in the crash and was trapped in the car. The father had some more minor injuries, but he says Noah was unhurt. Because the car was partially in the road, the father was concerned they might be hit from behind by another car, so he got Noah out and took him to about here and had him climb up in the rocks a little, where he'd be out of the way. Dad told Noah to stay put, then went to check on his injured wife. He called 911 and sheriff's deputies and paramedics responded. Deputy Ellis remembers seeing Noah waiting by the side of the road here when he arrived, but by the time firefighters began cutting up the SUV to allow access to his injured mom, he had disappeared."

A buzz of conversation rose from the volunteers, but died down again when Danny raised his hand. "Anna and her search dog, Jacquie, are on their way, but she was in Junction when the call went out, so we'll start without them. Noah is four feet tall, weighs forty-six pounds and has light brown hair and hazel eyes," he said. "He's wearing blue sweatpants and a green T-shirt and blue tennis shoes."

"He probably saw something that distracted him, he went to investigate, and he got lost," Carrie Stevens said. "That's the kind of thing my son would do."

Danny nodded. "I thought of that, too." Harper remembered that Carrie and Danny lived together, and she had two children from a previous relationship. "Pair up and spread out," he directed. "I want three teams on the three hiking trails that branch off from the trailhead where some of us parked. The rest of you, search both sides of the road. Climb up or down where you can, but be careful. Look for anything that's disturbed—rocks overturned, a child's footprint, anything he might have dropped. And be careful. Any questions?"

Caleb Garrison stuck up his hand. "You said someone ran them off the road? Do they know who?"

Deputy Shane Ellis had moved to stand beside Danny. "The dad described a white Jeep, traveling at a high rate of speed. It was northbound and came around the curve in the southbound lane. The mother had to swerve to avoid hitting it, skidded on the gravel and slammed into the cliff."

Harper winced. "I take it the Jeep didn't stop," Danny said.

Shane shook his head. "It didn't stop, and the dad doesn't remember any other cars passing by immediately after the accident. One man stopped after the dad called 911, but once he heard help was on the way, he continued on."

"Noah hasn't responded to his father's or the deputies' calls for him," Danny said. "He may have fallen, or he might simply be afraid of strangers. Keep those things in mind as you search. Good luck."

Harper teamed up with Christine and they began their search along the shoulder of the highway opposite the cliffs. The shoulder was only about a foot wide here, with no guardrails, and a steep drop-off into a deep canyon. Harper kept her eyes focused on the rough terrain below. "Would a little boy try to climb down those rocks?" she asked Christine. "It's so steep."

"Maybe," Christine said. "I mean, some kids are pretty fearless. Still…" Her voice trailed away as they looked down the long, steep slope. Harper didn't want to think about what could happen if Noah slipped on a loose rock, or lost his balance and went tumbling.

"I hope they find whoever was driving the car that ran them off the road and file charges," Christine said as they continued slowly along the shoulder. "The speed limit is twenty-five miles per hour in this section for a reason."

"There are a lot of white Jeeps around," Harper said. But even as she spoke, an image flashed into her mind of the white Jeep she and Ryker had followed on that mountain backroad—the one they were sure contained Kim, Mick and Charlotte. They had been driving much too fast, as well. Was it possible this was the same Jeep?

"Noah!" Christine cupped her hands around her mouth and shouted. The name echoed back at them, but they heard no reply.

They moved on to a rock outcrop that jutted from the shoulder, forming a small platform just big enough for a person to stand on. But currently, the platform was occupied by a yellow-bellied marmot. The furry rodent, as big as a house cat, was flattened on its belly in the sun. It sat up at their approach, but made no move to run away. "Seen a little boy around here?" Christine asked.

The marmot blinked, and let out a high-pitched squeak. Christine took a step toward it and it dove off the side of the platform and disappeared between the rocks below. Harper moved closer to see if she could spot where the marmot had gone, but another movement farther down the slope distracted her.

"Noah!" she shouted.

Christine hurried to her side. "What is it?" she asked. "Do you see something?"

"Down there, under that tree. Does it look like a person to you?" A small person, with blue sweatpants and tennis shoes, lying very still. "Noah!" she shouted again, unable to keep the frantic note from her voice.

Other volunteers gathered around them. Danny moved in, binoculars in hand. Harper held her breath, still staring at the figure far down the slope. Danny lowered the binoculars. "I think it's him," he said. "And I think I saw him move."

Everything happened very quickly after that. A team began rigging ropes to descend to the boy, while others gathered safety gear and first aid supplies. Tony and Danny consulted on the best way to bring up the boy, depending on his injuries. "I'll climb down to him," Ryan said.

"Let me go first," Sheri said. "He might be less afraid of a woman."

"You'll both go," Danny said. "It will take two of you to get him safely into the litter."

Sheri descended first, rappelling the last third of the way down what looked to Harper like a straight drop. Ryan followed and met her at the base of a small tree, which had apparently stopped Noah's fall.

"Let me through, please." A brown-haired man in his thirties, with a bandaged head and blood-splattered clothing, pushed between the volunteers. "I'm Noah's dad," he said. "Have you really found him?"

Danny put a hand on the man's arm, as if to hold him back. "Our volunteers are checking him out and figuring out how best to bring him up."

The man stared down at the scene below. Noah was hidden by Sheri and Ryan as they bent over his body. "Please tell me he's not dead," he whispered.

Danny's radio crackled. He turned to Harper, who was closest. "You stay with Mr. Ericson," he said. "Look after him." Which she took as code for *Don't let him do anything stupid*.

Danny walked away and Harper moved in next to Mr. Ericson and wondered if she should try to distract him. "You look like you were injured in the accident," she said. "Are you okay?"

"I'll be okay when my boy is safe." His eyes never wavered from the scene below.

Danny returned, looking less tense than before. "Sheri and Ryan say Noah is conscious and talking to them. He said he went over to look at a marmot and slipped and fell. They think he may have a broken arm, and he bumped his head, so that will have to be checked out. But he's lucid and his vital signs are good. They're going to stabilize the arm and get him into a helmet and secured in the litter and bring him up."

"Thank God." Mr. Ericson staggered and Danny and Harper steadied him on either side.

"Why don't you sit down," Danny said. "You can see

Noah as soon as they bring him up." He helped lower the man to the ground. "Stay with him," he said again to Harper.

She sat beside Mr. Ericson. "Noah will have a great story to tell for the rest of his life," she said. "About the time he slid off a mountain and got hauled up by search and rescue."

"His mom used to joke about putting a leash on him. He's such a live wire. Just so interested and curious about everything."

"He's going to be okay." She hoped that was true. Children were resilient, right? "How is your wife?" she asked.

"Shattered kneecap, sprained wrist and some cuts on her face from broken glass. She'll be okay." He glanced over his shoulder, but from this vantage point, they couldn't see the wreck. "The car is totaled, of course. Not that that matters. As long as my family is safe."

"I understand another car ran you off the road?"

"A white Jeep. It came flying around the curve in our lane, going way too fast. My wife had to swerve to avoid it. Next thing I know, we slammed into that wall. We weren't going very fast, but still." He shook his head.

"Did you get a look at the driver?"

"It was a man, but I couldn't tell you more than that. And there was a passenger. A woman, I think."

"Anyone else? Any children?"

"I don't know. It happened so fast."

A cheer went up and Harper and Mr. Ericson both stood in time to see Noah, cocooned in the litter, an orange safety helmet almost obscuring his face, start up the slope. Less than five minutes later, the litter slid onto the shoulder of the road. Mr. Ericson hurried to see his son. "Daddy!" Noah said, and squirmed.

Mr. Ericson knelt beside the litter. "Just be still," he said.

"You're going to get to ride in the ambulance. We'll go see your mom."

"Is Mama okay?"

"She's going to be just fine. She'll meet us at the hospital."

Paramedics moved in to take over and Harper turned away. She walked back down the road, toward the wreck site. A wrecker was hooking onto the SUV, leaving a trail of broken glass and metal behind. She looked down the road, trying to picture the scene Mr. Ericson had described, the white Jeep barreling toward them.

"He's lucky she steered toward the cliff and not the canyon."

Gage Walker joined Harper in watching the wrecker. "He said it was a white Jeep, with a man and a woman in the front seat," Harper said. "He didn't know if there was anyone else in the car."

"There are a lot of white Jeeps in the country," Gage said. "And there's nothing unusual about a couple in a car."

"Ryker and I saw Kim and Mick in a white Jeep with Charlotte," she said. "They were driving very fast for the roads we were on."

"We're looking for them," Gage said. "And we'll look for this vehicle too, but we don't have much to go on."

She looked up at him. "Do you believe that I saw Kim and Mick and Charlotte?"

"Yes."

"I'm not sure the FBI did."

"They're practiced at not revealing anything they're thinking," he said. "That doesn't mean they don't believe you. But it's a good idea to remain skeptical. Some people do lie."

"I know it was Kim and Charlotte I saw. I didn't get a good look at the driver, but I think it was a man, and we know Kim has been traveling with Mick."

"No one is giving up on finding them," Gage said. "A lot of people—law enforcement and regular citizens like you—are still looking."

"The FBI think they're in Utah."

"They're looking in Utah, but I think they're looking here, too. They talked to Ryker for a long time yesterday afternoon."

"He's a fellow law enforcement officer. Did they tell him anything? Do they have any leads?"

"I don't think so."

She looked around at Deputy Ellis and Jake Gwynn talking with Hannah and a couple of other search and rescue volunteers. "Where is Ryker now?" she asked.

"He went home. I think being at the sheriff's department, knowing we weren't getting anywhere with our search, was getting to be too hard on him."

"He's not going to feel any better sitting at home, missing her."

"No. But he can be with his parents. I think they need him now."

"This must be so horrible for them all."

"You should stop by and see them. They would probably appreciate it."

"You mean, like, take a casserole?" That was what people did in a crisis, wasn't it—take food?

"I doubt Ryker is interested in casseroles, but he might appreciate a friend to talk to."

Right. But nothing she said was going to make him feel better. Only getting Charlotte back would do that.

A RESERVE DEPUTY arrived at Ryker's house midmorning on Thursday with a box Ryker was required to sign for. Ryker took the box upstairs to the room he used as a home office and lifted the lid. Stacks of folders and envelopes, each labeled with a seven-digit case number, half-filled the space. This was supposedly everything related to Aiden Phillips's disappearance.

Ryker removed the contents and began flipping through them. Some photos of the open window and the ground beneath it, as well as Aiden's room, and his empty bed. Transcriptions of the interviews with Ryker, which he didn't bother to read. He also set aside the envelope labeled Body Photos.

He came to a sheaf of papers identified as an interview with Margery Kenner, and settled in to read. With the precision of the school teacher she had been for so many years, Mrs. Kenner described her interaction with Ryker immediately after he discovered Aiden was missing. "He was really upset. Frantic," she said.

"He didn't do anything to harm Aiden, I'm sure of it," she added. "I saw them playing ball earlier that evening. Ryker was good with him. Patient. He never left the house that night."

When pressed, she explained that Ryker's motorcycle was loud and he parked it in front of Aiden's house, directly across from her bedroom window. She hadn't slept well and had the window open. "I would have heard him if that motorcycle had moved an inch. And how is he going to carry a little boy on a motorcycle anyway? It's ridiculous."

He smiled, picturing Mrs. Kenner berating the deputy. When asked if she had seen anyone else near the Phillipses' house that night, she said, "Only one vehicle went down the street, a red Ford pickup." She said she thought the truck might belong to a local handyman, Gary Langley. He had repaired her porch the week before, so she remembered the truck, but she couldn't be sure it was his. He lived on the other side of town.

A chill shuddered through Ryker. Langley was the old man who had approached him outside the sheriff's department the night Charlotte was kidnapped. Even in a small town, it was an eerie coincidence.

He searched through the file to see if the sheriff's department had ever interviewed Langley. He found a brief mention of the man in a report: "Mr. Langley said he was not in the Phillipses' neighborhood that night, and in any case, he sold the truck a week prior, to a man in Texas."

Ryker frowned. He could find nothing in the files to show that anyone had followed up to verify the date of the sale of the vehicle, or any explanation of why it had been sold to someone out of state.

There was nothing else of interest, so he turned to his laptop and did a search for Gary Langley. He found a dozen references, none of which seemed related to the handyman.

The doorbell rang and Ryker tensed, and listened as his dad answered the door. "Harper! Come in! It's good to see you."

Ryker made it to the top of the stairs in time to see his father embrace Harper. His mother entered the picture and she too hugged Harper. "Come in and have some coffee. Or a soft drink or tea?" His mother took Harper's hand and pulled her toward the kitchen.

"Hello, Harper."

She stopped and looked up, and he felt the impact of her gaze like a physical touch. "Hello Ryker. I hope you don't mind me stopping by."

"Of course not." He hurried down the stairs to meet her.

"I can't stay long," Harper was telling his parents when

he joined them in the kitchen. "I just wanted to see how you were all doing. And talk to Ryker for a minute."

"We're all pretty miserable, as you can imagine." Wanda released Harper's hand. Steve moved to put his arm around her. "Ryker told us you saw Charlotte in that Jeep when you two were in the mountains. Did she look okay?"

"She looked fine. I mean, I only caught a glimpse of a girl with long blond hair in the back seat of the vehicle."

"Was she in a car seat?" Wanda asked. "We always make sure she's in her booster seat whenever we're in the car."

"I... I don't know." Harper sent Ryker a desperate look.

"Come on upstairs," Ryker said, and turned to lead the way.

Harper followed him. Behind them, he could hear his father softly talking to his mother, probably telling her to leave the two of them alone. He understood she was desperate for any positive news about Charlotte, but her obvious pain was tough to deal with, especially for someone as empathetic as Harper.

"You're not working today?" he asked when they reached the landing at the top of the stairs.

"I'm supposed to be. I got called out for search and rescue early this morning, so I'm late getting to the office. I just stopped by for a few minutes to tell you about the call."

He tensed. She hadn't stopped by just to shoot the breeze about a traffic accident or a lost hiker. "What was the call?"

"A missing little boy."

She must have read the horror on his face, because she rushed to add, "It's okay. He had just wandered away from his parents and slipped and fell. A tree stopped his fall and he probably broke his arm, but he's going to be fine."

"That's good." He never wanted to see his daughter hurt, but if she came away from this ordeal with nothing more than a scare and an arm that would soon mend, he would be relieved. "So what did you want to tell me?"

She glanced over her shoulder toward the bottom of the stairs. They could still hear the murmur of his parents' conversation. "Is there some place more private we can talk?" she asked.

"Come in here." He led her to the room he had set up as a home office, with a desk and computer. Her gaze immediately fixed on the smaller desk adjacent to his. "Charlotte likes to color or pretend to do schoolwork while I'm busy on the computer," he said. He had to force the words past a knot in his throat.

Harper faced him, her back to the desk. "The little boy belonged to a couple who were injured in a car accident. They were southbound near the Ruby Falls section of Highway 60 when a white Jeep came around the curve and crossed in their lane. The woman, who was driving, swerved to avoid a head-on collision and ended up slamming her SUV into the cliffs. Fortunately, they all should recover from their injuries."

"A white Jeep. Did they see who was driving?"

"They said a man was driving, with a woman passenger. They couldn't see into the back seat. It all happened very quickly. But I remembered how fast the Jeep we saw was going, despite the rough road."

He rubbed the back of his neck. "There are a lot of white Jeeps. It could be a coincidence."

"Or it could be Kim and Mick." She rested her hand on his shoulder. "Anyway, I thought you'd want to know. I wish I could do more to help."

He wanted to lean into her touch, to let someone else take part of the weight he was carrying. "You are helping," he said. He covered her hand with his own, holding her there, close to him. "I'm glad we're friends again. I've missed you."

"I've missed you, too."

"Do you think about her? Our daughter?" The little girl they might have had together had been on his mind lately, another lost child of his.

"I do," she said. "I wonder what she would look like. What she would be like."

"Yeah. Sometimes I wish things had worked out differently."

"Then you wouldn't have Charlotte."

"No." But he might have had two daughters. Who knew?

She moved away, breaking the tie between them. The physical one, anyway. Their past connected them, no matter what happened in the future. "I have to get back to work," she said.

"Thanks for stopping by."

"You know you can call me anytime. I mean it."

"I know." But was that the right thing to do—make her share in this sorrow, when she had already endured plenty of her own?

"I'll see myself out."

He stood there until he heard the front door close softly behind her. His phone rang and he answered it. "You need to get down here," Gage said, his voice clipped. Grim. "There's been a development."

Chapter Twelve

Gage refused to elaborate, only repeated that Ryker needed to come to the sheriff's department as soon as possible. He was waiting when Ryker arrived and pulled him into an empty conference room. "What's going on?" Ryker asked, searching Gage's expression for any clues, but finding none. "Have you found Charlotte? Is she okay?"

"We haven't found Charlotte," Gage said. "But Dwight is bringing in Kim. She flagged down a Jeep up past Galloway Basin. When the driver heard who she was he had sense enough to call 911."

A rush of adrenaline staggered Ryker. "Kim was by herself? Where are Charlotte and Mick?" He clenched his fists to keep from grabbing Gage by the shoulders and shaking the answers from him.

"We don't know anything else. Dwight is bringing her here for questioning. She didn't resist when he and Jamie arrived to arrest her. I wanted to tell you before someone in town spotted her and passed the word along to you. I didn't want you doing anything rash."

"What did you think I would do?" Ryker asked.

"I don't know. But in your shoes I would be pretty upset. Better to have you here. As soon as we know anything about Charlotte's whereabouts, I promise you will, too."

"Thanks for that."

Somewhere down the hall, a door opened and voices rose. Ryker turned toward the sound. "I want to see her," he said.

"Not until after we've questioned her."

Ryker knew this was the proper way to do things, and the best way to ensure that Kim's eventual prosecution stood up in court. But the idea of having to wait to find out where his daughter was ate at him. "I'll send someone in to wait with you," Gage said, and left the room.

Ryker paced. Gage had been so insistent that he come to the sheriff's department right away that he hadn't changed clothes. He was wearing jeans and a T-shirt, the clothing emphasizing his role here as just another civilian.

The door to the interview room opened and Jamie Douglas entered. The department's sole female deputy, Jamie was a tall, slender brunette with a reputation as a tough, smart cop. Like Ryker, she had grown up in Eagle Mountain. She was a few years older than Ryker, but he remembered her from school. "Hello, Ryker," she said. "Do you want a cup of coffee or anything?"

"No thanks. I'm wired enough without the caffeine."

Jamie sat, but he continued to pace. "Did you draw the short straw, having to babysit me?" he asked. "What does Gage think I'm going to do—run in there and attack Kim? He should know me better than that."

"I'm here to keep you company while you wait." She leaned back in the chair, deliberately casual. "We can talk about whatever you like, though I thought maybe you'd want to hear what happened when we arrested Kim."

He stopped, then dropped into the chair across from her. "Tell me," he said.

"We met the Jeep at the turnoff onto the county road," she said. "The driver pulled over and we asked him and

Kim to step out of the car. They both climbed out. Kim held up her hands and stood there, not resisting. She looked like she'd had a hard time of it, frankly."

"What do you mean?"

"Her clothes were filthy, she had scratches on her arms and her hair was a mess. I asked her about the scratches and she said Mick had pushed her out of the car and driven off."

"Where was Charlotte?"

"Kim said Charlotte was with Mick. She said she had run after the car, trying to get to Charlotte, but Mick just sped up. She fell, chasing him, and that was how she got so dirty and scratched up."

"Why did he throw her out of the car?"

"She said it was because she wanted to take Charlotte back to you. That made Mick mad, so he left her out there in the middle of nowhere. She said he had done it before— left her alone with nothing to punish her—but he always came back, usually after a few minutes, or sometimes after a few hours. She said she thought she had been there two hours or more when she saw the Jeep driver and decided to flag him down and ask for help."

"Where are Mick and Charlotte now?" Ryker said. That was the only question that really mattered.

"She said she doesn't know. They knew their tent was being watched, so they couldn't go back there. She had wanted to drop Charlotte off in town and leave with Mick, but he refused."

"Why would he refuse?" Ryker asked. "It's not like he was ever interested in Charlotte before. I always thought he was the main reason Kim stayed away."

"She didn't say. After we got her in the cruiser and gave her some water she didn't say much of anything at all, except to insist that she doesn't know where Mick or Charlotte are right now."

"They must have been staying somewhere since they left their camp," Ryker said.

"I asked her if there was somewhere we could take her, to pick up the rest of her belongings," Jamie said. "I was hoping that might lead us to Charlotte. But Kim just said no. And after that, she clammed up."

He rubbed the back of his neck. "Why did she take Charlotte in the first place?"

"Gage and Travis will find out as much as they can," Jamie said.

"What about the feds? Are they on their way to question her?" Once the FBI arrived, Kim would be even further out of his reach.

"I don't think they've been notified yet."

"They'll be involved sooner rather than later," Ryker said.

"Declan and Shane are driving all the Jeep roads near where we picked up Kim, looking for any sign of the white Jeep or any kind of encampment," she said. "They'll stop anyone they see and ask about Mick and Charlotte."

Maybe they would get lucky and find their new hiding place, but Ryker wasn't one to count on luck. "Did Gage find out anything more about Mick Davis?" he asked.

"I don't know," Jamie said. "He didn't mention it."

He probably wouldn't have said anything to Jamie if he had, Ryker thought. He got up and began to pace again. Jamie pulled out her phone and began scrolling. Somewhere in the distance a phone rang. A door opened and closed. Muffled voices swelled, then faded, the words indistinguishable.

The door to the interview room opened and Dwight Prentice stuck his head in. The lanky blond, thirty-four years old, had been with the department longer than anyone except Travis and Gage. "Ryker, could you come with me?"

Ryker followed him into the hallway. "Kim asked to talk to you," Dwight said.

"Good." He had a lot of things he wanted to say to her, but he reminded himself the most important thing right now was to listen.

"Are you armed?" Dwight asked him.

"No." He had been in such a hurry to get here, he hadn't taken his gun out of the safe he kept it in at home.

Dwight looked pained. "You know I have to check."

"I know." He held out his arms and allowed Dwight to frisk him. He was furious with Kim, but he would never have tried to kill her. But his fellow deputies had to always assume the worst in order to prevent tragedy.

He followed Dwight down the hall to another interview room. Gage opened the door for them, and the sheriff looked up from the table, where he sat across from Kim.

Jamie had been right—she looked rough. She had muddy smears down her cheeks and her eyes were red-rimmed, as if she had been crying. Her hair was a snarled nest, and one knee of her jeans was ripped, and not in a fashionably deliberate way. "Oh, Ryker, I'm so sorry," she moaned, and put her head down on the table and began to sob.

Travis stood. "You can sit here," he said.

Ryker took the seat and looked across at his ex-wife as she continued to sob. Most of the heat of his anger had dissipated. She was such a pathetic figure, not worth the energy it would take to muster any hatred.

Long minutes passed, her sobs the only sound in the room. Dwight hadn't come in, leaving Travis, Gage and Ryker to watch her. After a while, the sobs subsided, and she raised her head. She didn't say anything, so Ryker asked, "Where is Charlotte?"

"I don't know." Her voice sounded scratchy and raw. "If I did, I promise I would tell you."

"Where do you think she is?"

"I don't know that either!" Her voice rose on the last word, into a wail. Travis rested his hand on Ryker's shoulder, whether to steady him or because he feared Ryker might lunge across the table and throttle her, he didn't know. The sheriff needn't have worried about physical violence. Ryker wasn't going to lay a hand on Kim. She wasn't worth the effort. "Why did you take her?" he asked.

"Because I'm her mother. Mick agreed it was time. He had found this mining claim we were going to live on, off-grid. Charlotte was going to live with us. That was the plan all along. I told you when I left."

"I never agreed to the plan," he said.

"But I'm her mother." She sat up straighter, shoulders squared, and glared at him. This show of indignation might have been comical under other circumstances.

He wasn't going to waste time arguing the point. "Is she all right?" he asked.

"She's fine. She's having a wonderful time."

"You stole her away from her home. You took her from her family and friends. How could she be happy?" So much for his attempt to remain unemotional.

"Mick and I are her family, too. She was having fun with us."

"Mick isn't related to her. What is he going to do to her?" He had to force the words out, all the terrible possibilities behind them closing his throat.

She slumped. Ryker stared at her, frustration warring with fatigue. "Why did you want to talk to me?" he asked finally.

"I don't want you to think I'm a bad person," she said. "I wanted to tell you I'm sorry. I was trying to do the right thing and bring her back to you when Mick threw me out."

"Why did you change your mind about keeping her?"

"It's not that I didn't want her anymore, it's just that we weren't quite ready to have her with us. I guess I got a little overexcited and jumped the gun. Mick said he had a place for us to live, but it was just a shack and a tent. Not really the kind of place to bring a kid."

"Where was that?" he asked.

"I already told the sheriff about it. But we didn't stay there long. Mick decided we needed somewhere a little farther off the beaten path. But then we only had the tent, and I never realized it gets so cold in the mountains at night, you know?"

"You should have called me. I would have come to get her."

"I couldn't do that. I mean, you're a cop. Mick didn't like that. So I told him we could just drop her off in town and someone would make sure she got back to you."

This was a child she was talking about, not a package to be left at lost and found. But he reined in his anger. "Why didn't you do that?"

"Mick didn't want to do that. We argued and that's when he ended up leaving me by the side of the road. I was sure he would calm down and come back soon, but he didn't. And I was getting awfully thirsty out there, so I flagged down a guy for help. Only he had to go and call 911." She let out a long sigh. "But I guess it's for the best."

"It's not for the best if Charlotte isn't home safe," Ryker said.

"You think I'm an awful person and I'm not!" She began to cry again, but her tears didn't move him.

"Where are Mick and Charlotte now?" he demanded.

"I don't know." She buried her face in her hands.

He kept his fists clenched at his sides, wanting to shake her. "Where did you stay last night?"

"We slept in the Jeep. This morning he said he had found a new place for us to stay, but he didn't say where. But you don't need to worry. I'm sure he'll take good care of her."

"She belongs with me. You never should have taken her."

"Why are you being so mean to me?" she wailed.

He looked over at Gage. "I've had enough."

Gage opened the door and Dwight entered. "You need to come with us now," Dwight said, and took Kim's arm.

Her eyes widened in alarm. "Where are you taking me?"

"Downstairs, to the booking room and the holding cells," Dwight said. "You'll stay there until we can arrange transport to Junction."

"But you can't arrest me. I haven't done anything wrong."

"We've already told you you're charged with the kidnapping of Charlotte Vernon," Travis said. "We have you on tape saying that you understand the charges and your rights. I can read them to you again if you like."

"But I cooperated with you," she said. "I answered all your questions. And you can't charge me with kidnapping my own daughter."

"You don't have custody," Ryker said. "You haven't even seen Charlotte in three years."

"I'm still her mother."

"You need to come with me," Dwight said. "Stand up now."

She stood, but she looked furious. "I want a lawyer," she said.

"You have that right," Travis said. "We'll make the arrangements as soon as you're booked."

Dwight and Gage led her away, leaving Travis and Ryker alone. He felt utterly drained. "Did she tell you any more than she told me?" Ryker asked.

"No."

"What's this about a mining claim they were going to live on? Did Mick buy a place?"

"It doesn't sound like it," Travis said. "I think he had the idea that if they squatted there long enough, they could assume ownership. Or maybe he thought nobody would know, or he could scam someone into letting them stay. How did Kim seem to you?"

"What do you mean?"

"Is she how you remembered her?"

He tried to think back to the woman he had married. The one who had charmed him and made him believe they could make a life together. "I didn't marry her because I was in love with her," he said. "She was pregnant and I believed the baby was mine and I wanted to be there for her and the baby. She was pretty and outgoing and fun to be with, so I thought we could make it work. She was always a little...erratic. Very enthusiastic about one thing, then she would drop that and move on to something else. But once she met up with Mick..." He shrugged. "She became enthralled with him, and that doesn't seem to have changed."

"I can't decide if she's really that much under his control or if she's faking it," Travis said.

"I think she's that much under his control," Ryker said. "For what it's worth, I always thought he was behind her abandoning Charlotte. I wasn't happy about the two of them getting together, but I never thought she would turn her back on her baby. She was a good mother before she left with him." That knowledge was one thing that had kept him from losing it entirely after Charlotte disappeared. For all her faults, Kim had taken good care of Charlotte before she left, and he had held on to the hope that those motherly instincts still flourished inside her.

Gage returned to the room. "She's quieted down now," he said.

"Did you find out anything about Mick Davis?" Ryker asked. "Any reason the FBI might be worried about him?"

Gage looked past Ryker to the sheriff. "Davis has never been convicted of any offense related to children," Travis said.

"But?" Ryker asked.

"But he was questioned about the disappearance of a little girl in Gilcrest last year, where he and Kim were living at the time," Travis said. "A witness reported a man who fit his description seen with the girl about the time she disappeared. Nothing came of it. He was questioned and released."

Ryker's mouth was dry. "What happened to the little girl?" he asked.

"She's never been found."

"It may not mean anything," Gage said. "You know how these things work. Law enforcement questions a lot of people who turn out not to be related to the crime."

Right. Ryker had been one of them. But it didn't mean Mick wasn't involved in whatever happened with that little girl, or that he would take good care of Charlotte.

"We're putting everything into looking for him and Charlotte," Travis said. "We're sending up a helicopter as soon as it can get here from Delta. I'm asking every off-duty and reserve deputy to help. No one has said no."

"I can help." Ryker stood.

"You know that's not a good idea," Travis said.

If Ryker had been in Travis's shoes, he would have said the same thing. Law enforcement couldn't risk an enraged or distraught father confronting Mick and sending the situation spiraling out of control.

"I know it's hard," Gage said. "You need to find something else to focus on while we're doing our jobs. Did you see anything in the file I sent over?"

Ryker took a deep breath, and pulled his attention to Aiden's file. "Do you remember that handyman, Gary Langley?"

"What about him?" Travis asked.

Ryker explained about the man who had approached him the evening of the day Charlotte disappeared, and about Margery Kenner's mention of him in her statement. "The file states Langley told the sheriff's deputies that he sold the truck, but I couldn't find anything showing anyone followed up on the sale of his truck. Did he really sell it before Aiden disappeared, or did he get rid of it afterward?"

"He lives on a few acres east of town," Gage said. "I think he inherited the property from his family. He's been on disability for years."

"He said he had an accident at work the year after Aiden went missing," Ryker said. "I thought that was odd—he kept mentioning Aiden. Why didn't they look at him more closely at the time of Aiden's disappearance?"

"I'm not excusing them, but it was a small department, with few resources and not much experience," Travis said. "If I remember right, they followed up with him about the truck, he said he had sold it, and that's as far as it went."

"And they had already decided that I was the one who killed Aiden," Ryker said.

Travis nodded.

"Wasn't Langley related to one of the deputies back then?" Gage asked. "Married to his sister, or something?"

"Maybe so," Travis said. "He doesn't have a criminal

record that I'm aware of, but I promise I'll look at him a little more closely. Though it may not be right away."

"I understand," Ryker said. He didn't want anything distracting from the search for Charlotte. "But when you get a chance. It would be good to have some closure for Aiden's parents."

"In the meantime, go home and try to stay positive," Gage said. "You have to trust us. We've got your back."

But none of them were Charlotte's father. No matter how much they cared, he would always care more. No matter how much they fought, he would fight harder.

He left the sheriff's department but he didn't drive home. Instead, he headed east out of town, to the address he pulled up for Gary Langley. The property was a flat, scrubby acreage dotted with sagebrush. The house, a square wooden structure with flaking white paint and a metal roof streaked with orange rust, sat atop a small rise, a white van parked out front.

Ryker stopped his truck behind the van and sat for a moment studying the house. No dog barked and everything was so still he might have thought the property was unoccupied, except he saw the blinds move. A few moments later the door opened and Langley, leaning on a thick wooden cane, stepped out.

Ryker got out of his truck and walked up to meet Langley on the porch. "Deputy." Langley tipped his head in acknowledgment. "What can I do for you?"

"We talked that first day my daughter went missing," Ryker said. "I'm sorry I didn't remember you then. I was still in shock, I guess. But later, I remembered. You used to drive a red pickup, didn't you? For your handyman business?"

"I did. But why would you remember that?"

"I was a nineteen-year-old gearhead. I paid attention to

cars and trucks. I really liked yours. That red color—whatever happened to it?"

"I sold it. It looked nice, but I wanted something that would hold more tools. I ended up buying a van. I still have it." He nodded toward the battered white van in the driveway. "I had it converted to hand controls to make it easier for me to drive."

"I guess it was foolish of me to hope you still had it." Ryker attempted to look sheepish. "Who did you sell it to?"

"A fellow from Texas. But that was years ago. He probably got rid of it a long time ago."

"You never know. You don't remember his name, do you?"

"No, I don't." Langley scowled, the expression almost lost in the deep folds of wrinkles and jowls.

"What year did you sell it to him?"

"I don't remember. A long time ago."

"But you still had it when Aiden went missing."

"No, I sold it before then."

Ryker nodded. "Someone told me they thought you still had it then. They saw you driving it—probably helping search for Aiden."

"They were wrong." Langley shifted, the cane thumping hard on the porch floor. "Don't you have better things to do than to worry about an old truck? Shouldn't you be out searching for your daughter?"

"You're right. I'm just trying to stay busy while I wait for the sheriff's department to coordinate the search. Since I'm Charlotte's dad, they don't want me too directly involved. I won't bother you anymore. Thanks again for all your help."

He left, never completely turning his back on the older man. As he slid into his truck he glanced toward the porch. Langley was still there, glowering at him. He had made it a point to mention his disability again. Was that merely a habit, or did he want to emphasize how incapable he was of doing anything harmful? Maybe he was now. But when Aiden was alive, Langley had been a hardy, strong man. Ryker remembered something about him coaching youth soccer. He might even have known Aiden.

He started the truck and backed out of the driveway. Maybe Langley had nothing to do with Aiden's disappearance, but someone should have checked. Instead of deciding Ryker was guilty and focusing only on him, someone should have done a better job of searching for Aiden's killer. It might be too late to find whoever was responsible now. But that didn't mean it wasn't worth trying.

Chapter Thirteen

Harper was back at search and rescue headquarters Thursday evening for regular training. Attendance at these sessions was mandatory for rookies like her, and most of the veterans attended as well, if they were able. "Jake isn't here tonight because everyone at the sheriff's department is putting in overtime to look for Charlotte Vernon," Hannah shared when they were all settled in an assortment of folding chairs and cast-off sofas in the concrete-floored main space of headquarters.

"Where are they searching?" Harper sat on the edge of her chair. "Has there been a new sighting?"

"I don't know," Hannah said. "But he asked us to all be ready to go out again if we're needed."

"We could help now." Anna rested one hand on the head of her search dog, Jacquie. The black standard poodle stood by her side, ears pricked at the word *search*.

"They're not ready for us yet," Danny said. "But they could need us later. So have your gear ready to go. For now, let's focus on reviewing best practices for transferring an injured person into a litter."

Harper tried to keep her mind on the instructions for moving a person from a vehicle to a litter, or from the ground to a litter. Depending on the patient's condition, they had to be stabilized, fitted with safety gear, and moved in a way that wouldn't worsen any injuries. She studied the slides Danny projected onto the wall, and made notes to review at home, but all the while her mind was on Charlotte and Ryker. Was he out with the search crews now, or had the sheriff insisted he remain home, waiting? Either way, how agonizing it must be for him. Charlotte had been gone a week with people who were strangers to her, even if one of them was her mother.

"Let's take a break, then we'll come back and practice some of these transfer techniques." Danny shut down the slideshow and people began to stand and stretch. Harper moved into a back hallway and called Ryker. The phone rang five times before going to voicemail. "Hey, I'm at a search and rescue meeting and heard the sheriff's department has everyone out searching for Charlotte. I hope this means they're close to finding her. Call me when you get a chance." She ended the call, then sent a text with the same message.

"Something wrong?" She looked up to find Hannah standing in front of the door to the ladies' room.

"I was just trying to call Ryker to see if he knew what was going on with the search for Charlotte." She slid her phone into the pocket of her jeans.

"Jake didn't tell me much," Hannah said. "I never know if that's because he doesn't know any more, or if he's keeping sheriff's department business confidential. Probably a little of both."

"Something must have happened, to send them back out on the search," Harper said.

"I think you're right," Hannah said. "I just don't know what that is." She put her arm around Harper. "Waiting and not knowing is awful. I was really glad for this meeting tonight to distract myself."

They returned to the meeting, where Hannah and Ryan assumed the roles of injured accident victims and the others worked in teams to assess, stabilize and transfer them. It took a lot of strength and teamwork to do the job right, without hurting either themselves or their patients. By the time the evening ended, Harper felt she had had a real workout.

She checked her phone on the way to her car. Ryker hadn't answered her message. She sat in the front seat of her car, torn between the desire to drive to his house and make sure he was all right and the knowledge that it was after nine o'clock and she wasn't sure their rekindled friendship was at the drop-by-any-time stage. She started the car and resigned herself to heading home when her phone dinged.

Just got your message. I'm heading out to search now.

Where are you going?

I'm starting near Jack's Peak.

She had to think a moment to place the site. It was rugged country she had visited only once, on a long-ago hike with friends. Are you okay? It's really late.

I'm going to spend the night at a trailhead and start at first light.

She had a million questions to ask him, but settled for the one that mattered most. Is there anything I can do to help?

She waited a long, agonizing minute for his reply. Her heart hurt when she read it, the words so weighted with hope and fear: Say a prayer we find her. Before it's too late.

RYKER STUDIED THE map of the mining district spread out on his bed. On it, he had circled the Ida B Mine, where Harper had found Charlotte's hair ribbon. Though Kim hadn't been sure of the name of the place, he believed this was the claim Mick had intended to squat on. He had also circled the place where he and Harper had found the abandoned camp. Finally, he had drawn a red *X* at the intersection where deputies had arrested Kim. The three sites were all within a five-mile radius in the Galloway Basin Mining District. Though it was possible Mick might have decided to move on after abandoning Kim, Ryker was betting that he had found a new hiding place within the district.

The sheriff had probably studied a similar map and come to the same conclusion, but Gage had checked in when they shut down the search due to darkness to report they had found nothing. They planned to resume their efforts in the morning and focus on the eastern half of the district, a network of narrow roads pockmarked with small mining claims.

Those were also the roads most frequented by tourists, who hiked among the mining ruins photographing the rusting equipment and falling-down shacks, or searched among the debris for iron spikes, hand-cast nails and other souvenirs of the past—even though signs pleaded with people to leave all artifacts in place.

Even though these sites were most likely to offer habitable buildings, Ryker reasoned that Mick would avoid crowds and head to more remote locations. That meant the west side of the district, with its steeper, less-used roads and fewer abandoned mines. He used a highlighter to trace a route into this area, then folded the map and tucked it into the side of his pack. He had food and water, rain gear and first aid supplies. He was prepared to spend the night out if he had to, but he had purposely packed light. If he found Charlotte, he would need to carry her as well as the pack.

Maybe he was wasting his time. Mick could be two states away by now. Charlotte's Amber Alert was still active, and the sheriff would have updated the bulletin with the information that she was traveling with a lone male. If they got lucky, someone else would spot the pair and contact law enforcement.

But Ryker had to do something. He couldn't sit at home waiting any longer.

His headlights cut a narrow path up the rocky road leading to his first destination, a long-abandoned operation designated on the map as the Lucky Six Mine. Ryker drove as far as the trailhead for a popular hike up Jack's Peak and parked. From this point the road grew much rougher, with sharp, narrow turns and steep drop-offs. He would need better light to navigate it safely.

He rolled down the window and shut off the engine. Silence wrapped around him, the darkness so complete it was as if someone had thrown a blanket over him. Gradually, he was able to make out the shadowed outlines of rocks and scrubby trees beyond the parking area, and some of the tension in his chest released. He breathed in deeply, taking in the scent of dust and piñon.

A high wail rose in the distance, jolting him to attention and standing the hairs along his arms on end. A series of yips descended the scale and he recognized the song of a group of coyotes. They sounded very close, though he knew sound carried far in the clear air, echoing off rocks, so that it was hard to tell from which direction the noise originated.

Could Charlotte hear these same noises? Was she frightened by them? He tried to remember if they had heard coyotes before. He wished now he had taken her camping so that the night sounds of the wilderness were more familiar to her, and not frightening.

When Charlotte had first disappeared, he had comforted himself with the thought that she would be all right with Kim. For all her faults, she had been a good mother in Charlotte's early years. Now he didn't even have that solace. Charlotte was alone with a man who had been a suspect in the disappearance of another little girl. Maybe he had nothing to do with that crime, but what if he had?

He pushed the thought away. He wouldn't be able to function if he started playing that awful *what if* game. He needed to stay focused on Charlotte—on finding her and getting her to safety. To do that, he needed to sleep, and be ready to hike hard at first light.

HARPER SET HER alarm for 3:00 a.m. She slipped out of bed as quietly as possible, then dressed and collected the pack she had filled the night before with food, water, extra clothing and first aid supplies. She left a note for her parents. *Gone to help search for Charlotte.* Then she tiptoed outside to her car and set off toward the mountains. On the way, she called her office and left a voicemail explaining she needed to take a personal day.

She passed no other cars this time of night, and once out of town, the darkness was complete. Stars glittered between the peaks of distant mountains, which were little more than gray smudges against the sky. She watched carefully for her first turnoff. She had memorized the directions to the Jack's Peak trail, but there were no road signs out here and if she missed a turn or mistakenly took the wrong road, she would be lost within minutes. GPS was useless on these backroads, and within minutes of leaving the highway she had no cell signal anyway. She gripped the steering wheel more tightly and stared out the windshield, praying she was doing the right thing.

The roads grew progressively rougher as she climbed in elevation. Deep ruts and protruding rocks forced her to proceed at a crawl, gritting her teeth as she navigated tight turns. Her Subaru wasn't exactly designed for this kind of terrain. After one particularly nerve-racking passage she was debating parking the car and hiking the rest of the way when her headlights illuminated the back of a truck.

She pushed the car a little faster, and soon was able to verify it was Ryker's truck. Triumph surged through her and she tapped her horn, intending to alert him to her arrival.

But he didn't appear. By the time she parked, she realized the truck was empty. She shut off the engine of her car and realized the sky was lighter, the outlines of rocks and trees and mountain peaks more distinct against a sky that was fast transforming from gray to lavender to pink.

She looked around, wondering which direction he had traveled. The trail ahead was the one she had taken on that long-ago hike, up to the top of Jack's Peak. That didn't seem a likely destination for a couple fleeing with a little girl. That left the road past this parking area. She walked over to study it more closely and grimaced. Calling it a road would be overstating the situation. Twin rocky tracks led across more rocks, some the size of footstools. No way would her car get down that safely. Ryker's truck, on the other hand, probably could have navigated the route. So why hadn't he taken it?

She returned to her car and shouldered her pack and started down the road. She hadn't gone far before she discovered the reason Ryker had not driven this way. A rock-slide cascaded from a cliff on the right, burying the track hip-deep in stones and making it impassable. She studied the pile of rocks, looking for footprints, or any indication that Ryker had come this way.

She didn't find anything. Maybe she was wasting her time. Then again, she didn't have anything better to do today. She tightened the straps of her pack and began climbing.

She hiked for an hour after scaling the rockslide. The sun rose, warming the air, and she settled into a comfortable rhythm. She told herself she would go for another hour before she turned back. This was good training for rescue, even if she didn't find Ryker.

They had gone hiking once together in high school. What was the trail they had taken? Up on Dakota Ridge, she thought, a wooded trail in the fall, through showers of red and gold aspen leaves. It looked like something out of a romance movie, or at least it had felt like that to her, so young and so in love. They had stopped for a picnic lunch in a sheltered spot off the trail and ended up making love on that carpet of leaves, Ryker's coat spread beneath them. That might even have been the day their child was conceived.

She was walking head-down, lost in these memories, when a movement ahead startled her. Ryker stepped out from behind a boulder. "I thought someone was following me," he said. "Harper, what are you doing here?"

RYKER COULDN'T SAY he wasn't happy to see Harper, though acknowledging that felt selfish. Mick Davis was a convicted felon who might be dangerous. Having Harper here meant she might be at risk. So he didn't tell her how good it was to have her here. "You shouldn't be here," he said.

"Why not?" She met his gaze, unruffled. Stubborn. He remembered that same expression on her face when she had told him she was pregnant. Young as she was, she had been so certain she was making the right decision, so confident in her ability to see a tough thing through to the end. "I want to help, and two sets of eyes are better than one. Not to mention, it's safer to hike with a partner. And when we find Kim and her boyfriend, it will be the two of us against the two of them—better odds."

The sheriff must have done a good job of keeping the news about Kim quiet. "Kim isn't with Mick anymore," he said. "She was arrested and brought in yesterday afternoon. Charlotte is alone with Mick."

She looked exactly the way he had felt when he had heard the news—as if someone had punched her in the gut. She hugged her arms across her stomach and stared at him. "You don't think he'll hurt her, do you?"

"I don't know. All I know about the man is his criminal record, and that's more than enough to make me worried."

She straightened, visibly pulling herself together. "Where do you think they are?"

He looked up the road they were on. "I plotted all the points where they have been seen on a map. There's a mine at the end of this road that looked like a good place for him to hole up. Kim said they were looking for old mining claims with structures on them where they could live."

"How far is the mine from here?" she asked.

"A couple more miles, I think."

"It's a long way to walk with a little kid. And I didn't see any sign of the white Jeep, or any other vehicle, back at the trailhead."

"I'm wondering if he didn't drive up here before that slide blocked the road." He kicked at a rock in one of the ruts. "Even before the slide, the road was almost impassible, but the lack of traffic might have appealed to him. And he's shown a penchant for reckless driving." One more way he was endangering Charlotte.

"Then let's go." Harper set out walking. He caught up with her. "Where is Kim now?" she asked.

"I don't know. Probably on her way to jail in Junction."

"How did they manage to arrest her? Or are you allowed to say?"

"She said Mick kicked her out of the car and abandoned her on the side of the road. She flagged down a car and the driver called 911. She said it wasn't the first time Mick had left her somewhere like that, but he had always come back before."

"She must have been frantic, being separated from her daughter like that," Harper said.

"She seemed more upset about being arrested than worried about Charlotte." He tamped down his anger against Kim. He needed to focus on Charlotte, not his ex-wife. "She said Mick wouldn't hurt Charlotte, but I'm not so sure."

Harper moved over to link her arm with his. "You must be worried sick, but you're doing everything you can. And you're not the only one looking. Hannah said the sheriff has called in every available deputy to search for Charlotte, and search and rescue volunteers are on standby."

"I know. The sheriff sent me home to wait, but I couldn't sit idle and do nothing."

"Neither could I. That's why I came looking for you."

He looked down into her eyes and it was as if he was eighteen again. She had been the one person he had felt had truly understood him back then. Maybe things hadn't changed that much. "It helps, having you here," he said.

"Then I'm glad to be here." She squeezed his arm, then moved away again, picking up the pace.

They climbed a steeper section of the road and emerged

on a flat bench of land. A three-foot section of iron track jutted from a pile of rocks to their right, and the rusted shell of an ancient boiler crowned another pile of crumbling rocks, the bright ocher color identifying this as the waste rock left over from mining. Fifty feet beyond, the remains of a small shack leaned drunkenly to the left, its roof caved in, windows and door vacant holes in the weathered gray logs that remained. "Is this where Mick thought they could live?" Harper asked.

"I'm pretty sure this is the Lucky Six Mine," Ryker said. "This is the place I picked out on my map, though Kim swore she didn't know where Mick intended to go." He turned a slow circle, surveying the area. A few scrubby piñons dotted the mostly barren landscape. "The road ends here, so he would have had to park and walk if he wanted to go any farther."

Harper moved toward the shack. "I don't think anyone is living in here," she said as she peered into the open doorway. "It's full of broken boards and rusty metal roofing."

Ryker picked up a chunk of the mine waste and weighed it in his hand. "There are a couple of other places we can look, if you're up for it."

"Sure. Let me duck over behind those rocks and pee, then we can head back." She pointed to a pile of boulders at the edge of the bench.

"Okay." He turned his back on the boulders and looked up the hill, past the shack. He could just make out a narrow footpath that led up the hill and around another outcrop. Should they go a little farther and check out whatever was up there? But it didn't make sense that Mick would have come all this way on foot, especially with Charlotte in tow.

Then again, the man had been quick to ditch Kim, who had lived with him for three years. How long would it take before he decided a four-year-old was too much trouble? The thought of Charlotte left alone in the wilderness blurred his vision for a moment.

A shout from Harper brought him back to himself. He spun around in time to see her run out from behind the boulders. "Come look at this!" she shouted, and motioned for him to join her.

He jogged over to her. She grabbed his hand and pulled him behind the boulders. There, wedged between the rocks and a stout piñon, was a dirty white Jeep.

Chapter Fourteen

Harper stared at the abandoned Jeep, throat tight. "They were here," she said, almost whispering, as if Mick Davis might be close enough to hear her.

"They're still here somewhere." Ryker moved toward the Jeep, then stopped and shifted his pack until he could extract a pair of nitrile gloves from it. "I'm going to take a look inside."

She moved in close behind him, careful not to touch anything, but wanting to see what he found. The smell of cigarette smoke and stale food hit them as soon as Ryker opened the front passenger door. Over his shoulder, she studied the worn black upholstery and dusty floor mats almost obscured by piles of food wrappers, crushed soft drink cans, empty plastic water bottles and cigarette butts. "He didn't leave the keys," Ryker noted. He peered under the seat. "Nothing here but more trash."

He moved to open the rear passenger door. Harper couldn't see as well into this space. "More trash," Ryker said. "Wait a minute." He leaned in and emerged seconds later holding something small and white. Harper's throat closed again as she recognized a child's sock—white with pink rosebuds at the cuff.

Ryker stared at the sock, and she wondered what he was

thinking. Was he angry? Afraid? Sad? Probably all of the above. "If they're here, we'll find them," she said. "I could hike back down until I get a cell signal and call for help."

He hesitated, frowning, then shook his head. "I don't like the idea of you heading out by yourself with Mick possibly nearby. He's probably armed."

"I don't like the idea of leaving you up here alone, either," she said.

"We'll look around together," he said. "If we see anything, we'll both go back and get help." He closed both vehicle doors, easing them shut so that they scarcely made a sound. Then he moved around to the driver's door, opened it, leaned in and released the hood. He moved around to the front of the vehicle, reached in and yanked out a tangle of wires. "That will slow him down if he comes back." He eased the hood down until it closed with a soft click.

Harper scanned the area around them. Silence closed in—the silence of a long-deserted area. "Where do you think they are?" she asked.

"There's a trail just past that old building," he said. "Let's see what's up there."

Tension vibrating through her, she followed him up a narrow, rocky path that scarcely passed for a trail. She fought to keep her balance as loose rocks rolled beneath her feet. If she was having this hard a time making it up here, what would it have been like for Charlotte? Had Mick carried her? That is, if they were even up here. She couldn't see any sign that anyone else had come this way, but how would she know? Footprints didn't show in the dry, rocky soil.

Ryker stopped and put out a hand to halt her. "I see some buildings up ahead," he said.

She moved up beside him, and put her hand on his back to steady herself. She peered in the direction he indicated and could just make out the side of a log cabin, and one section of its rusty metal roof. "We need to get off this trail." Ryker spoke with his mouth close to her ear, his voice soft, sending a shiver down her spine. "Mick might be watching for someone to come up this way."

She nodded, then followed as he moved off the trail and began picking his way on an indirect route toward the log building. He kept below the ridge as they hiked in a wide arc, then began to climb once more. At the top of the ridge they emerged behind what proved to be a trio of log cabins.

These buildings were in better shape than the one nearest the parking area. One had a roof that looked intact, and though none of them had real windows, the walls were upright, if unchinked, and two of them had doors. Harper sniffed the air. "I smell woodsmoke," she whispered. There was no sign of smoke near any of the cabins now but perhaps last night, when temperatures would have dropped, someone had lit a fire to cook dinner and keep warm.

"Stay here," Ryker said. "I'm going to try to get closer."

She shook her head. "We need to stay together."

He scowled, but rather than argue, he turned and started toward the nearest cabin, the one with the intact roof and a door. She followed, moving as quietly as possible, every nerve tense, ears straining for the sound of anyone nearby. They reached the rear of the cabin and pressed their backs against the rough wood. Then Ryker inched toward the window opening, the rough wooden frame empty of glass. She darted past him to take up a position on the other side so she could look inside also.

It took a moment for her eyes to adjust to the dim interior. The floor was dirt, streaked with thin bars of sunlight showing through the gaps between the unchinked logs. At first, it appeared empty, then she focused on what appeared to be a heap of sleeping bags and blankets in the far corner. She reached out and gripped Ryker's arm. "They were here!" she whispered.

He nodded, and leaned in to examine the space more thoroughly. The air smelled of old wood and dust, and the stronger aroma of wet ash from an extinguished fire, though she couldn't see signs of any blaze within that one bare room. Perhaps they had lit a campfire outside, to the front of the cabin.

Ryker tapped her arm and indicated they should move on. She started to turn away, but as she did so, something moved over by the blankets. She grabbed Ryker's hand and pulled him back, then pointed into the cabin. As they stared, the blankets definitely shifted. She caught a glimpse of a small hand, and a flash of blond hair.

Ryker vaulted over the windowsill and raced to the pile of blankets. "Charlotte," he called, and pulled back the blankets. "Charlotte, honey, are you all right?"

The child blinked up at him, then reached up with her arms. "Daddy!" she called, and Ryker scooped her up, blankets and all.

Harper blinked back tears as she witnessed this reunion. "It's okay, sweetheart," Ryker said, smoothing back Charlotte's hair. "You're safe with me now. I'm going to take you home." He moved toward the door, but before he reached it, it burst open.

A wiry man with short blond hair and a scruffy beard filled the doorway. He hefted an axe in one hand. "Put her down," he ordered. "Do it now or I'll kill you."

RYKER HADN'T SEEN Mick Davis in years but he had no doubt the blond threatening him now was the man Kim had left him for. Charlotte began to sob, and Ryker tightened one arm around her and took a step back, toward the window. He kept his gaze on Mick and that axe, and debated whether or not he could draw his gun from beneath his jacket without putting his daughter in danger.

The light streaming through the window shifted. He didn't look over, but hoped Harper was retreating out of harm's way. Mick gave no sign he had noticed, his gaze remaining fixed on Ryker and Charlotte. Time to end this stare-down. "I'm going to take my daughter and leave," Ryker said.

Mick took a firmer grip on the axe. "And I told you to put her down."

Ryker could feel the weight of the gun at his back, but he couldn't risk Charlotte. She shifted against him and made a whimpering sound, and he cradled her head in his hand, wanting to comfort her and needing to protect her. To get her to safety. "What do you want with her, Mick?" he asked. "She'll just slow you down when you try to get away."

"She's my little insurance policy. To get to me, they risk hurting her and no one wants that, do they?" He hefted the axe higher and took a step toward them.

Charlotte wailed, and the light shifted again as Harper moved into the doorway behind Mick. She clutched a rusty iron bar in both hands. Before Ryker had time to react, she brought the bar down hard on the back of Mick's head.

He toppled like a felled tree, the axe trapped beneath him. He groaned, and tried to push himself up on hands and knees. Ryker kicked him hard in the chest and he crumpled again, then Ryker raced past him out the door. Harper stood, both arms wrapped around herself, looking shaken.

"We need to get out of here," Ryker said.

She nodded, but continued to stare past him at Mick.

Ryker looked back over his shoulder and watched Mick

rock up on all fours, groaning. Then he turned back to Harper. "Come on." He touched her shoulder.

He jogged away from the cabin, relieved to hear her right behind him. When they were a hundred yards or so from the cabins he paused to get his bearings. They needed to work their way off this ridge, back toward the trail that eventually led to the parking area and his truck. A shouted curse from Mick jolted him to action once more. He whirled to momentarily face the cabins—and Mick. The other man shouldn't be standing after the blow Harper had given him, but somehow he was on his feet and staggering after them. But he wouldn't be able to run. All he and Harper had to do was put more distance between themselves and Mick and hike the two miles to his car. Not the easiest thing he had ever done, but not impossible, either.

A whistling sound cut the air, and air rushed past his left shoulder, followed by the sharp report of gunfire. "He's shooting at us!" Harper cried.

Ryker bent over, shielding Charlotte with his body. "Run for cover!" he shouted.

HARPER DARTED INTO a clump of trees at the very edge of the clearing. She huddled behind the gnarled trunk of a juniper, the silvery bark peeling away like flowing hair. Was the trunk stout enough to stop a bullet? She peeked between the trees, looking back toward the cabins. Mick Davis, blood matting his hair and staining one side of his face and beard, held a large pistol and stalked toward them.

Ryker crashed through the trees to join her. He dropped to his knees behind her and shoved Charlotte toward her. "Charlotte, you remember Harper, don't you?" he said. "She's going to take care of you for a minute, but I'll be right here."

Harper gathered the girl close. "Hello, Charlotte," she said, and forced a smile. She moved farther into the cover of trees. Charlotte stared at her with wide, frightened eyes, but didn't say anything. Ryker pulled a gun from beneath his jacket at his back and moved to steady himself behind the juniper's wide trunk.

Harper startled at the first shot, even though she had known it was coming. Charlotte covered both ears with her hands and squeezed her eyes shut. Her trembling vibrated through Harper, who pulled her close and spoke in her ear, in what she hoped was a soothing tone. "It's going to be okay," she said. "Your dad is going to take care of us."

"He's back in the cabin." Ryker duckwalked to them. "We need to move. Can you carry her for a little bit, in case I have to return fire again?"

She shuddered at the idea of more bullets flying, but nodded. "Of course."

He helped her stand, and she settled Charlotte more comfortably on her hip. The child was heavy, but not any heavier than the full packs she had carried on search and rescue missions. "We're ready," she said.

Ryker led the way, not back to the path, but threading through the trees and rocky uplift. They had to move slowly, picking their way around obstacles, but no more bullets whistled past them, and she didn't hear anyone pursuing them. They were traveling downhill, and she reasoned that Ryker was taking them on a route that would eventually meet the road they had come in on. They moved quickly, not speaking. After a while, he took Charlotte again. The little girl put her arms around his neck and laid her head on his shoulders, but didn't say a word.

Harper thought they had been walking forty-five minutes to an hour when Ryker abruptly stopped. "What is it?"

she asked, hurrying to stand beside him. Then she saw that the ground fell away in front of them.

"We're cliffed out," he said. "We'll have to backtrack."

Charlotte started to cry. Ryker shifted her to his other hip. "We're not going back to Mick," he said. "You're safe with me."

"Can we stop and rest a little?" Harper asked. "Maybe get something to eat and drink, and think about what we need to do next?" The sun was high in the sky now and her stomach grumbled.

"Good idea." He set Charlotte on her feet. "Do you need to use the bathroom, honey?" he asked.

She nodded. "I'll take you," Harper said. She offered her hand and Charlotte took it. The two picked their way over fallen tree limbs and scattered rocks to a sheltered spot in a thicket of shrubs. When they had both relieved themselves, Harper smoothed back Charlotte's hair and looked into her eyes. "How are you feeling?" she asked.

"Scared."

"I'm a little scared, too," Harper admitted. "But your dad and I are going to protect you and we're going to get you back home." She had a dozen questions she wanted to ask, about what exactly had happened to this child, but now wasn't the time to ask them. It wasn't even her place to ask them. She would need to leave that to Ryker. "We probably have a lot more walking to do to get to where your dad has parked his truck," she said instead. "Are you up for it?"

Charlotte bit her lower lip. "Can we eat something first?"

"Yes. Absolutely. Come on, let's get back to your dad."

Ryker had removed his pack and had some of the contents laid out on the ground—two water bottles, a half-dozen protein bars, two sandwiches and a couple of apples.

He looked up at their approach. "I've got ham and cheese," he said.

"I've got peanut butter and jelly." Harper removed her own pack. "And candy bars."

Charlotte looked livelier than she had all day. "Can I have a peanut butter and jelly sandwich?"

"Of course. And if you're still hungry after you eat it, we'll split a candy bar." She sat cross-legged on the ground and Charlotte copied the posture. Harper distributed the food and Ryker unwrapped his own sandwich. Then he cut up one of the apples and passed out slices. When she was done eating, Charlotte wiped her hands on her dress and looked at Ryker. "Do you know where Mama is?"

Ryker looked flummoxed by the question. "Your mom is safe," he said. "You do know she wasn't supposed to take you away from me like that, don't you?"

"I know."

Ryker didn't look any happier. Harper could almost see his calculating what to ask next. "Were you surprised to see your mom?" Harper asked.

Charlotte turned to her. "She said she was going to take me to get ice cream." She looked back to Ryker. "She said it was okay with you."

"It wasn't," Ryker said. "If she had come to me and asked, I would have arranged for all of us to visit together. I never tried to keep your mother from you, no matter what she might have told you."

"She said it was her turn to take care of me now. Her and Mick." She made a face, like she had eaten something sour.

"You don't like Mick," Harper guessed.

She nodded.

Ryker leaned toward her, rigid with tension. "Mick didn't hurt you, did he?"

Harper held her breath, waiting for the answer. Charlotte shrugged. "He didn't hit me—though he said he would if I didn't do what he said. He yelled a lot—at me and at Mama. I didn't like that. And I was really scared when he pushed her out of the car and kept me with him. I kept telling him I wanted to go home." She began to cry, and Ryker gathered her close, pulling her into his lap and rocking her.

He looked over her head and met Harper's gaze, and the pain in his eyes made her want to weep, too. She settled for moving closer and rubbing Charlotte's back. "It's okay," she said. "Your dad isn't going to let anything happen to you."

After a while, the little girl's breathing grew more even. Harper thought she had fallen asleep.

"Do you know where we are?" Harper asked Ryker.

He looked up at the sun high overhead in a sky the color of forget-me-nots. "If we keep heading east, we should hit the road," he said. "But we have to find a way down the ridge."

"What about Mick? Do you think he's still following us?"

"I don't know," he admitted. "But you hit him pretty hard. He's bound to have a concussion. I doubt he's moving all that quickly. And he doesn't really need Charlotte. If I was him, I'd take the chance to get away while I could."

"But you disabled his car."

"I did. I hope that will slow him down. All I really care about now is getting Charlotte home. The rest of the force can deal with Mick."

He put one arm around her. "I'm sorry you got dragged into this."

"I'm not," she said. "I don't like to think what would have happened if I hadn't sneaked up behind Mick and hit him." The sound of that metal bar striking his skull wouldn't leave her anytime soon. The moment had been awful, but not nearly as awful as it would have been seeing him use that axe against Ryker or Charlotte. "If he had a gun all that time, why did he threaten you with the axe?" she asked.

"I think he had probably gone to chop wood, so he had the axe in his hand at the time. I guess he thought it would be enough." He squeezed her shoulder. "I take back what I said before. I'm not sorry you're here. And not just because you went after Mick with that iron bar."

She leaned against him. Being here with him and Charlotte felt right. They were a good team. "We should get going," he said. "I want to get back to the truck before dark. The sooner we're away from Mick, the better I'll feel."

She nodded, and shoved herself to her feet. She wanted to be away from Mick, too, though she hated to end this moment with Ryker—just the two of them and Charlotte, without anyone else to interfere.

Chapter Fifteen

Friday morning, Deputy Jamie Douglas glanced at the woman next to her as they waited for the elevator that would take them to the basement-level holding cells. "Do you really think this will work?" she asked.

Adelaide Kinkaid, the sheriff's department's office manager, looked down at the cardboard tray containing two cups of coffee and a cinnamon roll. "I think it's worth a try. I'm good at getting people to confide in me. If they don't know me well, they assume I'm a harmless old woman."

She grinned and Jamie suppressed a laugh. Even though she was in her sixties, Adelaide never acted old, and she had a well-deserved reputation of knowing almost anything worth knowing about the goings-on in town, from the details of coming events to idle gossip. If anyone could get the information they needed, it would be her.

They rode the elevator down and passed through two sets of locked doors to the booking area and the two small holding cells, only one of which was occupied. Kim Vernon looked up at their approach. "It looks like you're going to be with us a little longer," Jamie said. "We're waiting for room to open up at the jail in Junction."

"I brought you some breakfast." Adelaide held up the tray. "And some company, if you're interested."

Kim stood and moved to the bars of the cell. "Who are you?"

"Adelaide Kinkaid. I'm a civilian who handles clerical work here at the station." She pulled a chair up to the bars and sat. "I heard about what happened to you and well, I've got a daughter about your age and a granddaughter Charlotte's age. I figure you must be beside yourself, being separated from her like this." She pushed the coffee cup through the opening of the bars. "I've got cream and sugar here if you want. And a cinnamon roll."

"Just cream, thanks." Kim accepted the little tub of cream and the roll, and settled on the end of the bunk, still eyeing the two women warily. Her intake sheet said she was twenty-nine, but she looked older, like someone who hadn't lived an easy life. What makeup she had put on at some point was mostly smeared off or collected in the creases around her eyes, and dark roots two inches long showed along the part of her hair. She was thin—almost bony— and dressed in a T-shirt and elastic-waist shorts.

"I have to stay here because Adelaide is a civilian," Jamie said. "But I feel for you. I've got a little girl, too. I just came back to work after my maternity leave and it's hard enough being away from her during my shift. I can't imagine being forced to leave her the way you were. And not knowing where she is."

Kim sipped coffee. "I'm sure Mick won't hurt her," she said. "He just has a bad temper, sometimes. And I forget myself and annoy him. He'll get over it. He always does."

"I couldn't help noticing the bruises on your arm." Adelaide nodded to the purpling patches showing below the sleeve of Kim's T-shirt. "Did Mick do that?"

Kim covered the bruises with her hand. "He would never lay a hand on Charlotte," she said. Jamie's stomach clenched as she read the doubt in the other woman's eyes. They really needed to find Charlotte, and if it took pretending to be friendly to the woman who had put her in danger in the first place, Jamie was willing to do it.

"Still, he isn't her real parent," Adelaide said. "You are. A little girl needs her mother."

"That's what I keep telling these cops." Kim sat up a little straighter. "They act like I'm some kind of criminal for wanting to take care of my little girl."

"Charlotte is such a beautiful child," Jamie said. That, at least, wasn't a lie.

Kim smiled. "She is. A lot of people say she favors me."

"Yes, I can see that," Adelaide said. "I know a lot of people are out looking for her. I hope they find her soon. I'm sure she really misses you."

"She was crying when Mick pushed me out of the Jeep," Kim said. She blinked rapidly, her eyes shiny.

"That wasn't right of him," Adelaide said. "Especially when all you wanted was to take care of your little girl."

"I know." Kim pinched a piece from the cinnamon roll, but didn't eat it.

"Where do you think he went?" Adelaide asked. "I mean, do you think he came back to try to find you after you got a ride from that guy in the Jeep? Or did he go back to your camp?"

"We were moving to a new place," Kim said. "But I don't know where we were going."

"He didn't even tell you that?" Adelaide looked disapproving. "Men. They don't really know how to communicate, do they?"

Kim laughed. "Isn't that the truth? I have to ask twenty questions to get anything out of Mick. It makes him so angry sometimes, but if he would just tell me what's going on in the first place it would save us all so much trouble."

"So he never said where this new camp was?" Adelaide asked.

Kim ate the piece of cinnamon roll and chewed thoroughly before she said, "Even if he had, I wouldn't have recognized the name. I'm not from around here."

"There are a lot of old mines up in that area," Adelaide said. "I haven't driven up there in a while, but I remember some of them even had buildings on them—little cabins that almost looked like you could move right in."

Kim nodded. "That's what we were looking for. Some place we could settle down and make a home. You know, live off-grid. We didn't want to bother anybody. We thought we had found a place, but after one night there we realized it was too close to popular Jeep roads. People were up there all the time. We couldn't have that. I mean, we were looking for peace and quiet, where we could get away from everybody."

"So I guess you decided to head farther into the mountains, away from the popular trails," Adelaide said.

"Exactly. Mick said he had found a new place on the map. It had three almost-complete cabins we could choose from. There was water nearby, and it was open, so we could add solar panels and maybe even have a little garden in the future. It sounded like just what we were looking for."

Jamie made a mental note of this. This could help narrow the search, even if Kim didn't come up with a name.

"You didn't worry about hikers interfering with you?" Adelaide asked. "People always want to poke around those old mine ruins."

"Mick had that all figured out," Kim said. "He said the road up to this place was really narrow and not used much, but after we got up there he would trigger a rockslide over the trail so no one could follow."

"Wouldn't that mean you would be trapped, too?" Jamie asked.

"He said he could drive over or around the rockslide. Most people wouldn't attempt it, but he could do it." Kim frowned. "He takes a lot of risks, driving. It scares me sometimes, but he always gets where he needs to go."

"That does sound like the ideal place to get away from it all," Adelaide said. "I wonder which mine that is."

"He may have said the name but I don't remember," Kim said. "Maybe something with a number in it?" She wrinkled her nose. "I'm not sure I have that right. I was trying to get Charlotte to eat her breakfast and I wasn't paying much attention. That was what set Mick off, actually. He didn't like me paying more attention to Charlotte than to him."

"Of course your daughter had to come first," Adelaide said.

"If they had more woman cops, maybe I wouldn't be in this cell," Kim said. "Men just don't understand."

Adelaide stood. "It was nice chatting with you. I'd better get to work now."

"I'll let you know when Junction is ready for your transfer," Jamie said.

Neither woman said anything until they were in the elevator again. "Do you think we can find that mine she was talking about?" Jamie asked.

"The sheriff has a map of the mining district with all the old claims marked on it," Adelaide said. "She gave us a pretty good description, with those three cabins and water nearby."

"Mick might not even have gone there," Jamie said.

"He might not. But this is the best lead I've heard of, so

it's definitely worth sending someone up there to check it out." Smiling, Adelaide led the way out of the elevator. She pulled out her phone and hit speed dial. "Sheriff? Jamie and I have been talking to Kim Vernon. She told us some things you need to hear."

GETTING BACK TO the road proved more difficult than Ryker had anticipated. Though he was sure they were traveling in the right direction, they repeatedly encountered obstacles that prevented them from moving in anything close to a straight line—a deep gully, an abrupt drop-off, or a soaring cliff face they weren't equipped to scale. Harper didn't say anything, but her silence and exhausted expression made him feel guilty once more for putting her through all of this.

Charlotte grew increasingly fussy. She didn't want to be carried, but when allowed to walk, would sit down and refuse to go any farther. She burst into tears more than once, and Ryker felt her frustration.

The sun was setting when Harper suggested they stop and make camp. "Walking around in the dark is too dangerous," she pointed out. "Better to build a campfire and settle in for the night. We'll do better if we start fresh in the morning."

By himself, Ryker probably would have pressed on, but one look at his daughter's tearstained face and Harper's sagging shoulders convinced him she was right.

Harper chose the campsite in an area sheltered by a large boulder on one side and a clump of brush on the other. "I took a class as part of my search and rescue training on how to build a makeshift camp," she said as she picked up fallen limbs and moved rocks to clear an area for them to settle in. "When we go out on a search or respond to assist someone injured in the wilderness, we might have to spend the night out." She slipped off her pack and removed two small packets. "These are emergency bivy bags," she said, turning the packet so that he could read the label, which showed a person inside a bright orange sleeping bag cinched around his body. "I only have two, but Charlotte will probably do better tucked up with one of us."

"What else do you have?" Charlotte knelt on the ground beside the pack and watched as Harper pulled out more items.

"I have a water filter, a first aid kit, a whistle and fire-starting materials." Harper laid these items out alongside her pack. Charlotte picked up the water filter and examined it. "Also a mirror that can be used to signal someone, an aluminum splint, another candy bar, some nuts, packets of drink mix, extra socks, a collapsible metal cup and a multi-tool."

Charlotte focused on the small pile of food. "I'm hungry," she announced.

"I still have one sandwich, one apple and a couple of protein bars in my pack," Ryker said. "And one of those space blanket things."

"Great," Harper said. "We should be able to get pretty comfortable. Let's start with a fire, then we'll pull together a picnic supper."

Charlotte pitched in to help collect tinder and smaller pieces of wood for their campfire. "I watched Mama and Mick build fires," she said, and dropped a handful of pine needles in the middle of the rock circle Harper had constructed as a fire ring.

Ryker soon had a fire going, and Harper spread the space blanket and the two bivy bags along one side of the fire. They sat on them and she divided their food, giving each of them a portion of sandwich, nuts, apple and candy.

"We'll save the protein bars for breakfast," she said. Then she mixed some of the powdered drink mix in the metal cup and passed it to Charlotte. "It's not a lot of food, but it's pretty well balanced, nutritionally."

Ryker bit off half his share of the candy bar and chewed.

"Daddy, you're not supposed to eat the candy first," Charlotte said. She was nibbling one corner of her quarter sandwich.

"I'm not too worried it's going to spoil my appetite," he said. He could have eaten three sandwiches after all the hiking he had done today.

Charlotte giggled. He hadn't meant to be funny, but hearing her sound so happy and normal lifted his spirits.

They finished eating and Charlotte settled beside Ryker. The light faded, sending them deeper and deeper in shadow, until he realized he could make out little beyond the circle of their fire. Charlotte lay down and was soon sleeping. He folded one side of the space blanket over her.

Harper moved closer. "Tomorrow we'll get to the road," she said. "And if we don't, maybe we'll see a plane. There's bound to be some aerial searches by now."

"I shouldn't have set out to find her on my own," he said. "I should have urged the sheriff to look here. If you hadn't been there to stop Mick…"

"Don't!" She clutched his arm. "You did what you did with the best of intentions. You wanted to find Charlotte. And it worked out. One night out here isn't going to hurt any of us."

He looked down at his sleeping daughter. She was curled on her side against him, breathing evenly. She was dirty, her clothes ragged and her hair tangled, but she didn't appear traumatized by what had happened. "I didn't want to leave Mick," he said. "But getting Charlotte to safety was more important."

"You disabled his car. He's not going to be able to get far."

"You're right. I guess I'm just a worrier." He blew out a breath. "Maybe it comes with being a cop. You know all the ways a situation can go bad."

"And you became a parent. I think that probably makes you worry more. Children are so vulnerable."

He turned to study her, the side of her face visible in the flickering light from the fire. "What happened with our baby?" he asked. "I never knew, exactly. That is, if you don't mind talking about it."

"I don't mind." She stared into the fire for a moment, then said, "I was six months pregnant. I felt huge and awkward, and really tired sometimes, but I was getting excited, too. My aunt, who I was living with, talked a lot about putting the baby up for adoption, but I didn't think I wanted to do that." She looked at him, then away. "I had this fantasy that I would have the baby, get back home to Eagle Mountain and find you, and you would insist that we be together. A real family. I didn't think my parents would be able to keep you away from your daughter, which meant they couldn't keep you away from me, either."

"I thought about getting on my motorcycle and going to Florida to look for you, but I worried you wouldn't be happy to see me. Maybe you agreed to leave because you believed I really had hurt Aiden."

"No!" She gripped his arm. "Leaving you was awful, but it was even worse because you were going through such a terrible thing alone."

"Not exactly alone. My parents stood by me, and there were other people." He covered her hand with his own. "But you were the one I wanted."

"My parents made me leave," she said. "My mom said we were going to see friends. She put me in the car and the next thing I knew, we were at the airport. I pitched such a fit, and I didn't calm down until my mom told me we were just going to Florida for a few days to see my aunt. She pitched it as a chance for me to get away and decide what I wanted to do with my life. It wasn't until the next day that I realized they weren't going to let me come home until after the baby was born. And they refused to let me get in touch with you. My aunt watched me like a jailer. She didn't let me have a phone or go online. After a while I just stopped trying. And after I lost the baby, I was too sad to come back. I was so angry with my parents, and I felt guilty and confused." She shook her head. "When I did finally get back to Eagle Mountain..."

"I wasn't here. It didn't seem worth hanging around without you here," he said. "And even after the sheriff said I wasn't a suspect in Aiden's death, there were still people who believed I must have been involved. Going somewhere else to school was a chance to make a fresh start. But I never forgot about you."

"I never forgot about you, either." She blew out a breath. "Anyway, I don't really know what happened with the baby. One day I was fine. The next day I felt really tired and kind of queasy, but I didn't think anything of it. I woke up in the middle of the night and I knew that something wasn't right. I was cramping and bleeding. I screamed for my aunt and it took her a while to calm me down. She took me to the hospital but before we even got there I knew it was too late. The doctor said I had miscarried. He didn't know why. He just said sometimes these things happen."

He slipped his arm around her shoulder and pulled her close. "I'm sorry," he said. "I used to think about you and the baby. I didn't know if it was a boy or girl. The idea of being someone's father was scary. But I liked it, too. I wanted the chance to do the right thing. To be a good dad."

"You're a good dad to Charlotte."

"I try. But it's hard not to make mistakes. And I worry about her not having a mother. My mom does her best, but it's not the same. I would never have intentionally kept Kim out of her life. If she had come to me and said she wanted visitation, or even shared custody, I would have tried to work something out. I want what's best for Charlotte. But now—now I could never trust Kim. And I don't want Mick having anything to do with my kid."

"Will Kim go to jail?" she asked.

"Probably. That's not for me to decide. I'll do my best to see that Mick serves time, for threatening us with that axe, and then shooting at us. And if I find out he laid a hand on Charlotte…" Anger closed his throat, so that he couldn't finish the sentence.

Harper rubbed his back, a soothing gesture. He became aware of the heat and pressure of her hand, and her soft curves pressed against his side. "Do you remember the time we hiked up on Dakota Ridge?" she asked.

Heat flooded him at the memory. "It's not the hiking I remember," he said.

She laughed, a throaty, sexy sound. "It felt so daring to sneak back into the woods like that and make love outdoors," she said. "So exciting."

"I was worried you'd think it was too risky," he said. "Or that you wouldn't be comfortable out in the open like that."

"I was a little nervous," she admitted. "But I was with you. That was all that really mattered." She turned her face to his and he kissed her, as if more than ten years hadn't passed since that afternoon in the woods. Her lips were as soft as he remembered, and she still felt just as tantalizing pressed against him. She shifted to face him, and slid her arms around his waist. He deepened the kiss, her mouth hot. Needy. Her breasts beneath his palms were fuller than they had been then, but his own response was as urgent as ever—that feeling of wanting so much, balanced on the edge of control.

A whimper beside them reminded him they were not alone. Harper pulled back. "Charlotte needs you," she said, and looked away.

He turned to his daughter. She was still sleeping, but more restless now, whimpering and tossing her head. He laid a hand on her side. "It's okay, honey," he said. "I'm right here."

Charlotte didn't open her eyes, but she settled. "Probably just a bad dream," Harper whispered.

He looked up and met her gaze, the reflection of the campfire sparking gold in her brown eyes. She smiled, a hint of regret in the expression. "We should try to get some sleep," she said. "We have a big day tomorrow."

She turned away and crawled into one of the bivy bags, then lay with her back to him. Tomorrow he hoped they would be home and safe. And then what? What would happen to him and Harper? Could they try again to regain what they had lost, or had too much time passed and too many things happened for that to ever be possible?

Chapter Sixteen

"Ryker is missing. I'm worried about him." Wanda and Steve Vernon had been waiting for Sheriff Travis Walker when he showed up at the sheriff's department a little after eight o'clock Saturday morning. Adelaide summoned him to the lobby before he had even poured his first cup of coffee. He found Ryker's parents pacing the small reception area. Wanda didn't bother to say hello before voicing her concerns.

"When did you last see him?" Travis asked.

"Night before last." Steve Vernon had his son's dark hair and square chin, though his eyes were a lighter brown and his skin more weathered. "He said good-night and went upstairs, but I saw his light was still on when I went up to bed."

"I thought I heard him leave close to midnight," Wanda said. "I was lying there in bed, unable to sleep, and I heard the stairs creak, then the back door. I thought he was going for a drive to clear his head. I was waiting for him to return, but I must have finally drifted off. When we got up Friday morning, he wasn't there, but he often leaves before we're awake. I was annoyed when I didn't hear from him all day, but when he didn't show up for dinner, or after that, I got really worried. I wanted to call you right then, but Steve persuaded me we should wait."

"I figured he was out searching for Charlotte," Steve said. "I didn't want to embarrass him by contacting his boss."

Travis had spent most of the previous day in a spotter plane, flying over the mining district in search of the white Jeep Mick Davis was supposedly driving, or anything else out of the ordinary. Most of his deputies had been assigned to patrol the network of Jeep roads in the mountains. No one had come up with anything. "I was out all yesterday, searching," he said. "I didn't see any sign of Ryker or his vehicle."

Wanda hugged her arms across her chest. "I can't believe this is happening—first Charlotte, now Ryker." She had striking features, with high cheekbones in a heart-shaped face, her long, dark hair just beginning to show gray at the temples.

Travis had a vague memory that she had once been a local beauty queen. Miss Rayford County or something like that. "I assume you've tried calling and texting him?" he asked.

"Of course. But I'm not getting any answer."

Steve rubbed his wife's shoulder. "If he's in the mountains, he probably doesn't have cell service."

Wanda shrugged off his hand. "Ryker said Mick Davis has a criminal record, but he wouldn't tell me what for. What if he went after Ryker? Either because he's Charlotte's dad or because he's a law enforcement officer?"

"We don't have any reason to believe Mick has anything personally against Ryker," Travis said.

The front door to the sheriff's department opened and Valerie Stanick entered. She stopped and frowned at the Vernons, then focused on the sheriff. "Harper didn't come back to her apartment last night," she said. "She's not answering her phone, and she didn't show up for work yesterday. That's not like her at all."

Wanda clutched her husband's arm. "Maybe Harper is with Ryker."

"What would she be doing with Ryker?" Valerie put a definite chill behind her words. Like Wanda, Valerie had the kind of beauty that didn't fade with age. Her blond hair was swept back off her forehead and her hazel eyes seemed capable of looking right through a man. Travis found himself squaring his shoulders and standing up a little straighter as he faced her.

"Harper has been helping Ryker search for Charlotte," Wanda said. "They spent at least one afternoon driving around the mining district, searching for them. Harper didn't tell you?"

Valerie's lips tightened. She addressed the sheriff. "Where is Ryker now?"

"We don't know." Steve Vernon spoke up. "We came here to report that he didn't come home last night."

"And you think he just ran off with my daughter? Eloped?"

"Of course not!" Wanda's voice rose. "Ryker wouldn't leave town as long as Charlotte is missing. He wouldn't. I'm sure the two of them are somewhere, looking for her." She turned to the sheriff. "But what if Ryker's truck broke down, or they got lost hiking?"

"If Harper is hurt, I blame your son," Valerie said to Steve.

"Ryker hasn't done anything wrong," Wanda protested.

"Ryker would never hurt Harper," Steve said. "He cares about her a great deal. He always has." He looked sadder, and older, as he spoke.

"I'll ask my deputies to keep a lookout for them," Travis

said. "We're sending a drone up in some areas today to do some lower-altitude searches."

"Have you heard anything at all about Charlotte?" Wanda asked.

"When we picked up her mother, she said Charlotte was with Mick Davis," Travis said. "We don't know any more than that at this time."

Wanda couldn't see Valerie's face from where she was standing, but Travis could. Valerie looked as if she was on the verge of sobbing. He put a hand on Wanda's arm. "I promise we'll look for Ryker. And for Harper. I'm sure you're right and the two of them are hunting for Charlotte. I'll keep you posted."

Steve moved in to take his wife's arm and steer her toward the door. "Thank you, Travis," he said, and they left.

Valerie nodded, and hurried after them.

Adelaide moved in and handed Travis a cup of coffee. "I'm concerned that Wanda is right and Ryker and Harper are lost or have had car trouble," she said.

"I'll alert the deputies to be on the lookout for them while they're searching for Charlotte." Travis turned toward his office.

"I hope we find that little girl soon."

"I do, too." He knew all the statistics about missing persons—the longer someone, especially a child, stayed missing, the less chance of finding them. Trails went cold. And anything could happen in the rough country where Charlotte and Mick had last been seen.

HARPER SCOOTED CLOSER to the campfire, trying to warm her icy hands. She had forgotten how cold even summer nights could be at this elevation. The bivy bags had kept them from freezing last night, but they hadn't offered much in the way of comfort. She had awakened every couple of hours, sore and stiff from lying on the hard ground. She had heard Ryker tossing and turning, too. Only Charlotte had slept soundly.

When Ryker had risen shortly before dawn to feed sticks and broken tree limbs into the fire, Harper had joined him and tried not to think about how wonderful a cup of coffee with cream and sugar would be right now. She and Ryker had shared part of the remaining bar, along with an energy gel that was probably past its prime but better than nothing. When Charlotte woke, Harper made her a cup of cocoa from a packet she found at the bottom of her pack. The adults drank water, and Harper washed down a couple of ibuprofen from her first aid kit, though it did little to relieve the headache that pounded at her temples. *We're going to be home in a few hours*, she reminded herself. She was going to shower, eat and take a nap. By tomorrow all of this misery would be only a memory.

Ryker sat on a section of log across from the little blaze and studied a map he had spread out across his knees. "I think we're in here somewhere," he said, and stabbed his index finger at the map.

Harper moved over until she could see the position he indicated among the contour lines of the map. "If we head east, then south, we should reach this drainage here," he said. He indicated another spot on the map. "If we follow that, we should reach the road here." His finger traced a path to the dark line that designated the road. "From there we can walk back up the road about half a mile to the parking area where we left our cars."

It was a lot of walking, over rough terrain, but knowing they had a plan lifted Harper's spirits. "That's terrific." She rested her hand on his shoulder, enjoying the reassuring strength of him. Last night by the fire she had felt so close to him. As if they were starting to mend the rift that had separated them for so long. She told herself not to get her hopes up, but her heart wasn't listening to logic.

"Finished!" Charlotte, wrapped in one of the bivy bags, held their single cup aloft. A faint chocolate moustache adorned her upper lip, along with a few crumbs from one of the protein bars.

"That's great." Harper took the cup and smoothed back the girl's hair, which was a mess of dirty tangles. "How are you feeling this morning?"

"Okay." Charlotte looked to her father. "Are we going home today?"

"We are." He stood, then scooped her into his arms. "We're going to go home and your grandmother is going to make you whatever you want for supper."

"Pizza!" Charlotte didn't hesitate in her choice. "And trees, with butter."

Ryker laughed, then, seeing Harper's puzzled look, said, "Broccoli is Charlotte's favorite vegetable."

"They do look like little trees," Harper said. She smiled at Charlotte, who answered with a grin. Harper's heart flipped over in her chest. Even if she didn't already care for Ryker, she was completely besotted with his little girl.

They packed up camp, made sure the campfire was extinguished, then set out, Ryker regularly checking the map he had downloaded to his phone to make sure they stayed on course. If she had been fed and caffeinated, Harper might have enjoyed the hike more, but she was grateful for the mild weather and the mostly-downhill route they followed. She walked behind Ryker, with Charlotte between them, and passed the time admiring his strong shoulders beneath his pack, narrow hips and attractive backside. She smiled to herself, remembering sitting behind him in high school chemistry and amusing herself this same way.

When Charlotte began to tire, they took turns carrying her. Harper balanced the little girl on one hip. She wasn't a very large child, and seemed so vulnerable with her tangled hair, dirty clothes and scraped knees. A wave of tenderness washed over Harper as she held the child close.

Charlotte studied her, and Harper wondered what she was thinking. The scrutiny was unnerving, so she tried to break the tension with conversation. "What's your favorite color?" she asked.

"Pink. What's yours?"

"Blue."

"Blue is my dad's favorite color, too."

Harper nodded. She had known this, though she hadn't thought about it for a long time. "I guess pizza is your favorite food," she said. "What kind?"

"Cheese," Charlotte said. "Dad likes sausage."

Harper nodded. She remembered that from the pizzas the two of them had shared in school. Back then, Ryker could eat an entire large pizza by himself and never seem full.

But never mind what she already knew about Ryker. Here was her chance to discover things she didn't know. "Does your dad read to you?" she asked. "Bedtime stories?"

"Sometimes. Grandma reads to me most of the time. Dad sometimes sits with me while she reads, when he doesn't have to work."

Harper pictured the three of them—the little girl tucked into bed, Ryker on one side and Wanda on the other. A little family. Would there ever be room for another woman in that scene? Room for her?

"Daddy is a sheriff's deputy," Charlotte said. "He helps people when they're in trouble."

"Yes, he does."

Charlotte studied her a moment longer, her gaze traveling over each detail of Harper's face. Harper remained still, wondering what this little girl thought of her. "What do you do?" Charlotte asked when she had completed her inspection.

"I draw maps," Harper said.

Charlotte's forehead wrinkled. "How do you do that?" she asked.

"Do you remember the map your dad was looking at this morning?" Harper asked. "He was figuring out which way we needed to walk to get back to his truck. Lots of lines on a piece of paper?"

Charlotte nodded, though she still looked doubtful. "That's what I do," Harper said. "I draw maps like that one. Or maps of towns that show where the houses and streets are located. Or pictures of hiking trails. Or ski trails."

Clearly, Charlotte was unimpressed. "Do you have a dog?" she asked.

"No. Do you?"

"No, but I want one. Do you think when I get home Grandma and Grandpa will be so happy to see me, they'll let me get a puppy?"

Harper suppressed a laugh. If it were up to her, she would run straight out to find a puppy for this little darling. "You never know," she said instead.

"I want to get down now," Charlotte said, so Harper set her carefully on the ground and she ran ahead to catch up with Ryker.

They hiked for three hours, scarcely stopping to switch off carrying Charlotte, or to drink the last of their water. Harper's head and shoulders and back and legs ached, but she kept putting one foot in front of the other, focused on getting to the truck. She could sit down there. Lock the doors. They would be safe. The memory of Mick brandishing the axe, then firing a gun at them had disturbed her dreams, and all morning she had found herself searching their surroundings for any sign of him.

The drainage had been formed from snowmelt trickling down during the spring thaw. It was dry now, littered with loose boulders and the stubby new growth of saplings and shrubs. They had to pick their way as the elevation dropped, avoiding loose rocks and unstable soil. The sun beat down and a fly repeatedly buzzed in Harper's ear. She swatted it away and focused on their destination. A little before noon they emerged onto the road. She had been taking another turn carrying Charlotte, and Ryker took the child from her. "Not much farther to go now," he said.

When they drew in sight of the parking area a short time later, her heart beat faster as she recognized her Subaru, looking dusty and a little forlorn by itself on the side of the road. "Where is your truck?" she asked Ryker.

"I don't know." He picked up his speed, trotting the final hundred yards, then stopped in the spot beside her car where his truck had been parked.

Harper looked all around them, but there was no sign of the truck. "We disabled Mick's Jeep so he couldn't get away in it," Ryker said. "He must have hiked here and stolen my truck."

"We still have my car." Harper pulled the keys from the side pocket of her pack and pressed the button on the fob to unlock the doors. All she wanted was to get the three of them back to the safety of town.

Ryker set Charlotte on the ground and slipped off his pack. "As soon as we have a cell signal I'll call the sheriff and let him know Mick probably has my truck."

Harper slid into the driver's seat and inserted the key into the ignition. Then she merely sat for a moment, enjoying the feeling of sitting down on a soft surface. Ryker settled Charlotte in the back seat and fastened the seat belt over her hips. "We don't have a booster seat for you," he said. "But we'll have to make do for now. You have to promise to sit back and be still."

"I promise."

Harper turned the key in the ignition. *Tick, tick, tick...*

She stared at Ryker, wide eyed. "Pop the hood," he said.

She reached under the dash and pulled the handle to release the latch. He got out and raised the hood and peered into the engine compartment. He swore.

"Daddy said a bad word," Charlotte said.

Harper got out and joined Ryker at the front of the car. "What's wrong?" she asked.

"He ripped out every wire he could reach," he said. "Someone did. But I'm sure it was Mick. And he flattened three of the tires."

She hadn't even noticed the tires in her eagerness to sit inside the car. She might have said a few bad words herself, but she didn't have the energy. "What do we do now?" she asked.

He lowered the hood. "We're going to have to walk. At least until we get a cell signal and can call for help."

She could have lain down then and there and wept, but that wouldn't help anything. Ryker must have read her thoughts from her expression. "I'd offer to go for help by myself," he said. "But I don't like the idea of leaving you and Charlotte alone, in case Mick comes back."

"No. We stay together." She went back to the driver's seat and leaned in. "Charlotte, honey, my car is broken," she said. "We're going to have to walk until we can call for help."

Charlotte began to cry, and Harper felt tears well in her own eyes. "I know, honey. I feel that way, too," she said. "But we're just going to have to do it. No pizza until we do."

Charlotte sobbed harder. Ryker leaned in, unbuckled her, and pulled her close. She continued to sob as he led the way down the road. Harper locked the car, with their packs inside, and followed. One foot in front of the other. And hoped Mick Davis didn't decide to come back.

Chapter Seventeen

Jamie stifled a yawn, and shifted in the driver's seat of her sheriff's department SUV. Her daughter had been fussier than usual last night, with Jamie and her husband, Nate, taking turns getting up with her. It had taken a very hot shower and a lot of hot coffee to get going this morning, but the thought of Ryker's little girl out there somewhere with a man who wasn't her father had spurred her on. Today, she decided to focus on some of the more remote roads in the mining district. Dwight had said he had driven up there the day before yesterday and discovered the road to the mine blocked by a rockslide, making it unlikely that Mick Davis and Charlotte were up there. But Jamie had felt compelled to check it out for herself. Maybe Davis had cleared a path around the rockslide, or there was another route they hadn't explored yet.

She was making her way up the county road toward the Jeep route when a black Ford pickup passed her on the left. Jamie stared hard at the vehicle. That looked like Ryker's truck. She pressed down harder on the gas, trying to catch up. She came around a curve in time to see the truck turn onto the same Jeep road she had been headed for. She made the turn also, and tried to get close enough to read the license plate number. Dust boiled up beneath the truck's tires, obscuring the plate.

The sheriff had sent a call out earlier that Ryker and Harper Stanick were both missing. "We think they were searching for Charlotte, but they may have run into car trouble so be on the lookout," the sheriff said.

Jamie sped up, gritting her teeth as the SUV bounced up the washboarded road. She could see the truck more clearly now, though she still couldn't read the license plate. The back window was streaked with dirt, but she could make out a single occupant, wearing a dark windbreaker, much like the black Rayford County Sheriff's Department jacket Jamie herself wore. And the driver's hair was covered by a black knit cap. Hadn't she seen Ryker in a similar cap recently?

She tried to get closer, but the truck pulled away, kicking up gravel that hit her windshield. She let off the accelerator and flashed her lights, but the truck didn't stop, so she hit the siren. One loud whoop. The truck sped up even more.

As if he was trying to get away from her.

She pulled to the side of the road and shifted into Park, then keyed her radio. Signal repeaters positioned around the county were supposed to enable communication from anywhere, but depending on the terrain and the weather, they weren't always reliable. "Dispatch, this is Rayford County Sheriff's Department Unit 16."

"Hello, Jamie. What can I do for you?" Dispatcher Sally Graham's friendly voice responded.

"I'm headed south on the road up to the Jack's Peak trailhead. I'm following a truck that looks like the one Ryker drives. And there's a man in the cab who could be Ryker, but he's not stopping, even though I let him know I'm behind him."

"Hang on, I'm going to connect you with the sheriff."

As she waited, Jamie stared at the cloud of dust ahead that marked the truck's progress. Ryker or whoever was driving the vehicle was well above the posted speed limit of twenty-five miles per hour for these Jeep roads. In some places, even twenty-five was too much speed for the narrow, rutted tracks and sharp curves.

"Jamie, you think you've spotted Ryker?" Travis's clipped voice came on the line.

"Yes, sir. He passed me on the county road and turned onto the Jeep road up toward the Jack's Peak trail."

"You're sure it's Ryker?"

"No, sir. It looks like his truck, but I can't get close enough to read the license plate, and I can only tell you there's a person driving who appears to be a man about Ryker's height and build. But he was clearly trying to get away from me. He wouldn't stop even when I flashed my lights and hit the siren."

"Any passengers in the vehicle?"

"Not that I could see."

"Can you still see the vehicle?" Travis asked.

"Just the dust cloud he made. But I don't know of anywhere around here to turn off the road."

"Proceed cautiously," Travis said. "I'll send backup out your way."

"Have you heard anything from Ryker or Harper?"

"Not yet. Whoever this is, keep your distance until backup arrives."

"Yes, sir." She ended the transmission and steered her SUV back into the road. Ryker had no reason to run away from her, so maybe whoever was driving that car wasn't him. But if that was true, what had happened to Ryker?

RYKER SHIFTED CHARLOTTE from one hip to the other and trudged across the uneven terrain, keeping parallel to the road as much as possible, but out of sight of any driver—particularly Mick Davis—who might pass. Every joint in his body ached, and his head pounded. He was furious at Mick and Kim, and at himself, too. If he had taken the trouble to investigate Mick more thoroughly when Kim first got together with him, maybe he could have been better prepared for the possibility that the two of them might try something like this. At the very least he could have prepared Charlotte to resist an attempt by Kim to take her without permission. He had wanted to believe the best of his ex, but that attitude had put their daughter in danger.

He glanced over his shoulder at Harper, who walked with her head down, back bent. She looked weary and defeated, and guilt stabbed at him. He had put her in danger, too. As if he hadn't put her through enough in their time together, what with the surprise pregnancy, her parents' disapproval, her banishment to Florida, and his inability to be with her when she needed him most. He had been thrilled to find she didn't harbor resentment for all of that, but now he had pulled her into this mess. He wouldn't blame her if she didn't want anything to do with him after this.

She lifted her head and smiled. "Do you need me to take Charlotte for a bit?" she asked, and hurried to catch up with him.

"Do you want Harper to carry you for a little bit?" he asked Charlotte.

"No." Charlotte pressed her forehead into his shoulder.

"Maybe you'd like to get down and walk on your own for a little bit?" Ryker asked.

"No!"

Harper's eyes met his, her expression sympathetic. "She's probably worn out," she said.

They were all worn out. Ryker dug his phone from his pocket and checked to see if he had a signal yet. Nope. And his battery was getting low. He had turned it off overnight to conserve the battery but now that it kept searching for a tower, it was draining fast.

Harper stopped and put a hand on Ryker's arm, stopping him. "I think I hear a car coming," she said.

He raised his head. Yes, that was the distant crunch of tires on gravel, and the whine of an engine straining up a grade. "Maybe we can catch a ride," he said.

"Unless it's Mick," she said.

He nodded. "Let's get out of sight and take a look. If it isn't Mick, we can probably run after it and get the driver's attention."

They moved farther off the road into a clump of sagebrush, and crouched down. Moments later, Ryker's own truck rocketed past, rocks pinging as they hit the undercarriage, suspension protesting as the vehicle charged in and out of ruts. "He's going to tear up my truck, driving like that on these roads," he said.

"Was Mick driving?" Harper asked.

"I didn't see who it was," Ryker said. "But it had to be Mick. He's probably heading back to the parking area to see if he can intercept us."

"He'll see our packs in my car and know we've been there," Harper said. "What do we do?"

"We keep walking, but we have to stay off the road and out of sight."

They stood and set out again, but Charlotte balked. "I don't want to walk anymore!" she wailed. "I'm tired and hot and hungry. I want to stop. I want to go home." She sobbed, tears dampening the front of Ryker's shirt.

He rubbed her back, frustrated by his inability to do anything to help her. "I know you're hungry and hot and tired," he said. "Harper and I are too. I promise, we're doing everything we can to get you home. But to do that, we have to keep moving."

"Let me take her for a while," Harper said. "That way you'll have both hands free."

She didn't say she wanted him to be able to draw his weapon if Mick returned, but he was sure she was thinking it. He certainly was. If Mick did return and find them, it would be up to Ryker to protect both Charlotte and Harper. He wasn't going to let anything happen to them.

Charlotte screamed as Harper peeled her away from Ryker, but Harper merely cuddled her close. She whispered in Charlotte's ear and before long the child calmed and clung to Harper. "I think we're ready now," Harper said.

Ryker turned to lead the way back toward the county road when he heard his truck returning, the roar of the engine rapidly growing louder. Once again, they dove for shelter, this time in a trio of piñons clustered close to the road.

The truck wasn't moving as fast this time. Ryker could clearly see Mick as he passed by them, the driver's window rolled down. A short distance past them, he stopped the vehicle in the middle of the road. "What's he doing?" Harper whispered.

Ryker shook his head. He reached back and eased his pistol out of its holster and brought it forward. The truck door opened and Mick slid out. He stood for a moment, looking around, then turned and began walking toward them. Sun glinted off the pistol in his hand.

He stopped when he was only a few feet from them and

aimed the gun at the clump of trees where they waited. "Get out of there and stand up slowly," he said. "Don't try anything."

Harper stared at Ryker, wide-eyed. Charlotte whimpered and reached for him. Ryker shook his head. He still wasn't sure Mick knew they were here. Maybe he was only guessing.

"Do it!" Mick shouted, and fired the gun. Bark tore from one of the tree trunks as the bullet hit it. Charlotte screamed so loudly Ryker worried she had been hit. "She's okay," Harper said. She smoothed the girl's hair. "She's okay."

"Stay down," Ryker said. He laid his pistol on the ground, right beside Harper, then slowly stood, his hands in the air.

"The woman and the girl, too," Mick said. "Now!"

Harper popped up, Charlotte beside her. Harper gripped Charlotte's hand.

"Throw out your gun," Mick ordered. "I know you've got one."

Ryker looked down at the pistol. "It's on the ground," he said. "I have to bend down to pick it up."

"Leave it, then, and step out here."

They did as he ordered, Ryker first, then Harper and Charlotte.

"Why didn't you leave when you could?" Harper asked. "You had the truck. You could be in New Mexico by now."

"I came back for Charlotte," he said. He wore a battered black baseball cap that shielded his eyes from view, but his words alone were enough to send a shiver down Ryker's spine.

"What do you want with her?" he asked.

"I like her. And I think she'd be useful. If I've got her with me as a hostage, the cops will have to let me go to save her. No one wants to see a little girl get hurt."

"You'll never lay a hand on her," Ryker said.

"You talk tough, but I'm the one with the gun. Come out here before I decide to shoot you. Or maybe I'll shoot your girlfriend. How would you like that?"

Harper glanced at Ryker. Then he realized she wasn't looking at him but past him, down the road. Then he heard what had caught her attention. The crunch of tires on gravel.

"Hurry up!" Mick shouted.

Ryker took a step toward the truck. Harper started after him, then stopped. He looked back to see her crouched on the ground, next to Charlotte. She stared into Charlotte's face. "You need to run," she told the little girl. "As fast and as far away from Mick as you can. Your dad and I will distract him, then we'll catch up with you later."

Charlotte looked up at Ryker. He nodded. "Run," he said, keeping his voice soft, but trying to convey the urgency of the matter.

Harper stood and Charlotte ran. Ryker bounded down the slope to the road, hoping his movements would distract Mick. "Hey!" Mick shouted, and raised the pistol as if to fire. But the wail of a siren shattered the stillness, and he swiveled toward the sound. Two Rayford County Sheriff's Department SUVs hurtled toward them.

The first SUV slid sideways and stopped, blocking the road. Mick turned toward it, mouth open. He was still holding the gun, but he held it at his side, the muzzle pointed at the dirt. Ryker stared at the weapon for half a second before making his decision. He rushed forward and threw Mick to the ground.

The gun went off, the bullet striking the ground. Then Deputy Jamie Douglas was out of the SUV and she and Ryker subdued Mick. They had him handcuffed, face down in the road, when Travis and Gage Walker joined them.

Ryker nodded at the sheriff and his brother, then turned to look toward the roadside. "Charlotte!" he shouted.

"It's okay. We're both right here." Harper walked down the road toward them, Charlotte in her arms.

Ryker met them and took Charlotte, then put his free hand on her shoulder. "Are you okay?" he asked.

She nodded. "I am now. What about you?"

He fit Charlotte more securely on his hip, then took Harper's hand in his. Behind him, he could hear Jamie reciting the Miranda warning to Mick as she and Gage transferred him to Gage's SUV. "I'm okay now," he said. As okay as he'd ever be again.

RYKER WAS STILL holding Harper's hand when the sheriff walked up to them. "Your parents and Harper's mother were at the sheriff's department first thing this morning to report the two of you missing," he said. "Have you been with Mick Davis all this time?"

"We tracked him down to the Lucky Six Mine, where he'd set up camp," Ryker said. "We took Charlotte and got away on foot. We got off track and had to work our way back to the road. Mick was looking for us and spotted us. You all showed up just in time."

"Your truck passed me on the county road and turned off onto this Jeep trail." Jamie moved up beside the sheriff. "We had been alerted to look for you, but when you didn't pull over when I signaled you, I got worried enough to call for help."

"Come on," Travis said. "You can give your statements back at the office. Your parents are waiting for you."

They rode to town in the sheriff's SUV, Ryker in the front passenger seat, Harper in the back next to Charlotte in a car seat Travis unearthed from the back of the vehicle.

"My twins aren't big enough for this yet, but we keep a few spares at the department to hand out to people who might need them," he explained as he buckled it into the vehicle.

Harper studied the back of Ryker's head as they drove. Charlotte fell asleep and Harper felt if she closed her eyes and allowed herself, she might doze off, too. "You said my mother reported me missing?" she asked Travis.

"Yes. She walked in a few minutes after Ryker's parents came to ask us to look for him." He glanced in the rearview mirror, catching her eye. "When Ryker's mother said she thought you and Ryker might be together, your mother asked if the two of you had eloped."

"Eloped?" Ryker sounded horrified at the idea—because her mother had asked, or because he was appalled at the idea? Not that Harper wanted to run away this minute to get married, but his reaction made her queasy. Was the idea of the two of them married really so awful?

At the station, they had scarcely entered the front doors before Wanda and Steve Vernon surrounded them. "Charlotte, I'm so happy to see you." Tears streamed down Wanda's face as she gathered the little girl close.

Steve embraced his son. "I knew you'd find her," he said.

Harper took a step back, not wanting to intrude on this family reunion. She spotted her mother and father on the other side of the room and went to join them. Her father hugged her. "I'm glad you're okay, sweetheart," he said.

Valerie studied her daughter. "You look like you had a rough night," she said. She stared at Harper's hair, which probably needed combing.

"Did you really think Ryker and I eloped?" It wasn't the way she had planned to start the conversation with her mother—the words burst out on their own accord.

The line between Valerie's eyebrows deepened. "You've never behaved rationally around that man," she said.

"Ryker isn't *that man*," Harper said. "He's someone I care about. Very much."

Valerie started to speak, but Harper interrupted. "I'm an adult now," she said. "You can't send me off to Florida because you don't like the decision I made."

"Yes, you are." Her dad put his arm around her. "Your mom and I will be here for you, no matter what happens."

Valerie pressed her lips together. Harper couldn't tell if it was because she was trying not to say something she might later regret—or because she was trying not to cry. Valerie looked down at the floor, then up again, and said. "I wasn't trying to ruin your life when I sent you to Florida. I was trying to keep you from making a big mistake. You were too young, and I didn't think Ryker was the right man for you."

"Because you thought he had something to do with his cousin's death."

She flushed. "I wasn't the only one who believed that. And they never found anyone else who was responsible, did they?"

"Ryker didn't have anything to do with Aiden's abduction," Harper said. "The DNA evidence proved that, but I knew he wasn't capable of such a thing."

"I didn't know that," Valerie said. "And I had to protect you. When you have a child of your own one day, you'll understand."

Harper thought of how much she had wanted to protect Charlotte, and she hugged her mother. "It's okay, Mom. I don't think it hurt anything that Ryker and I both had time to grow up. And I'm sorry I worried you two."

"You're safe now," her dad said. "That's all that matters." He joined in the hug and Harper savored this feeling of closeness. As often as they had clashed, she could see now her mother's actions had come from a place of love. Time had given her a new perspective.

She hoped the years had given her courage, too. Courage to stand up to her parents, sure. But also courage to go after the man she wanted. Or at least to find out how he really felt about her, knowing she might not get the answer she wanted to hear.

THREE HOURS LATER, Ryker stood at the door to Charlotte's bedroom, watching her sleep. She lay curled on her side beneath her pink comforter, a daisy-shaped night-light giving off a soft glow. She smelled of strawberry bath gel, her clean blond hair spread out on her pillow. She had eaten pizza and ice cream, and had made it halfway through a bedtime story before she had fallen asleep. Ryker, having showered and shaved and eaten, should have been headed for his own bed. But energy buzzed through him, and his brain kept replaying scenes from the past few days, from the shoot-out with Mick Davis to last night's campfire conversation with Harper.

His mother moved in beside him. "I can't stop checking to make sure she really is still here," Wanda said softly.

"I know." He let out a long breath. "But she is here. And Kim and Mick are in jail. She's safe. We all are." Logically, he believed this to be true. It would probably take a little longer for his emotions to settle down and accept that, but he trusted it would come.

"What about Harper?"

He met his mother's gaze. Her expression was one he had seen so many times in his life, one that said she had an opinion on the situation under discussion, but wanted to hear his take before she gave advice. Whether he wanted her opinion or not, he was going to get it and no sense arguing. As she had said more than once when he was growing up, "I'm your mother and I have an obligation to try to teach you at least a little of what I know."

"Harper…is complicated," he said. "My job takes so much of my time, and Charlotte deserves the rest."

"Lots of people manage to juggle jobs and children and relationships."

"I know, but—"

Wanda laid a hand on his arm. "Do you love her?"

He hesitated only a few seconds before he nodded. "Yes."

"Then you should tell her."

He looked back at his sleeping daughter, a dozen reasons why that would not be a good idea filling his head.

"I think Charlotte would like to have a mother," Wanda said. "And I think you shouldn't be alone."

"If it doesn't work out between us, it will hurt Charlotte, too." And it would hurt him. That possibility frightened him more than he would ever admit.

"I remember the way the two of you were together, even when you were seventeen and eighteen. And I've seen the two of you together now. Don't let fear of something that probably won't ever happen keep you from being happy now."

He turned back to his mother. She smiled up at him. "Go on. Charlotte isn't going to wake up for hours, and you won't rest until you've seen Harper."

He kissed her cheek. "How did you get to be so smart?"

"I raised a smart boy. I had to keep up with you."

"Can I borrow the Jeep?" Ryker asked. "The evidence team is still going over my truck."

"Of course, dear. Tell Harper we said hello."

He retrieved the keys and walked out to the Jeep, parked at the side of the house. Movement in the bushes brought him up short and he pivoted toward the sound, just as Gary Langley emerged. The light from a window flashed on something bright as the older man lunged, and Ryker instinctively dodged out of the way, then felt the sharp edge of a knife slicing his arm.

Langley lunged again, but Ryker shoved back, then kicked one leg out to trip the old man. Langley fell hard, taking Ryker down with him. The two men rolled, the knife cutting Ryker again. He felt the sting, and the sticky warmth of blood, but adrenaline numbed the pain. He smashed his fist against Langley's jaw, then grabbed his wrist and bent it back. The knife rattled against the gravel of the driveway. Ryker knelt on the older man's chest and pinned both arms at his sides. "Try anything else and I swear I'll break your arm," Ryker said.

Langley blinked up at him, transformed once more from angry predator to weak old man. "I thought I could take you by surprise and silence you before anyone heard," he said.

"Why would you try to kill me?" Ryker asked.

"You were asking too many questions about things that happened a long time ago."

"You kidnapped Aiden and killed him."

Langley turned his head to the side. "I'm not saying anything."

Ryker rolled Langley onto his stomach, and used his own bootlaces to tie his hands. Then he stood and pulled out his phone to call the sheriff. "Gary Langley attacked me with a knife outside my home," he said.

The sheriff arrived a few minutes later, along with an ambulance. Steve and Wanda emerged from the house and Wanda turned pale at the sight of the blood running down

Ryker's arms. "It's okay, Mom," he said. "It's going to be okay."

Two deputies put Langley in restraints and the sheriff interviewed Ryker while Hannah cleaned and bandaged the cuts on his arms, none of which were very deep. "Your jacket protected you," she said as she applied rows of Steri-Strips across the longest wound. "But you'll need to be careful of infection, and make sure you're up to date on your tetanus vaccine."

She left them and Travis said, "I did some checking and Langley was asked to resign from his coaching position because there had been complaints he was paying the wrong kind of attention to some of the kids."

"Aiden played soccer for a little while," Ryker said. He buttoned up the new shirt he had asked his mom to bring from the house. "He probably knew Langley."

"I'm going to do some more digging. Aiden might not be the only child he harmed."

"That accident he had likely saved a lot of kids," Ryker said. "He probably thought he had gotten away with Aiden's murder, and then I came back and started asking questions."

"Questions that should have been asked years ago," Travis said. "We're going to check his DNA. If it's a match to that found on Aiden's body, he won't have a chance to hurt anyone else."

Ryker nodded. He had no doubt the DNA would be a match. He stood. "Is that all you need from me?"

Travis nodded. "Get some rest. We'll finish up the paperwork in the morning."

But Ryker had no intention of resting. He drove to Harper's apartment, grateful she had her own place. He thought he could deal with her parents when the time came, but he didn't really want them witnessing this particular conversation.

Harper answered the door wearing a clean T-shirt and shorts, barefoot with her toenails painted pink. Her hair was damp and her cheeks flushed, and the air around her smelled of vanilla. Her gaze shifted to the single bandage on the side of his face. "Ryker! Is everything okay?"

"Can I come in?"

"Sure." She held the door wider and he moved past her into a living room furnished with a sofa and chair, and what looked like an antique rocking chair. There were shelves of books and plants, and lots of pictures on the walls, from local landscapes to photographs of people he didn't know. "What happened?" she asked, and gestured to the bandage.

"Gary Langley attacked me outside my house tonight."

"Who is Gary Langley?"

"I think he's the person who kidnapped and killed Aiden. I've been looking into the case. He was a youth soccer coach and local handyman when Aiden was abducted. A neighbor reported seeing a truck that looked like Langley's the night Aiden disappeared, but it was never properly followed up on. Langley found out I was taking a closer look at him and decided to try to stop me."

"Ryker! You could have been killed."

"But I wasn't. And Langley is behind bars and will probably stay there for a long time. Maybe the rest of his life." That knowledge energized him, even though he ought to be exhausted. He looked around the room again, and focused on a large map that hung over the mantel of a gas fireplace. He moved closer and realized it was a map of Eagle Mountain, hand-drawn with all the local landmarks and businesses carefully labeled.

"Did you draw this?" he asked.

She came to stand beside him, close enough he realized the vanilla aroma was coming from her hair. "I did. You can get a copy of your own, on a smaller scale, from the visitor's bureau." She hugged her arms across her chest. "It was one of the first projects I did when I moved back. It helped me get to know my hometown again."

"I'm glad you came back," he said.

"Are you?"

Was that hurt he heard in her voice, or merely his own doubts coloring his interpretation? He turned to her. "I love you," he said. "I'm not sure I ever stopped but seeing you again, I knew. I just didn't know if that was enough to make up for all the mistakes I made before."

She dropped her hands to her sides, her expression puzzled. "What mistakes did you make? I'm the one who left town without even telling you where I was going."

"Because your parents wouldn't let you. I knew that. But I should have tried harder to find you. I left you pregnant and alone with strangers."

"I was with my aunt. And she was kind, even if she wasn't exactly thrilled to have me with her."

"But you had to go through losing the baby without me there."

"I did." She moved closer, and slid her arms around his waist. "But I never blamed you. I blamed my parents—especially my mom. But I never blamed you."

"Why not?"

She smiled. "I guess because I still loved you so much. In my eyes, you could do no wrong."

"If you had only known I was off getting involved with a woman I never should have gone out with, much less married. A woman who would leave me for an ex-con and return years later to kidnap our daughter and lead me to dragging you along to chase after her boyfriend, who could have ended up killing you." A tremor shook him at the last words, and Harper hugged him more tightly.

"What happened in the past isn't as important as what we do now," she said. "I love you and I love Charlotte, too. I want to be a part of your lives."

He looked into her eyes, and all the fear left him. He wanted to be with her. He wanted Charlotte to know her better. He wanted the three of them to make the family they had been denied before. All that hope didn't leave any room for worry and doubt. "I love you," he said, and kissed her.

In the fairy tales he sometimes read Charlotte, kisses were magical things, turning frogs into princes and waking sleeping beauties. Harper's kiss was like that, breaking the lock he had kept on his emotions. He didn't have to be anywhere or answer to anyone or worry that at any moment she might turn on him. All he had to do was be here with her and enjoy the feel of her body pressed to his, the softness of her lips and the heat that spread through him as she stroked her hands down his back.

She broke the kiss and smiled up at him. "Do you remember the afternoon we sneaked into your house when your parents were away, and made love in your bedroom?" she asked.

"Yes. I wanted you so much, yet I was nervous we would get caught." That afternoon had been both wonderful and awful, since he had felt cheated of the ability to fully enjoy it.

"No parents to interrupt us here," she said, a wicked gleam in her eye.

He took her hand and kissed her palm. "Where's the bedroom?" he asked.

Later, he couldn't have told anyone what the room looked like, except that the mattress was soft and the sheets cool and silky, and she was beautiful. She was different, yet the same, more mature, more confident, yet the same woman he had loved all along. Making love to her was new and exciting and so familiar. He remembered what she liked and how she made him feel. He wanted to touch and kiss every inch of her, yet his body—and her urgent movements and breathy sighs—told him neither of them wanted to wait the time that might take. He settled for kissing his way down her torso, then pausing to gaze up at her. "Do you have a condom?"

She laughed.

"What's so funny?"

She rolled over and opened the drawer of her bedside table and pulled out a strip of foil packets. "I was just thinking that as much as this all feels the same for us, we have at least learned to be a little more responsible." She tore off a packet and thrust it at him. "Just so you know, I bought these after that first day I ran into you, up on Dixon Pass at that accident call."

"Really? The first day?"

"I had hopes."

"Then let's see if we can make a few dreams come true. For both of us." He tore open the packet.

She lay back against the pillows, watching him with an expression that was more erotic than any touch. He rolled on the condom, then moved up to lie beside her. She trailed her fingers down his chest. "One day I'll draw a map of you," she said. "I'll annotate it with all my favorite parts."

"Such as?"

"Here." She kissed his shoulder. "And here." More kisses traced the muscles of his chest. "And definitely down here." She moved lower.

When he could restrain himself no longer, her urged her

up beside him once more. "Work on your map later," he said. "I don't want to wait any longer."

"No. We've waited long enough."

They came together without awkwardness, two people who knew what they needed and were as eager to give as they were to take. They didn't rush, but they didn't waste time, either. When she climaxed she made the same small, joyous sounds she had so long ago, and he couldn't help but smile. Then she reached down and touched him and his own release surged through him and he shouted her name. Which he had never done before, but this time, it felt right. The two of them together felt right, in a way that nothing had in a very long time.

Epilogue

"I promise to love and support you, to stand by your side, and to face together all the ups and downs that life may bring."

"And I promise to love and support *you*, to stand by your side, and to face together all the ups and downs that life may bring."

"By the power invested in me by the state of Colorado, I now pronounce you husband and wife."

Cheers erupted and a trumpet fanfare heralded the bride and groom's exit down the aisle. Harper and Ryker rose to stand with the rest of the guests as Hannah and Jake paraded past their family and friends. Ryker slipped his arm around her. "Were you taking mental notes for our wedding?" he asked.

Harper looked down at the diamond solitaire on the third finger of her left hand. She had only had it a few days, and she couldn't stop admiring it. "Maybe a few." She grinned up at him. "Charlotte has been giving me ideas, though."

"Charlotte has ideas for our wedding?"

"I told her I wanted her to be a bridesmaid, so she asked if she could wear a fancy pink dress. And she thinks I should wear flowers in my hair, like a picture in one of her favorite storybooks. And we should serve pizza at the reception, because everyone likes pizza."

"I like pizza," he said. Then he burst out laughing when he saw her expression. "Okay, no pizza at the reception, but how do you feel about pink dresses and flowers in your hair?"

"The idea is beginning to grow on me. What do you think?"

"I don't care what we do, as long as you and Charlotte are both there. You two are all I need."

"I think it was worth waiting to marry you to hear lines like that one." She kissed his cheek. "You were never this smooth in high school."

"I like to think I've learned a few things over the years." He slid his hand down her hip.

She caught his wrist and directed his hand to her waist. "Let's make our way to the reception."

"Are you in a hurry?" He followed her out of the chapel. The reception was being held at the Alpiner Inn, a short walk down the street.

"I was just thinking," she said. "Your mom isn't expecting you home until late, right?"

"My mom isn't expecting me home at all." He grinned. "Another nice thing about not being a teenager. I don't have to pretend I'm not spending the night with my fiancée."

"In that case, let's leave the reception as soon as we politely can."

"Something urgent you need to do?" he teased.

"Yes. I have a map I need to work on."

"Must be a special map."

"Oh, it is." She laced her fingers with his. "It's going to take me a lifetime to draw, so I need to devote myself to it."

"We should put that in our wedding vows," he said, and pulled her to him.

The guests who exited behind them had to veer around them while he kissed her, but Harper didn't mind. Not that many people in life got a second chance, and she and Ryker weren't going to waste this one.

* * * * *

A NOTE TO ALL READERS

From October releases Mills & Boon will be making some changes to the series formats and pricing.

What will be different about the series books?

In response to recent reader feedback, we are increasing the size of our paperbacks to bigger books with better quality paper, making for a better reading experience.

What will be the new price of Mills & Boon?

Over the past four years we have seen significant increases in the cost of producing our books. As a result, in order to continue to provide customers with a quality reading experience, the price of our books will increase to RRP $10.99 for Modern singles and RRP $19.99 for 2-in-1s from Medical, Intrigue, Romantic Suspense, Historical and Western.

For futher information regarding format changes and pricing, please visit our website millsandboon.com.au.

INTRIGUE

Seek thrills. Solve crimes. Justice served.

Available Next Month

The Sheriff's Baby Delores Fossen
Under Lock And Key K.D. Richards

....

Smoky Mountains Mystery Lena Diaz
The Silent Setup Katie Mettner

....

Black Widow Janice Kay Johnson
Safe House Security Jacquelin Thomas

Larger Print

Keep reading for an excerpt of a new title
from the Romantic Suspense series,
COLTON'S SECRET PAST by Kacy Cross

Chapter 1

Hannah Colton had more brothers than she knew what to
do with most days, but Wade had always been her favorite.
That's the only reason she took his phone call despite juggling crepe batter, a hot griddle pan and a five-year-old who
had moved to step three in her campaign to convince Hannah to get her a dog. Washington at Delaware hadn't been so
determined to win as Lucy was when she wanted something.

This occasion was what God had invented speaker-
phones for, if there was ever a doubt.

"Someone better be dying," she called in the direction
of the phone and winced at her poor choice of words, considering Wade had been the one to call when their father
had passed.

Not that any of them had mourned Robert Colton overly
much. Maybe the loss of what could have been, but their
father had made his choices long ago.

"Not this time." Her brother's voice floated from the
counter as Hannah expertly flipped the crepe to let it cook
on the other side for a precise one minute.

Most people only cooked crepes on one side when they
were meant to be filled, but Hannah preferred the golden
griddle-cooked color to be visible on both sides. It was this
attention to detail that infiltrated all her cooking techniques

over the years as she'd made her mark catering bigger and bigger events.

"Uncle Wade," Lucy broke in. "Tell Mama about the puppy you saw at Aunt Ruby and Uncle Sebastian's place."

Great. So Wade had been discussing the Great Dog Campaign with her daughter again. "Wade. What is the one thing I asked you not to talk about with Lucy?"

"Hey, Goose," Wade called to Lucy, ignoring Hannah's question. "Did you draw me another picture at school?"

"Oh, I forgot! I have it," Lucy announced and dashed from the room to presumably scare up the artwork in question.

"That was an inspired way to get her out of the room," Hannah told her brother wryly. "I hope it wasn't so you could start in on me about getting Lucy a dog. How much did she pay you?"

Wade laughed, and it did her heart good to hear the sound from someone who hadn't done much laughing until recently. Harlow had done that for her brother, and it thrilled Hannah to know that they'd found love again after giving up on each other in high school.

"It wouldn't kill you to get a dog. Betty Jane is a godsend, and you see how much Lucy has taken to her."

"Betty Jane is *your* dog," she stressed. She left out the part about why Wade had needed a therapy dog in the first place, though her brother's PTSD didn't seem to be nearly as touchy a subject as it had once been. "I'm up to my elbows in crepes for the Women Entrepreneurs of Wake County brunch. Did you have a reason for calling or did you just want to hear my lovely voice?"

"Uh, you called me?" he prompted. "Last night?"

Oh, dang. How could she have forgotten that already? The Great Dog Campaign was about to be renamed the Distract Mom Crusade, and she did not need any more of dog campaigns *or* distractions. "I did. Call you. I was just… I've got all these crepes. Hang on."

As quickly as she could, she plated up the remaining fifteen so she could chill them in advance of adding the mascarpone and strawberries. She had a little bit of time before she had to leave for the brunch at the civic center in Conners, where two of her employees, Judy and Todd, would meet her to help serve. As catering jobs went, this one was on the small side, but Hannah treated them all as if each client was her only one, plus she always managed the entire affair herself, regardless of the magnitude. That's why she had lots of repeat business and a steady stream of new customers via solid word of mouth.

Bon Appetit Catering was hers, and she'd built it from nothing. She wasn't just serving food at the Women Entrepreneurs of Wake County meeting—she was a standing member. She'd earned it.

She slid onto one of the stools lined up at the kitchen island where she did much of the prep work for her catering business, taking the phone off speaker in case little ears wandered into the room unexpectedly. Though it seemed as if Lucy had abandoned the kitchen in favor of her room, likely having fallen into a game or elaborate Barbie soap opera that was far more important than the picture she'd gone in search of.

"Okay," she said. "Hear me out."

"I don't like the direction this is headed," Wade groused, his voice shifting as if he'd found a spot to perch as well.

"What? I am a paragon of virtue and good sense." *Now* she was. Six years ago, no. But she'd done everything she could since then to atone for the unfortunate screw-up named Owen Mackenzie. "I would never bring up something that warrants the suspicion in your voice."

"You'd have to actually spell it out for me to hear it, Hannah Banana," Wade told her with a long-suffering sigh.

Fine. Yes. She needed to come out with her idea, but this was a delicate subject requiring careful wording. Especially if she hoped to convince her family, which was why she'd started with Wade. If she could sell him on it, he'd run interference with everyone else.

"Okay, so here it goes. I'm going to investigate Markus Acker."

"No. You are not." Wade's voice had taken on a hard edge that she imagined had made many a marine sweat during his time in the service. "End of subject."

"Un-end of subject," she countered, rolling her hand to mime lifting the imaginary restriction he'd just placed on the topic. "I need to do my part. Aunt Jessie is mixed up in this church that's really nothing more than a cult—"

"That's why you're not investigating him. He's a criminal. We know that much, but the extent of his crimes… We are not finding out what he's capable of with you as bait. Not happening."

Hannah sighed. So Wade could talk about bringing down Markus Acker but she couldn't? "This is my turn to help. None of the rest of you are caterers. I can easily figure out a way to cater an event for the church and use that as my foot in the door to do some additional investigation into the hold he has over Aunt Jessie."

This was necessary. Critical. Not only did she have a no-brainer excuse to finagle her way onto the Ever After premises, she owed her family for disappointing them. First, she'd married Owen, then she'd failed by not figuring out how to keep him around, at least for Lucy's sake. Sure, it wasn't technically her fault that Owen had turned out to be a low-life scum—her brothers' term, not hers, though she did find it fitting a lot of days.

Okay, maybe sometimes she thought it was *partially* her fault and that was her business. After all, she'd picked him. If she didn't carry that blame, who did?

No one else blamed her. She knew that. Rationally, anyway. Still, it felt like she had some atoning to do, and this was her shot. Wade could step aside.

"I cannot repeat this enough, Hannah," Wade said sternly. "Stay away from the church, don't try to contact Jessie, and for crying out loud, please do not walk up and introduce yourself to Markus Acker. If not for yourself, consider Lucy. She only has you."

"I know that," she countered, her mouth flattening as she internalized his point.

Did she really have the luxury of taking risks? No. If she had someone to help carry the load, then maybe, but that was a daydream she had no business harboring. Single mother forever or at least until Lucy went to college. That was her vow, and she was sticking to it.

But how big of a risk was it to cater an event and keep her eyes open?

"Han, promise me," her brother insisted.

"I promise," she intoned and crossed her fingers. "I won't contact Jessie and I won't accost Markus Acker in the middle of the street next time he jogs by."

"Mean it," he said gruffly, and she made a face at him even though he couldn't see her. Thankfully, Wade didn't notice that she'd left out staying away from the church, and she wasn't about to bring it up.

"I'm getting another call," she lied and then nearly yelped when her phone beeped to signal another call.

Maybe she should buy a lottery ticket since she seemed to be able to predict the future.

"I'll talk to you later, then. Tell Lucy Goosey I said to come over and play with Betty Jane."

She hung up without honoring that subject with a reply and switched to the other call from an unrecognized number, answering automatically because she'd already committed to it after mentioning the call to Wade. Normally she'd let an unrecognized number go to voicemail since it was usually someone wanting a quote for a catering job, which required a dedicated chunk of time to get all the details. She'd just deal with it real time as her penance.

"Hello?"

"Is this Hannah Colton?" the unfamiliar female voice asked. "Formerly Hannah Mackenzie?"

Something flashed across the back of her neck, heating it. She hadn't gone by that name in over four years. Not since Owen had hightailed it out of Owl Creek and probably Idaho as a whole, not that he'd bothered to tell her a blessed thing about his plans or final destination.

"Can I help you?" she countered instead of confirming the answer to the woman's question, because after all, Mackenzie was still Lucy's last name and until she knew exactly what the nature of this inquiry was, she would wait to share any information.

"I'm looking for Hannah Colton who was married to Owen Mackenzie. He's been in a terrible accident."

Hannah drove toward Conners, but not wearing her caterer's uniform, the smart white coat with the entwined *B* and *A* of her logo embroidered on the left breast. Instead, she'd scrambled to get Marcia to cover for her at the last minute at the brunch, dropped Lucy at her mother's house—which fortunately had always been in the cards due to the impending job—and then wandered around in a daze trying to remember how to breathe, let alone the four hundred things she still needed to get done. Because thanks to Owen, she was still a single mom.

Owen Mackenzie. A name from the past that she wished a lot of days would stay there. But she saw him every time she looked at Lucy. Lucy's features favored her mother's, but she had light brown hair, halfway in between Hannah's blond and Owen's dark brown. And she definitely had her father's eyes with her mother's green irises.

What she couldn't figure out was why the hospital had called her.

She and Owen hadn't spoken in years. If he had her phone number, it was news to her because he'd certainly never hit the call button even one time. Had he asked the hospital to contact her?

Okay, there were two things she couldn't figure out— why they'd called her *and* why she'd agreed to go see him in the hospital. She should have hung up and not thought a moment more about him. That's what he'd done to them.

But the lady who'd called indicated that there were complications from the accident and that it would be very beneficial for Owen to see her in person. In Conners. A stone's throw from Owl Creek, where Hannah and Lucy had been living the whole time without one single iota of contact from her ex-husband.

Curiosity, maybe, could be the driving factor here. Was he sorry he'd left them? It would be sweet to hear that. In fact, she had a serious fantasy about that exact thing. The second he saw her standing there, he'd fall to his knees, apologies pouring from his mouth profusely.

Of course, he had apparently been hurt in the accident.

There wouldn't be a lot of falling to his knees, unless he rolled out of the hospital bed inadvertently. Which she would take. She wasn't picky.

Hannah laughed at herself. Yes, she was picky. She wanted a full-bore apology, first to her, then to Lucy second. Then she wanted to spit in his face and turn on her heel to walk out the door so he could see what it felt like to have someone he'd depended on show him their back.

She drove as slowly as possible, telling herself it was due to the heavy snowdrifts on the sides of the plowed highway, but it was really to give herself time to settle. It worked, to a degree.

But when she got to the hospital, nerves took over. It would be a miracle if she didn't throw up at his feet, assuming he was ambulatory. She didn't actually know what condition she'd find Owen in. The lady on the phone had been so vague, continually repeating that the doctor wanted to talk to her in person.

After parking and finding her way to the correct floor, she crept down the hall to the room the receptionist had indicated, feeling like she'd stumbled into another world. One with a hushed sense of doom and urgency. She didn't care for the atmosphere at all.

A plate with number 147 next to a whiteboard was affixed to the wall. Someone had scribbled Owen Mackenzie on the white part with a marker.

The door was open. She forced herself to walk through it, her gaze automatically drawn to the figure in the bed.

Owen. Her fingers flew to her mouth.

His eyes were closed and he had a square bandage near his temple. There was so much white—his gown, the sheet, the bed, the walls. And machines. With beeping.

She scarcely recognized the way her heart was beating, this erratic thump that couldn't find a rhythm.

And then he opened his eyes and fixed them on her. She smiled automatically because *oh my God*, it was Owen. Ashen-faced and obviously in pain, but she had never forgotten that particular shade of brown framed by his lashes, like an espresso with just the right amount of milk to turn it a molten chocolate color.

His hair was longer, spread along his neck, and he should have shaved two weeks ago, but the scruff along his jaw had just enough edge to it to be slightly sexy. No. Not sexy. She slammed her eyes shut and drew in a shaky breath.

"Hello?" he rasped.

"Hi, Owen," she murmured and that was it. The extent of her brain's ability to form words. Her throat's ability to make sounds.

After all this time, after all the scenarios she'd envisioned, the tongue-lashing she'd give him if they were ever in the same room together again—that was all she could come up with? Lame.

"Are you one of the nurses?" he asked, blinking slowly. "Why aren't you wearing scrubs?"

Raising a brow, she eyed him. "It's me, Owen. Hannah. I know I've put on a few pounds, but come on."

Only five! Maybe seven, tops. Plus her hair was the same, since she hadn't changed styles in… Good grief. Had it really been four years that she'd been getting this exact same cut?

"Are we related? The hospital said they were trying to track down my family."

Confused, she cocked her head. "You're kidding, right? We're not related, not anymore, though I don't know that being married is actually the same as being related, come to think of it."

And now he had her babbling, which felt like par for the course. She'd been knocked sideways since the phone call back at home, and being here in this room with Owen hadn't fixed that any.

She had to get it together. This was her chance to make her fondest wish come true—Owen on his knees, begging her forgiveness, blathering about how sorry he was he'd left her. How much he missed her. How big of a mistake he'd made.

Then and only then could she hold her head up high and walk away. Forget this man and the way he'd made her question her judgment every hour of every day, which was not a great parenting skill, by the way.

She'd get that confession out of him or die trying. She opened her mouth.

"Ms. Colton, I presume?" Hannah glanced at the door where a white-coated older gentleman stood with an iPad. "I'm Doctor Farris. Mr. Mackenzie is unfortunately suffering from amnesia. We had hoped that seeing you might jog something loose, but based on what I just heard, that doesn't seem to have happened."

"Amnesia." The concept bounced around in Hannah's head, searching for a place to land, but she couldn't quite connect all the dots. "You mean he lost his memory? That's a real thing? I thought Hollywood made up that condition for dramatic purposes."

"Oh, no, it's very real." Dr. Farris smiled kindly. "It's also not very well understood or studied so a lot of times, we're a little unsure on how to treat it. Conventional wisdom says to give it time, and eventually everything will come back to him."

"Sorry… Hannah?" Owen called, his gaze searching hers as if desperately trying to recall even a sliver of a memory that included her. "I wish I remembered you, but I don't. I don't remember who I am either. Can you tell me?"

Oh, she could. Absolutely. She'd had four years and change to stew about how this man had treated her. He deserved to hear every last horrible thing he'd done to her. Every last tear she'd shed.

But instead, she sat down heavily in one of the bedside chairs and blurted out, "You're the only man I've ever loved."

Subscribe and fall in love with a Mills & Boon series today!

You'll be among the first to read stories delivered to your door monthly and enjoy great savings.

WE SIMPLY LOVE ROMANCE

MILLS & BOON

JOIN US

Sign up to our newsletter to stay up to date with...

- Exclusive member discount codes
- Competitions
- New release book information
- All the latest news on your favourite authors

Plus...
get $10 off your first order.
What's not to love?

Sign up at **millsandboon.com.au/newsletter**